Math made Easy

Grade 1

Ages **6-7**

Canadian Editor
Marilyn Wilson

DK

Numbers

Trace the numbers.

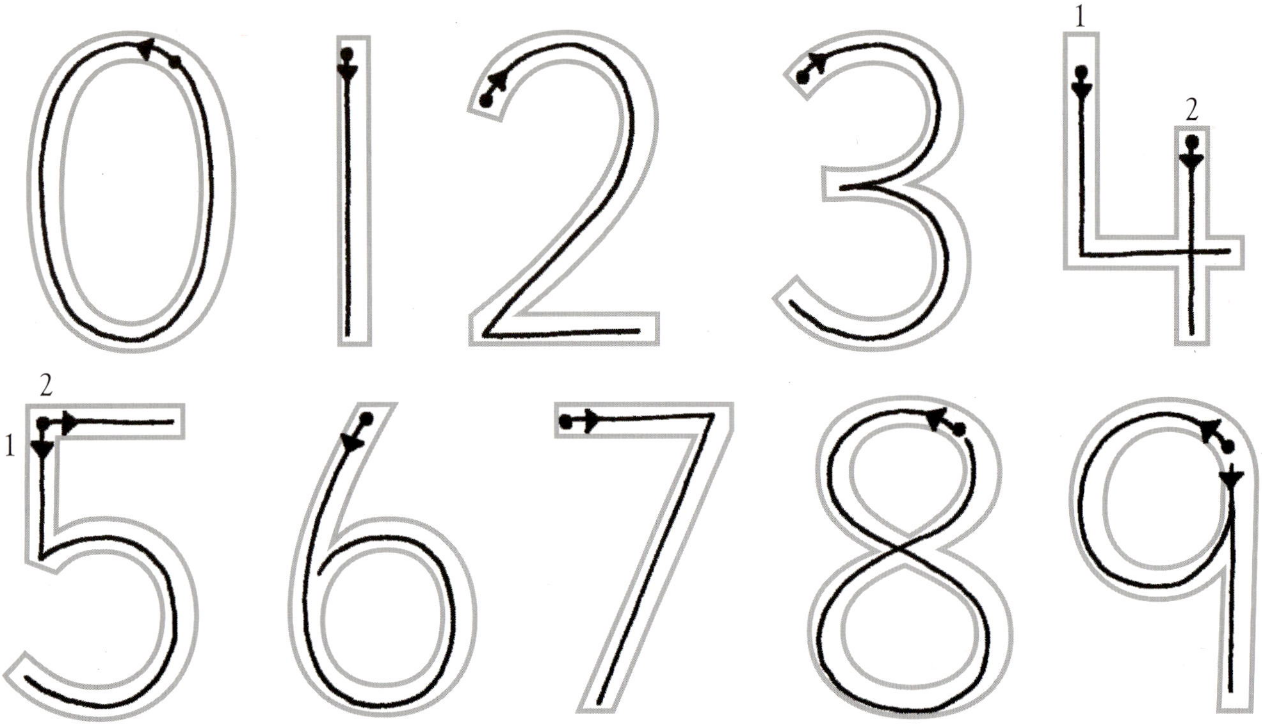

Write the numbers.

0 0 0 0

1 1 1 1

2 2 2 2

3 3 3 3

4 4 4 4

5 5 5 5

6 6 6 6

7 7 7 7

8 8 8 8

9 9 9 9

Progress Chart

This chart lists the topics in the book. Once you have completed each page, stick a star in the correct box below.

Page	Topic	Star	Page	Topic	Star	Page	Topic	Star
2	Numbers		13	Finding 10s		24	Subtracting	
3	Numbers and pictures		14	Tens and ones		25	Counting back	
4	Counting		15	One more or one less?		26	Sets	
5	Counting out loud		16	Ordering		27	Money	
6	Missing numbers		17	More than or less than?		28	Ordering stories	
7	Making 10		18	Greater or less?		29	Time	
8	Count by 10s		19	Comparing		30	Graphs	
9	Count by 2s		20	Halves		31	2-dimensional shapes	
10	Patterns		21	Quarters		32	3-dimensional shapes	
11	Adding machines		22	Adding up		33	Writing numbers	
12	Reading numbers		23	Adding animals		34	Counting	

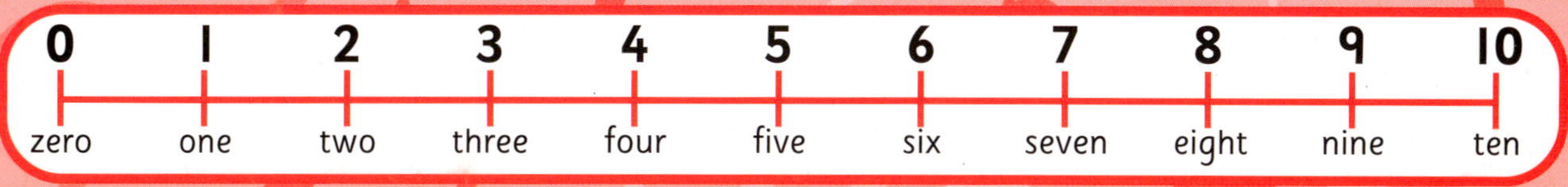

Page	Topic	Star	Page	Topic	Star	Page	Topic	Star
35	Counting on by 2s	☆	49	Expanded form	☆	63	Numbers	☆
36	Most and least	☆	50	Adding dice	☆	64	Numbers	☆
37	Counting by 10s	☆	51	Adding	☆	65	Addition	☆
38	Counting forward or back	☆	52	Crossing out	☆	66	1 less or 1 more	☆
39	Reading numbers	☆	53	Subtraction	☆	67	Tallies	☆
40	Tens and ones	☆	54	Sets of	☆	68	Using a table	☆
41	Comparisons	☆	55	Sharing	☆	69	Patterns of 2, 5, and 10	☆
42	Comparing money	☆	56	Addition properties	☆	70	More or less	☆
43	Spot the doubles	☆	57	Most and least likely	☆	71	Ordering	☆
44	10 more or 10 less	☆	58	Days and seasons	☆	72	Fractions of shapes	☆
45	Ordinals	☆	59	Using clocks	☆	73	Addition	☆
46	Ordering	☆	60	Favourite fruits	☆	74	Adding coins	☆
47	Halves and fourths	☆	61	Draw the other half	☆	75	Addition grid	☆
48	Place value	☆	62	Where's the bear?	☆	76	Doubles	☆

Page	Topic	Star	Page	Topic	Star	Page	Topic	Star
77	Fact families		91	Venn diagrams		105	Fact families	
78	Addition		92	Similar shapes		106	Adding money	
79	Subtraction		93	2-dimensional shapes		107	Using doubles	
80	Subtraction		94	3-dimensional shapes		108	Adding up	
81	Subtraction		95	Read, write, and draw		109	Count by 2s	
82	Real-life problems		96	Counting		110	Addition	
83	Real-life problems		97	Bar graphs		111	Addition	
84	Subtraction tables		98	Subtraction		112	Addition and subtraction	
85	Counting down		99	2s, 5s, and 10s		113	Real-life problems	
86	Clocks		100	Comparing		114	Real-life problems	
87	Digital clocks		101	Ordering		115	Addition	
88	Match the times		102	Subtraction		116	Clocks and watches	
89	Do you know?		103	Matching fractions		117	Puzzles	
90	Matching shapes		104	Money		118	Tables	

Page	Topic	Star	Page	Topic	Star	Page	Topic	Star
119	Venn diagrams		133	Estimating length		145	Properties of polygons	
120	Appropriate units of measure		134	Subtracting		146	Venn diagrams	
121	Symmetry		135	Simple tally charts and bar graphs		147	Most likely/ least likely	
122	2-dimensional shapes		136	Addition properties		148	3-dimensional shapes	
123	Equal value		137	Equations		149	Counting	
124	Shapes and places		138	Picture graphs		150	Finding patterns	
125	Numbers		139	3-dimensional shapes		151	Reading tally charts	
126	Counting by 1s, 10s, and 100s		140	Missing addends		152	Same shape and size	
127	Counting by 2s		141	Reading tables		153	Parts of a set	
128	Odd and even		142	Adding		154	Symmetry	
129	More and less		143	Reading a calendar		155	Measurement problems	
130	Fact families		144	Subtracting		156	3-dimensional shapes	
131	Fractions							
132	Adding							

Numbers and pictures

Count the animals, draw the dots, and write the number.

2

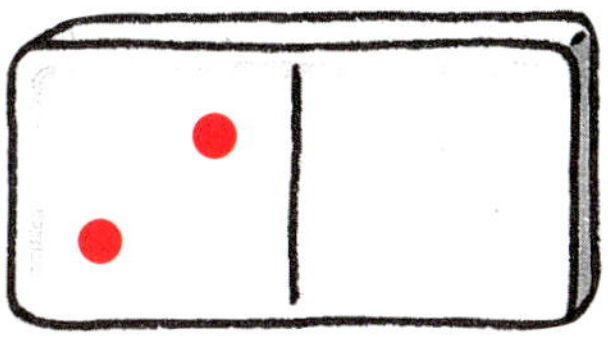

two

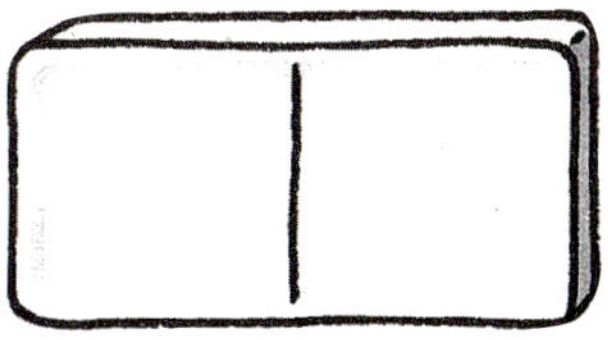

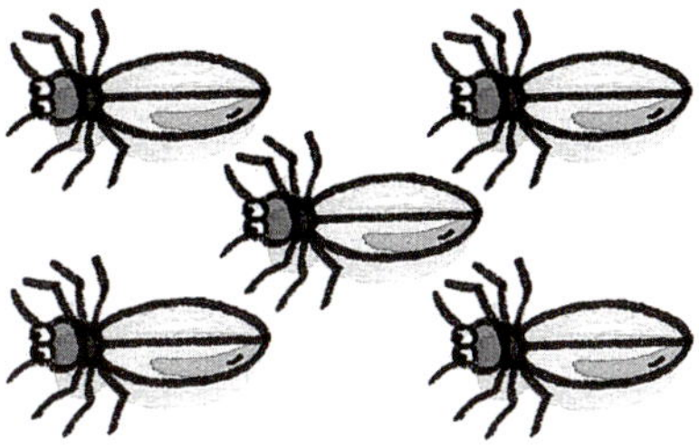

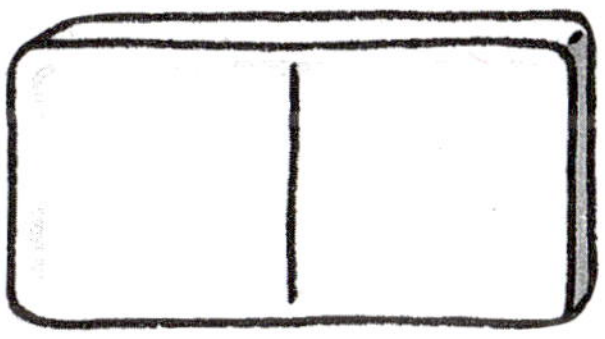

Draw your own examples.

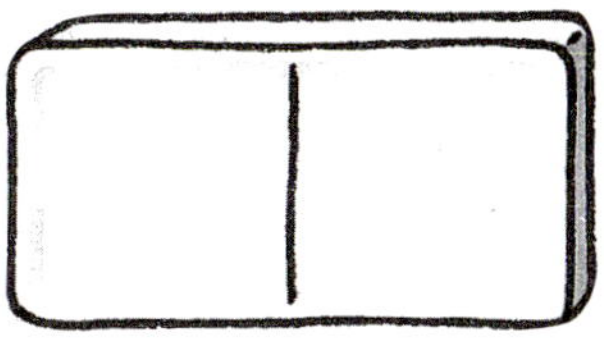

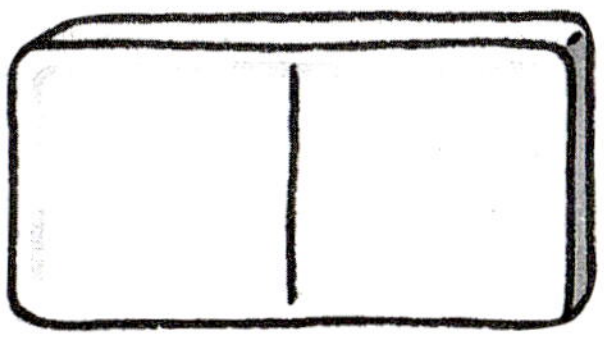

Counting

Connect each set to the correct number.

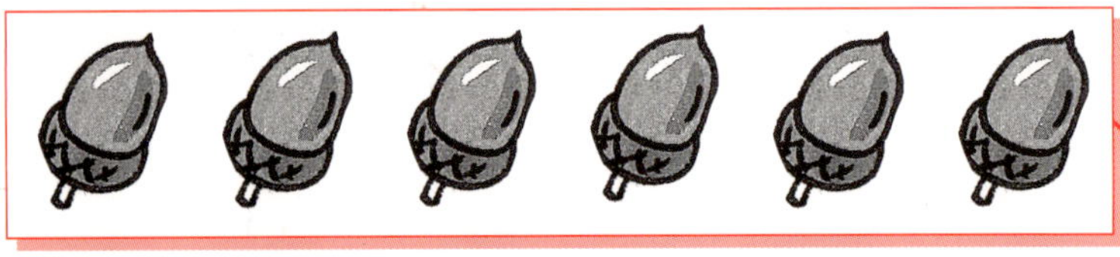

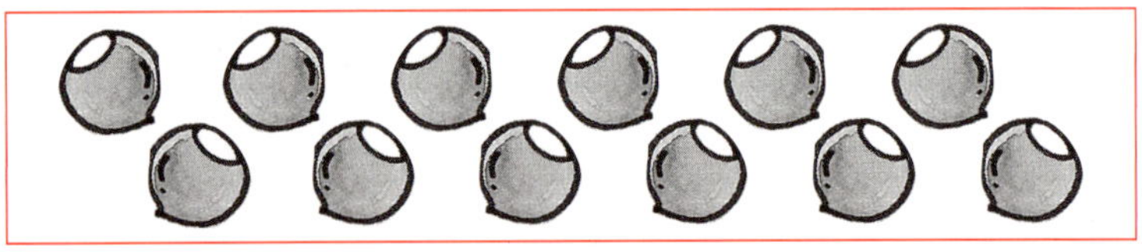

8

9

6

15

10

Draw your own set to match the number.

12

Count the beads.

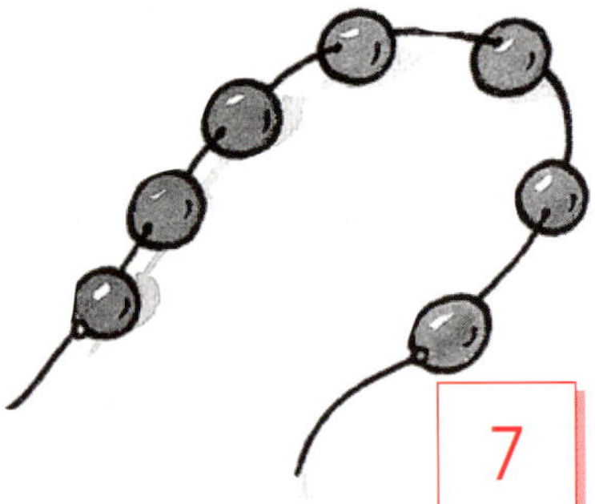

7

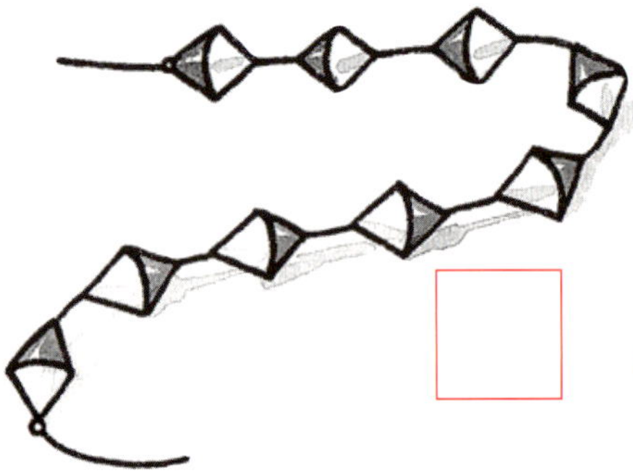

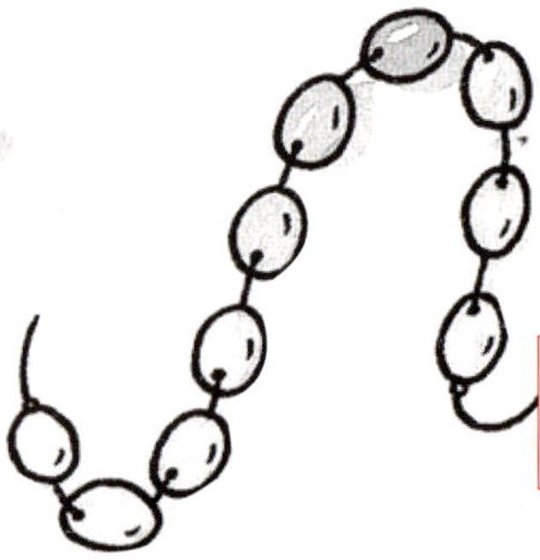

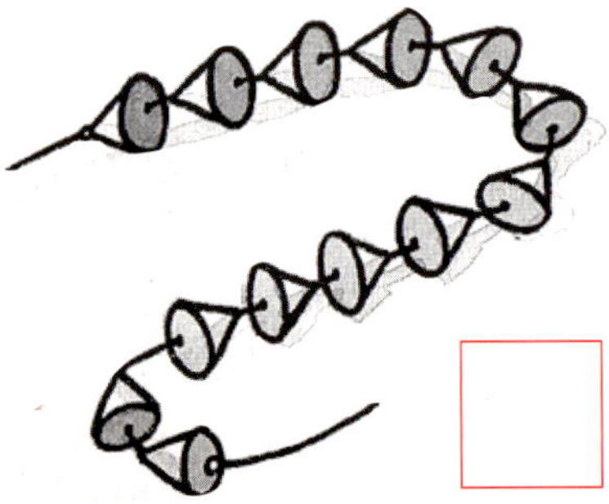

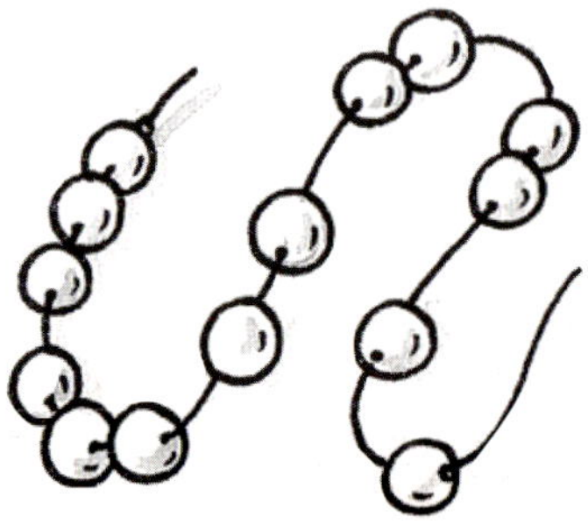

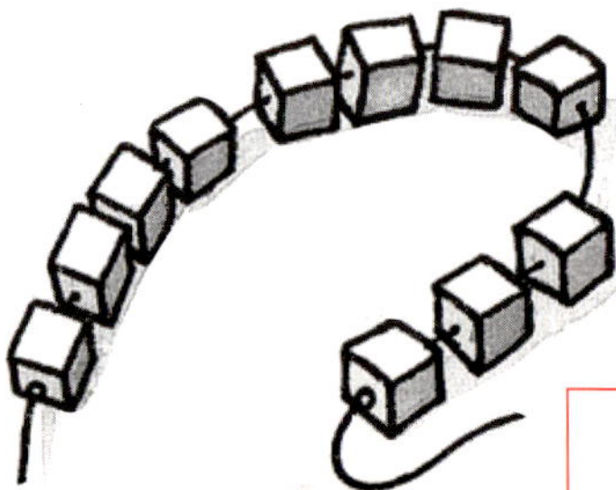

Counting out loud

Say and write the missing numbers.

Missing numbers

Write in the missing numbers.

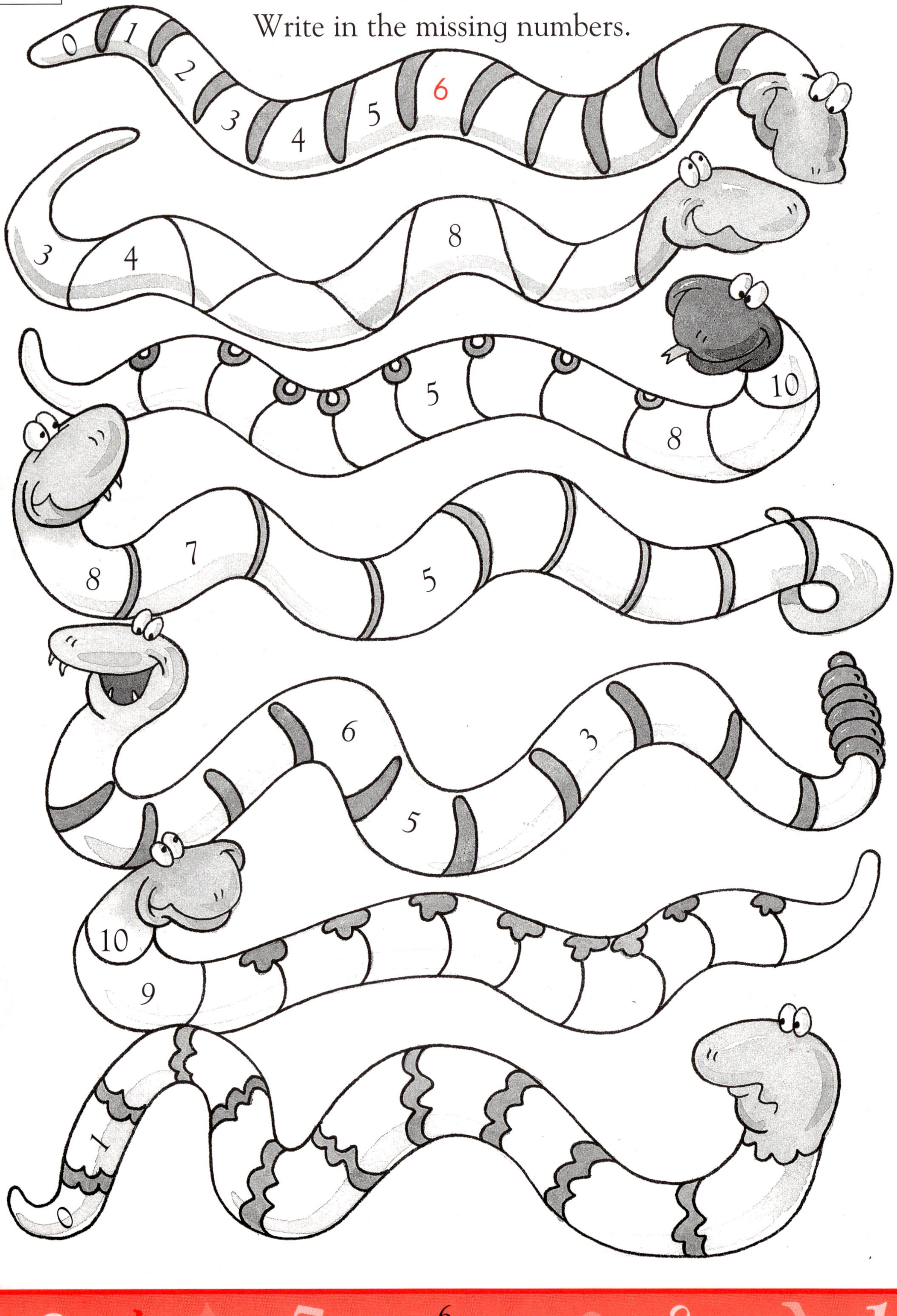

Making 10

Colour some fish red, and write the correct numbers in the boxes.

4 red 6 white

4 + 6 = 10

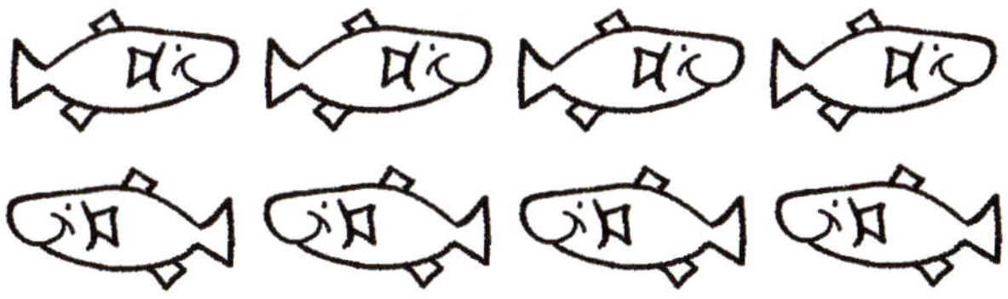

☐ red ☐ white

☐ + ☐ = 10

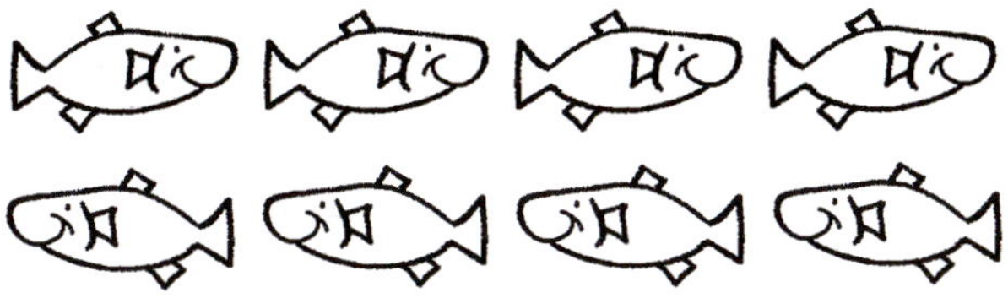

☐ red ☐ white

☐ + ☐ = 10

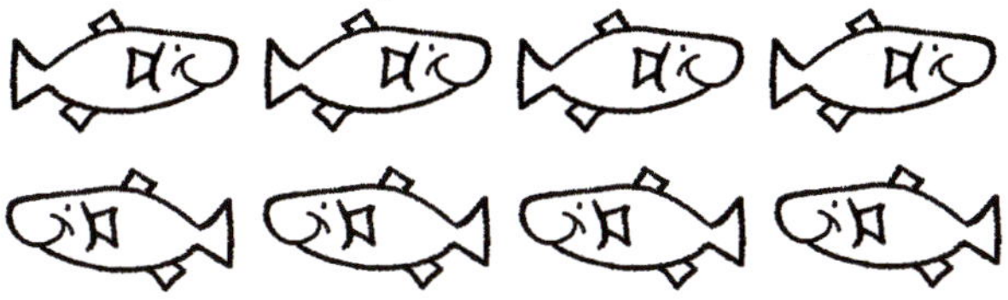

☐ red ☐ white

☐ + ☐ = 10

☐ red ☐ white

☐ + ☐ = 10

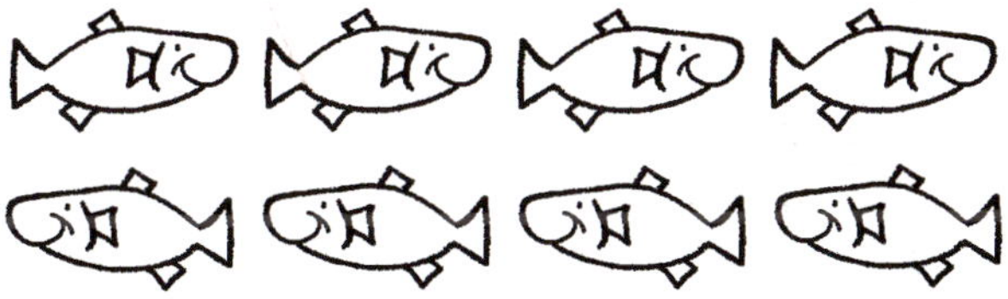

☐ red ☐ white

☐ + ☐ = 10

Write the missing numbers in the boxes to make 10.

10 + 0 = 10	6 + ☐ = 10	2 + ☐ = 10
9 + ☐ = 10	5 + ☐ = 10	1 + ☐ = 10
8 + ☐ = 10	4 + ☐ = 10	0 + ☐ = 10
7 + ☐ = 10	3 + ☐ = 10	

Count by 10s

Match the numbers to the words.

fifty	ten	thirty	twenty	forty

10	20	30	40	50	60	70	80	90	100

seventy	ninety	sixty	eighty	one hundred

Which numbers has the snail hidden?

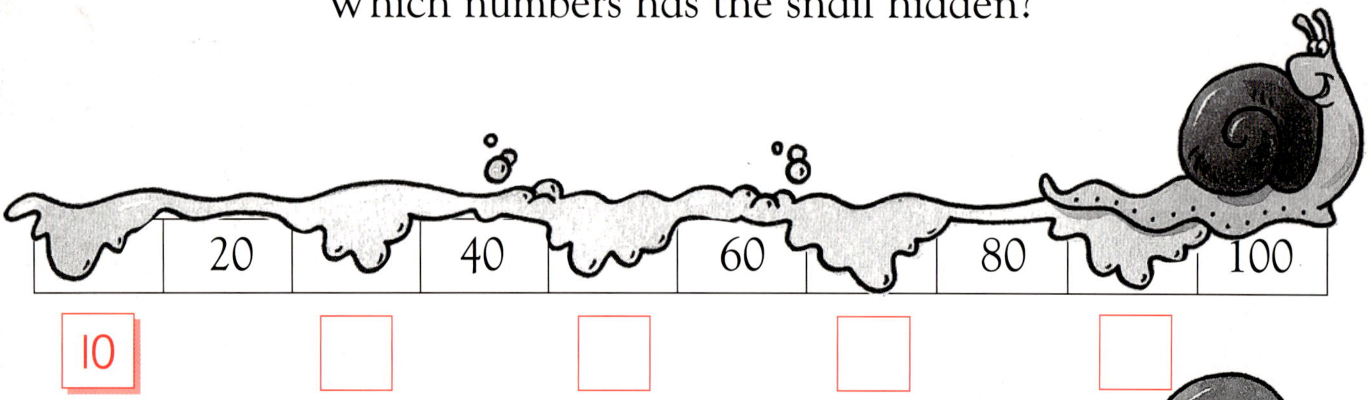

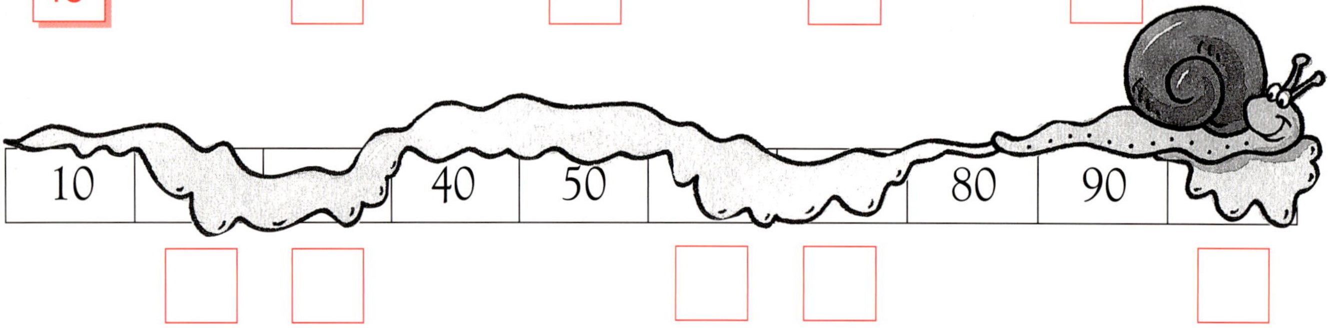

Help the snail follow the bricks in the right order.

Count by 2s

Fill in the "hops" and circle the even numbers.

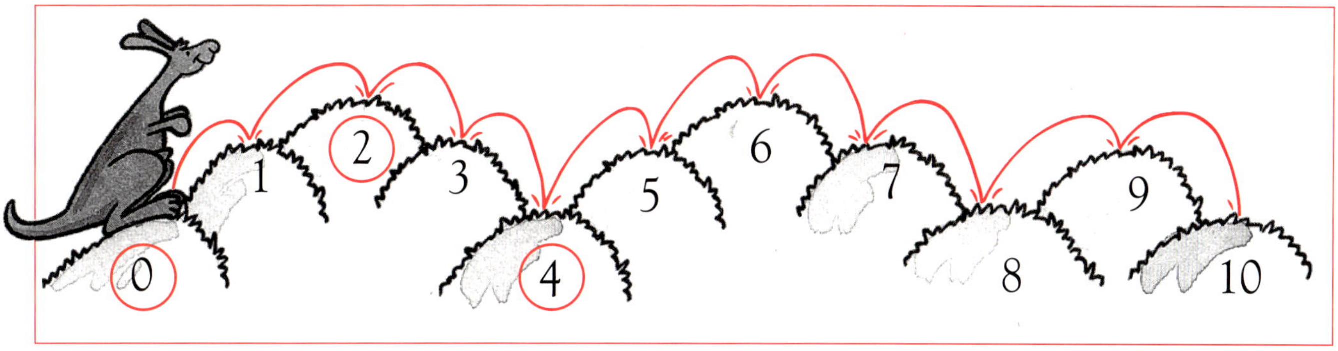

Colour the even numbers.

1	2	3	4	5
6	7	8	9	10
11	12	13	14	15
16	17	18	19	20
21	22	23	24	25
26	27	28	29	30

Connect the dots in order.

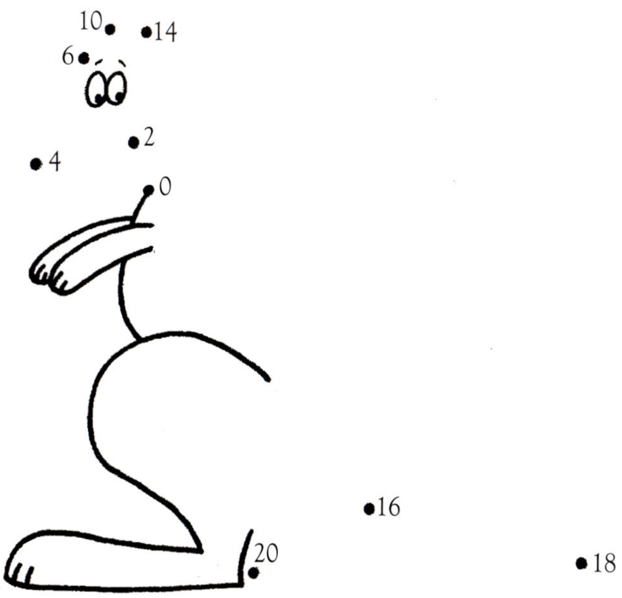

Patterns

Continue the pattern.

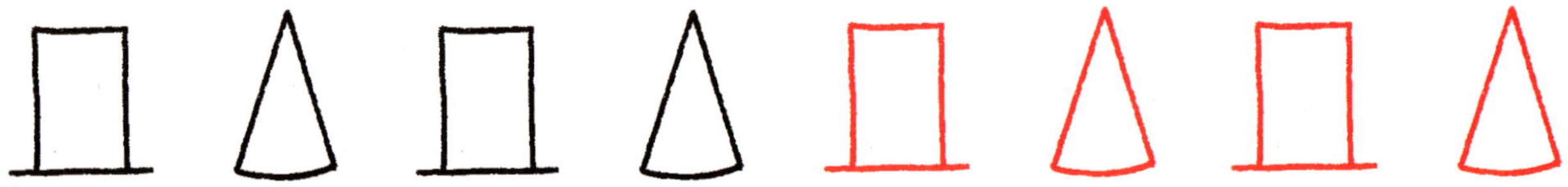

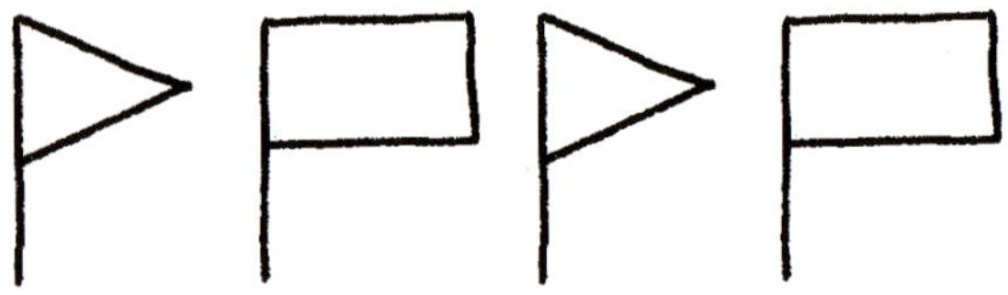

Make your own patterns.

Continue the number patterns.

2	4	6	2	4	6	2	4	6				
10	9	9	10	9								
1	3	5	7	1								
5	5	5	6	5								

Adding machines

Add the numbers, and write the answers.

1 → = 2
3 → = 4
5 → = 6
7 → = 8
9 → = 10

2 → = ☐
4 → = ☐
6 → = ☐
8 → = ☐
10 → = ☐

9 → = ☐
11 → = ☐
13 → = ☐
15 → = ☐
17 → = ☐

8 → = ☐
10 → = ☐
12 → = ☐
14 → = ☐
16 → = ☐

2 → = ☐
6 → = ☐
12 → = ☐
14 → = ☐
16 → = ☐

3 → = ☐
7 → = ☐
11 → = ☐
13 → = ☐
15 → = ☐

Reading numbers

Colour enough things to match the number in each box.

12

10

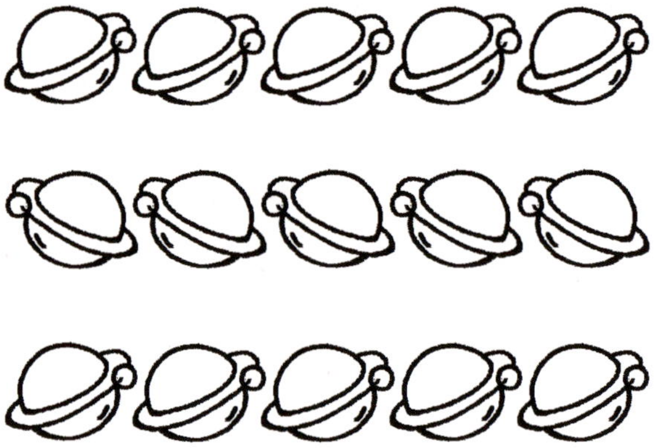

9

7

11

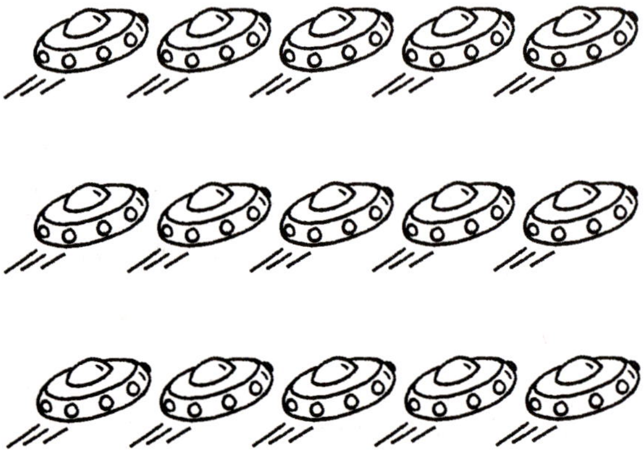

Draw your own example.

Finding 10s

Ring 10 items, and write the numbers.

12 = 10 + 2

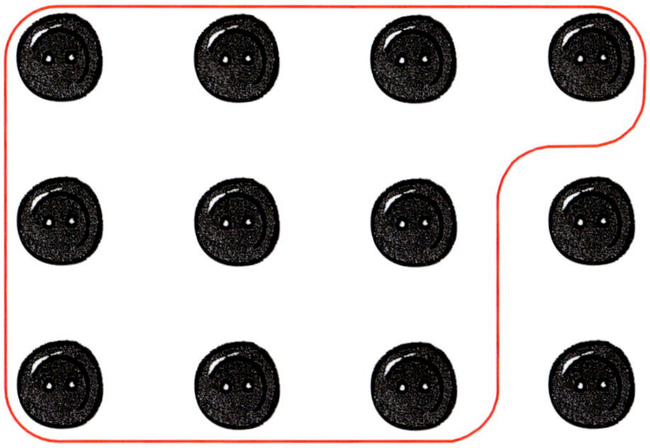

16 = ☐ + ☐

19 = ☐ + ☐

17 = ☐ + ☐

11 = ☐ + ☐

20 = ☐ + ☐

Tens and ones

How many tens and ones do you see?

tens	ones	tens	ones	tens	ones
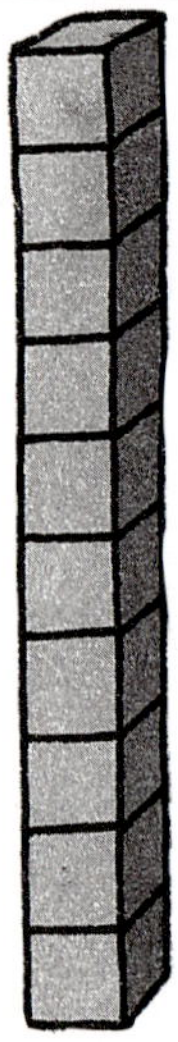		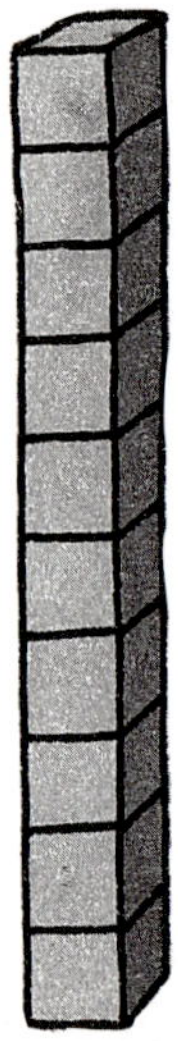		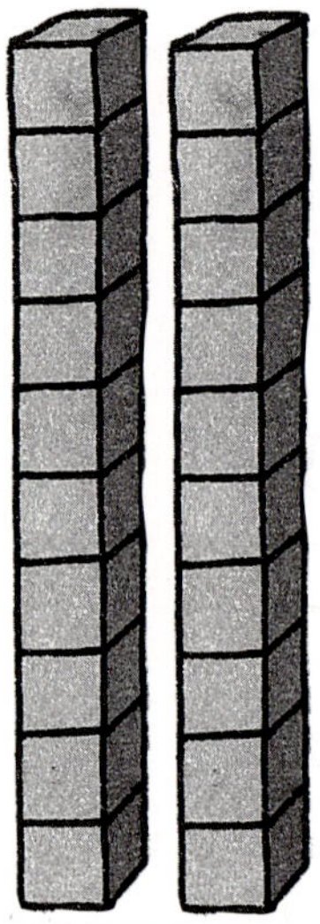	
1	4				

14

Draw the tens and ones.

tens	ones	tens	ones	tens	ones
1	9	1	5		3

19

One more or one less?

Write one less and one more than the numbers shown in the boxes.

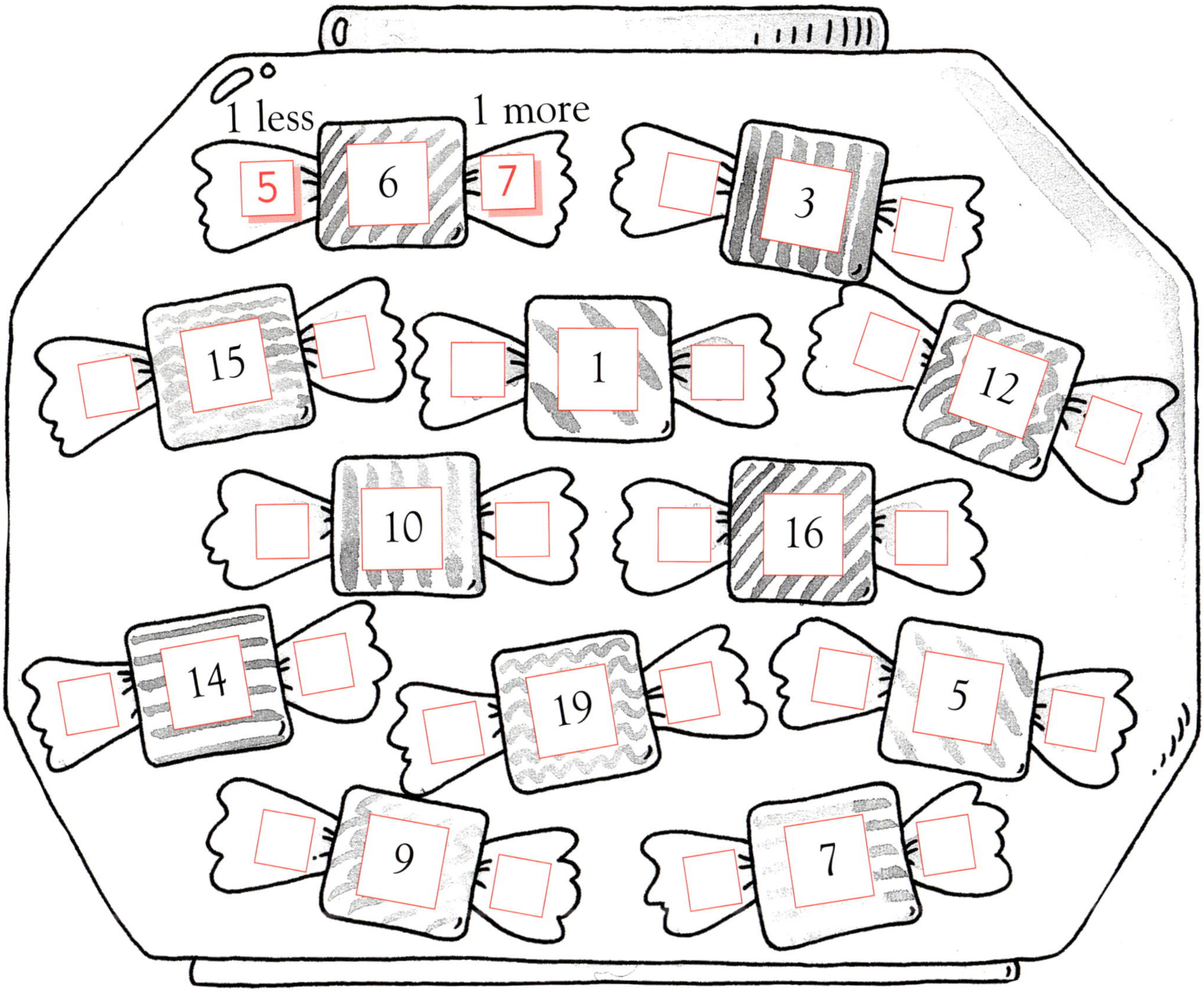

Draw one more or one less, and write the new number.

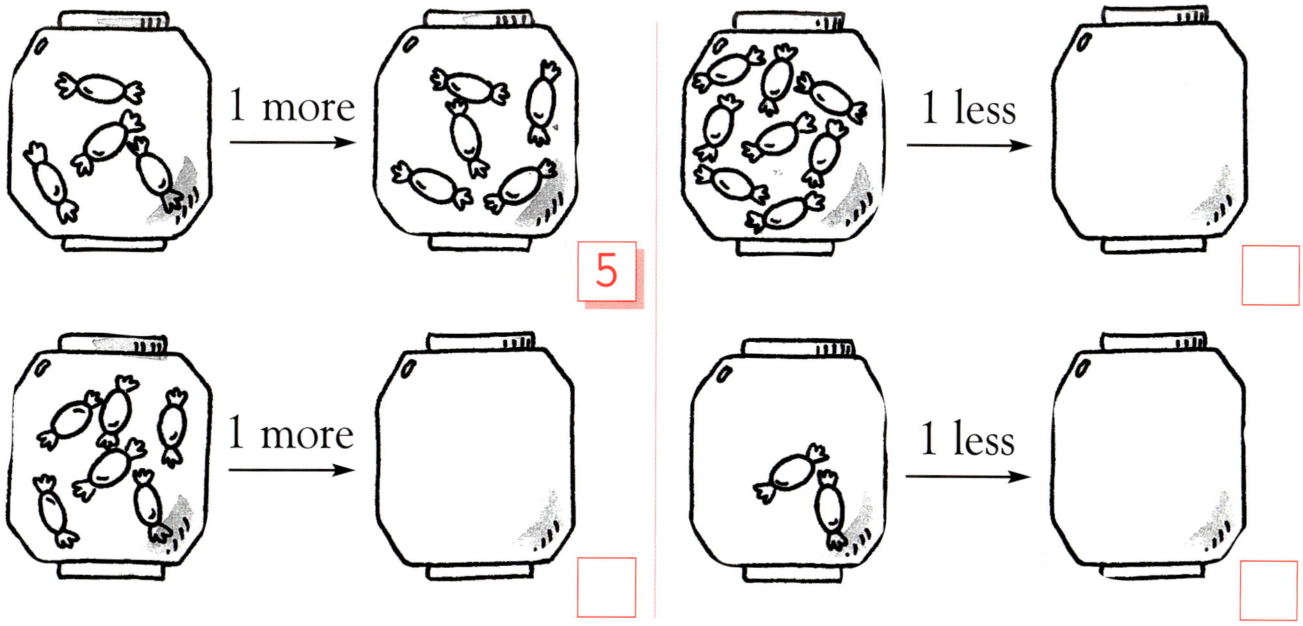

Ordering

Colour the prize ribbons.

4th= purple | 3rd= yellow | 1st= green | 6th= red | 2nd= blue | 5th= orange

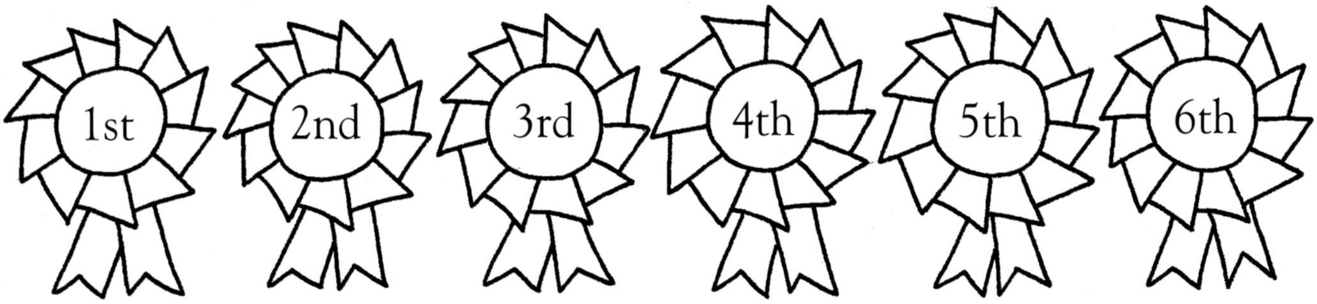

Which rabbit is 1st, 2nd, 3rd ...?

Which shape comes 1st, 2nd, 3rd ...?

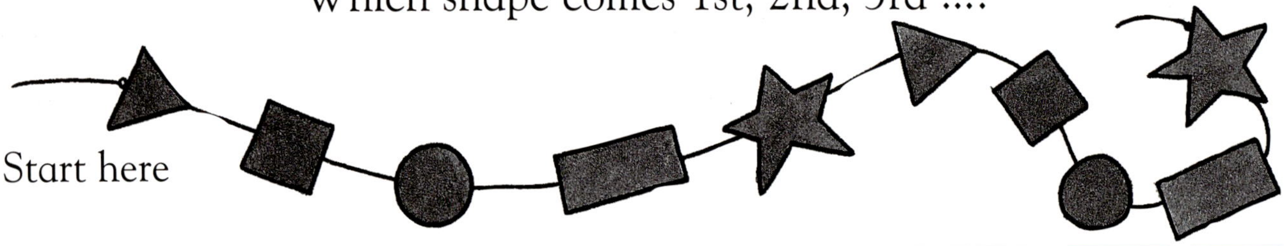

More than or less than?

Fill in the apples and numbers that make each sentence true.

5 is more than → 3

5 is more than → ☐

8 is more than → ☐

12 is more than → ☐

Fill in the flowers and numbers that make each sentence true.

6 is less than → 7

8 is less than → ☐

7 is less than → ☐

3 is less than → ☐

Greater or less?

Draw the hungry crocodiles.
They always eat the greater numbers!

6	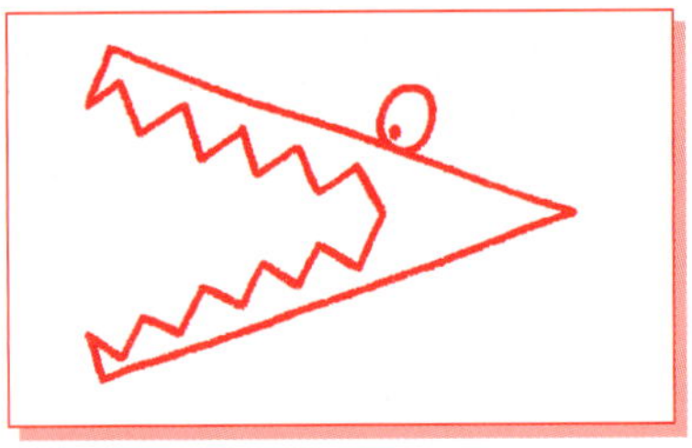	4	2	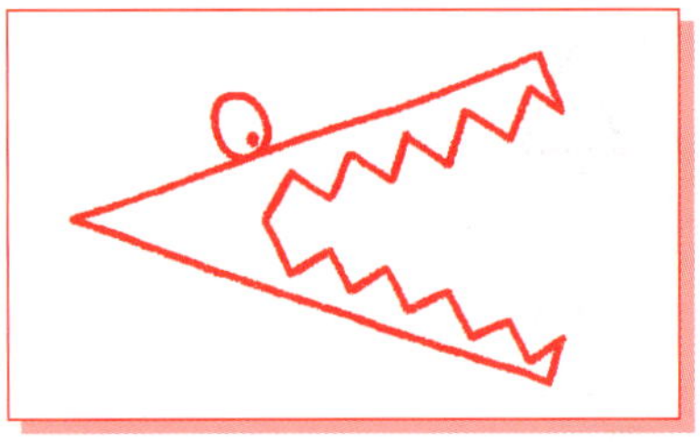	12
5		10	3		13
8		13	6		16
15		9	15		20
10		2	11		12
20		10	1		0

Comparing

heavier lighter bigger smaller longer shorter

Draw the pictures to make each comparison true.

 heavier than →  heavier than → 

[ ] lighter than → [ ] lighter than → [ ]

[ ] bigger than → [ ] bigger than → [ ]

[ ] smaller than → [ ] smaller than → [ ]

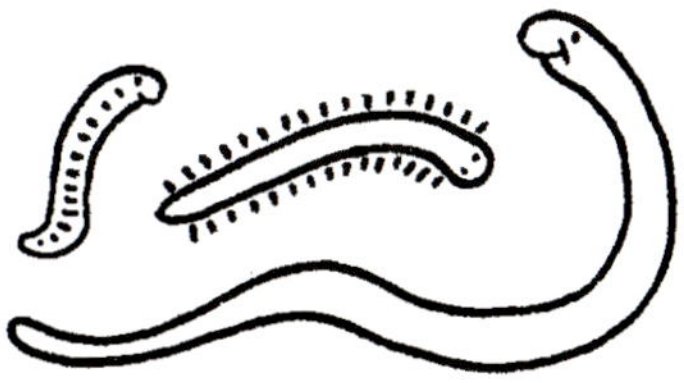

[ ] longer than → [ ] longer than → [ ]

[ ] shorter than → [ ] shorter than → [ ]

Halves

Colour one half ($\frac{1}{2}$) of each shape.

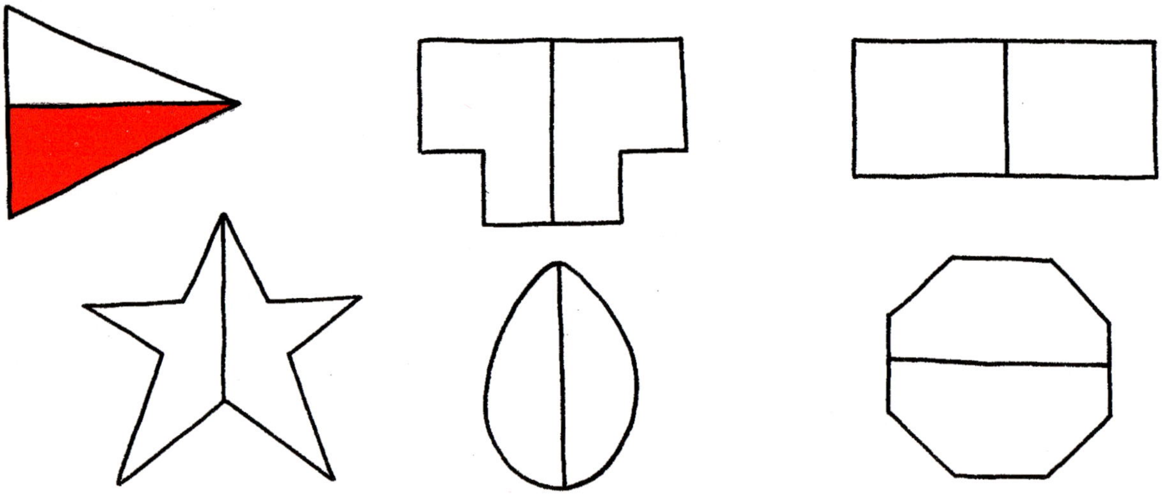

Write a ✓ in the box if $\frac{1}{2}$ the figure is shaded and a ✗ if less than $\frac{1}{2}$ is shaded.

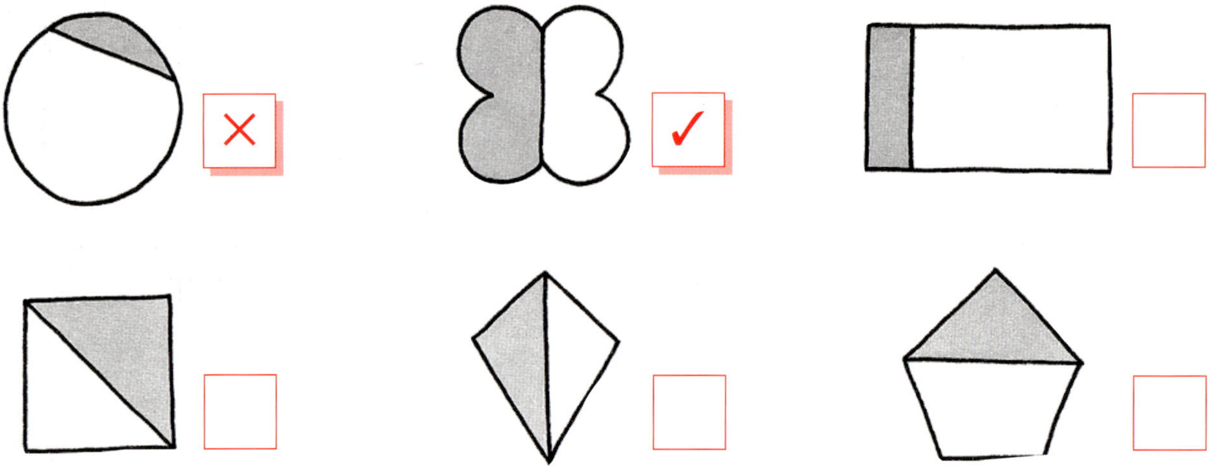

Colour one half ($\frac{1}{2}$) of each figure.

Quarters

Colour one quarter ($\frac{1}{4}$) of each shape.

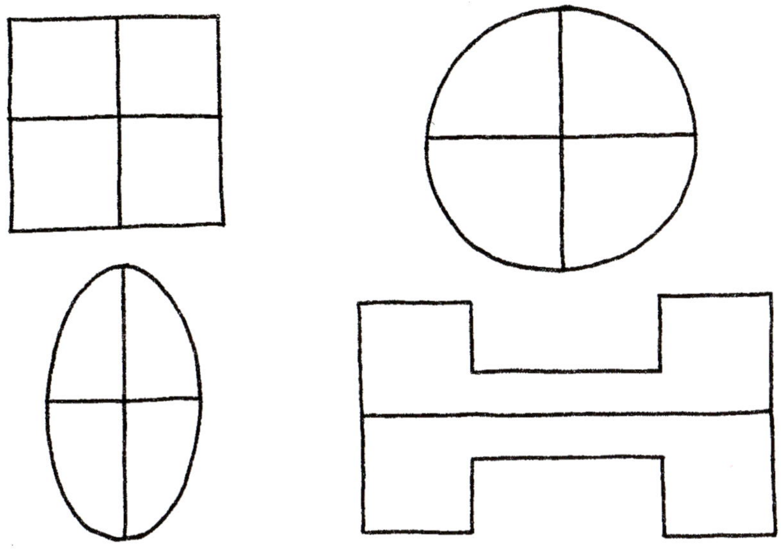

Write a ✓ in the box if $\frac{1}{4}$ of the figure is shaded and a ✕ if less than $\frac{1}{4}$ is shaded.

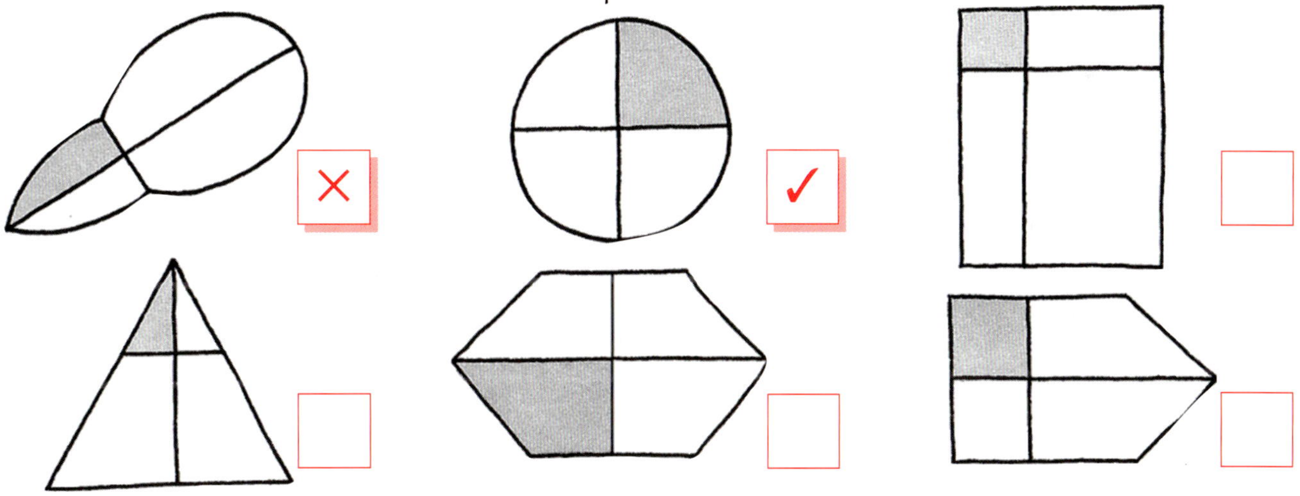

Colour one quarter ($\frac{1}{4}$) of each picture.

Adding up

Fill in the missing numbers, and add.

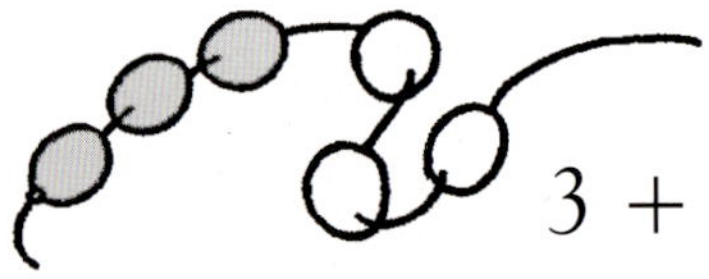

3 + 3 = 6

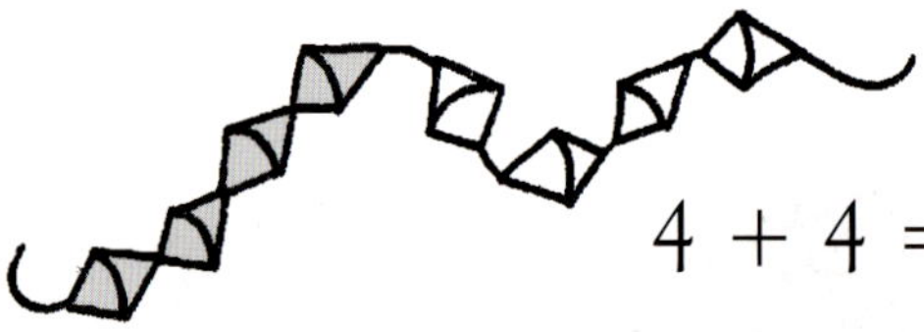

4 + 4 = ☐

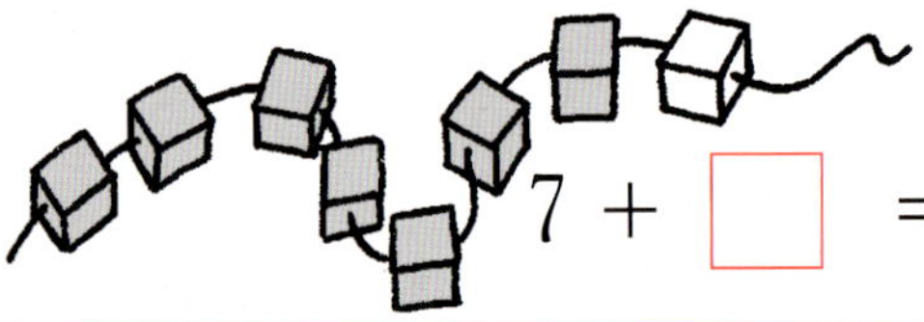

7 + ☐ = ☐

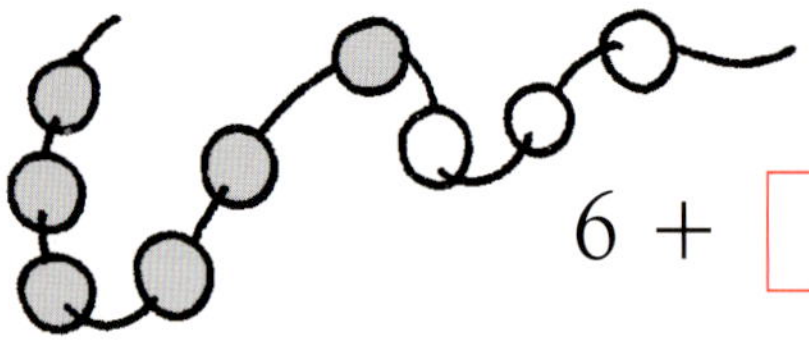

6 + ☐ = ☐

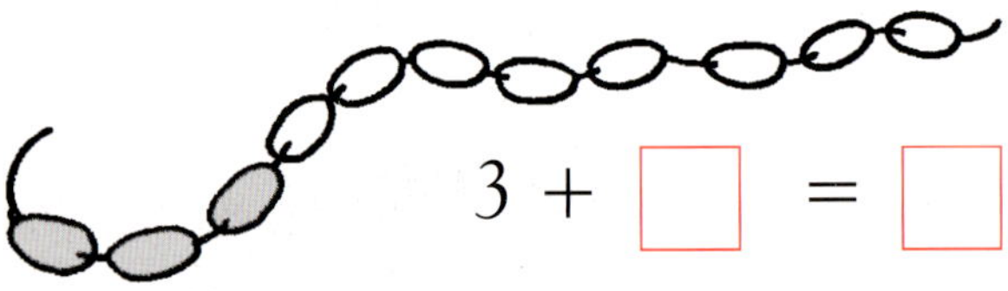

3 + ☐ = ☐

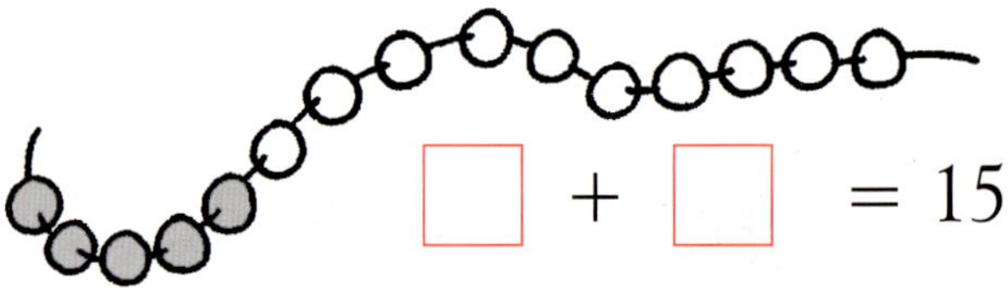

☐ + ☐ = 15

Count on to find out on which step the rabbit stops.

4 + 3 = 7

2 + 7 = ☐

8 + 2 = ☐

5 + 5 = ☐

Adding animals

Count and add the animals, and then write the new number.

2 + 6 = 8

☐ + ☐ = ☐

☐ + ☐ = ☐

☐ + ☐ = ☐

☐ + ☐ = ☐

☐ + ☐ = ☐

Fill in the missing numbers in the equations.

7 + 4 = 11	3 + ☐ = 12	6 + 6 = ☐
9 + 5 = ☐	2 + 8 = ☐	3 + 11 = ☐
9 + 3 = ☐	6 + ☐ = 10	13 + ☐ = 17
2 + ☐ = 5	16 + ☐ = 16	15 + ☐ = 19

Subtracting

Cross out the correct number of animals, and fill in the answers.

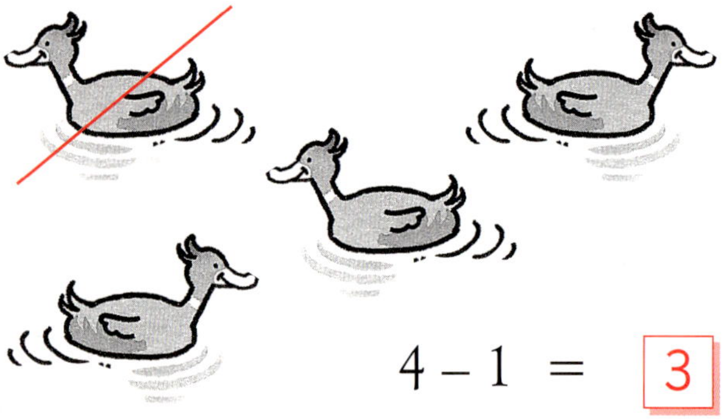

4 – 1 = 3

6 – 2 = ☐

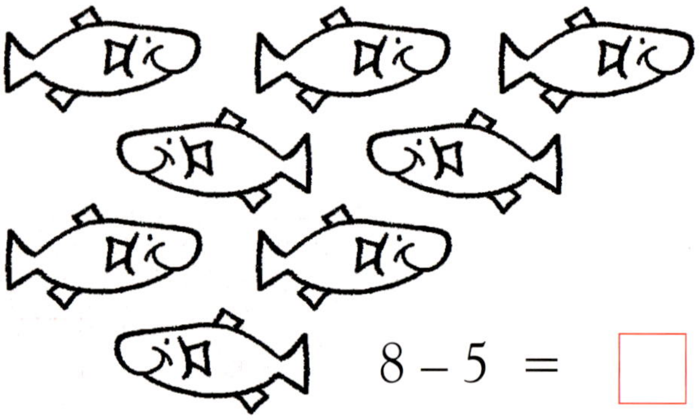

8 – 5 = ☐

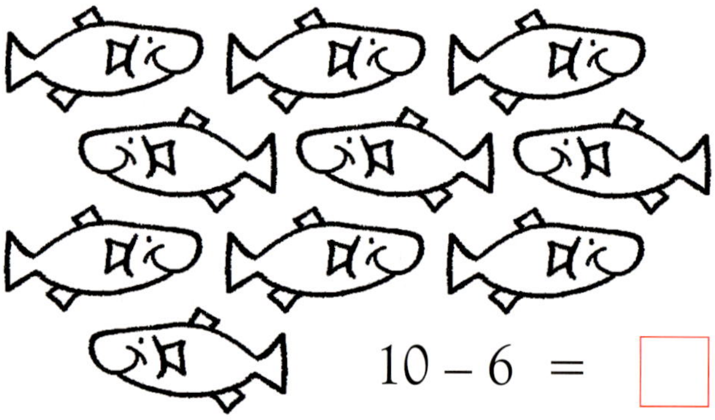

10 – 6 = ☐

Cross out the correct number of fruits, and fill in the answers.

8 – 3 = ☐

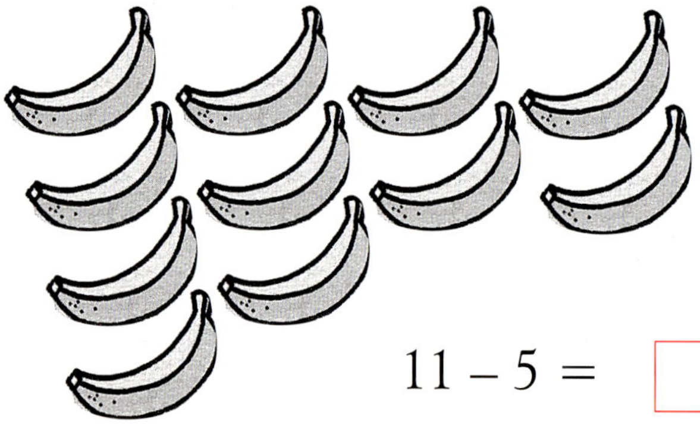

11 – 5 = ☐

13 – 7 = ☐

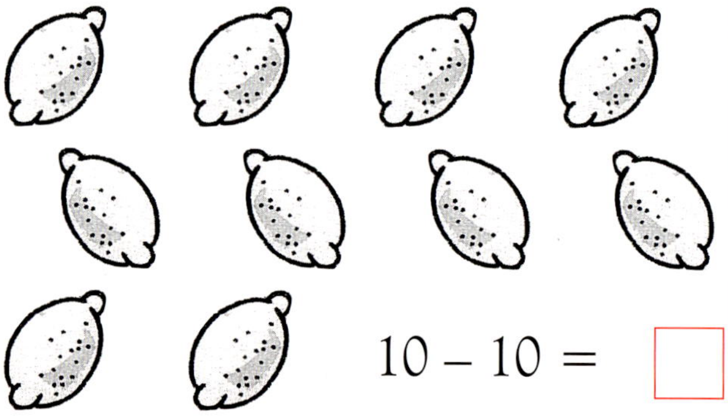

10 – 10 = ☐

Counting back

Count back to find out on which step the frog stops.

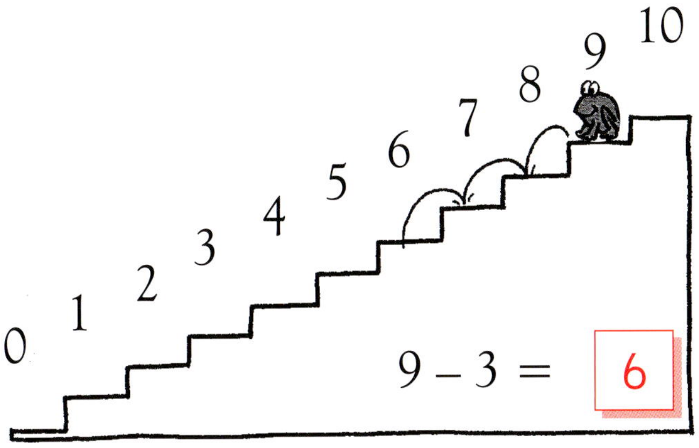

9 – 3 = 6

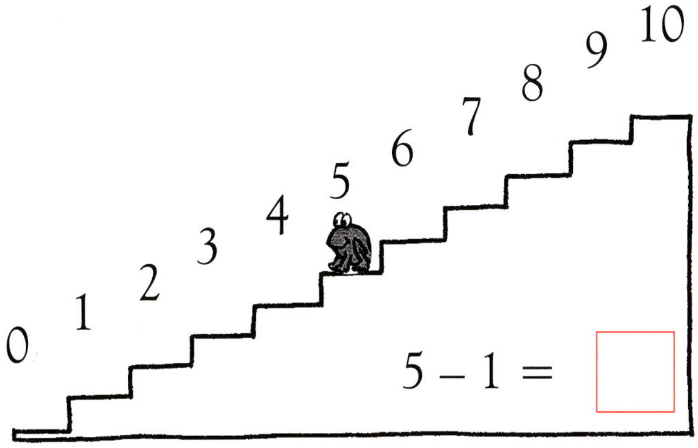

5 – 1 = ☐

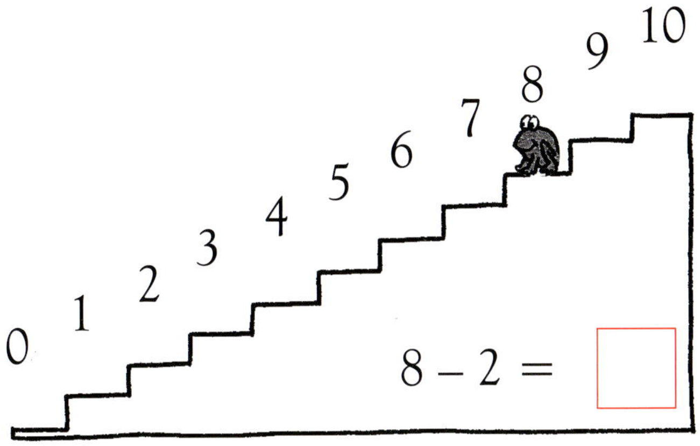

8 – 2 = ☐

7 – 0 = ☐

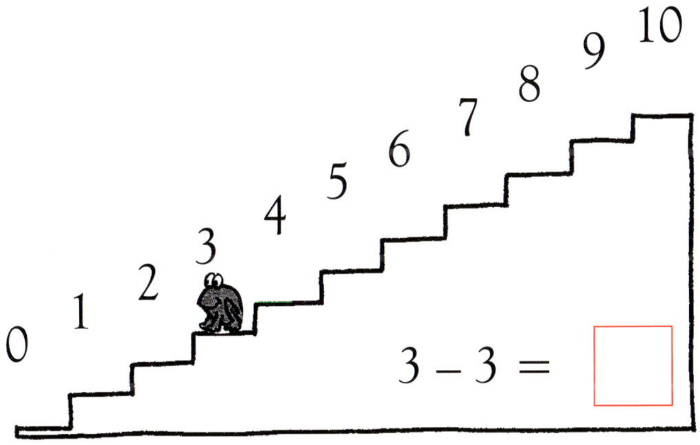

3 – 3 = ☐

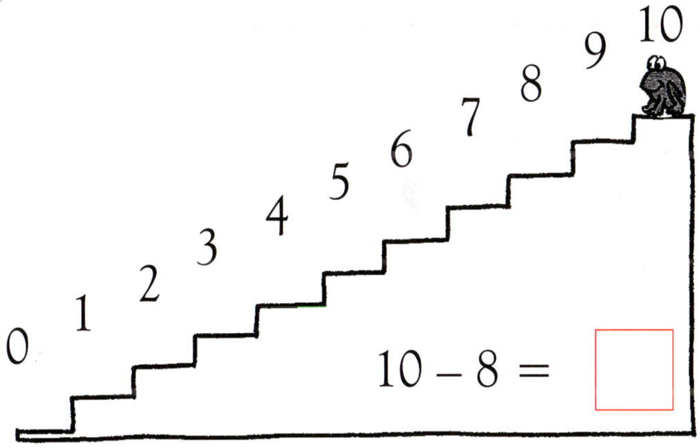

10 – 8 = ☐

Write the missing numbers in the boxes.

3 – 3 = 0	20 – 10 = ☐	9 – ☐ = 6	15 – ☐ = 5
5 – 4 = ☐	8 – 8 = ☐	5 – ☐ = 0	20 – ☐ = 4
15 – 4 = ☐	19 – 9 = ☐	6 – ☐ = 2	18 – ☐ = 11
10 – 9 = ☐	16 – 9 = ☐	10 – ☐ = 4	13 – ☐ = 10

Sets

Write the missing numbers in the boxes.

2 sets of 3 = 6

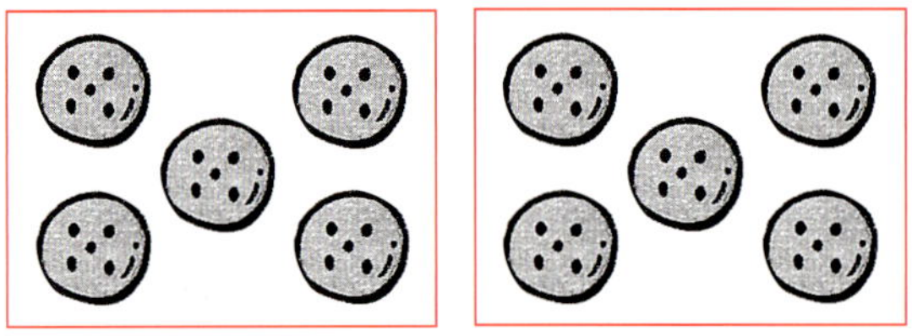

2 sets of 5 = ☐

3 sets of 4 = ☐

☐ sets of 2 = ☐

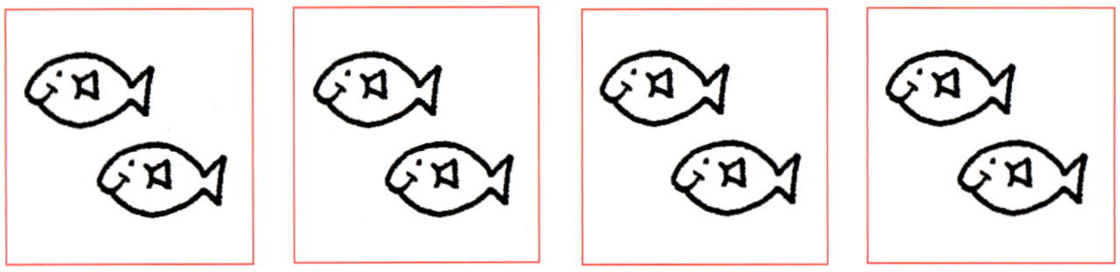

☐ sets of 2 = ☐

Draw pictures in the boxes to match the equations.

3 sets of 3 = 9

2 sets of 4 = 8

Money

Which coin?

Penny

Nickel

Dime

Quarter

How much?

3¢

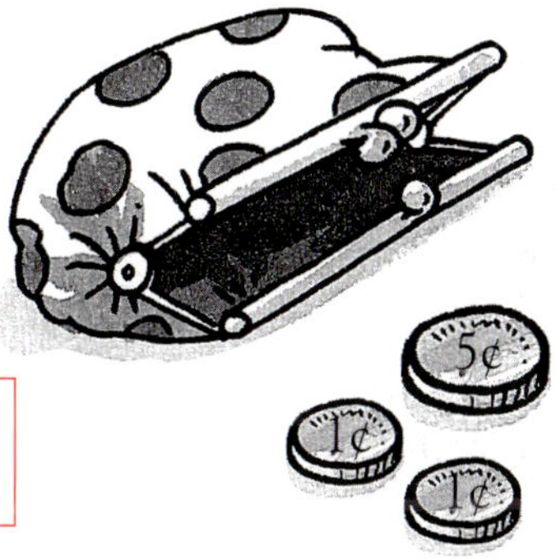

Put the correct change in the piggy bank.

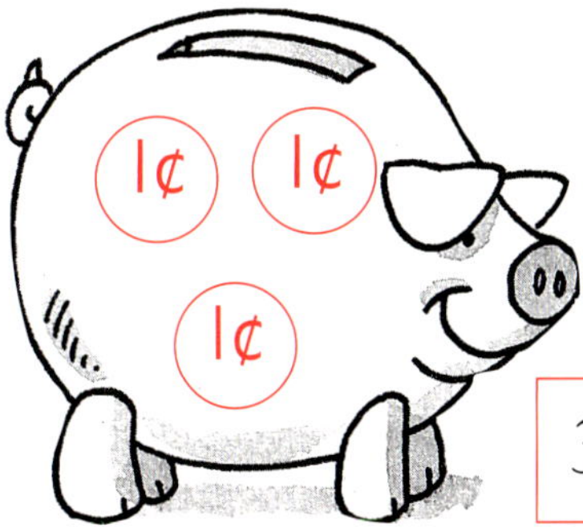

3¢

11¢

7¢

Ordering stories

Which happens 1st, 2nd, and 3rd?

 2nd  3rd  1st

 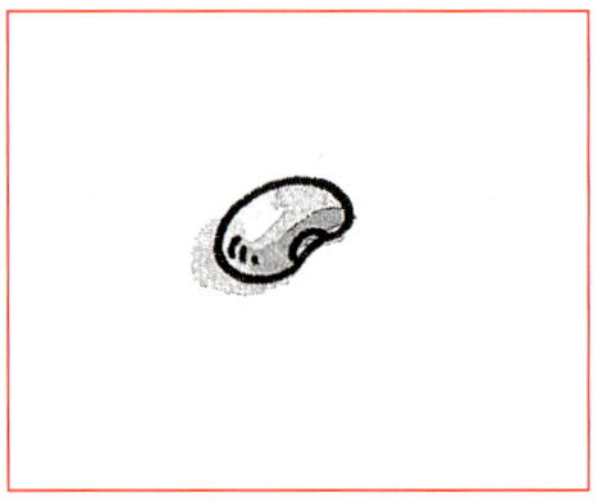 

  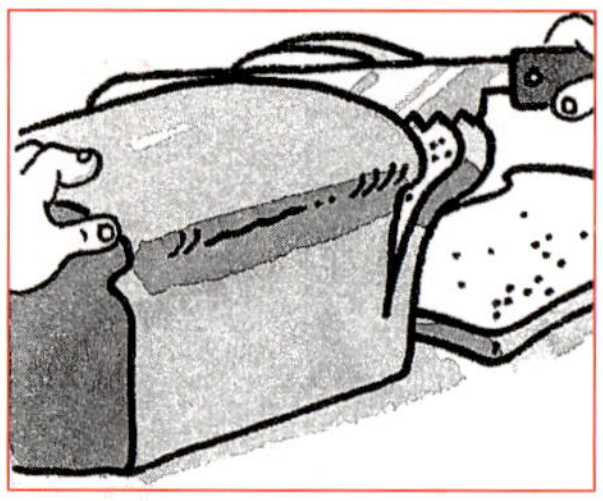

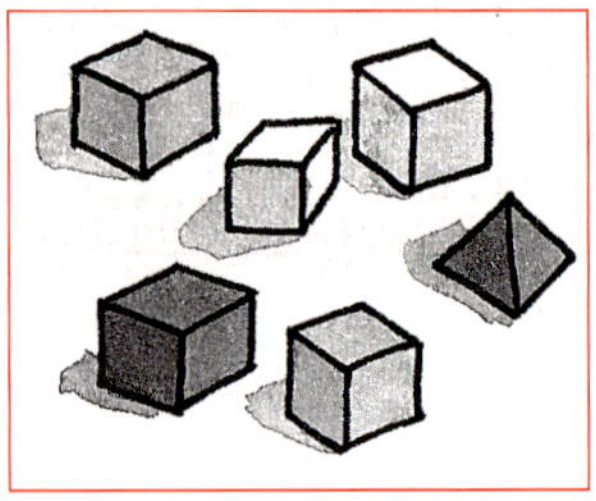 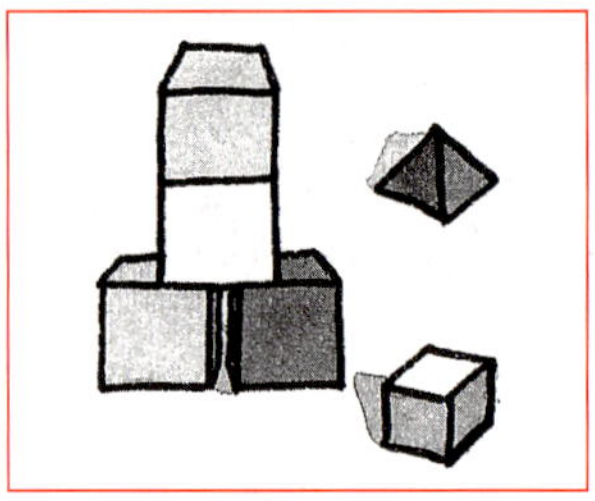 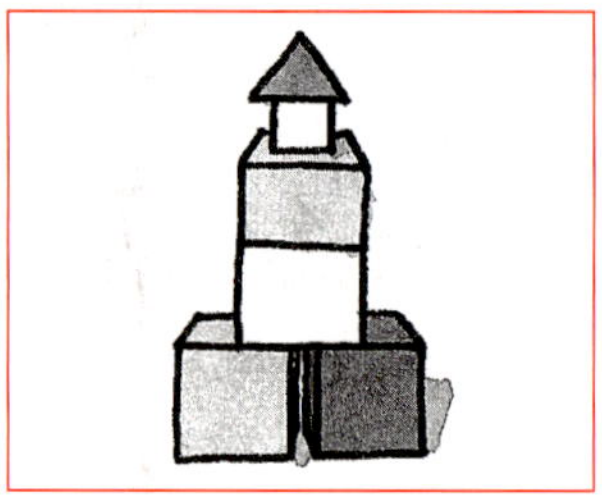

Match the pictures to the order in which they happened.

4th 2nd 1st 3rd

Time

Write the time in each box.

| 3 | o'clock | | o'clock | | o'clock | | o'clock |

Draw the hands on the clock faces.

4 o'clock   10 o'clock   1 o'clock   6 o'clock

Match the times to the clocks.

| 12 o'clock | 7 o'clock | 2 o'clock | 9 o'clock |

3-dimensional shapes

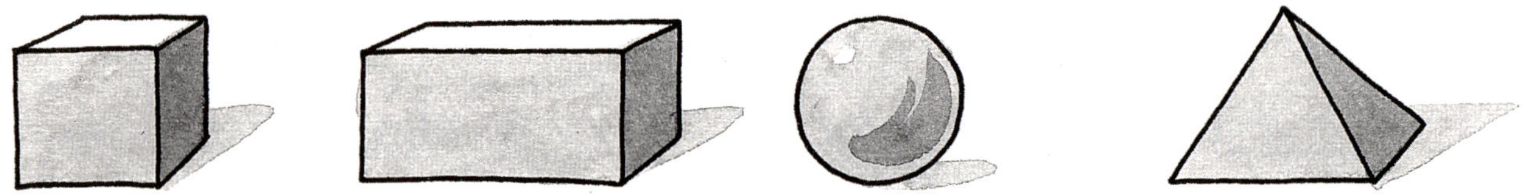

cube | prism | sphere | pyramid

Match the shapes to the names.

pyramid | sphere | cube | prism

How many?

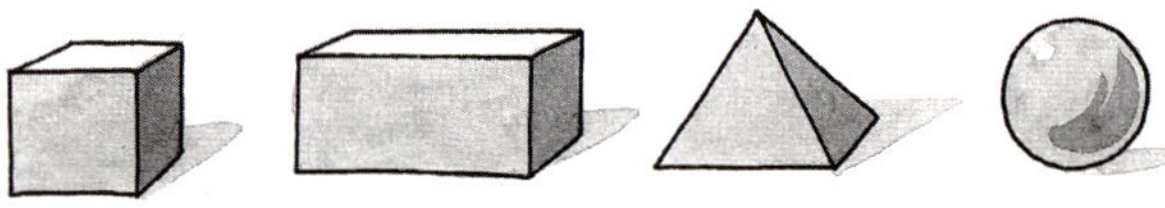

2			

How many?

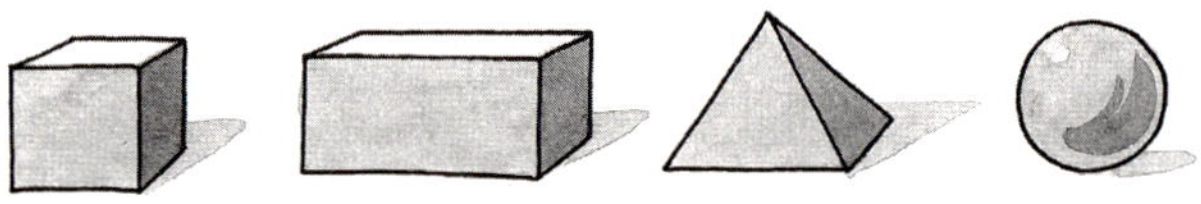

Writing numbers

Count, write, and say the number of letters.

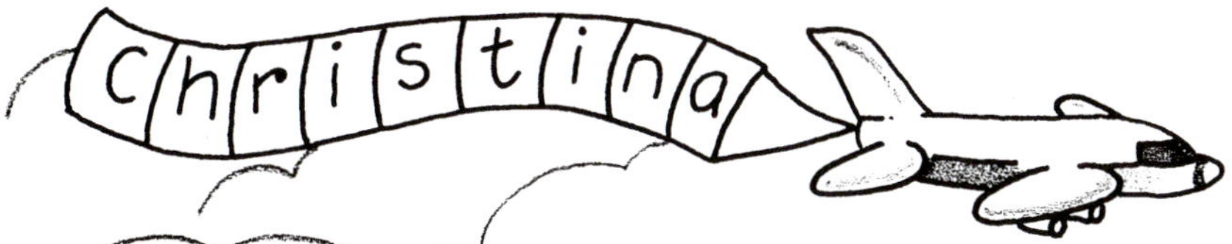

9 nine

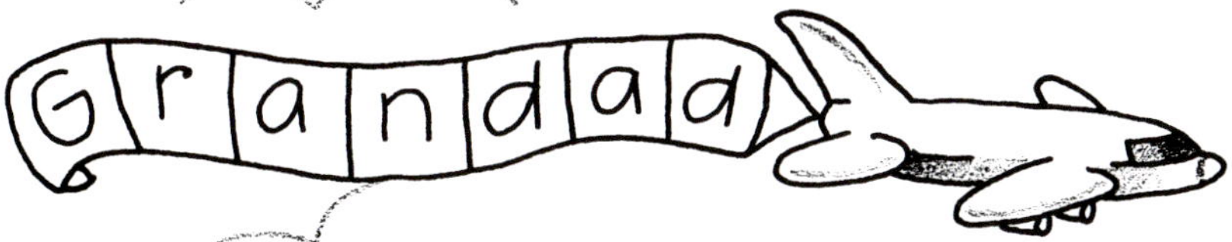

Write your name.

Make up your own message.

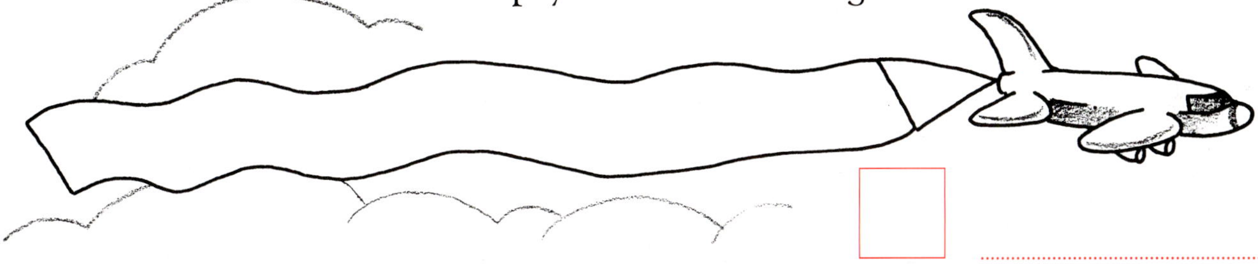

Counting

Write the missing numbers.

Counting on by 2s

Hop by 2s. Colour the squares.

What letters will you find? Say the numbers as you draw.

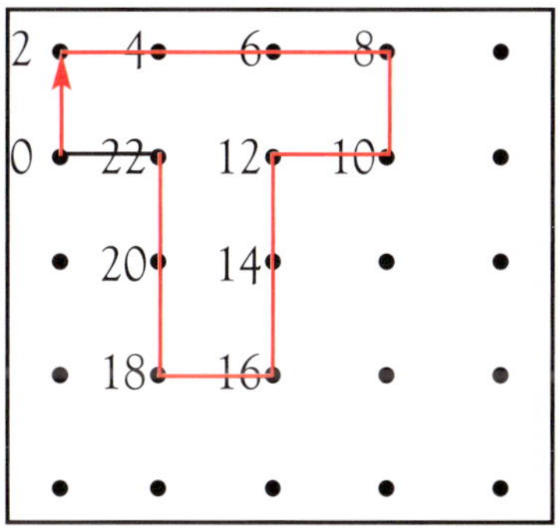

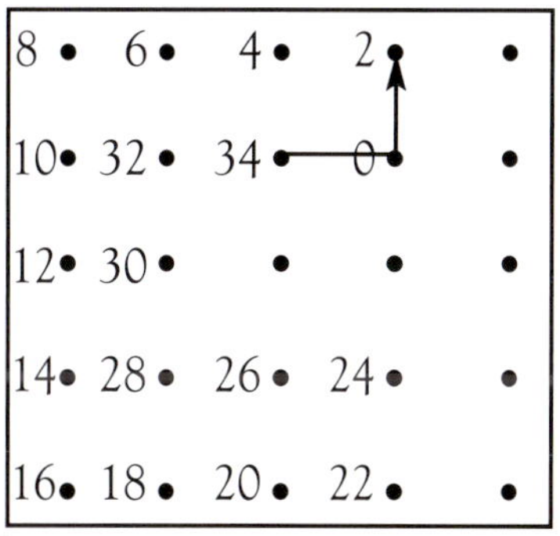

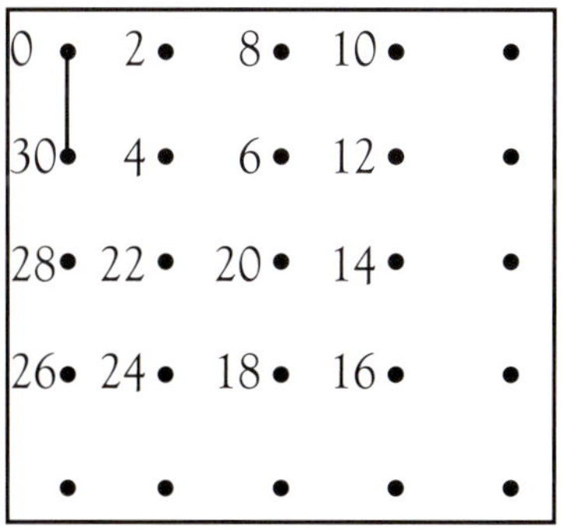

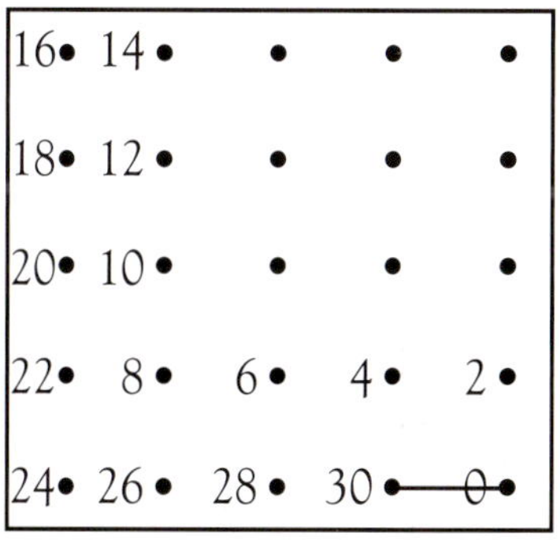

Write the numbers.

Even numbers

2 4 6 8 ☐ ☐ ☐ ☐ ☐ ☐

Odd numbers

1 3 5 ☐ ☐ ☐ ☐ ☐ ☐ ☐

Most and least

Circle the set with the most items in it.

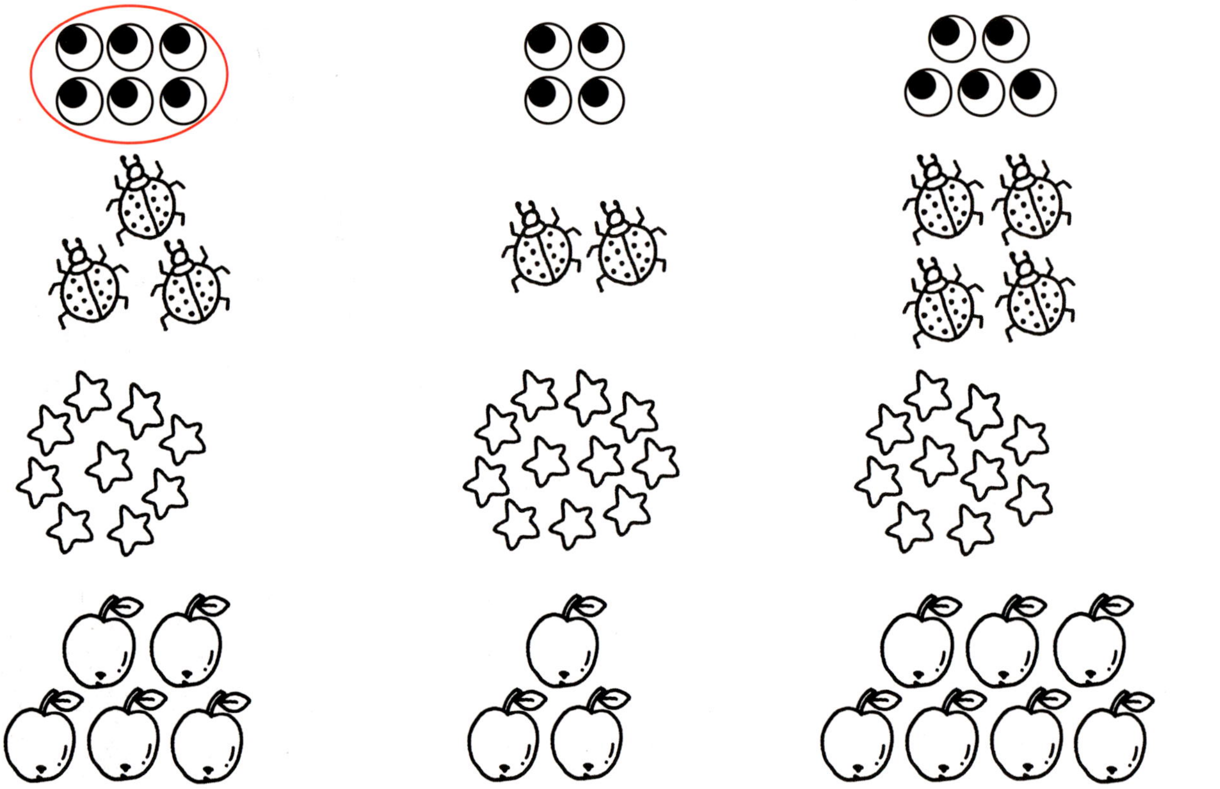

Circle the set with the least items in it.

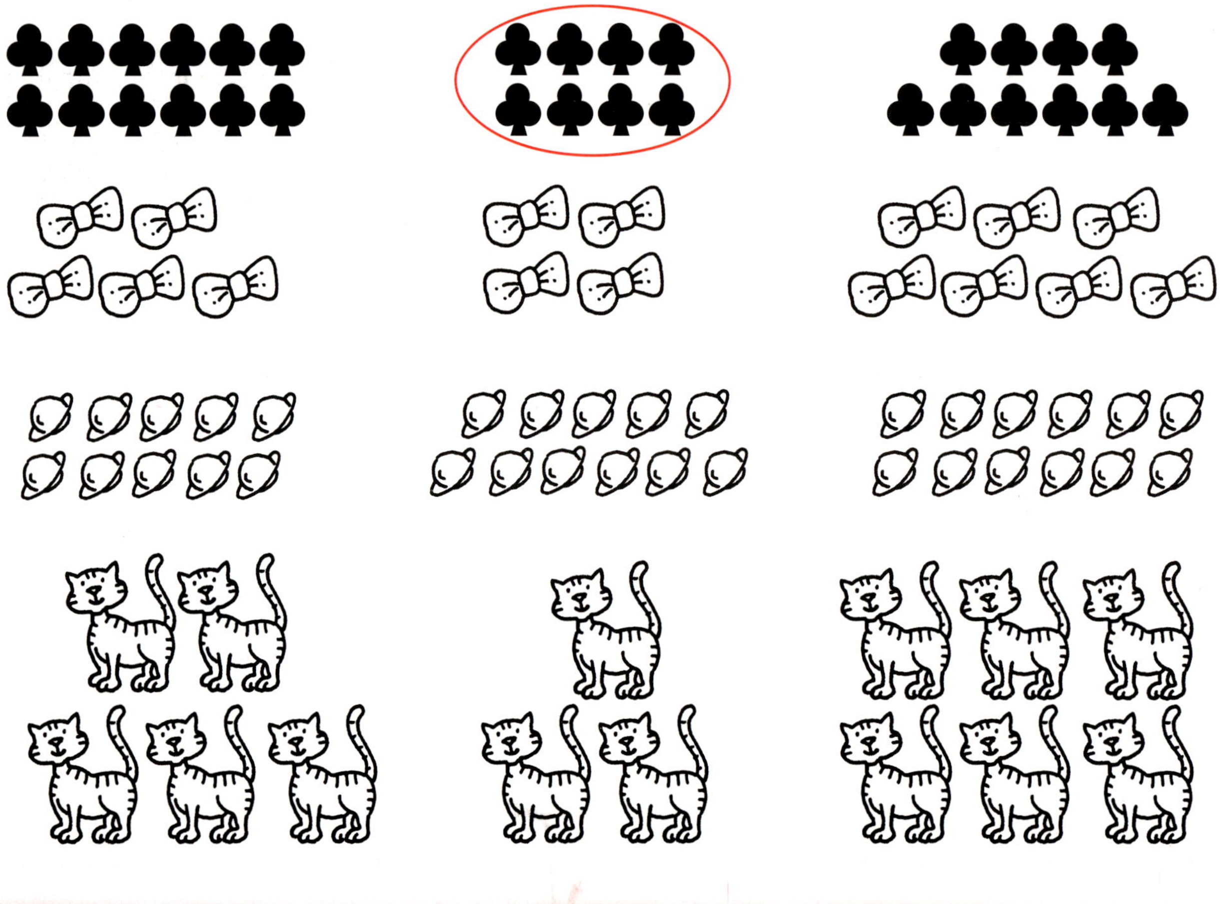

Counting by 10s

Use this number line to help you.

0	10	20	30	40	50	60	70	80	90	100
zero	ten	twenty	thirty	forty	fifty	sixty	seventy	eighty	ninety	one hundred

How many candies? Count, say, and write.

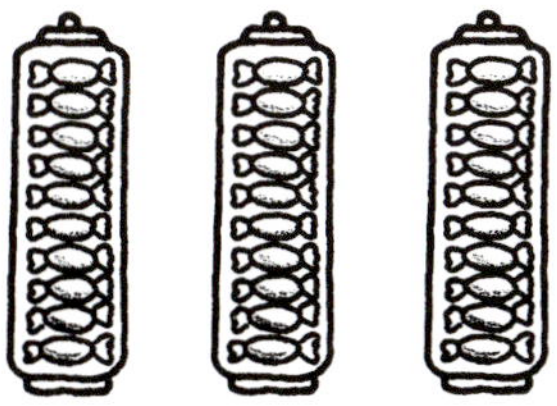

30 thirty

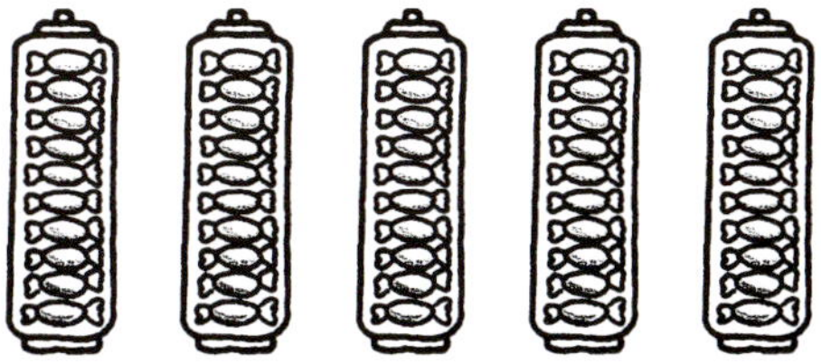

50 ....

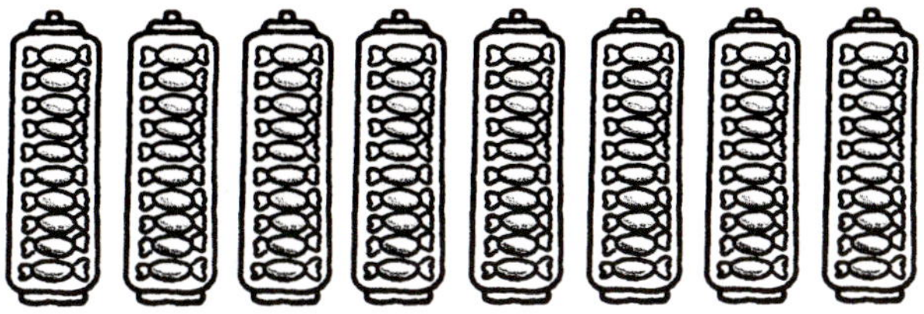

☐ eighty

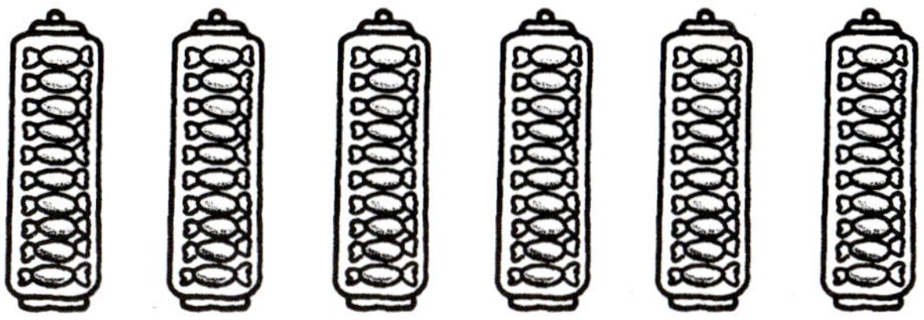

60 ....

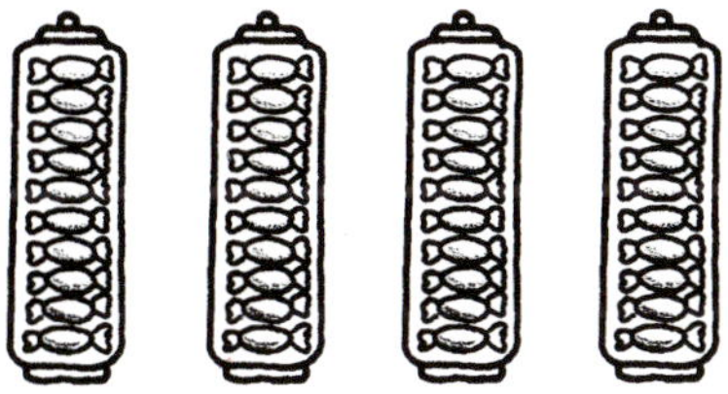

☐ ....

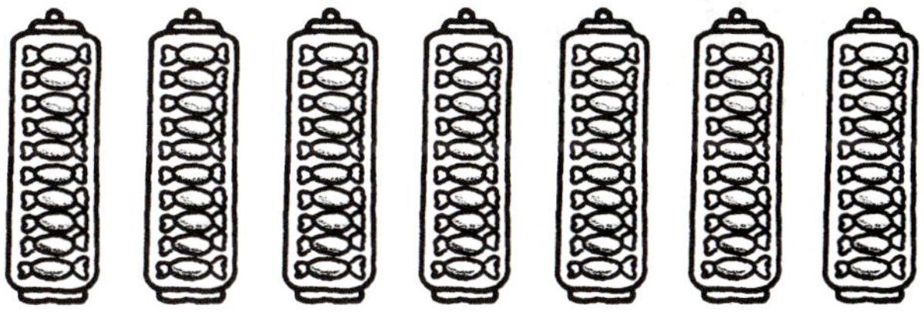

☐ ....

Put the numbers in the right order.

~~10~~ 60 100 50 ~~20~~ 70 90 30 40 80

10 20 ....

Greatest first

100 90 80 ....

Counting forward or back

Draw pathways by writing the missing numbers.

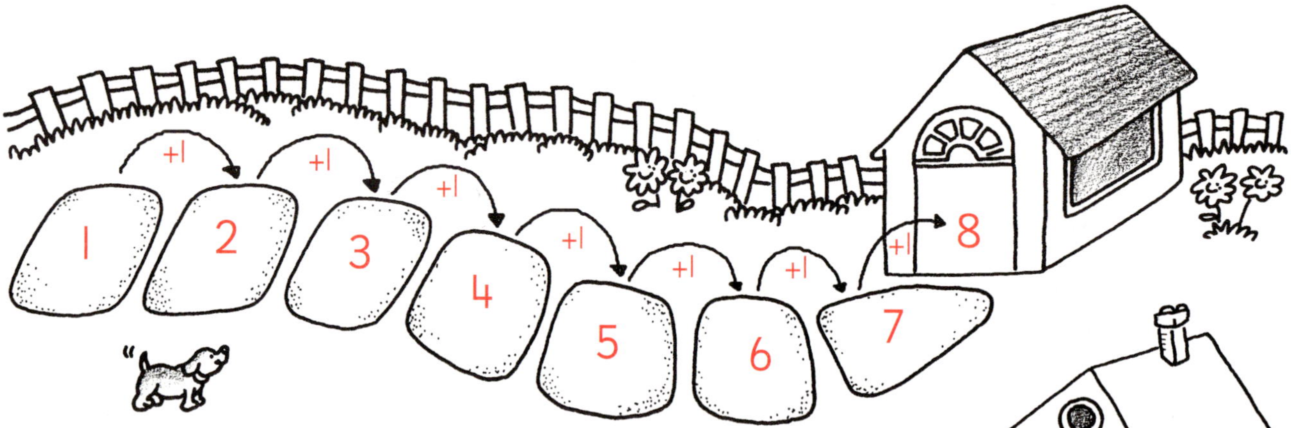

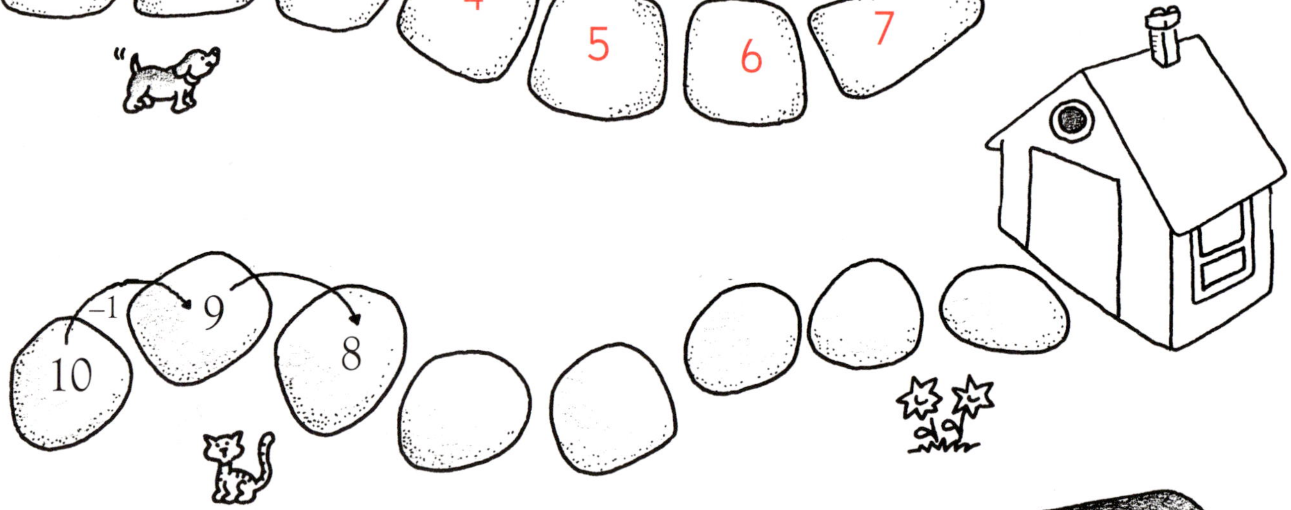

Reading numbers

Connect the numbers, and complete the drawings.

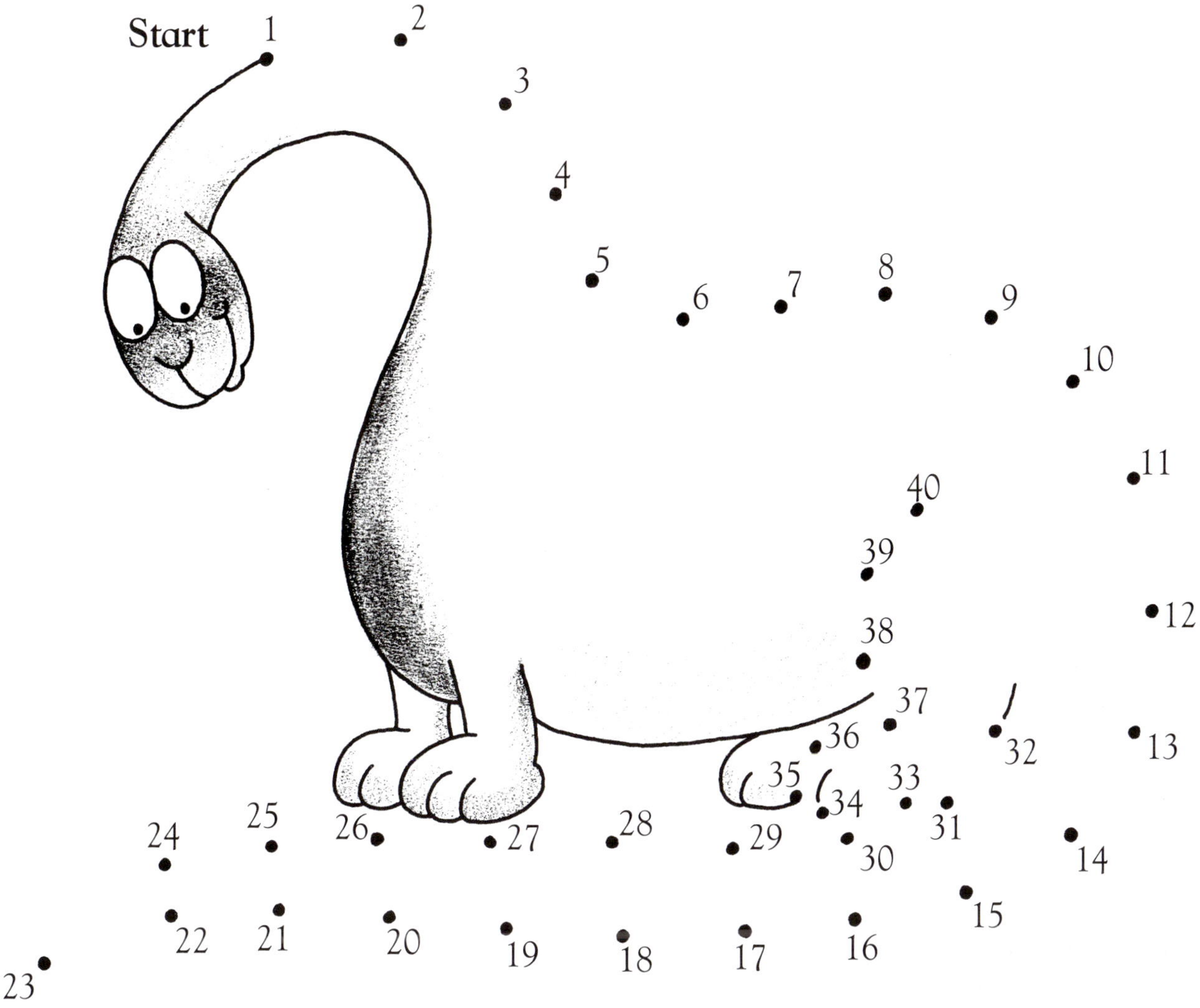

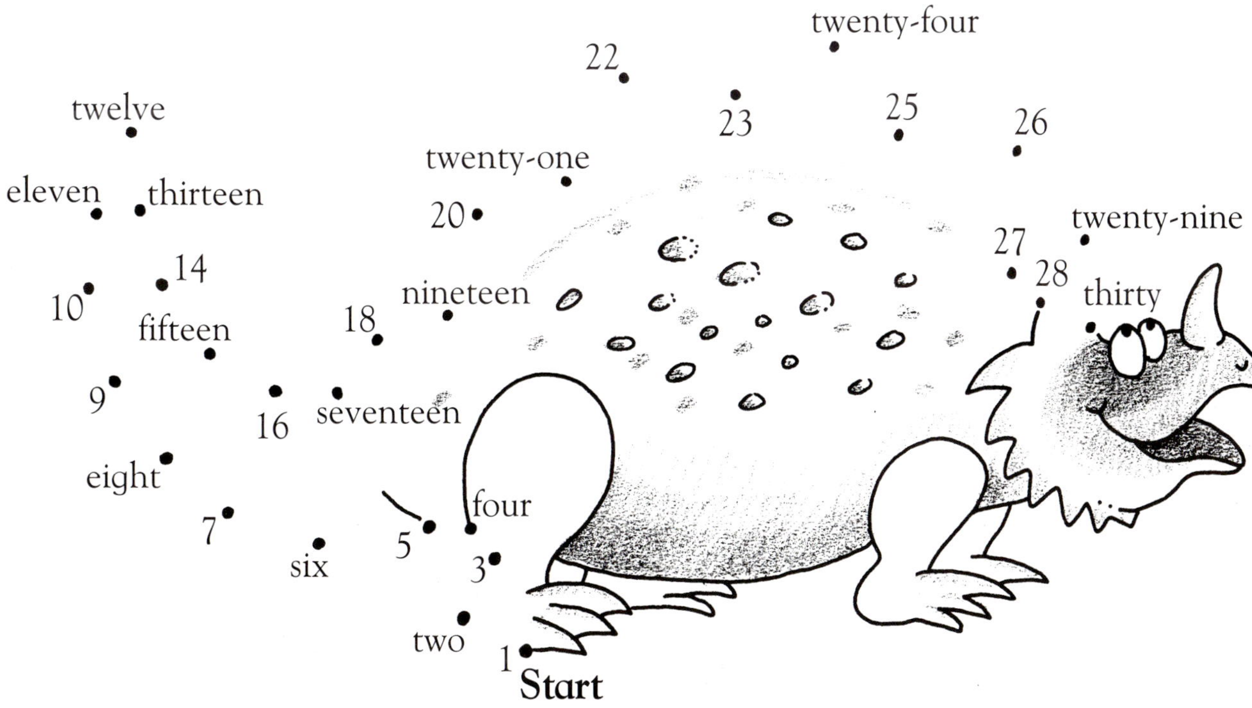

Tens and ones

Write the tens and ones.

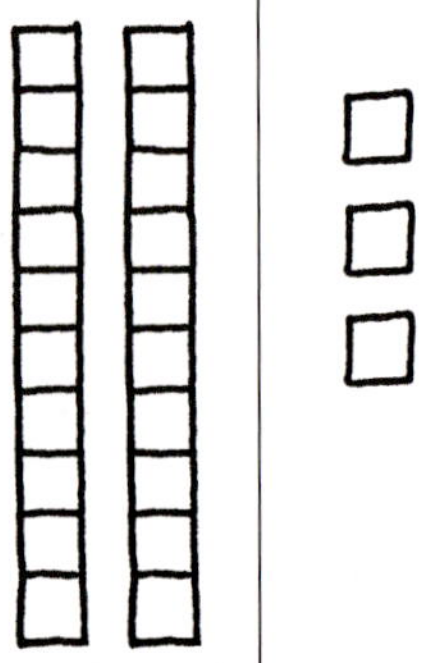

tens	ones
2	3

23

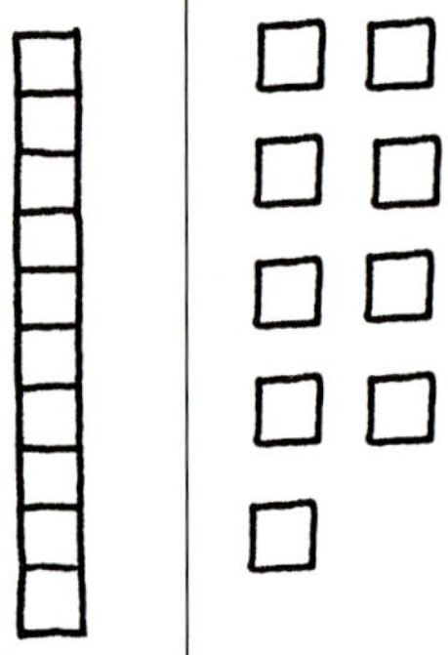

tens	ones

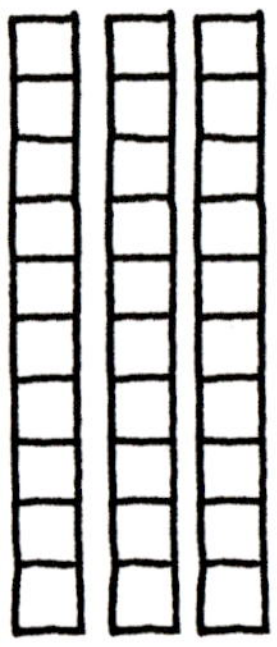

tens	ones

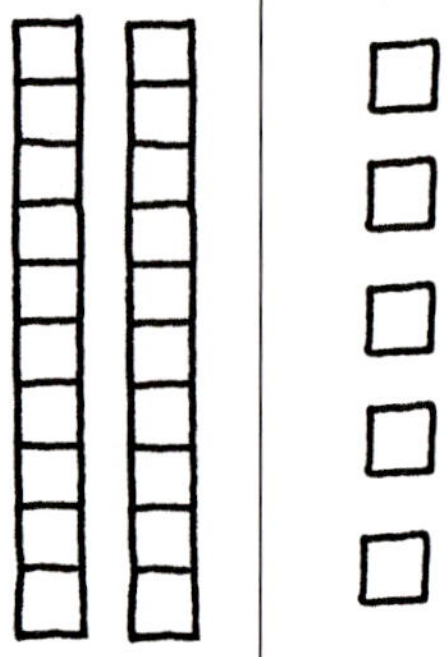

tens	ones

Draw and write the tens and ones.

tens	ones

29

tens	ones

34

Comparisons

Add the values, and write *is greater than* or *is less than.*

16 — is greater than → 9

12 →

→

→

Write the numbers that are 1 more, 1 less, or between.

1 less	between	1 more
20	21	22

1 less	number	1 more
	26	

number	between	number
19		21

1 less	number	1 more
	29	

1 less	number	1 more
	11	

number	between	number
30		32

Comparing money

Colour the one who has the most money.

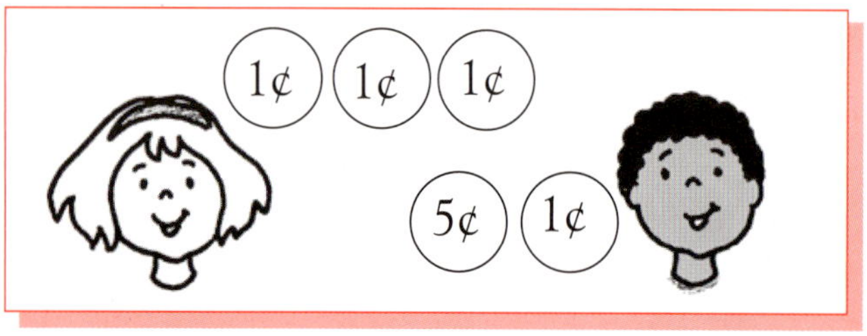

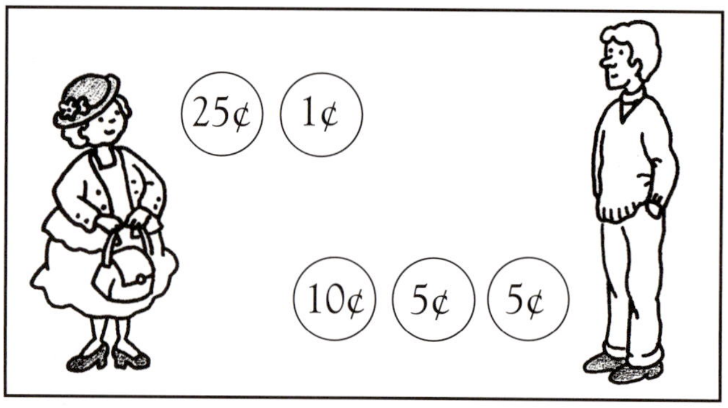

Draw some coins in the purses.

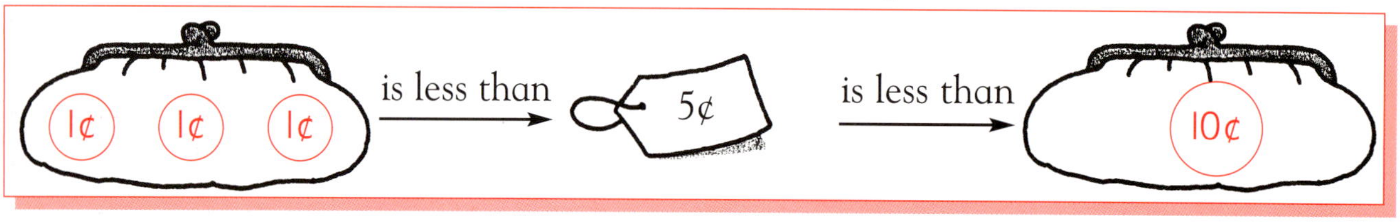

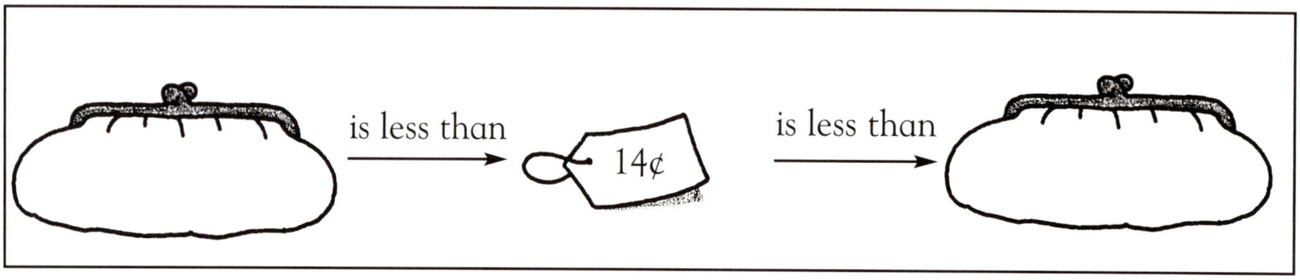

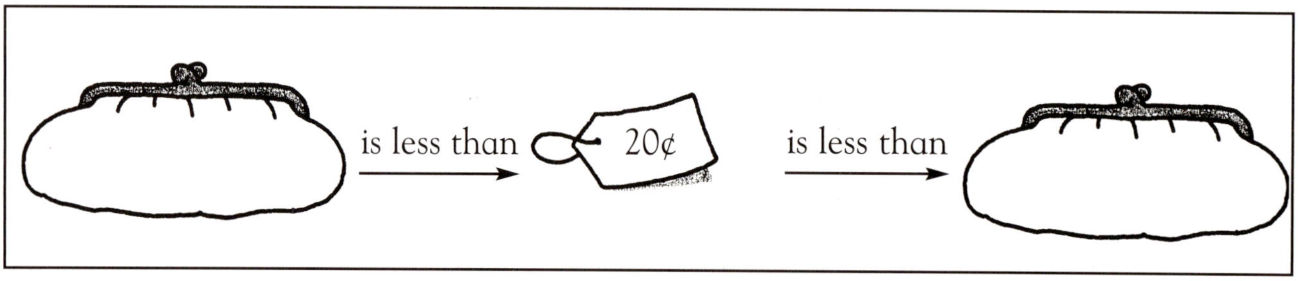

Spot the doubles

Draw the missing spots and write the numbers.

3 + 3 = 6

double 3 is 6

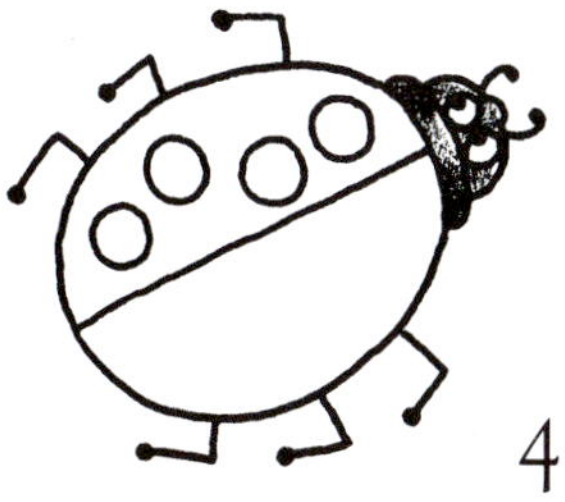

4 + □ = □

double 4 is □

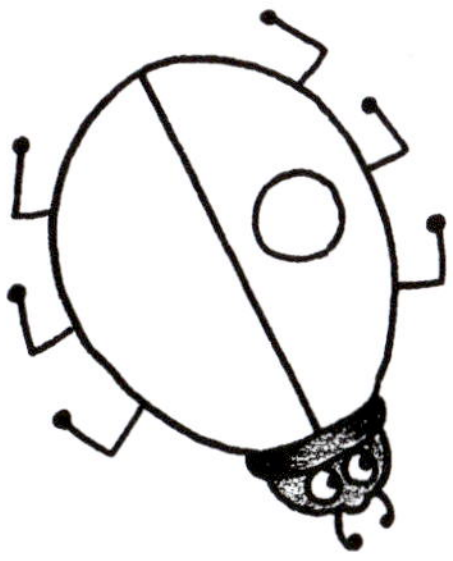

1 + □ = □

double 1 is □

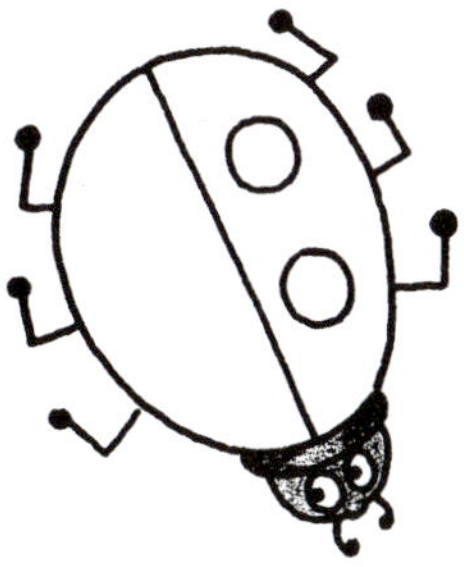

2 + □ = □

double 2 is □

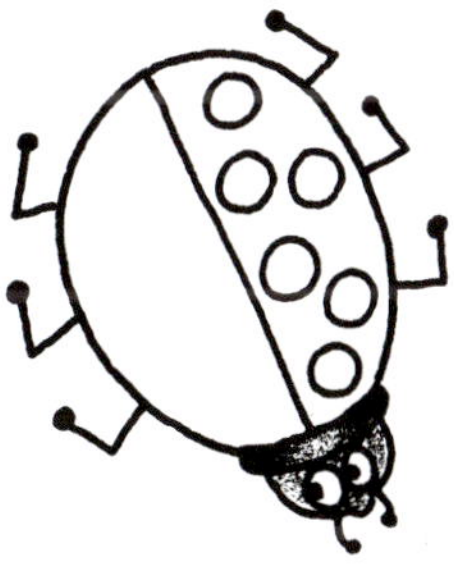

6 + □ = □

double 6 is □

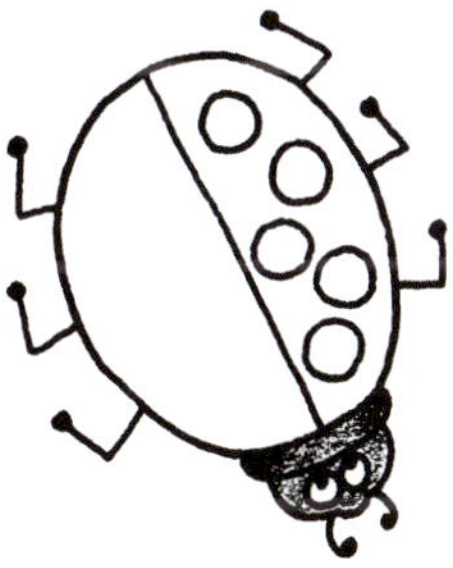

5 + □ = □

double 5 is □

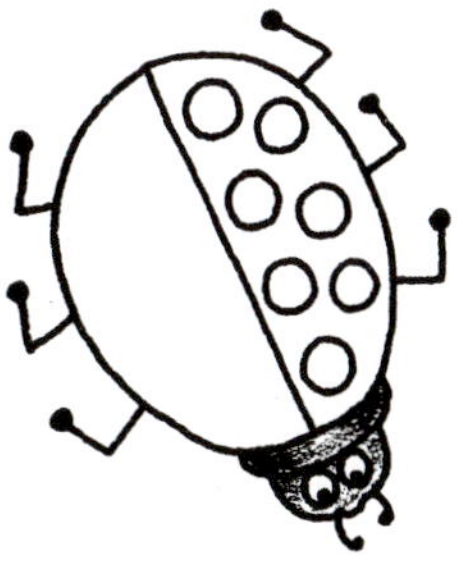

7 + □ = □

double 7 is □

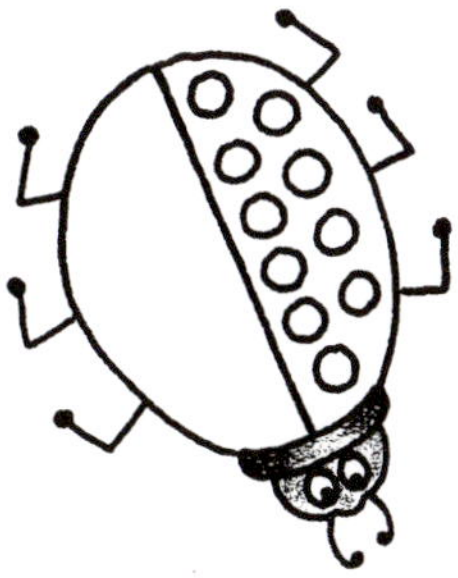

10 + □ = □

double 10 is □

10 more or 10 less

Draw a line to add 10 to each number on the rocket.

Draw a line to subtract 10 from each number on the rocket.

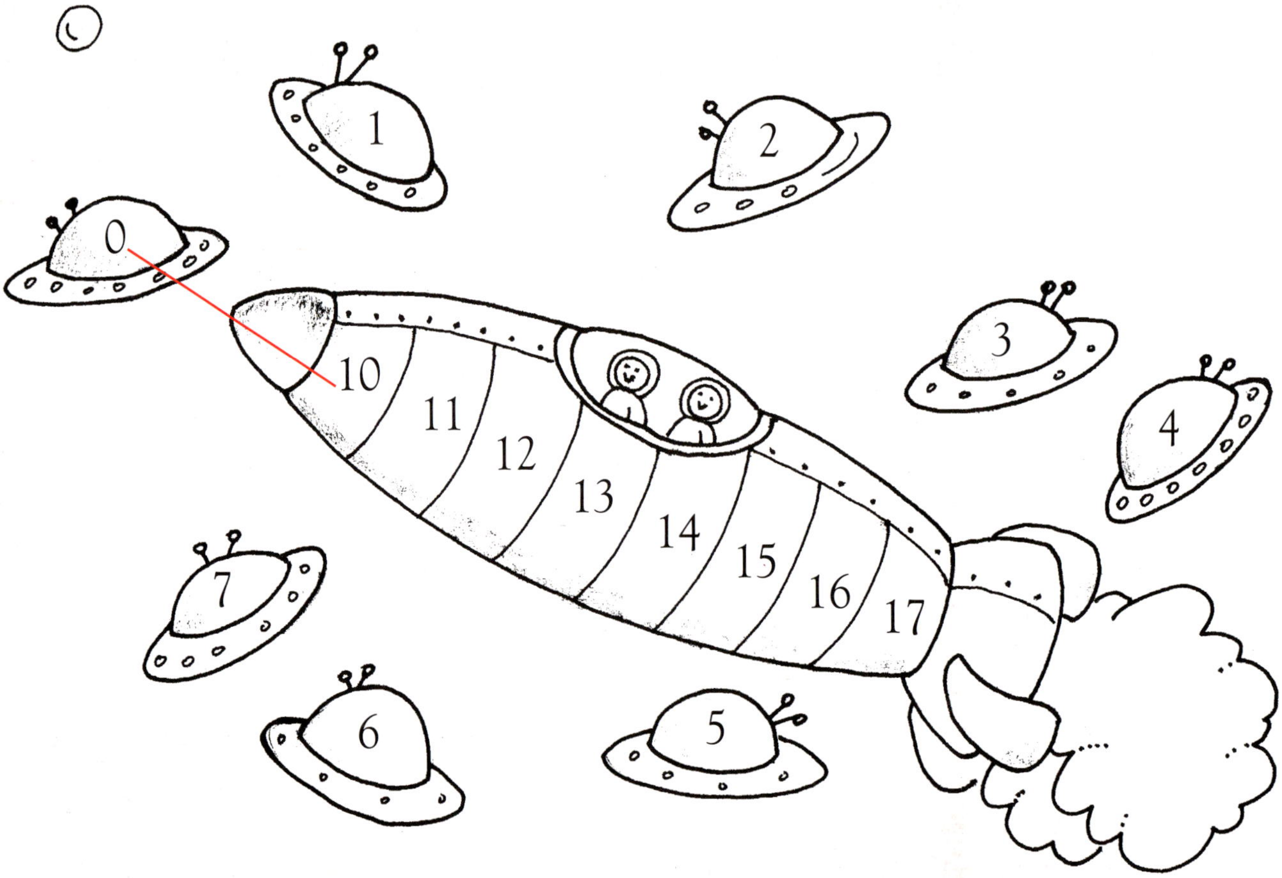

Ordinals

Colour the beads.

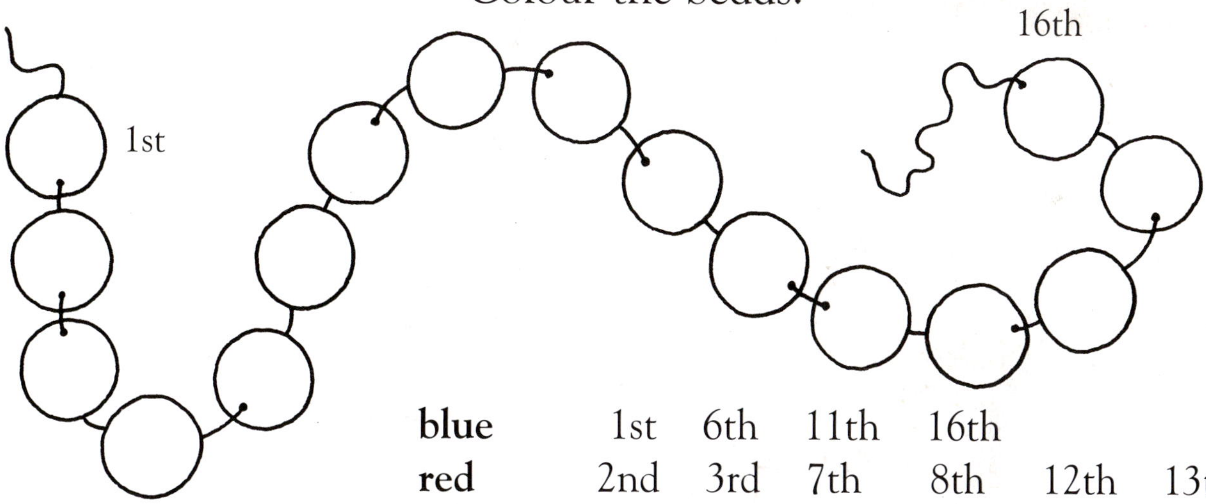

blue	1st	6th	11th	16th		
red	2nd	3rd	7th	8th	12th	13th
yellow	4th	5th	9th	10th	14th	15th

Write the positions.

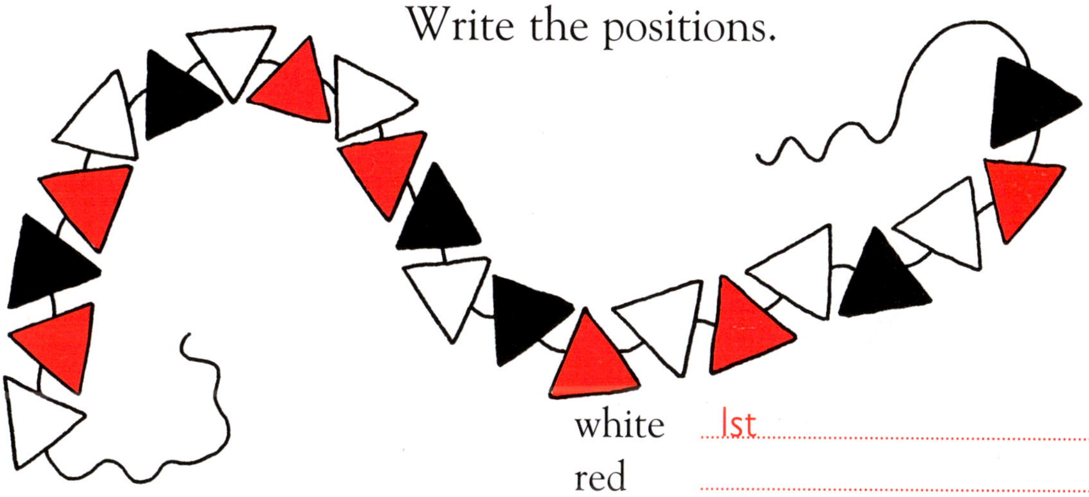

white 1st ....

red ....

black ....

Choose 3 colours. Make your own pattern. Write the positions.

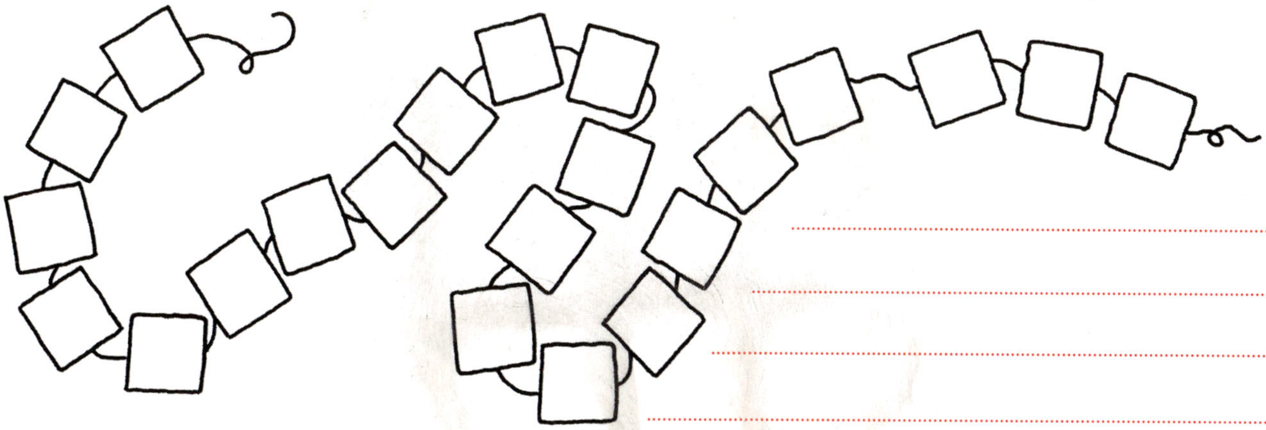

....

....

....

....

....

....

Ordering

Look for a pattern. Write the numbers in order.

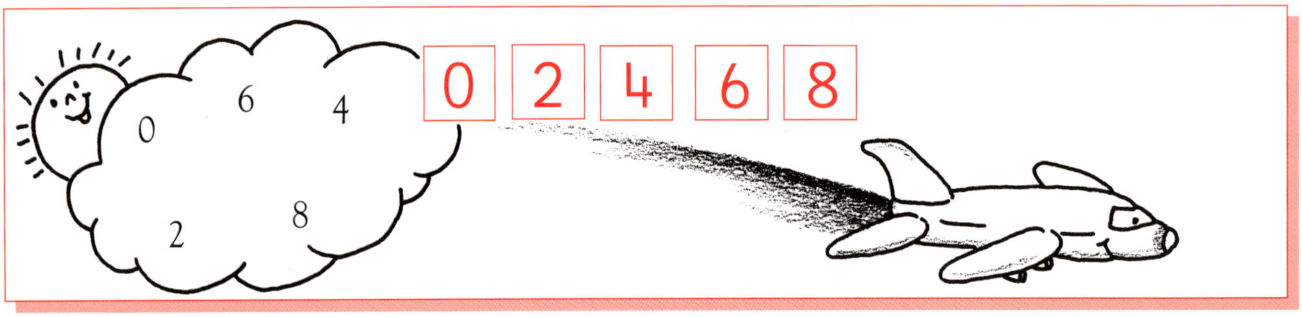

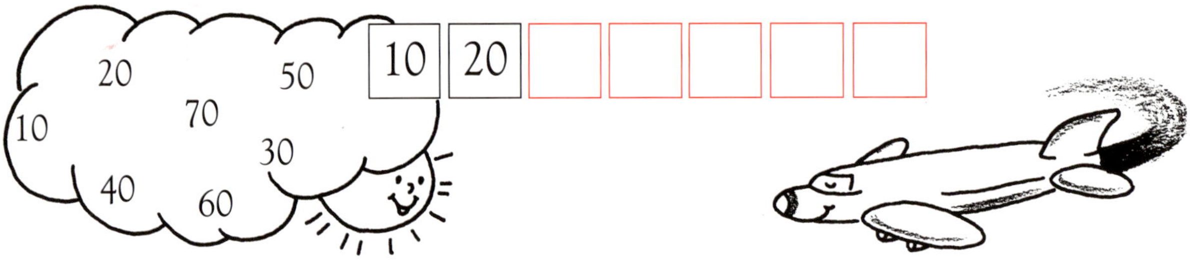

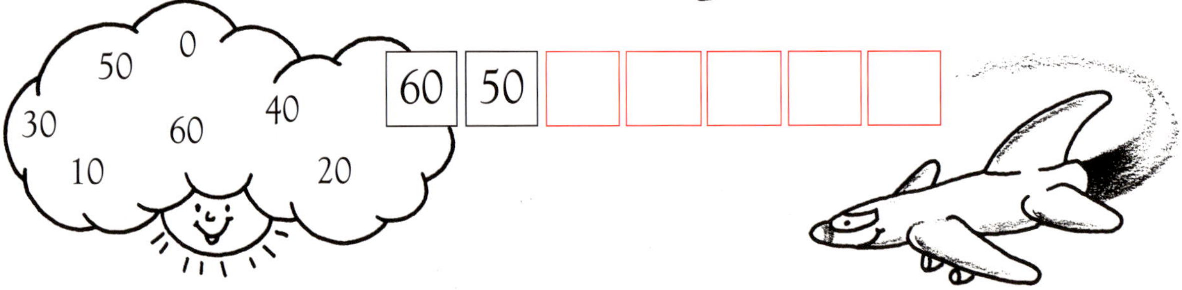

Halves and fourths

For each shape colour one half red or one fourth yellow.

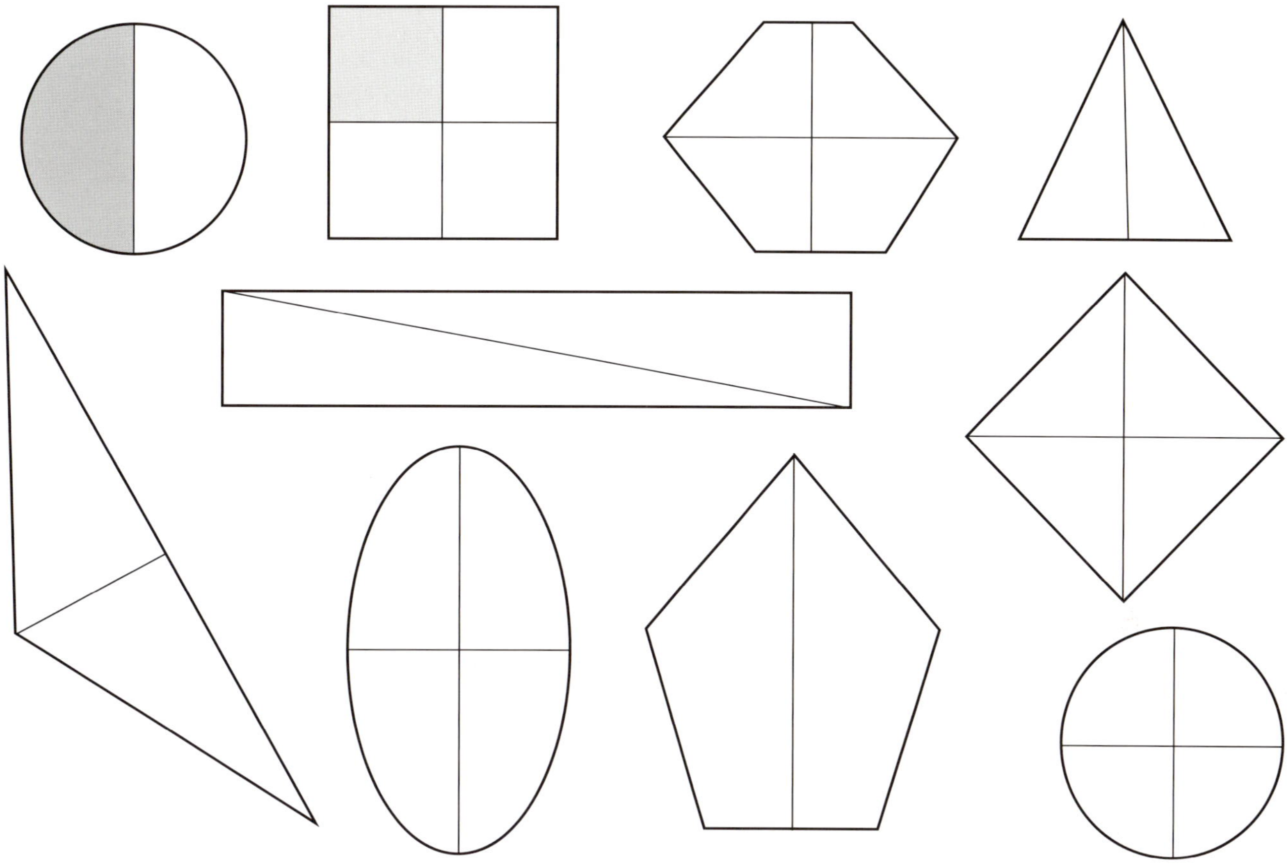

Halves or fourths?

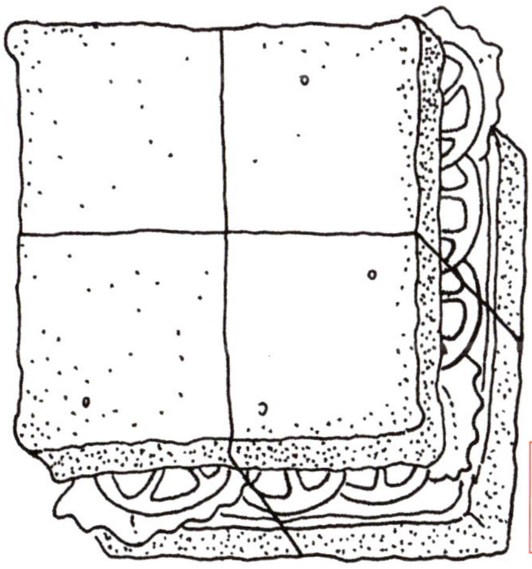

$\frac{1}{4}$

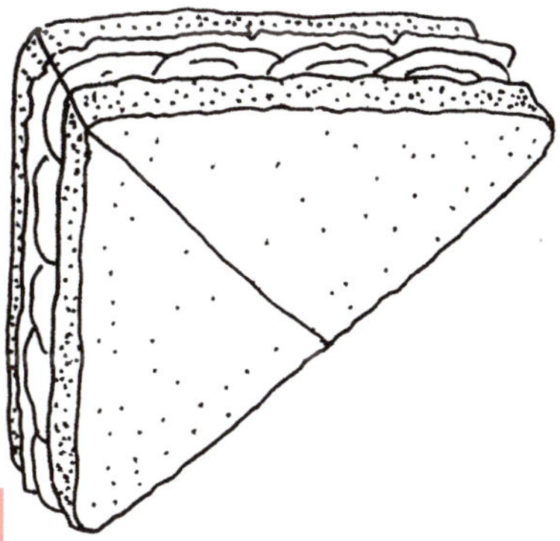

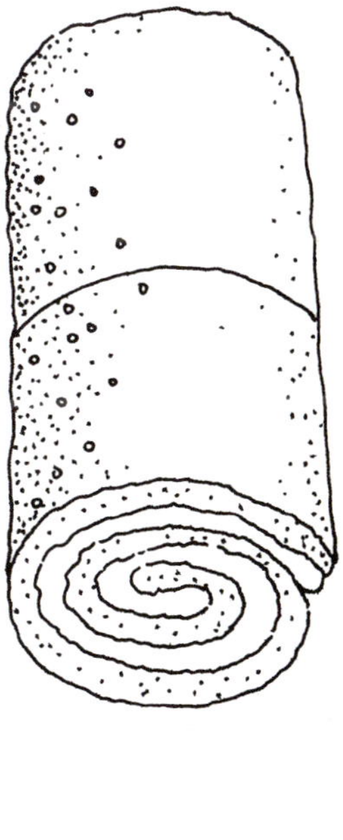

$\frac{1}{2}$

Place value

What is in the ones place in each number?

24	61	87	19
4	1		
65	68	13	42

What is in the tens place in each number?

30	94	10	69
3	9		
27	81	18	50

What is in the tens place in each number?

12	90	43	58
1			

Circle the number that has a 7 in the tens place.

57 79 70

Circle the number that has a 3 in the ones place.

34 93 30

Circle the number that has a 1 in the tens place.

10 61 21

Expanded form

Write each number as a sum of tens and ones.

54	=	50 + 4	12	=		88	=	
47	=		29	=		11	=	
75	=		51	=		44	=	
62	=		93	=		19	=	
25	=		74	=		36	=	

Write the missing number.

80	+	6	=	86	90	+	7	=	97
	+	3	=	33		+	1	=	61
10	+		=	15		+	8	=	58
20	+		=	22	70	+		=	79
	+	3	=	43	90	+		=	94

Adding dice

Count the dots on the dice.

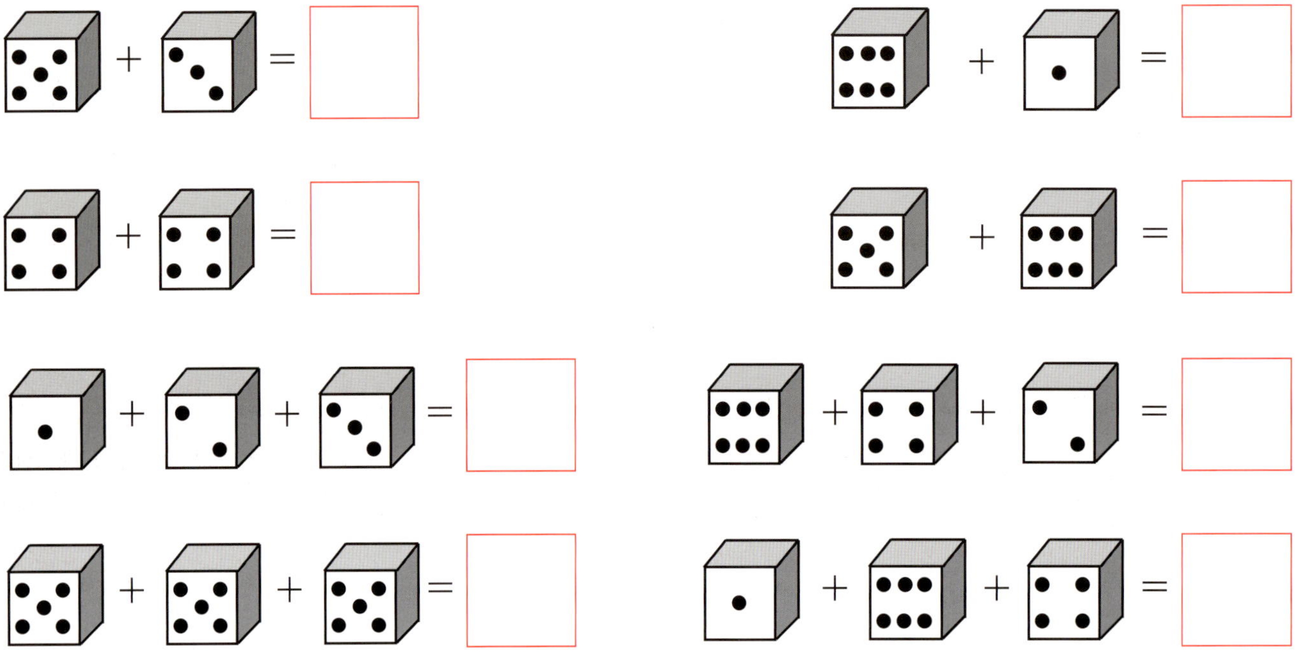

Make your own dice problems. You can roll real dice to help.

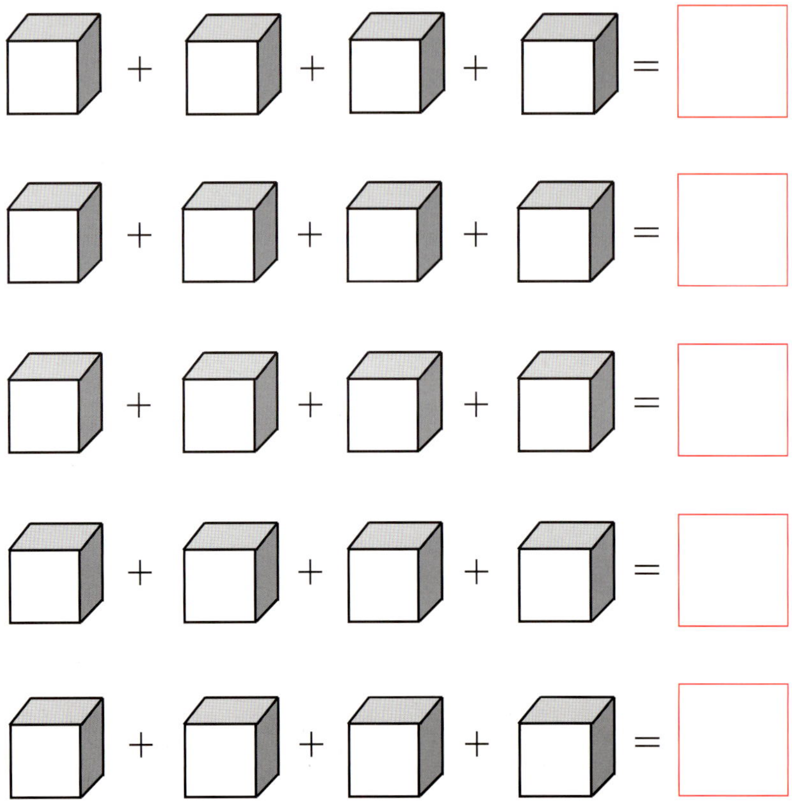

Adding

Add up the numbers on the socks.

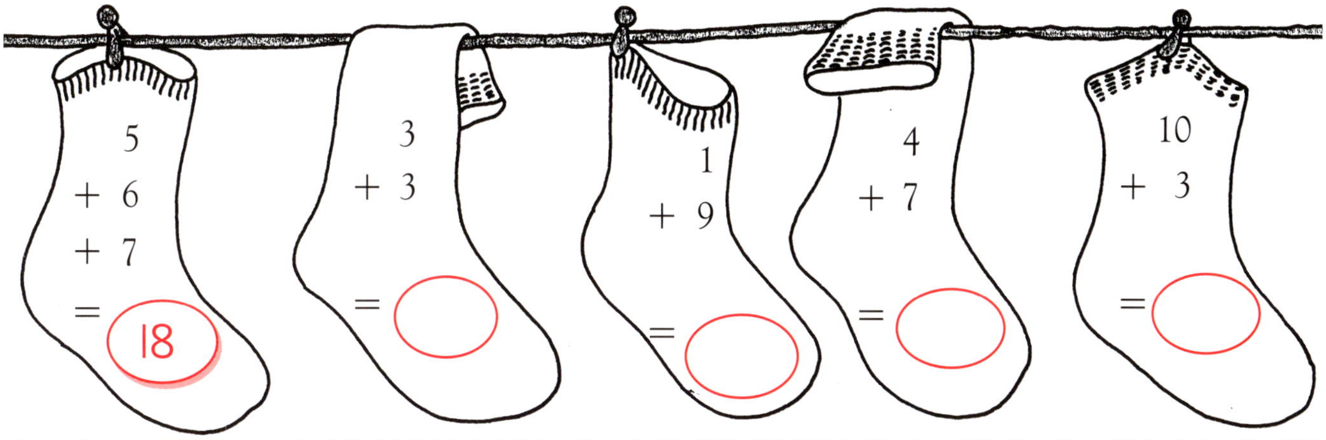

Add up the numbers on the towels.

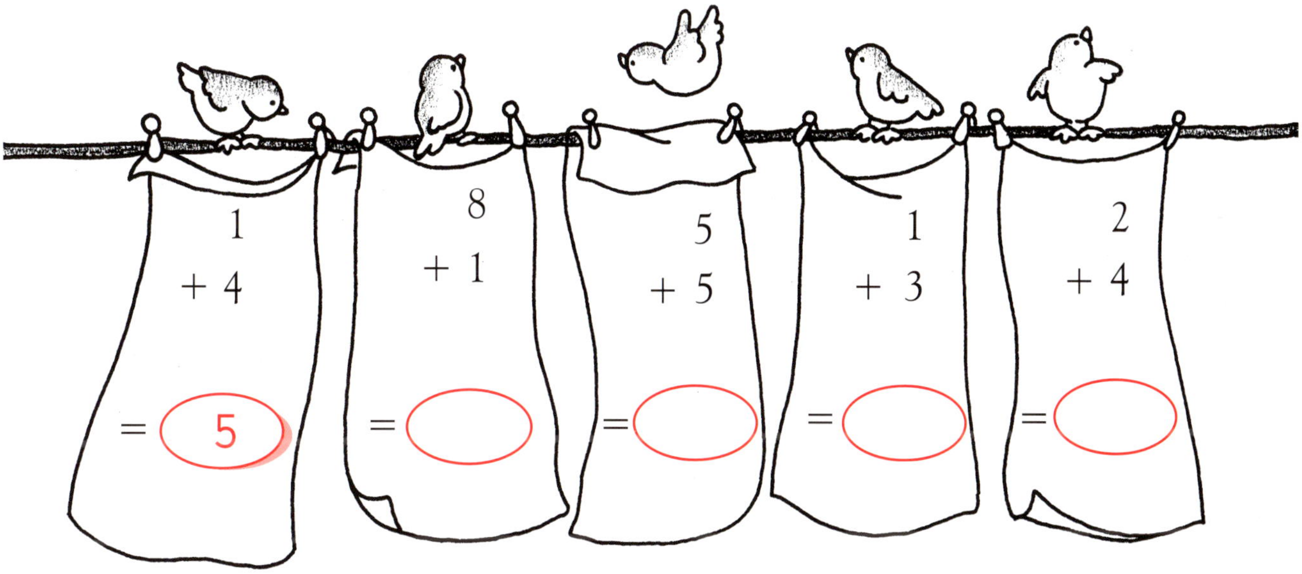

Make up your own number towels.

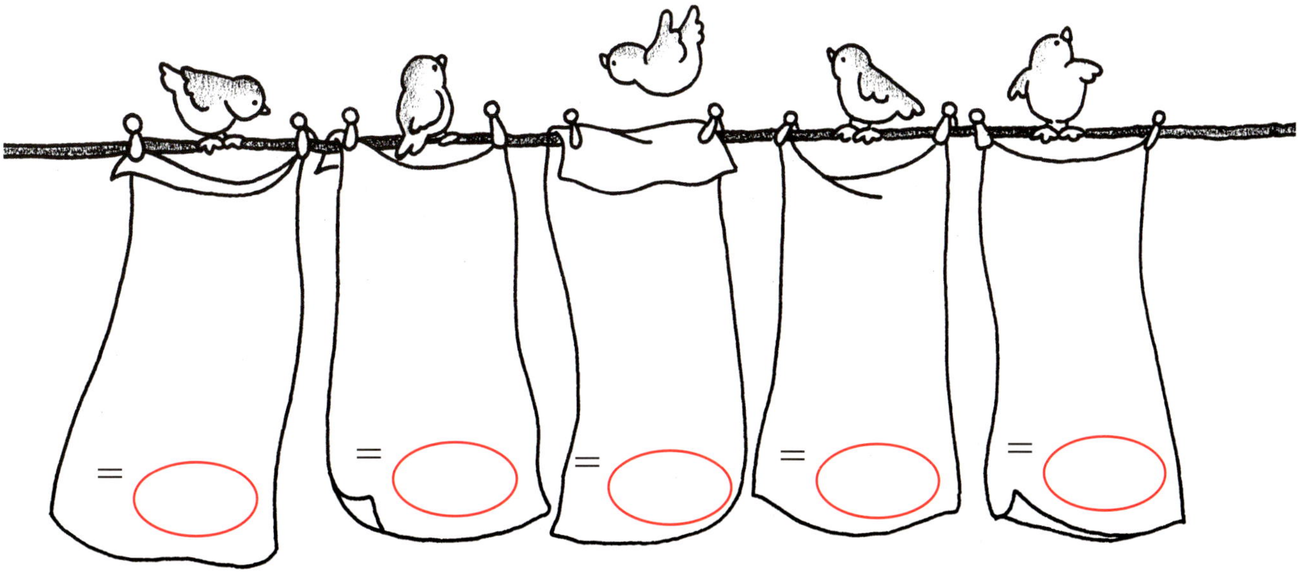

Crossing out

Cross out one type of shape in each box.

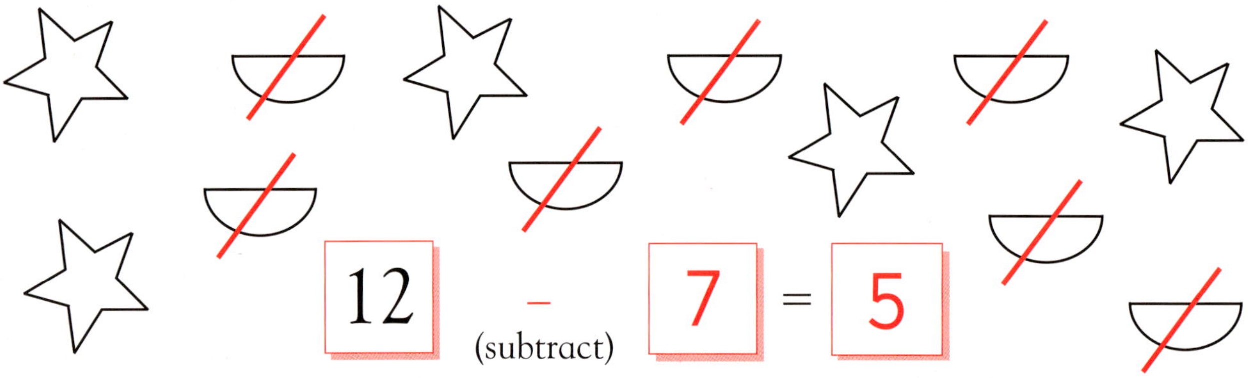

12 – (subtract) 7 = 5

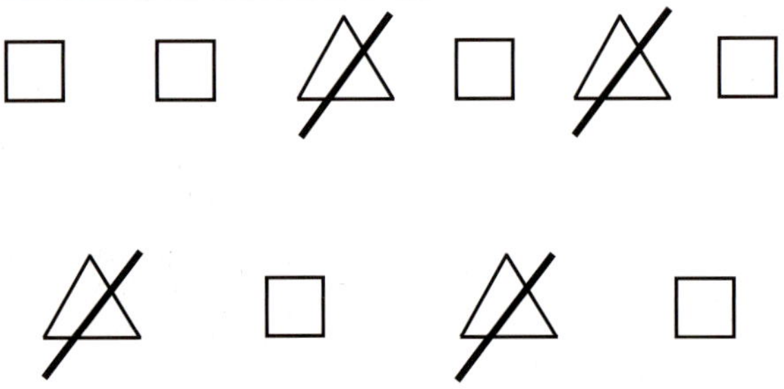

10 – ___ = ___

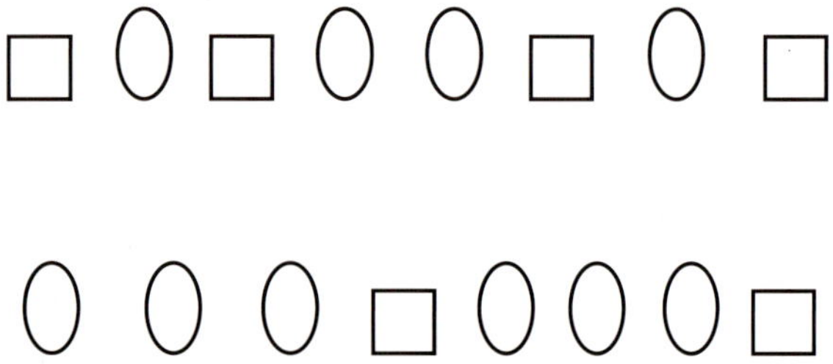

16 – ___ = ___

10 – ___ = ___

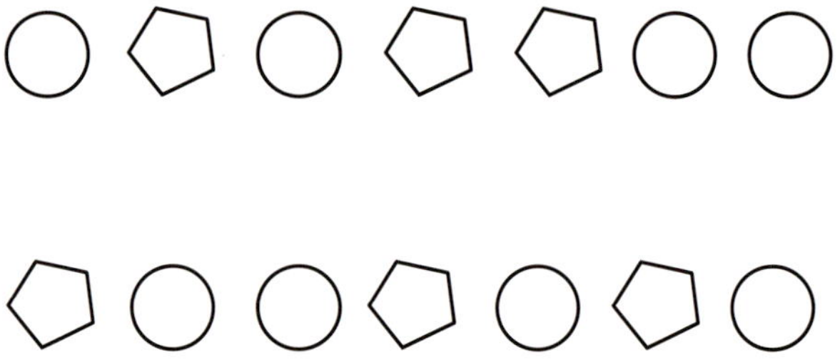

14 – ___ = ___

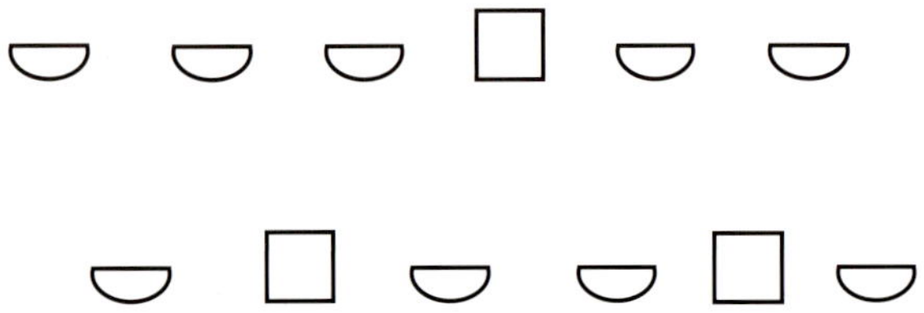

___ – ___ = ___

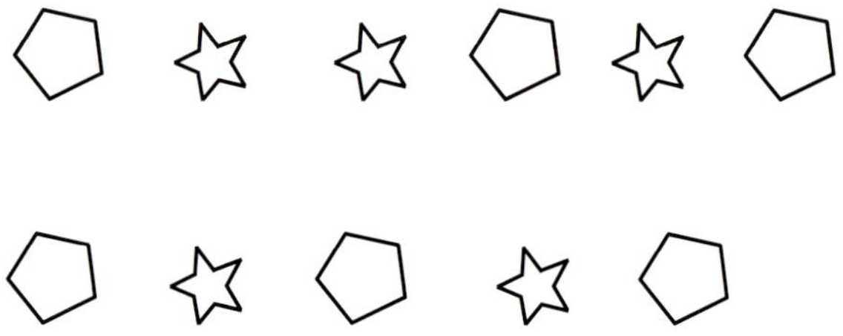

___ – ___ = ___

Subtraction

Say and count as you write.

10 altogether. How many in the tent?

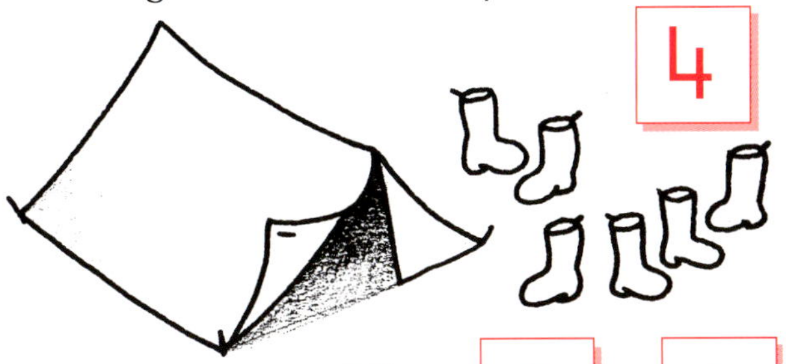

4

10 – 6 = 4

18 altogether. How many in the tent?

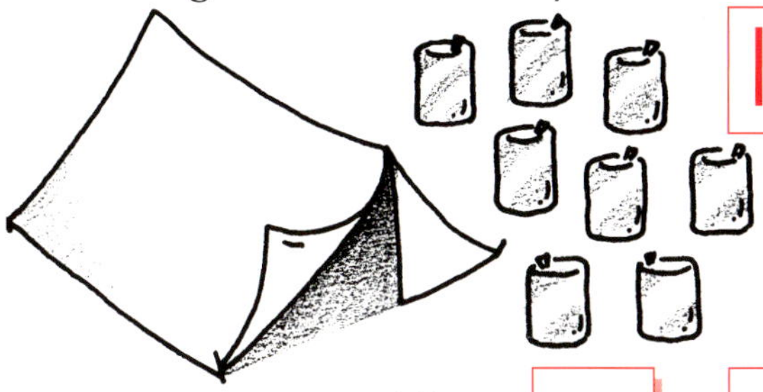

10

18 – 8 = 10

9 altogether. How many in the tent?

9 – ☐ = ☐

8 altogether. How many in the tent?

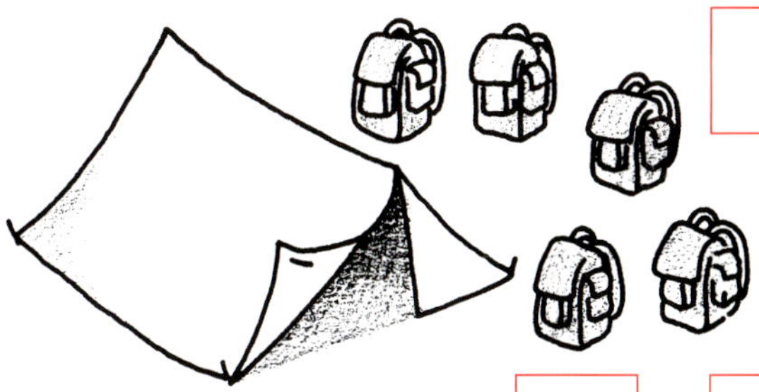

8 – ☐ = ☐

Say as you write.

16 – 4 = 12	18 – ☐ = 7	12 – ☐ = 2
15 – ☐ = 14	19 – ☐ = 5	15 – ☐ = 9
9 – ☐ = 4	17 – ☐ = 11	11 – ☐ = 10

Say as you write.

15 – 5 = 10	10 – ☐ = 0	16 – 0 = ☐
13 – 10 = ☐	20 – ☐ = 0	8 – 8 = ☐

Sets of

Say and count as you write.

4 + 4 + 4 = 12 legs

3 sets of 4 → 12

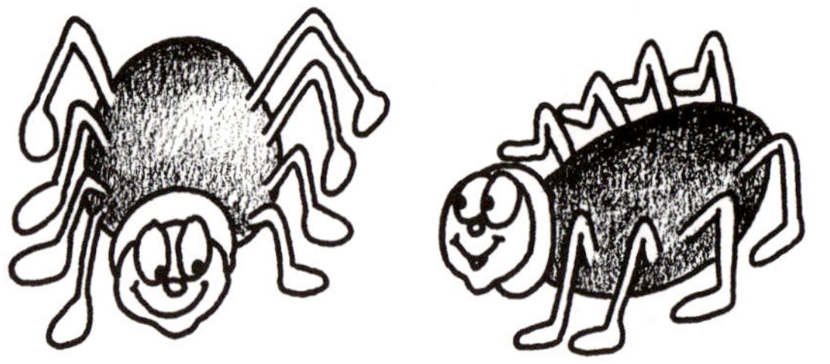

8 + 8 = ☐ legs

2 sets of 8 → ☐

5 + 5 + 5 + 5 = ☐ legs

☐ sets of ☐ → ☐

3 + 3 + 3 + 3 = ☐ legs

☐ sets of ☐ → ☐

2 + 2 + 2 = ☐ legs

☐ sets of ☐ → ☐

10 + 10 = ☐ legs

☐ sets of ☐ → ☐

Sharing

Share the food equally.

How many each? 2

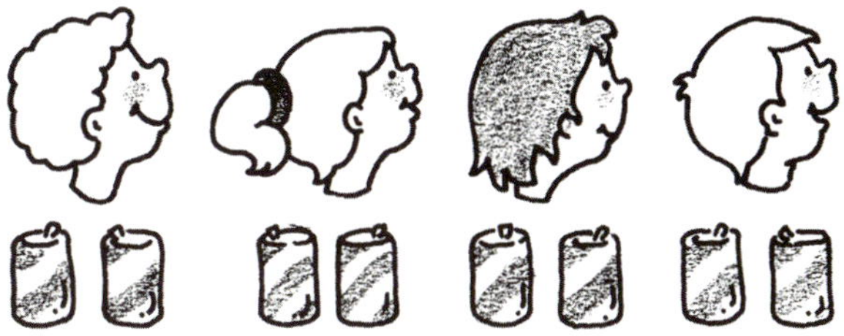

How many each?

How many each?

How many each?

Draw lines to share the picnic.

Addition properties

Write the missing number.

6	+	0	=	6	0	+	6	=	6
	+	7	=	17		+	10	=	17
11	+		=	11		+	11	=	11
4	+		=	12	8	+		=	12
13	+		=	19		+	13	=	19
	+	3	=	3	3	+		=	3

Circle the addition fact that has the same sum as 2 + 3.

1 + 5   3 + 2   4 + 2

Circle the addition fact that has the same sum as 5 + 8.

8 + 5   6 + 6   3 + 9

Circle the addition fact that has the same sum as 1 + 7.

8 + 2   2 + 5   7 + 1

Circle the addition fact that has the same sum as 10 + 6.

7 + 4   9 + 9   6 + 10

Circle the addition fact that has the same sum as 4 + 2.

1 + 6   2 + 4   3 + 2

Circle the addition fact that has the same sum as 9 + 5.

5 + 9   7 + 6   10 + 5

Most and least likely

What are you most likely to pick out of each bag? Circle the answer.

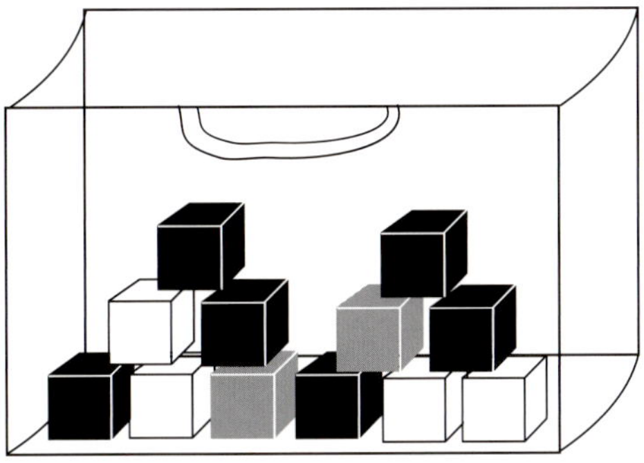

a black cube
a grey cube
a white cube

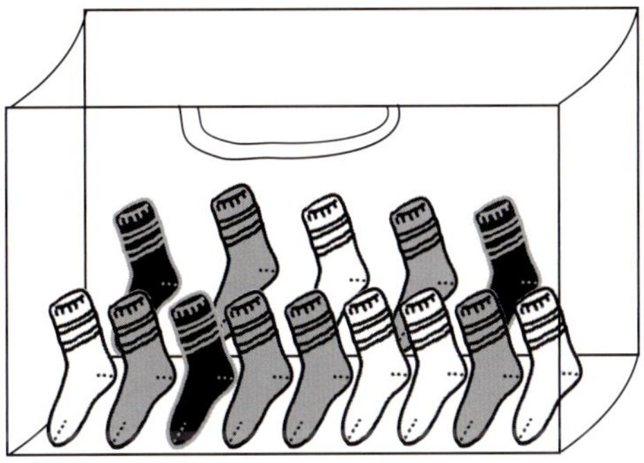

a black sock
a grey sock
a white sock

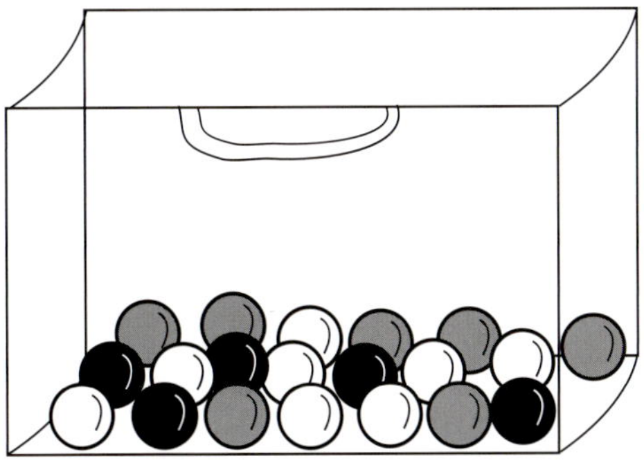

a black marble
a grey marble
a white marble

What are you least likely to pick out of each bag? Circle the answer.

a black tea cup
a grey tea cup
a white tea cup

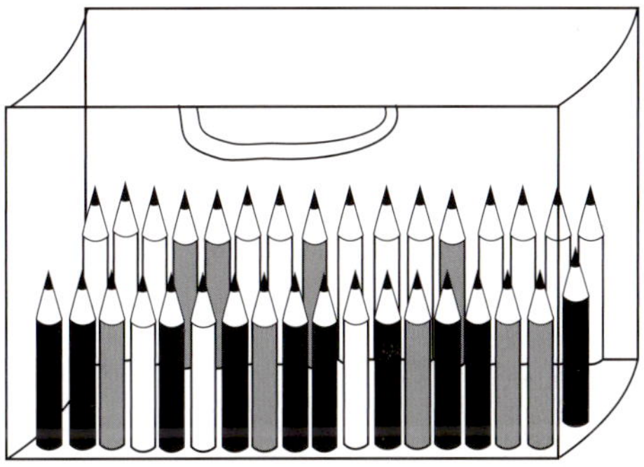

a black pencil
a grey pencil
a white pencil

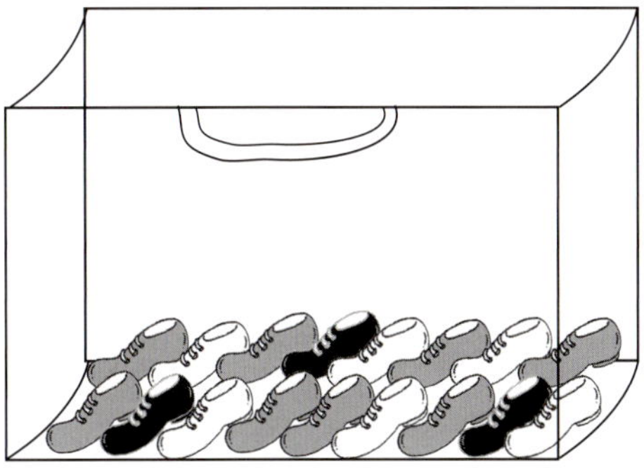

a black boot
a grey boot
a white boot

Days and seasons

Days of the week

Can you write them in order?

Monday Tuesday Wednesday Thursday Friday Saturday Sunday

Wednesday Thursday Fr

Saturday Sunday M

Thursday Friday S

Yesterday and tomorrow

yesterday	today	tomorrow
Tuesday	Wednesday	
	Monday	
	Thursday	
	Sunday	

Seasons of the year

Draw lines to connect each picture to a season.

Spring

Summer

Autumn

Winter

Using clocks

Write the time.

8 o'clock	half past 10		

Draw the hands.

   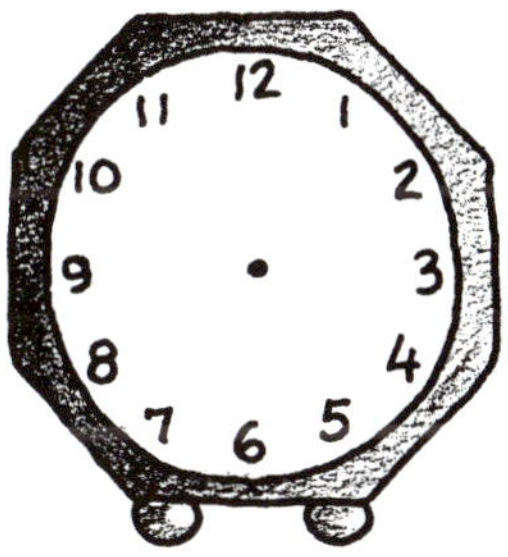

half past 7	1 o'clock	half past 9	half past 6

half past 1	11 o'clock	half past 8	2 o'clock

Favourite fruits

This table shows the favourite fruits of a class of children.

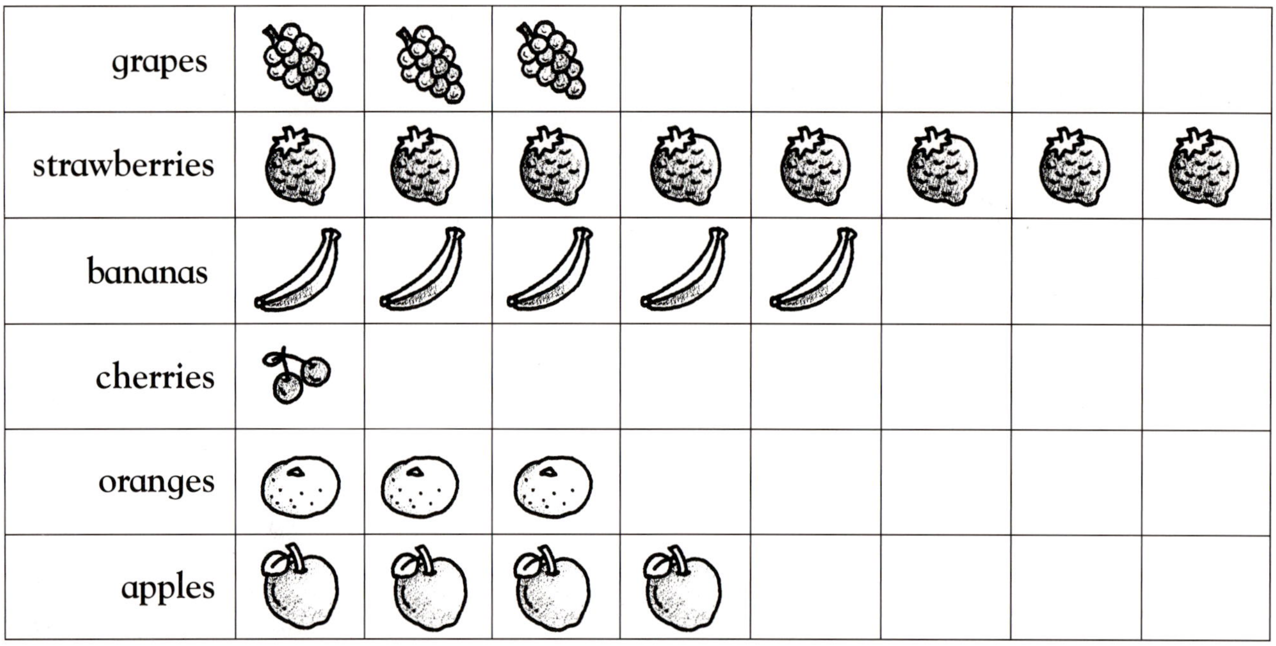

How many preferred each fruit?

Which fruit? Draw.

5 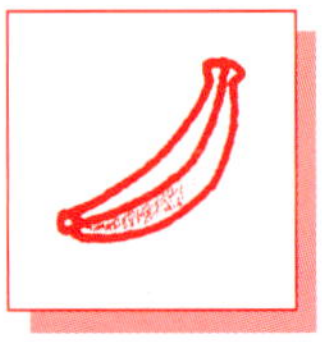

8

1

3

Say and draw.

The fruit chosen most often is ______.

The fruit chosen least often is ______.

More children chose ______ than ______.

My favourite is ______.

Draw the other half

Finish the pictures.

Make the two halves of the pegboards match. Colour them in.

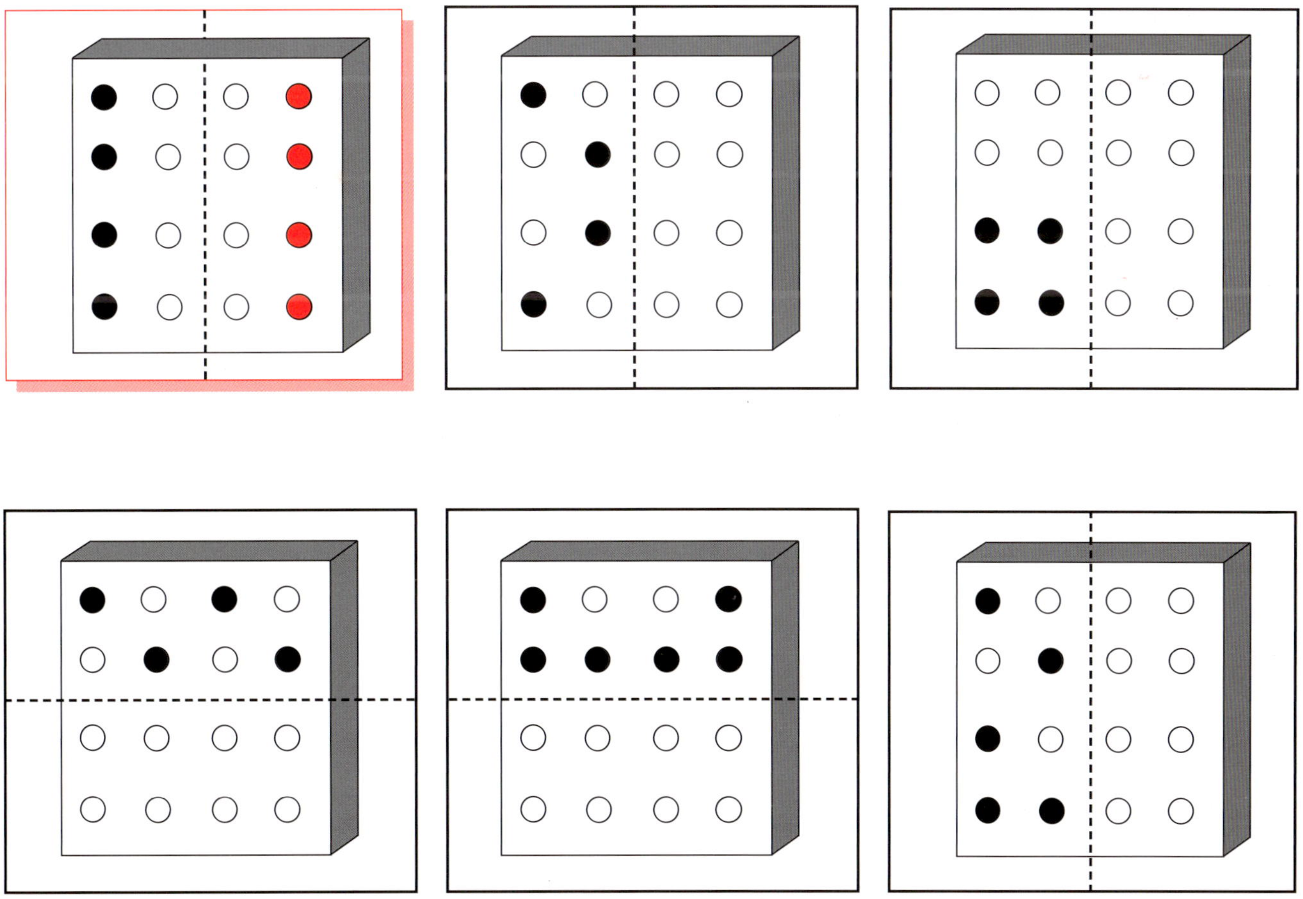

Where's the bear?

on yes
next to no

inside
on top

inside
up

behind
beside

on
in

in front
inside

under
behind

above
under

on
over

down
up

Numbers

Write the numbers.

0 0 0 0

1 1 1 1

2 2 2 2

3 3 3 3

4 4 4 4

5 5 5 5

6 6 6 6

7 7 7 7

8 8 8 8

9 9 9 9

Continue the pattern.

1 5 7 1 5 7

3 6 9 3 6 9

2 4 8 2 4 8

Numbers

Which numbers are the snakes hiding?
Say the numbers as you write the answers.

1	2	3	4	5		7	8		
11			14	15		17		19	20
21	22		24	25		27	28		30
	32	33	34	35		37	38		
41			44	45	46			49	50

9 10

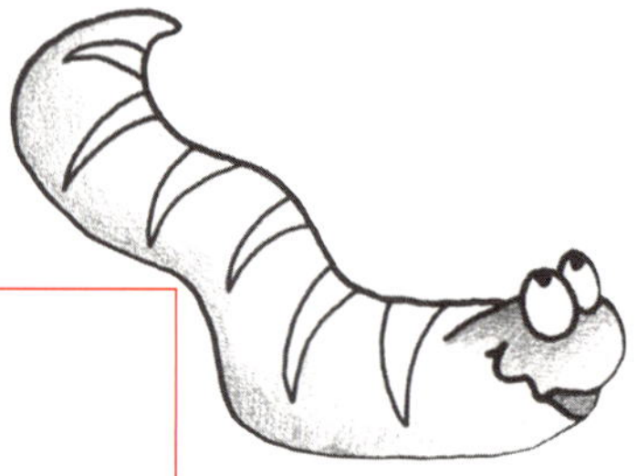

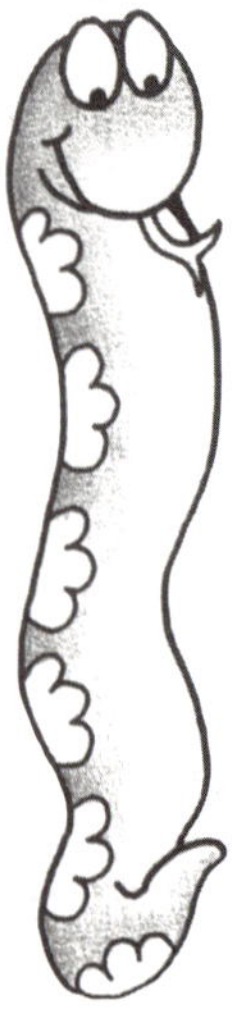

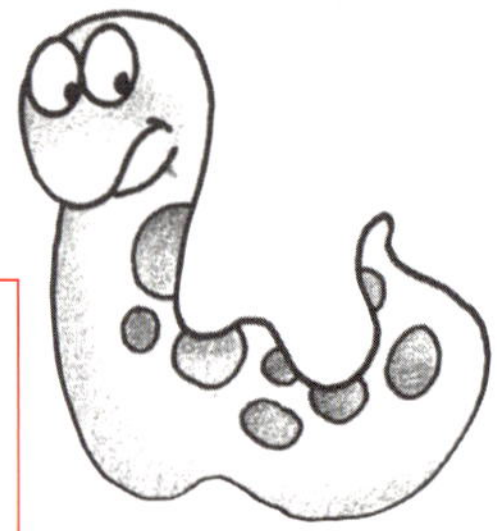

Addition

How many are there in all? Colour them in.

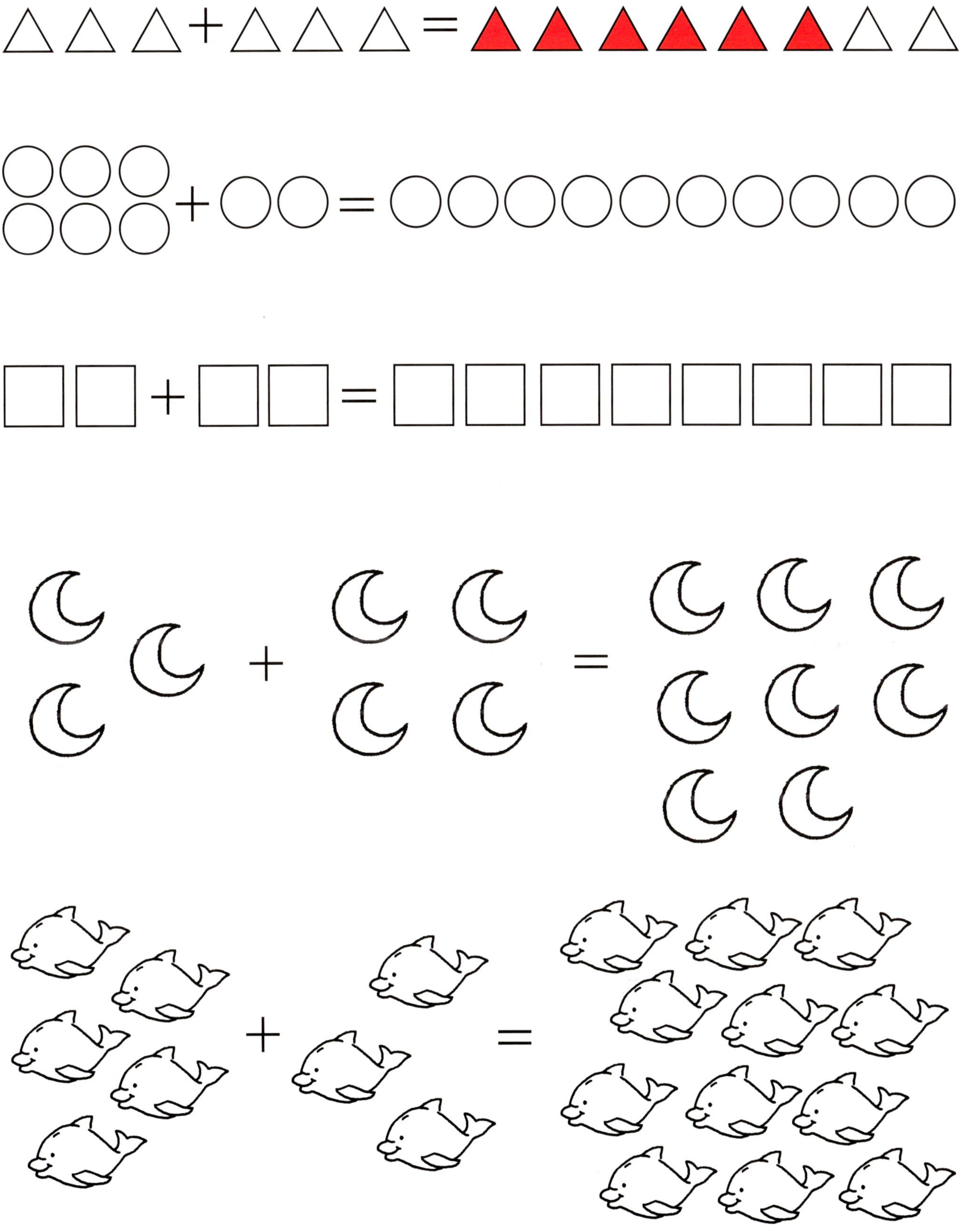

1 less or 1 more

Count, draw, and write.

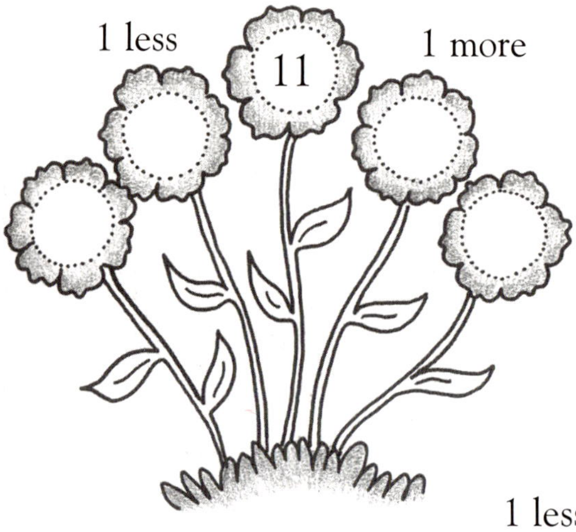

Tallies

Which tally marks show 13?

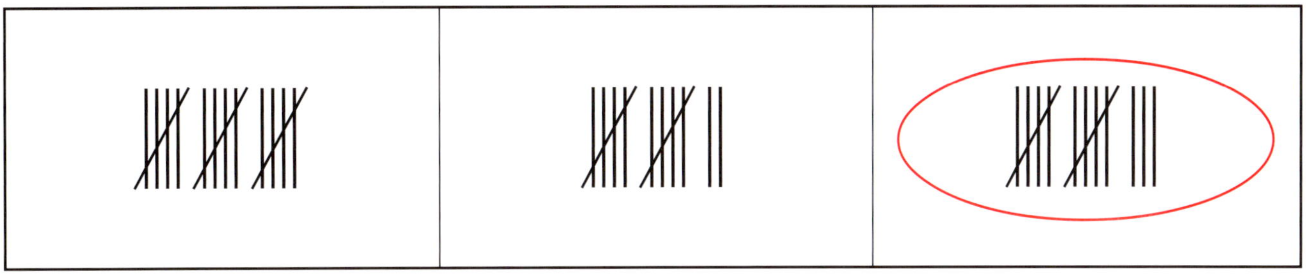

Which tally marks show 15?

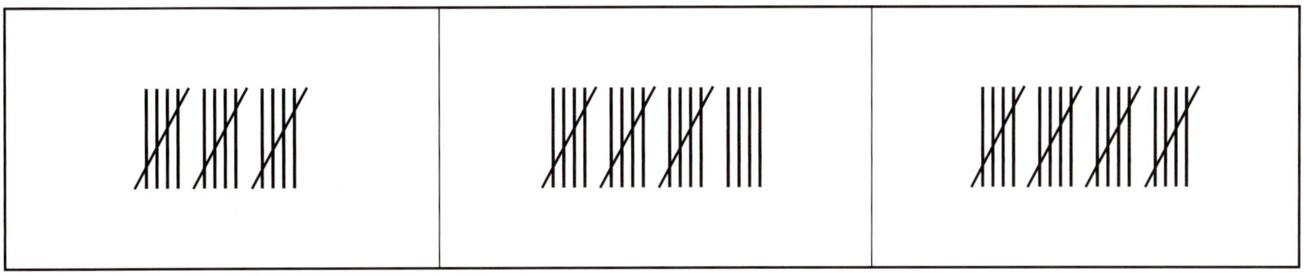

Which tally marks show 17?

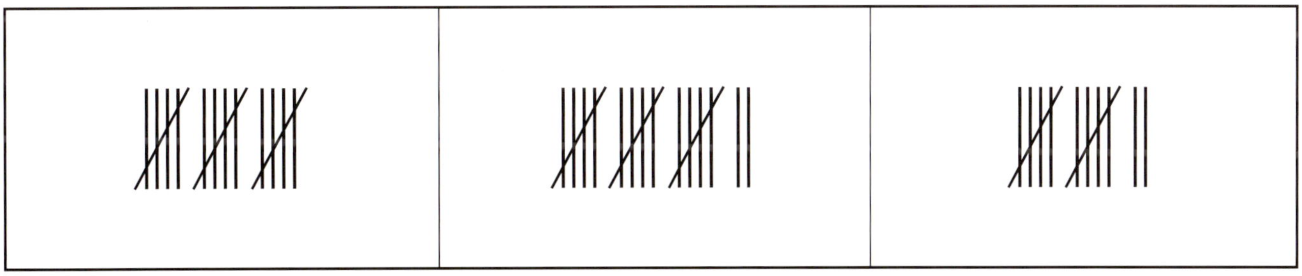

Which tally marks show 23?

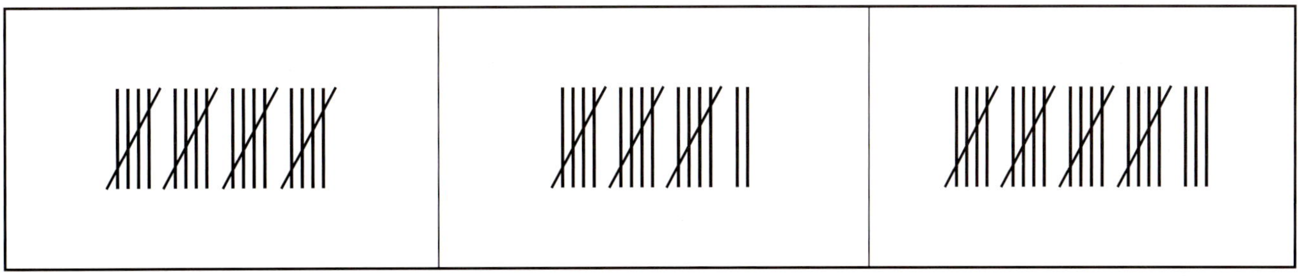

Using a table

Use the table to answer the questions.
Circle the correct answer.

Glasses of water

Name	Saturday	Sunday
Sasha	4	6
William	6	4
Anita	6	8
Nabi	5	7

Who drank less water on Saturday? Sasha Nabi

How many glasses of water did Anita drink on Sunday? 4 8 7

Who drank 7 glasses of water on Sunday? Nabi Anita

Who drank a total of 10 glasses of water? Nabi William

Who drank the most glasses of water? Nabi Anita

Who drank less water on Sunday? Anita Nabi

How many glasses of water did Sasha and William together drink on Saturday? 10 12

Patterns of 2, 5, and 10

Count, colour, and find a pattern.

Count by 2s and colour them red.

1	2	3	4	5	6	7	8	9	10
11	12	13	14	15	16	17	18	19	20
21	22	23	24	25	26	27	28	29	30
31	32	33	34	35	36	37	38	39	40
41	42	43	44	45	46	47	48	49	50

Count by 5s and colour them purple.

1	2	3	4	5	6	7	8	9	10
11	12	13	14	15	16	17	18	19	20
21	22	23	24	25	26	27	28	29	30
31	32	33	34	35	36	37	38	39	40
41	42	43	44	45	46	47	48	49	50

Count by 10s and colour them yellow.

1	2	3	4	5	6	7	8	9	10
11	12	13	14	15	16	17	18	19	20
21	22	23	24	25	26	27	28	29	30
31	32	33	34	35	36	37	38	39	40
41	42	43	44	45	46	47	48	49	50

More or less

Connect the spaceships to the planets and the rockets to the stars.

1 more

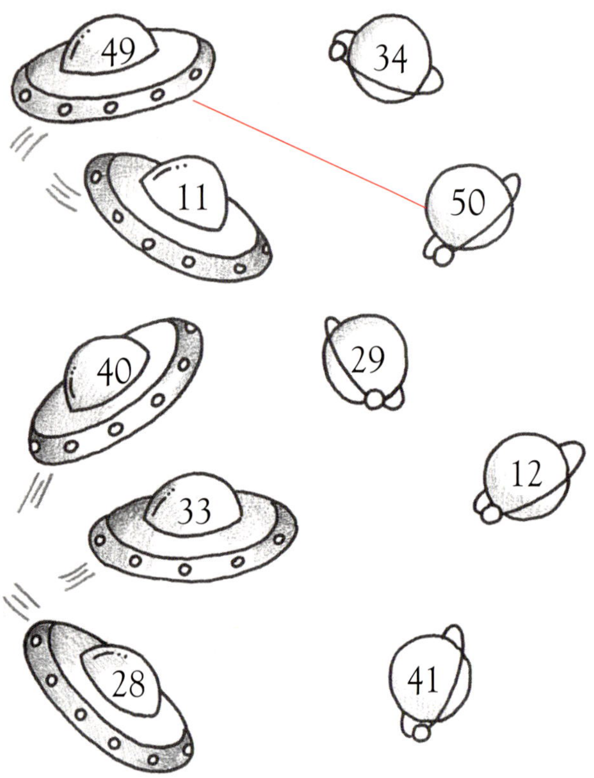

10 more

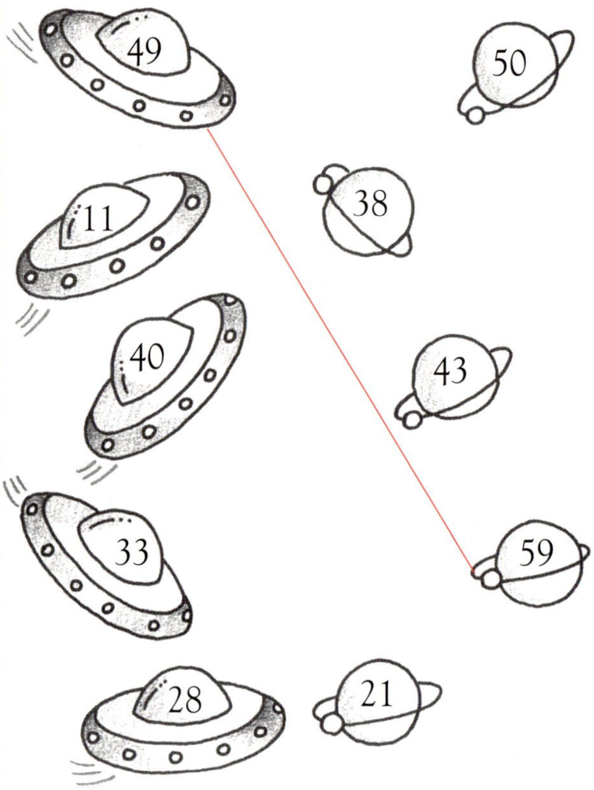

1 less

10 less

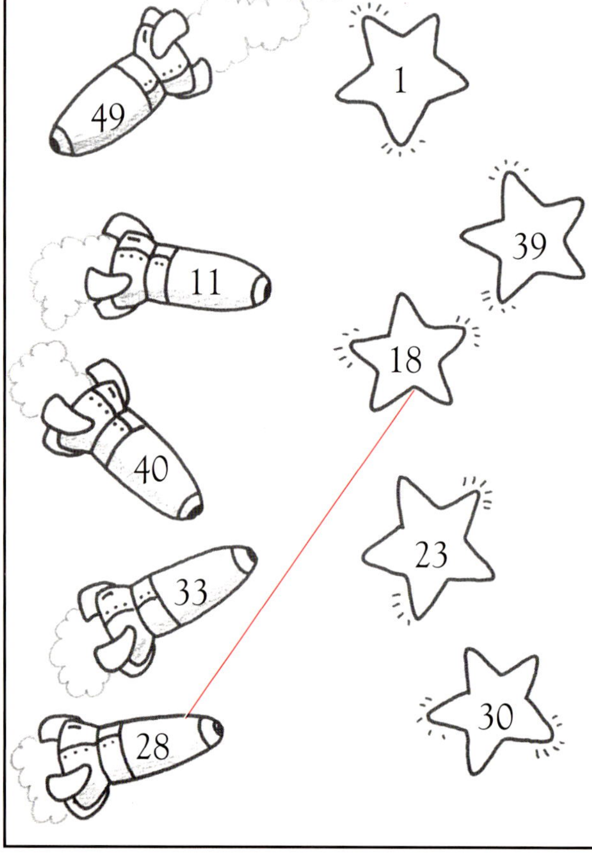

Ordering

Write the numbers in order.

smallest first

7	16	26			

greatest first

smallest first

greatest first

Fractions of shapes

Colour one third ($\frac{1}{3}$).

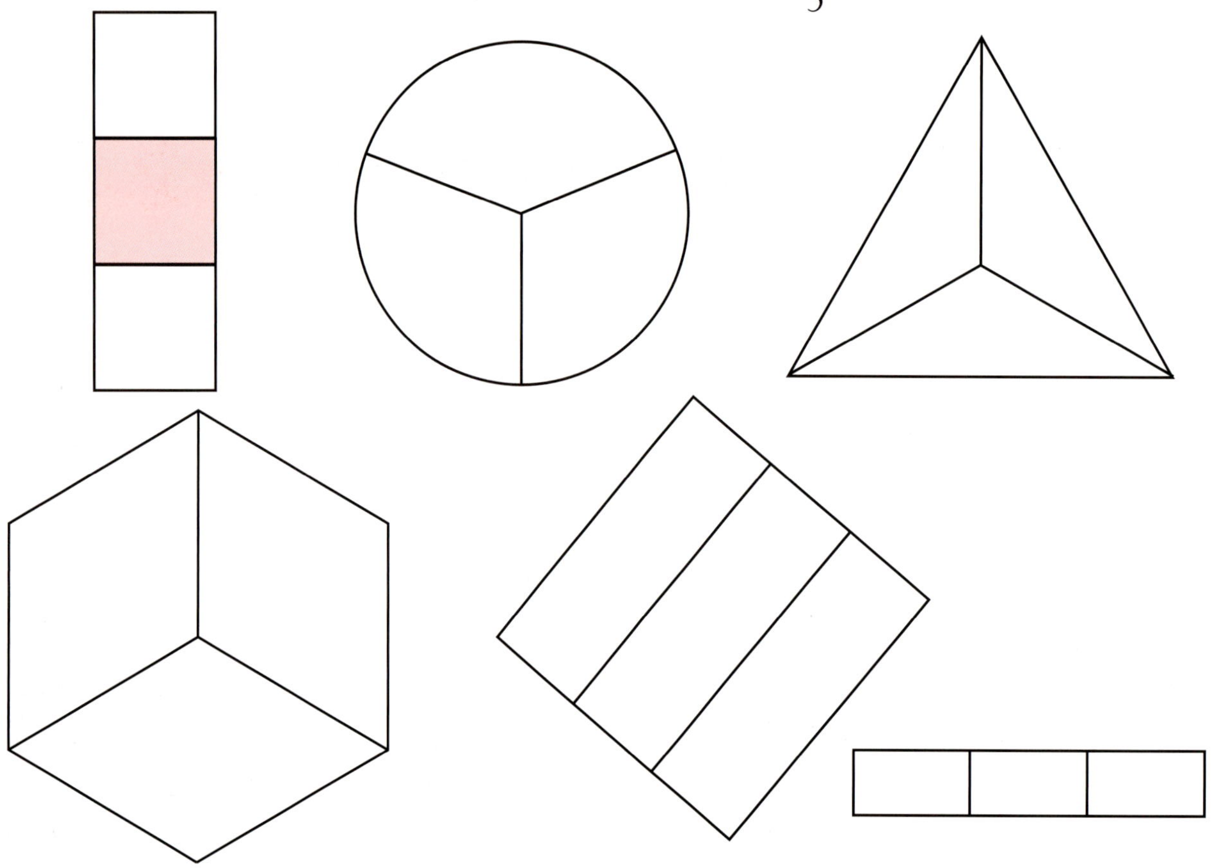

Is it $\frac{1}{3}$? Yes or no.

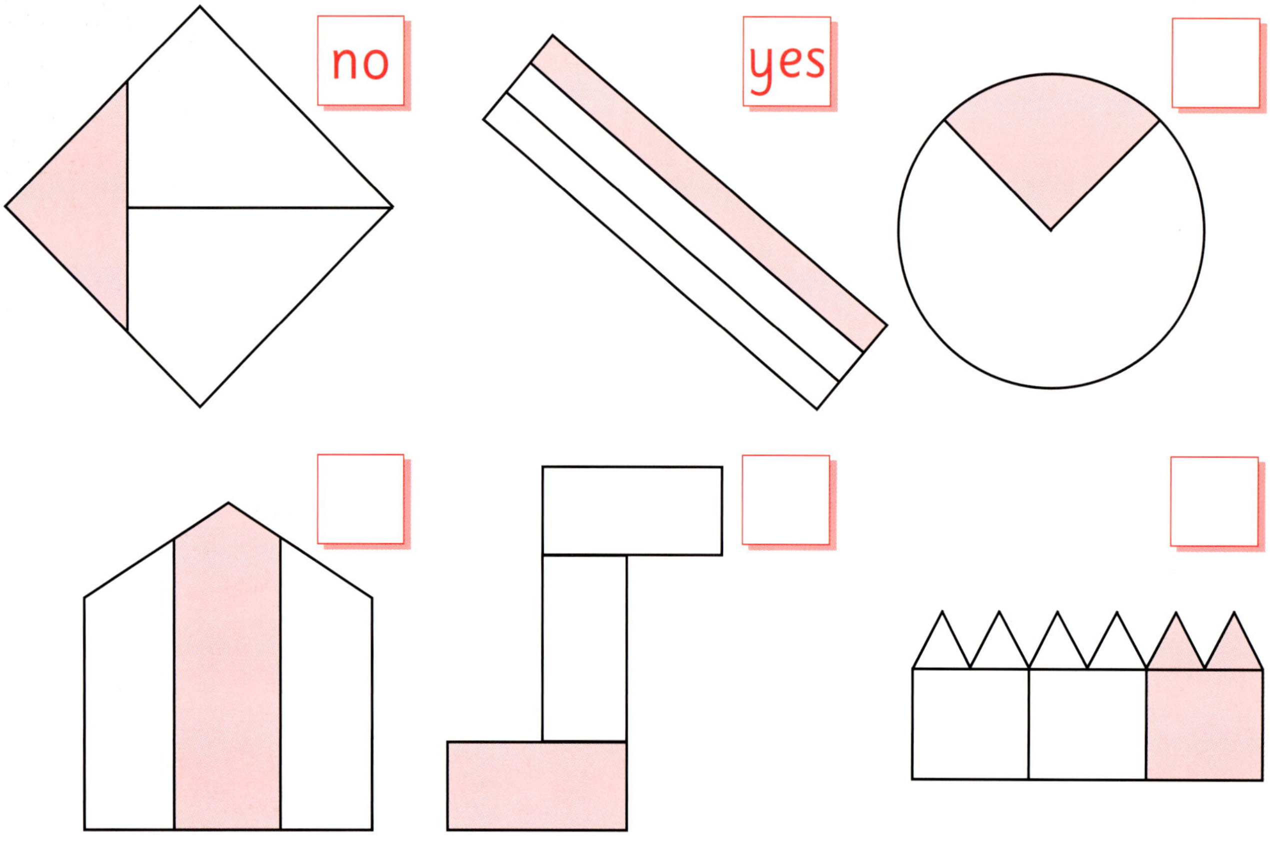

Addition

How many are there in all? Colour them in.

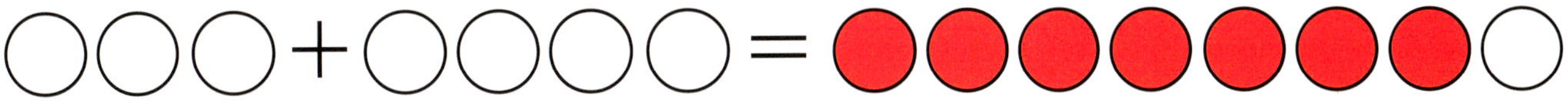

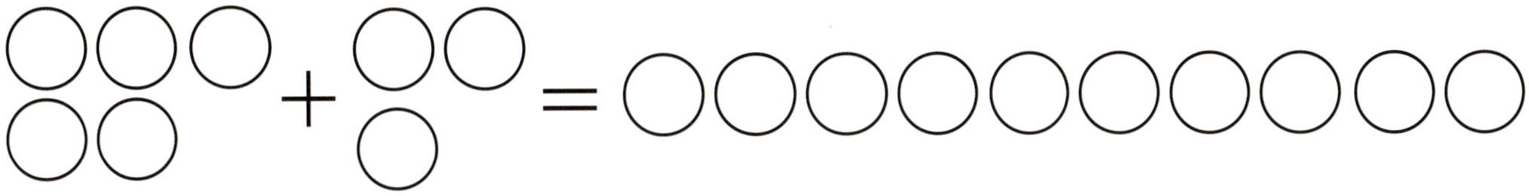

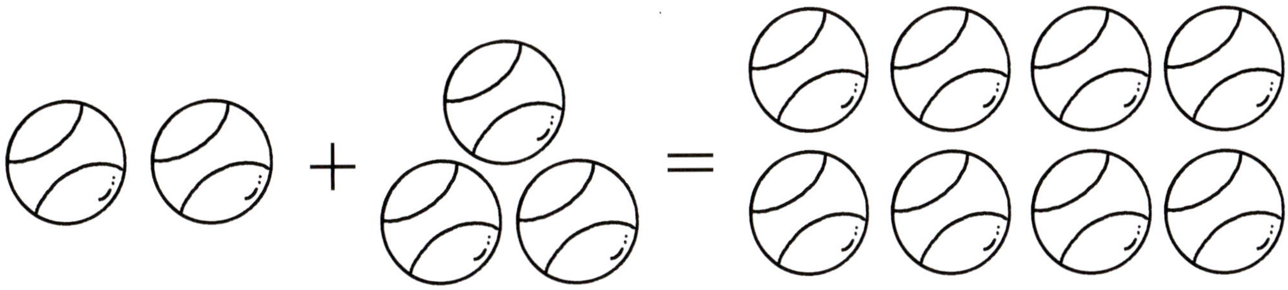

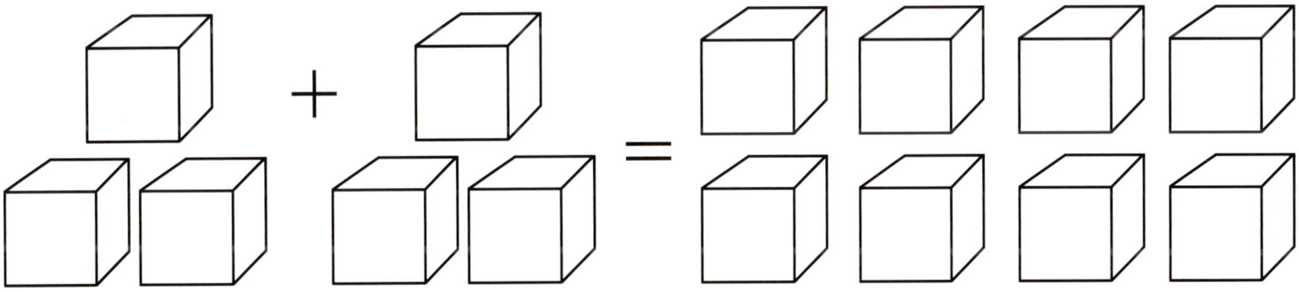

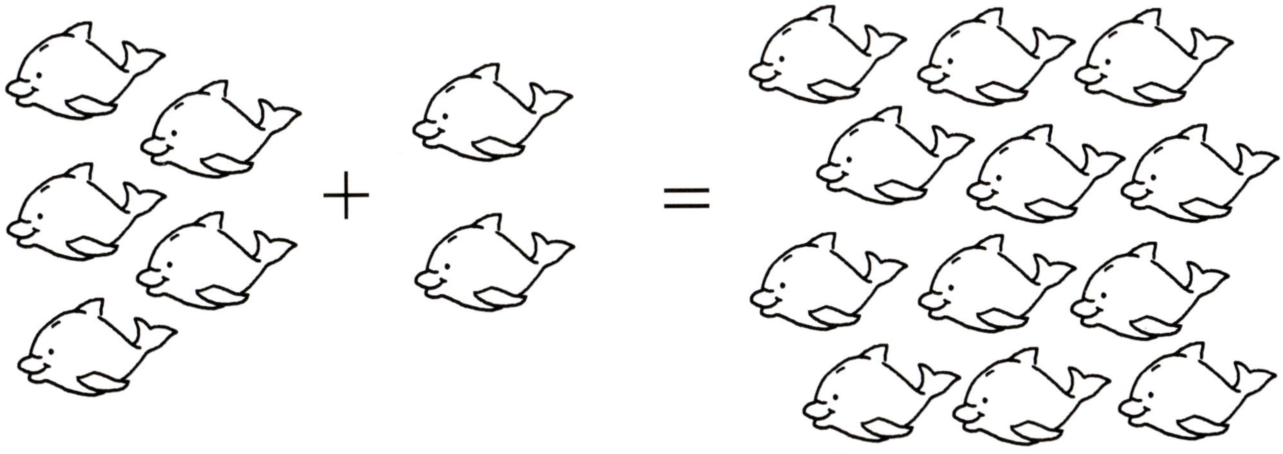

Adding coins

Use three coins each time.
How many different totals can you make?

10¢ + 1¢ + 1¢ = 12¢

25¢ + 5¢ + 1¢ = 31¢

Addition grid

Draw rings around the pairs of numbers that add up to 20.

15	5	3	10	10	4	19
8	6	20	0	9	1	10
12	13	7	12	0	16	1
4	5	10	16	4	5	10
9	2	18	7	20	3	10
11	3	3	1	0	11	9
17	1	1	19	3	18	11

Doubles

Write the missing numbers.

3 → 6
5 → 10
8 → 16

6 → ☐
10 → ☐
1 → ☐

2 → ☐
9 → ☐
4 → ☐

7 → ☐
11 → ☐
0 → ☐

What has been doubled? Write the missing number.

Double 4 is 8   Double 8 is 16

Double ☐ is 18   Double ☐ is 20   Double ☐ is 14

Double ☐ is 6   Double ☐ is 12   Double ☐ is 10

Double ☐ is 4   Double ☐ is 2

Fact families

Complete each fact family.

4, 5, 9

4	+	5	=	9
5	+	4	=	9
9	−	4	=	5
9	−	5	=	4

3, 4, 7

3	+	4	=	7
4	+	3	=	
7	−	3	=	4
7	−	4	=	

2, 4, 6

2	+	4	=	6
4	+	2	=	
6	−	4	=	2
6	−	2	=	

3, 5, 8

3	+	5	=	8
5	+	3	=	
8	−	3	=	5
8	−	5	=	

Addition

Add to find each sum.

$$\begin{array}{r} 13 \\ +\ 4 \\ \hline 17 \end{array}$$

Add to find each sum.

$$\begin{array}{r} 8 \\ +\ 1 \\ \hline \end{array} \quad \begin{array}{r} 3 \\ +\ 4 \\ \hline \end{array} \quad \begin{array}{r} 2 \\ +\ 6 \\ \hline \end{array} \quad \begin{array}{r} 0 \\ +\ 5 \\ \hline \end{array}$$

$$\begin{array}{r} 10 \\ +\ 9 \\ \hline \end{array} \quad \begin{array}{r} 10 \\ +\ 3 \\ \hline \end{array} \quad \begin{array}{r} 10 \\ +\ 4 \\ \hline \end{array} \quad \begin{array}{r} 10 \\ +\ 2 \\ \hline \end{array}$$

$$\begin{array}{r} 12 \\ +\ 3 \\ \hline \end{array} \quad \begin{array}{r} 16 \\ +\ 3 \\ \hline \end{array} \quad \begin{array}{r} 14 \\ +\ 3 \\ \hline \end{array} \quad \begin{array}{r} 12 \\ +\ 5 \\ \hline \end{array}$$

$$\begin{array}{r} 17 \\ +\ 1 \\ \hline \end{array} \quad \begin{array}{r} 12 \\ +\ 4 \\ \hline \end{array} \quad \begin{array}{r} 10 \\ +\ 7 \\ \hline \end{array} \quad \begin{array}{r} 11 \\ +\ 7 \\ \hline \end{array}$$

Subtraction

Subtract to find the difference.

$$\begin{array}{r} 14 \\ -\ 3 \\ \hline 11 \end{array}$$

Subtract to find each difference.

$$\begin{array}{r} 8 \\ -\ 1 \\ \hline \end{array} \quad \begin{array}{r} 5 \\ -\ 2 \\ \hline \end{array} \quad \begin{array}{r} 6 \\ -\ 2 \\ \hline \end{array} \quad \begin{array}{r} 5 \\ -\ 4 \\ \hline \end{array}$$

$$\begin{array}{r} 19 \\ -\ 7 \\ \hline \end{array} \quad \begin{array}{r} 13 \\ -\ 2 \\ \hline \end{array} \quad \begin{array}{r} 14 \\ -\ 4 \\ \hline \end{array} \quad \begin{array}{r} 19 \\ -\ 3 \\ \hline \end{array}$$

$$\begin{array}{r} 16 \\ -\ 3 \\ \hline \end{array} \quad \begin{array}{r} 16 \\ -\ 5 \\ \hline \end{array} \quad \begin{array}{r} 18 \\ -\ 7 \\ \hline \end{array} \quad \begin{array}{r} 17 \\ -\ 5 \\ \hline \end{array}$$

$$\begin{array}{r} 17 \\ -\ 1 \\ \hline \end{array} \quad \begin{array}{r} 14 \\ -\ 2 \\ \hline \end{array} \quad \begin{array}{r} 17 \\ -\ 4 \\ \hline \end{array} \quad \begin{array}{r} 17 \\ -\ 1 \\ \hline \end{array}$$

Subtraction

Subtract to find the difference.

$$\begin{array}{r} 80 \\ -\ 30 \\ \hline 50 \end{array}$$

Subtract to find each difference.

$$\begin{array}{r} 30 \\ -\ 20 \\ \hline \end{array} \quad \begin{array}{r} 50 \\ -\ 30 \\ \hline \end{array} \quad \begin{array}{r} 40 \\ -\ 20 \\ \hline \end{array} \quad \begin{array}{r} 20 \\ -\ 10 \\ \hline \end{array}$$

$$\begin{array}{r} 40 \\ -\ 30 \\ \hline \end{array} \quad \begin{array}{r} 50 \\ -\ 20 \\ \hline \end{array} \quad \begin{array}{r} 60 \\ -\ 40 \\ \hline \end{array} \quad \begin{array}{r} 90 \\ -\ 30 \\ \hline \end{array}$$

$$\begin{array}{r} 70 \\ -\ 30 \\ \hline \end{array} \quad \begin{array}{r} 90 \\ -\ 40 \\ \hline \end{array} \quad \begin{array}{r} 40 \\ -\ 10 \\ \hline \end{array} \quad \begin{array}{r} 50 \\ -\ 40 \\ \hline \end{array}$$

$$\begin{array}{r} 90 \\ -\ 70 \\ \hline \end{array} \quad \begin{array}{r} 80 \\ -\ 10 \\ \hline \end{array} \quad \begin{array}{r} 60 \\ -\ 50 \\ \hline \end{array} \quad \begin{array}{r} 40 \\ -\ 40 \\ \hline \end{array}$$

Subtraction

Subtract to find the difference.

$$\begin{array}{r} 87 \\ -\,34 \\ \hline 53 \end{array}$$

Subtract to find each difference.

$$\begin{array}{r} 39 \\ -\,27 \\ \hline \end{array} \quad \begin{array}{r} 58 \\ -\,32 \\ \hline \end{array} \quad \begin{array}{r} 44 \\ -\,11 \\ \hline \end{array} \quad \begin{array}{r} 27 \\ -\,17 \\ \hline \end{array}$$

$$\begin{array}{r} 46 \\ -\,33 \\ \hline \end{array} \quad \begin{array}{r} 59 \\ -\,46 \\ \hline \end{array} \quad \begin{array}{r} 75 \\ -\,31 \\ \hline \end{array} \quad \begin{array}{r} 88 \\ -\,14 \\ \hline \end{array}$$

$$\begin{array}{r} 77 \\ -\,33 \\ \hline \end{array} \quad \begin{array}{r} 93 \\ -\,22 \\ \hline \end{array} \quad \begin{array}{r} 67 \\ -\,53 \\ \hline \end{array} \quad \begin{array}{r} 38 \\ -\,22 \\ \hline \end{array}$$

$$\begin{array}{r} 99 \\ -\,79 \\ \hline \end{array} \quad \begin{array}{r} 82 \\ -\,70 \\ \hline \end{array} \quad \begin{array}{r} 69 \\ -\,69 \\ \hline \end{array} \quad \begin{array}{r} 47 \\ -\,46 \\ \hline \end{array}$$

Real-life problems

All the piggy banks need 30¢. Draw different coins in each one. You can use any coin more than once.

Real-life problems

6¢ 5¢ 4¢ 2¢ 1¢

Draw the stamps on the letters.
You can use any stamp more than once.

6¢ 4¢ 2¢

Ms. Heather Hedgehog
1 The Leaf Pile
Snowdrop Corner
Garden City

12¢

Doctor Dilly Dinosaur
6 The Swamp
Mud Town

20¢

Rachel Robot
999 Mechanical Mansion
Metalville

10¢

Cheeky Charlie Chimp
100 Banana Court
Giggleton
Apeland

18¢

Mr. Bertie Bear
The Toy Box
Betty's Bedroom
The Big House

11¢

Samuel Spider
Wonder Web
Grandpa's Greenhouse
South Central Garden

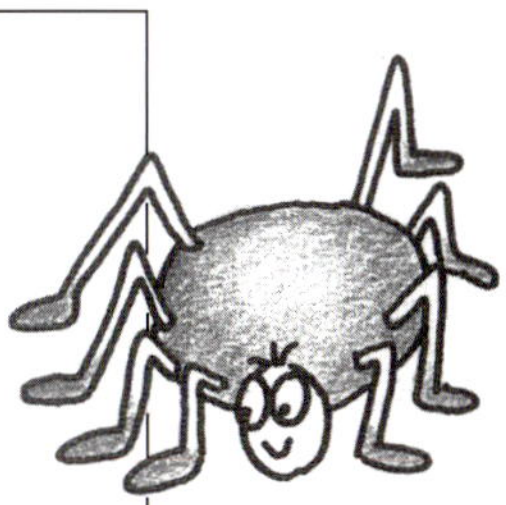

6¢

Subtraction tables

Finish each table.

–	2	3	5	10
11	9	8		
15	13			
20				

–	1	6	8	9
14				
19	18	13	11	
20				

–	0	4	7	11
12			5	
28			21	
18				

Counting down

The rocket can only lift off at zero.
Use subtraction to get to 0 in 4 moves.

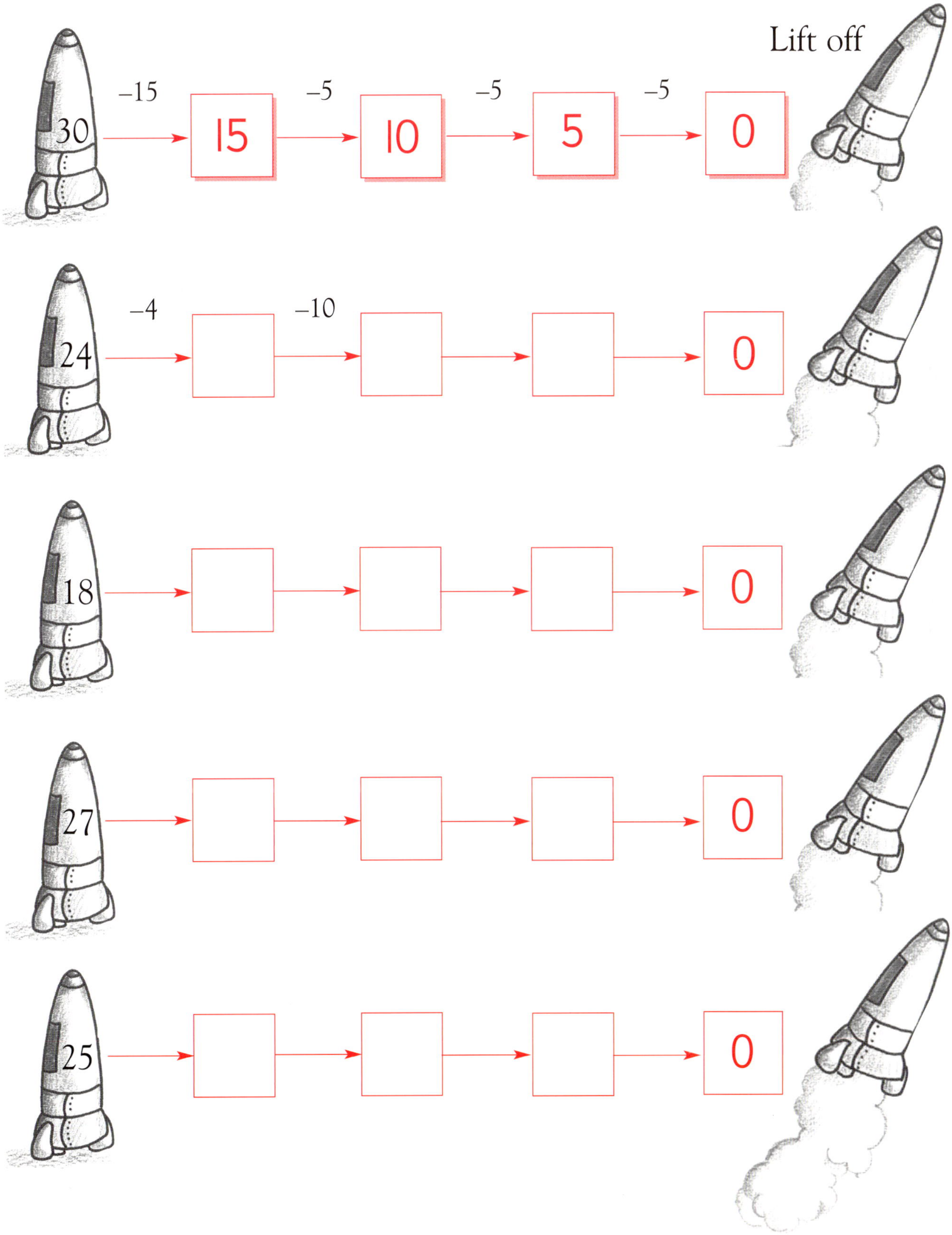

Clocks

Write the times under the clocks.

4 o'clock

Draw the hands.

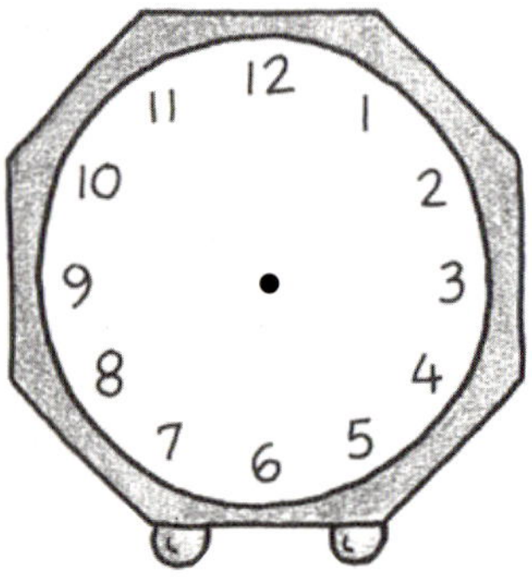

half past 7

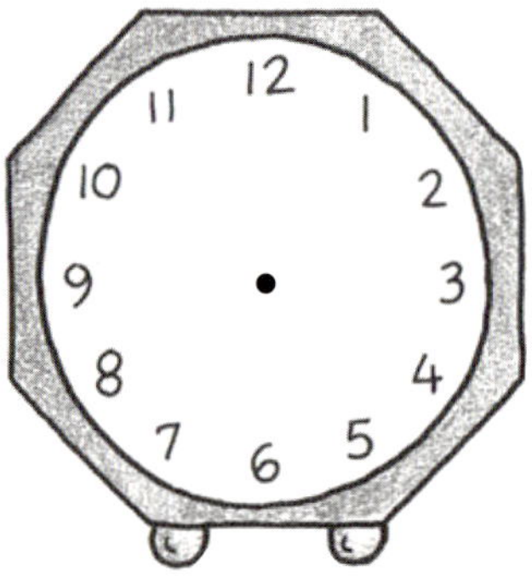

half past 2

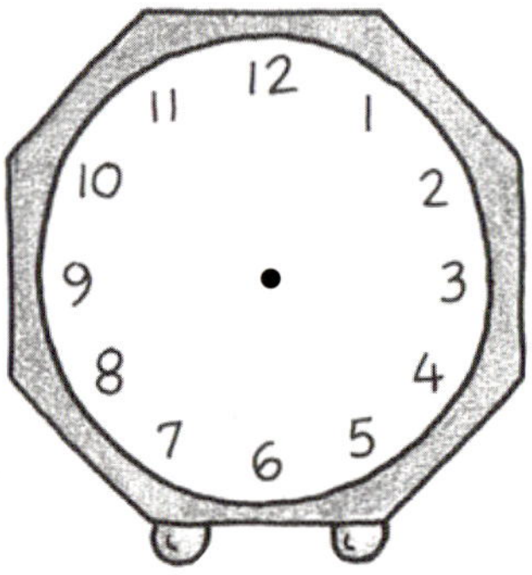

10 o'clock

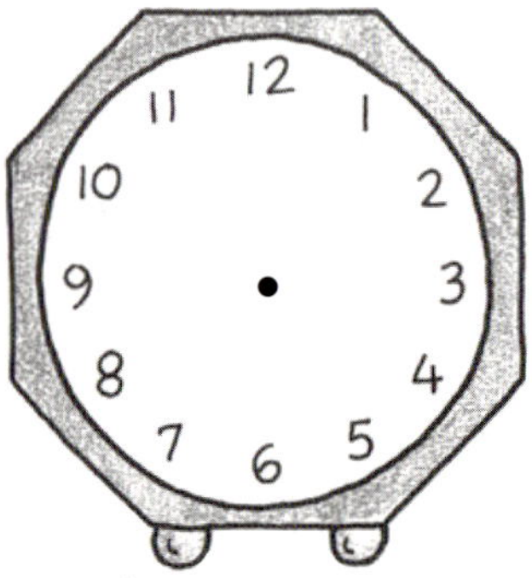

half past 11

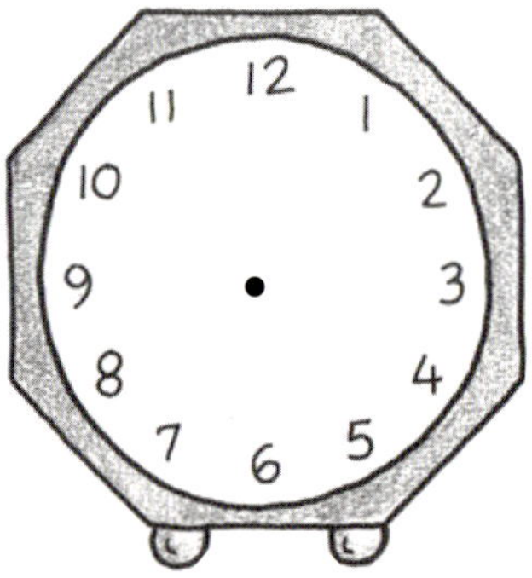

3 o'clock

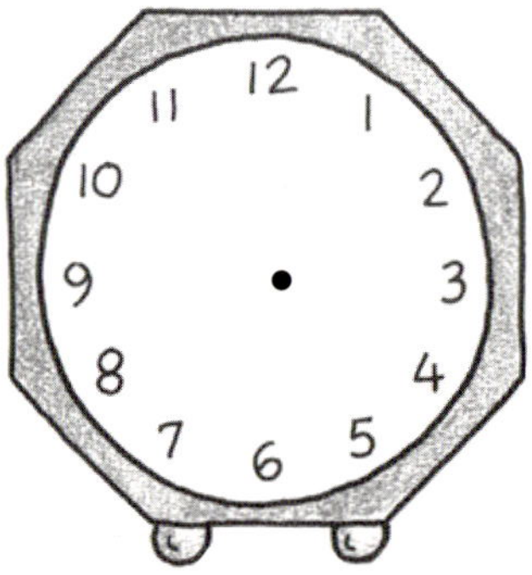

9 o'clock

Digital clocks

Write the times under the clocks.

half past 12

Fill in the digital times on the clock faces.

half past 11

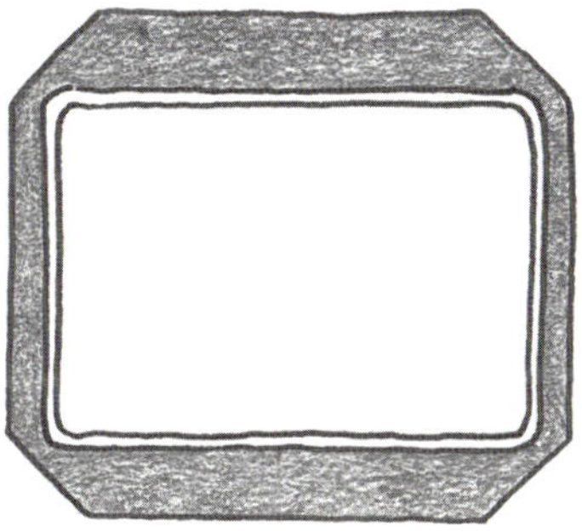

half past 1

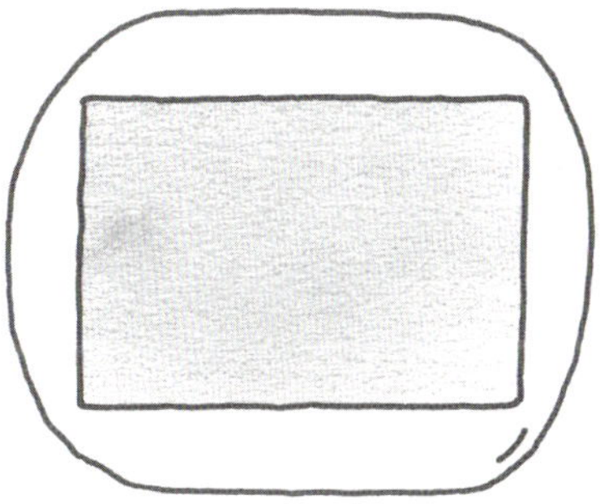

12 o'clock

half past 3

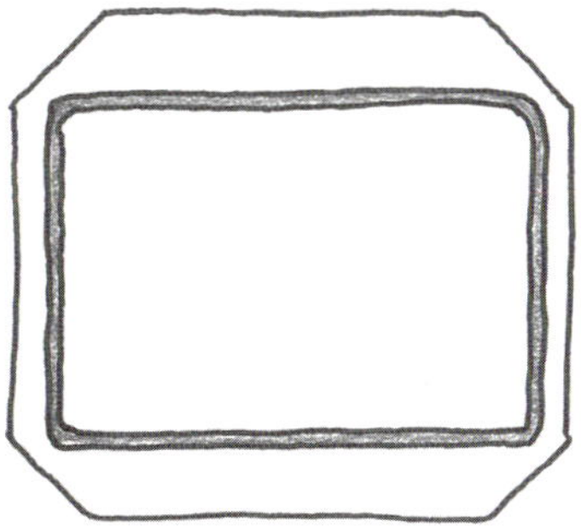

8 o'clock

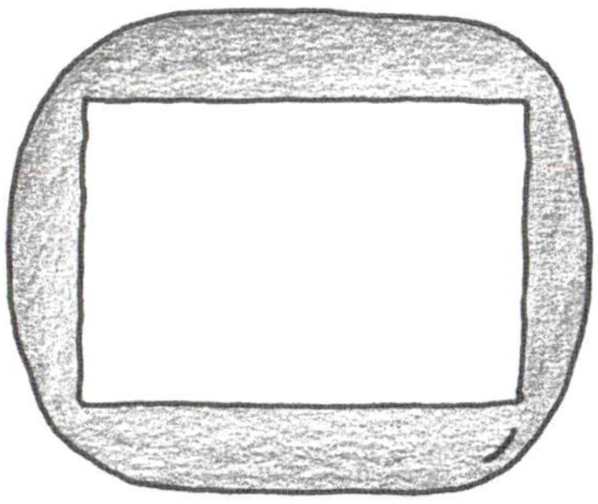

10 o'clock

Match the times

Draw a line to connect the matching times.

half past nine

half past 9

2 o'clock

6 o'clock

six o'clock

2 o'clock

half past six

9 o'clock

half past twelve

half past 6

nine o'clock

half past 12

Do you know?

Put the months in order by writing a number on each page.

How many ...

... seconds in a minute?		... minutes in an hour?	
... hours in a day?		... days in a week?	
... days in a year?		... months in a year?	

Learn this rhyme.

30 days have September,
April, June, and November.
All the rest have 31,
Except February alone
That has 28 days clear
29 in each leap year.

How many days are there in your birthday month?

Matching shapes

Ring the shape that matches the first shape.

Venn diagrams

Flowers with red petals

Flowers with white petals

How many flowers have ...

... red petals? 7

... white petals? 10

... both red and white petals? 2

Shapes with straight sides

Shapes with curved sides

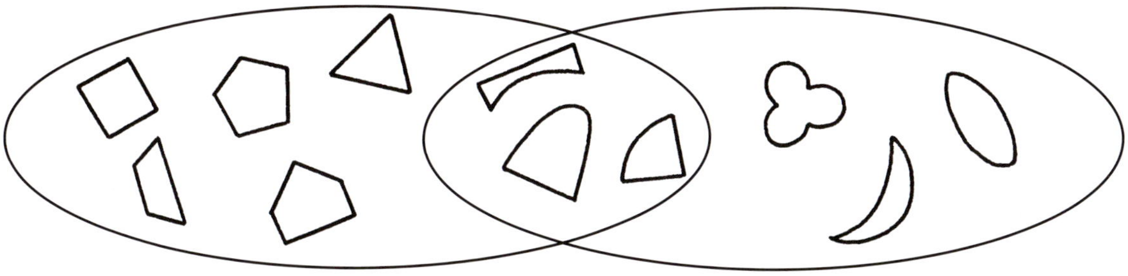

How many shapes have ...

... straight sides? ☐

... curved sides? ☐

... straight and curved sides? ☐

Odd numbers

Numbers greater than ten

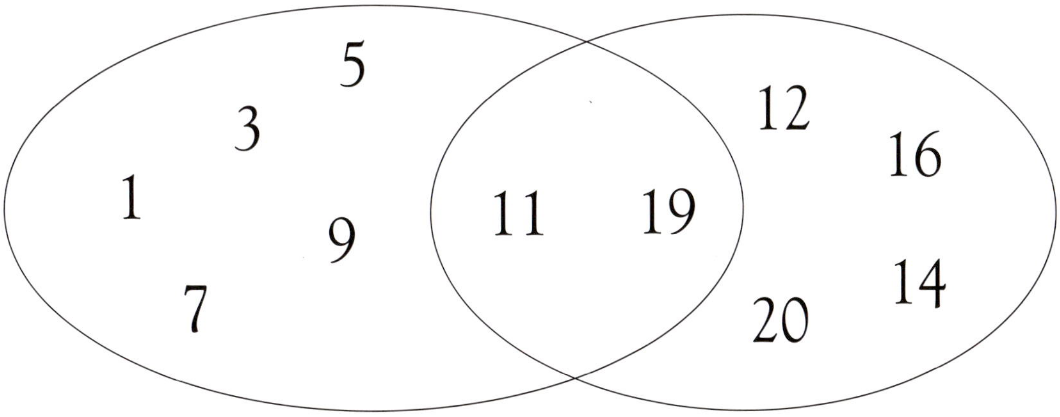

How many numbers are ...

... odd? ☐

... more than ten? ☐

... odd and more than ten? ☐

Similar shapes

Ring the shape that is the same but a different size.

2-dimensional shapes

Add the costs to find the cost of each picture.

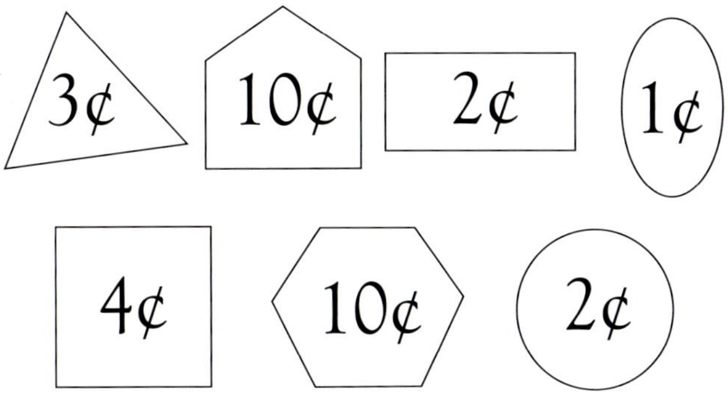

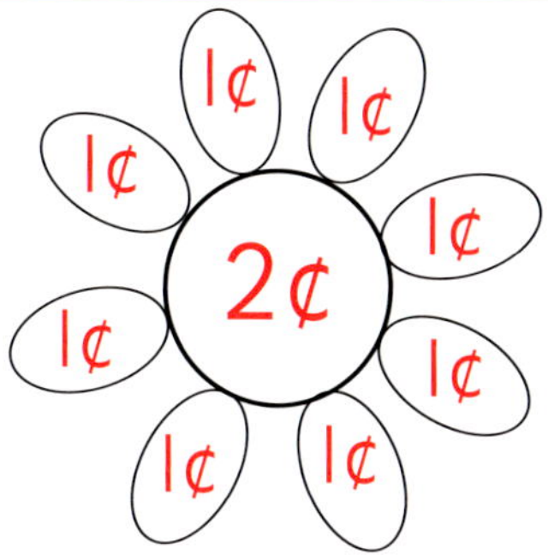

2¢ + 1¢ + 1¢ + 1¢ + 1¢ + 1¢ + 1¢ + 1¢ + 1¢ = 10¢

House

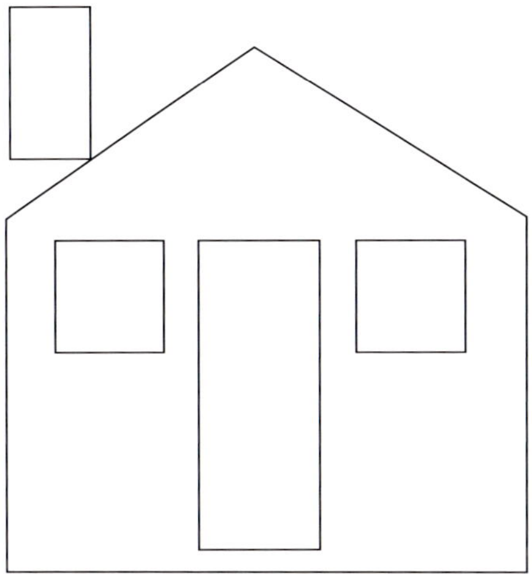

Bee and honeycomb

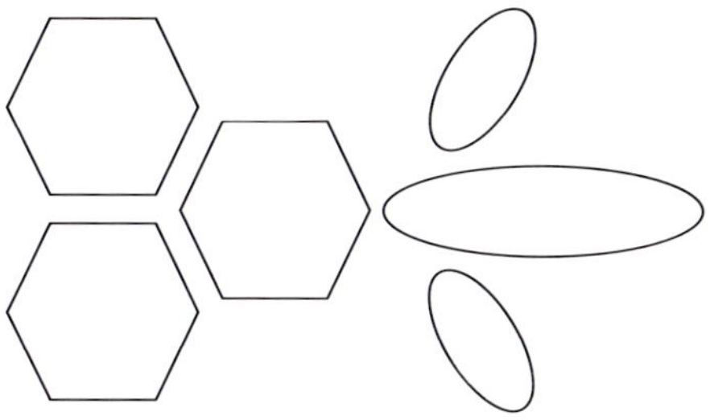

Teddy bear

Crown

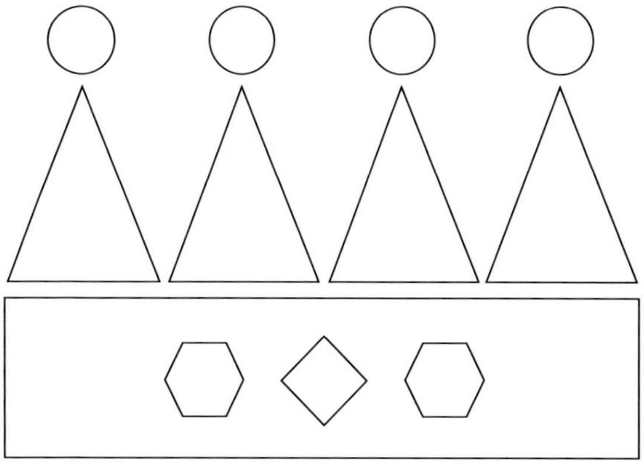

3-dimensional shapes

Label the 3-D shapes.
(cone, cylinder, pyramid, cube, sphere, rectangular prism)

cube ______ ______ ______ ______

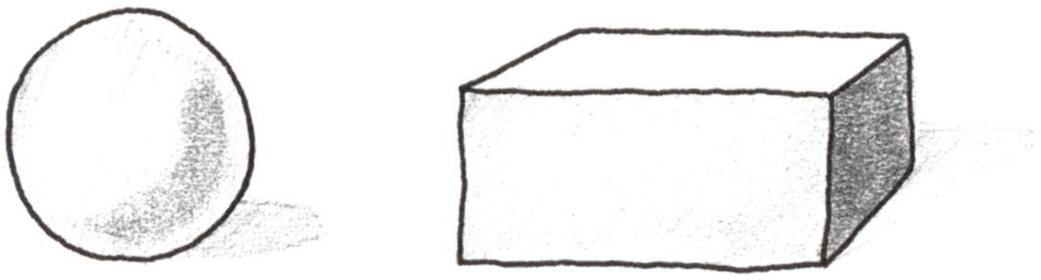

______ ______

How many of each 3-D shape?

cube [3] rectangular prism [ ] cone [ ] cylinder [ ]

pyramid [ ] sphere [ ]

Read, write, and draw

Write the numbers and draw the pictures.

16 sixteen

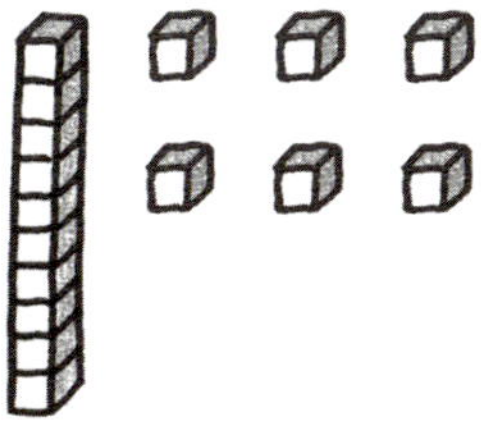

19 nineteen

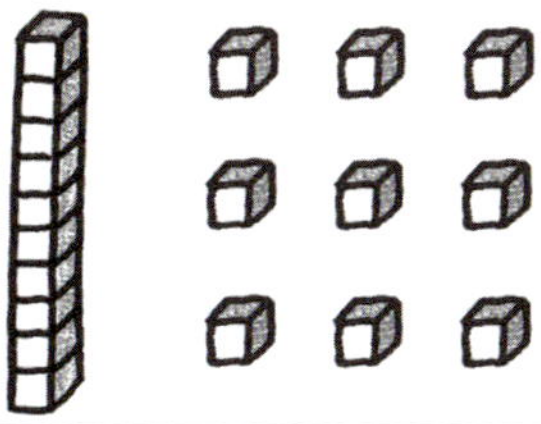

10 ten

12 twelve

21 twenty-one

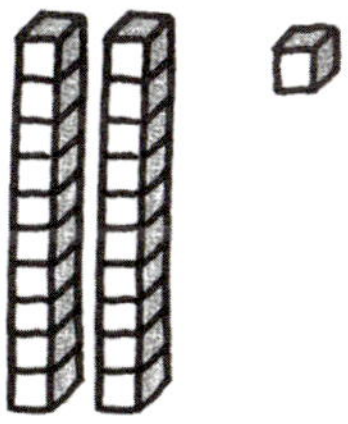

7 seven

50 fifty

Counting

Count on forward or backward by 10s.
Write the missing numbers.

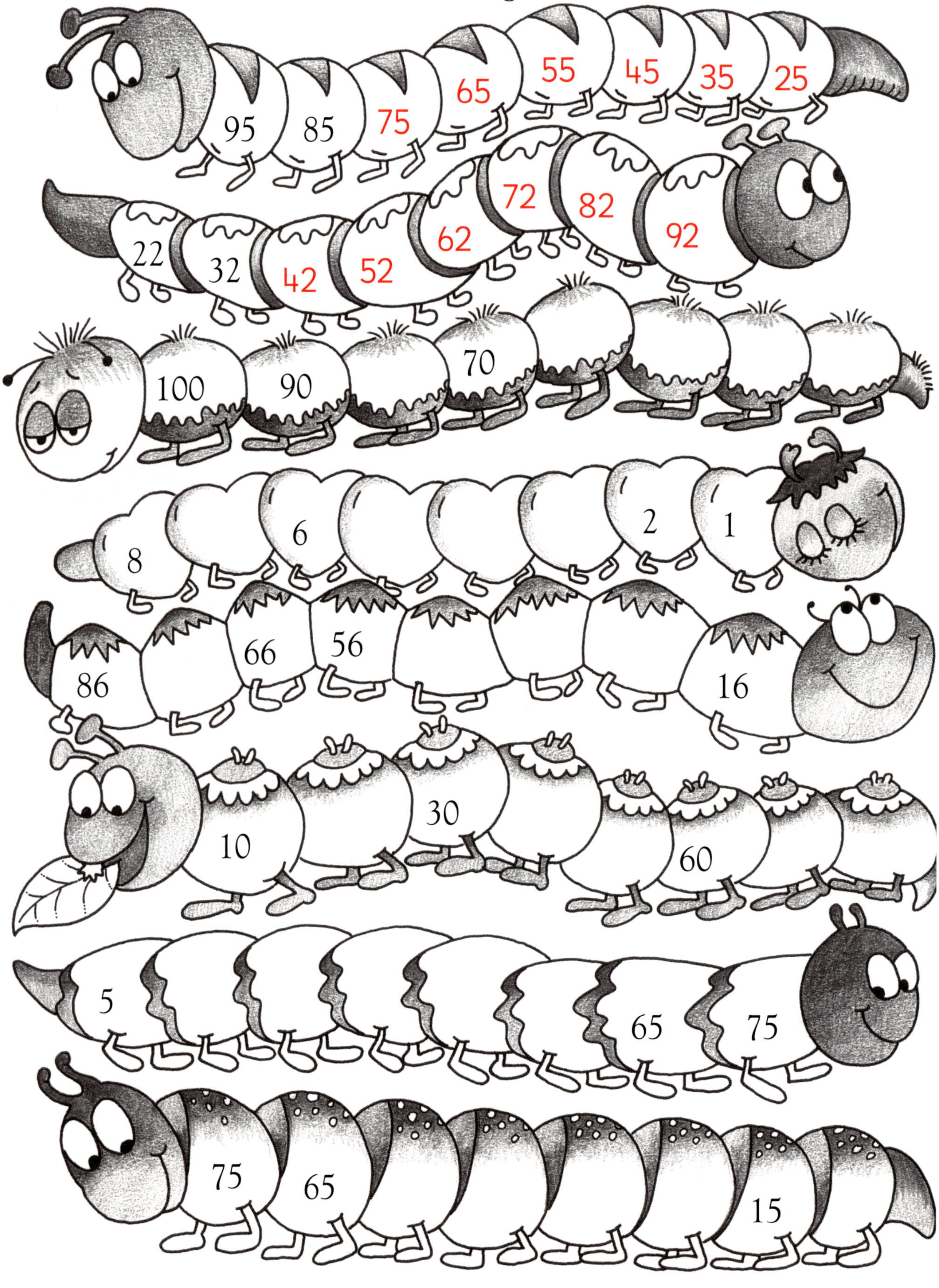

Bar graphs

Fruit

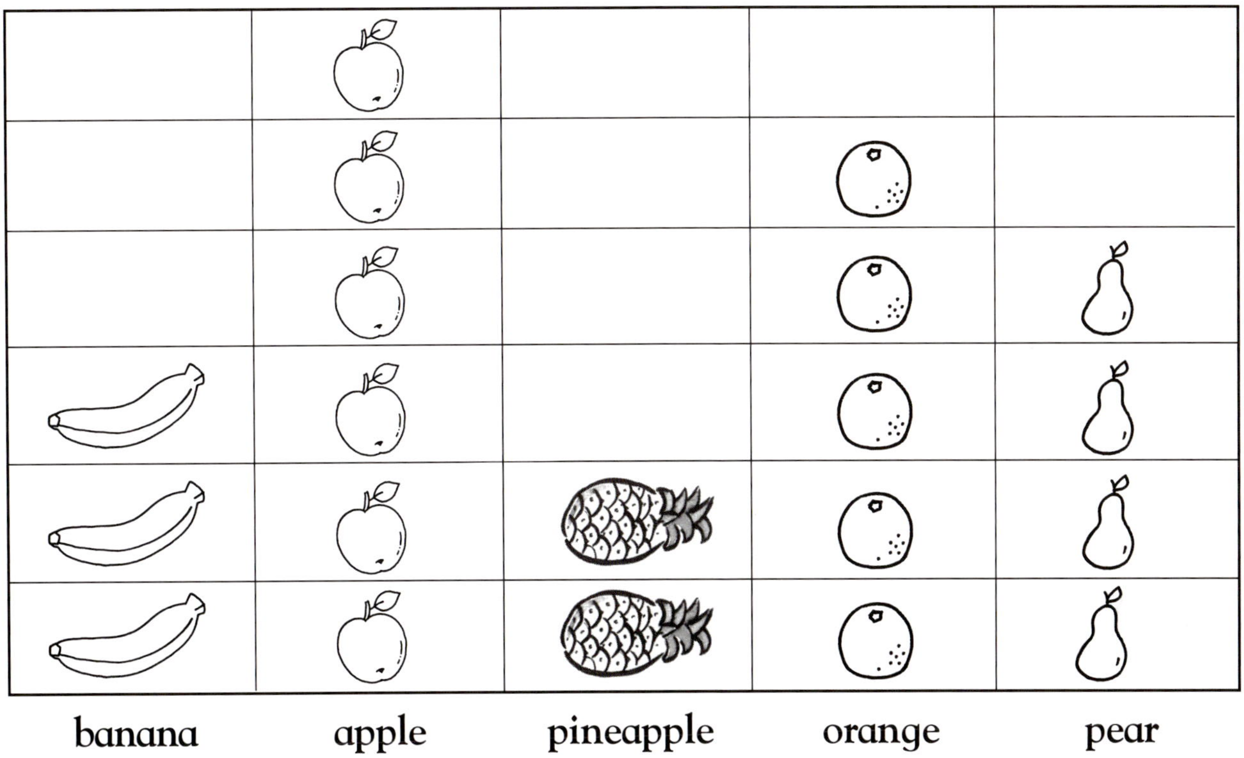

How many pears are there? 4 How many bananas are there? ____

The graph shows 6 ____. The graph shows 2 ____.

How many more oranges are there than bananas? ____

How many apples and pears are there altogether? ____

Ellen's marbles

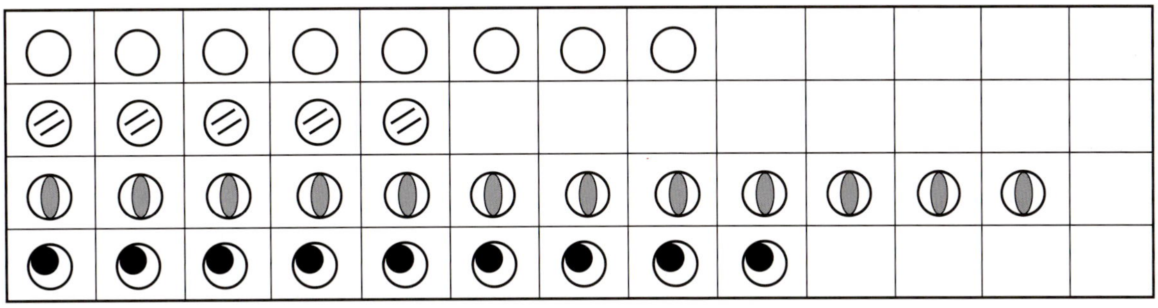

How many ⊘ does Ellen have? ____ How many ⦶ does Ellen have? ____

How many fewer ◕ than ⦶ does she have? ____

How many ○ and ⊘ does she have altogether? ____

Subtraction

If each child eats 1 slice, how many slices will be left? 5

If the children eat 6 slices, how many slices will be left?

If the children eat 8 slices, how many slices will be left?

If each child reads 1 book, how many books will be left?

How many books will be left if the children take 6 books altogether?

How many books will be left if the children take 9 books?

If the dog buries 1 ball, how many balls are left?

Write a subtraction sentence. 7 – 1 = 6

If the dog buries 3 balls, how many balls are left?

Write a subtraction sentence.

2s, 5s, and 10s

Count by 2s, 5s, and 10s to help you connect the dots.

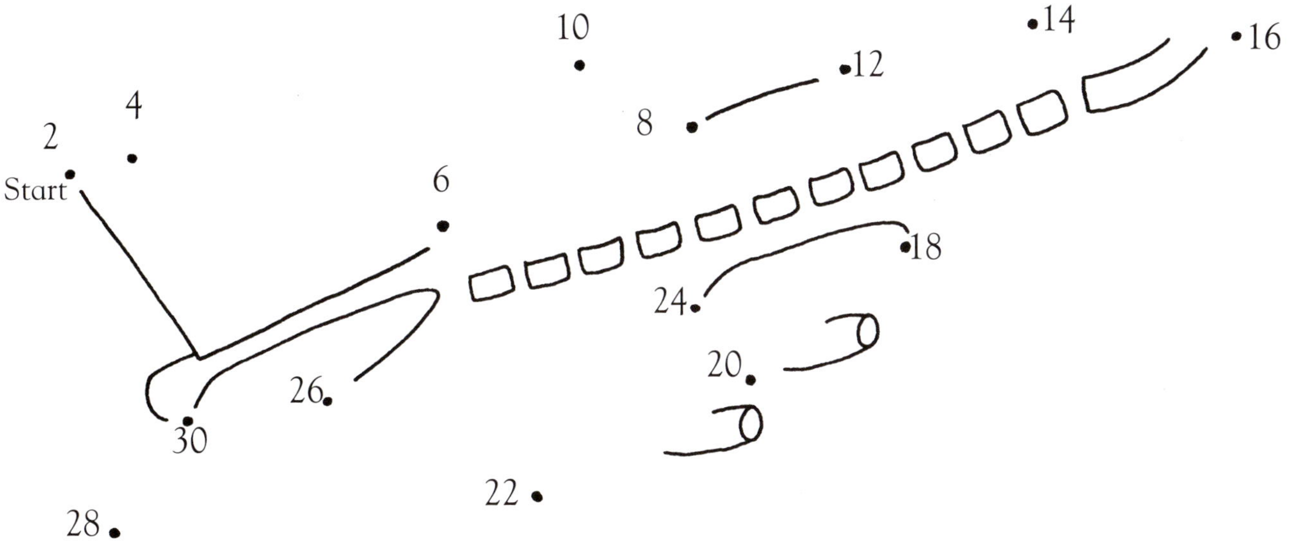

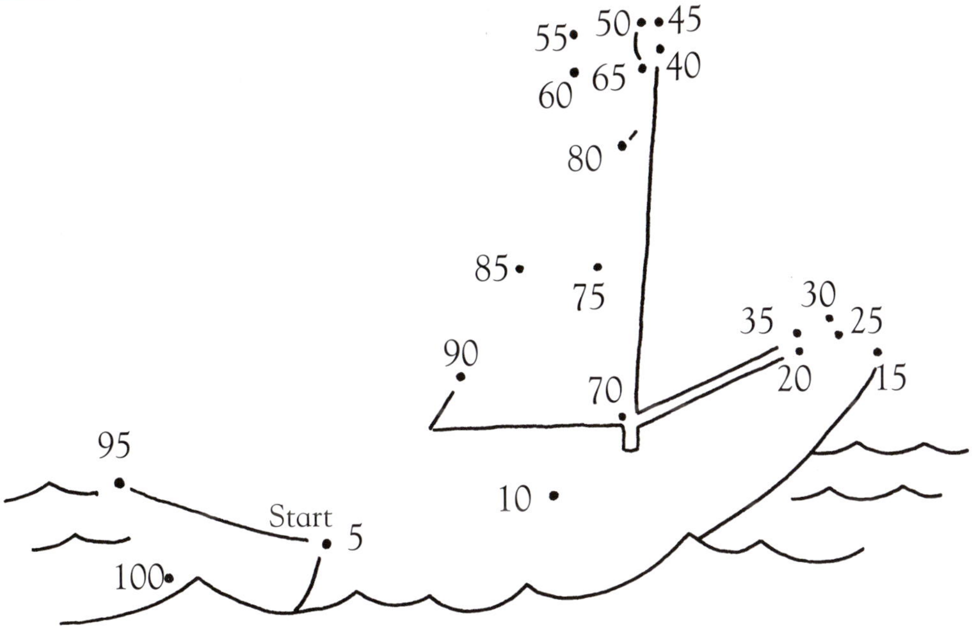

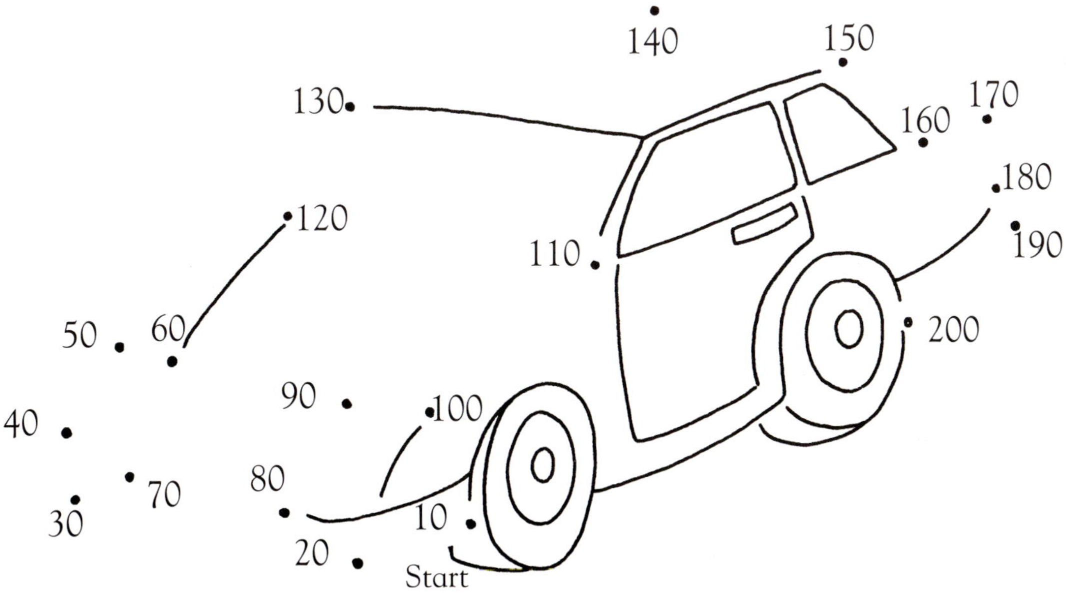

Comparing

Complete the boxes.

2 less	number	2 more
51	53	55

number	between	number
96	97 98	99

number	between	number
20		24

3 less	number	3 more
	30	

2 less	number	2 more
	29	

number	between	number
18		22

number	between	number
31		34

10 less	number	10 more
	19	

5 less	number	5 more
	25	

number	between	number
40		45

number	between	number
39		42

5 less	number	5 more
	15	

Ordering

Find the totals.

11¢

Write the totals in order, greatest first.

1st	2nd	3rd 11¢	4th	5th

Find the totals.

40¢

Write the totals in order, smallest first.

1st	2nd	3rd	4th	5th 40¢

Subtraction

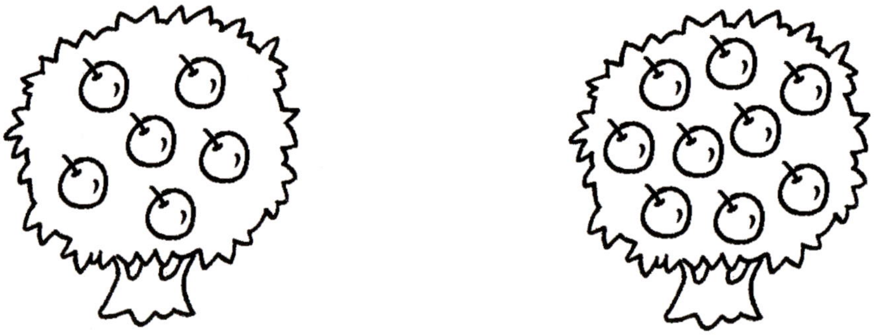

How many fewer apples
are on the left tree than on the right tree?

Write the subtraction sentence.

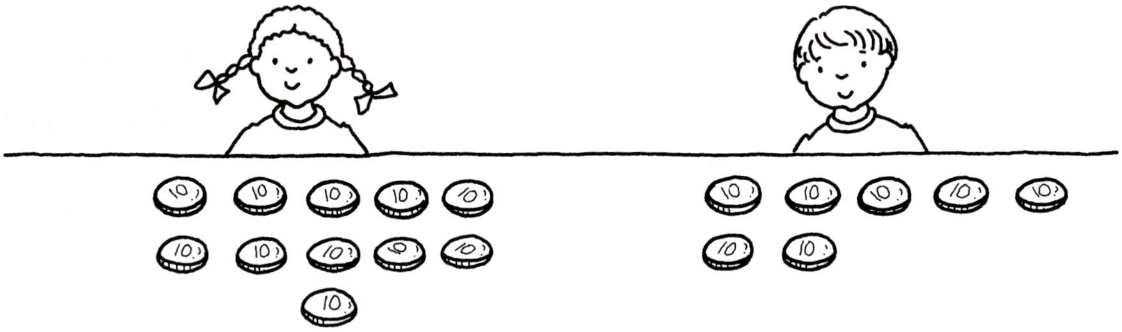

How many more dimes does Tasha have than Juan?

What is the subtraction sentence?

How many fewer bricks are
in the left stack than in the right stack?

What is the subtraction sentence?

Matching fractions

Colour all the matching squares.

Use yellow for halves.
Use orange for thirds.
Use green for fourths.

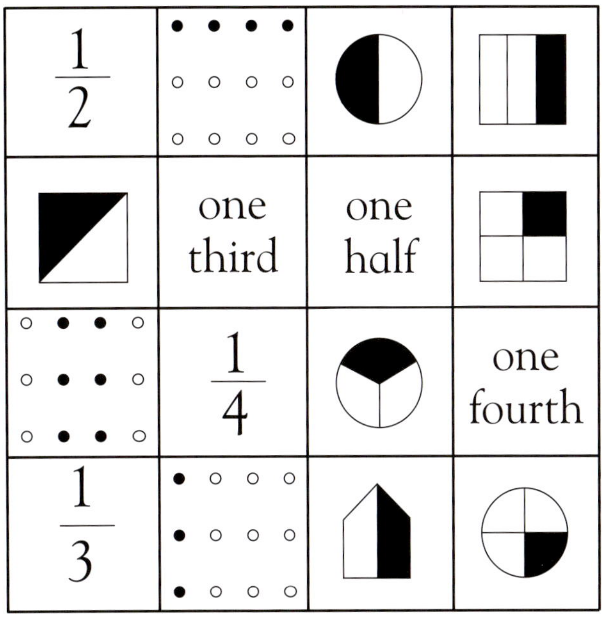

Label each part.

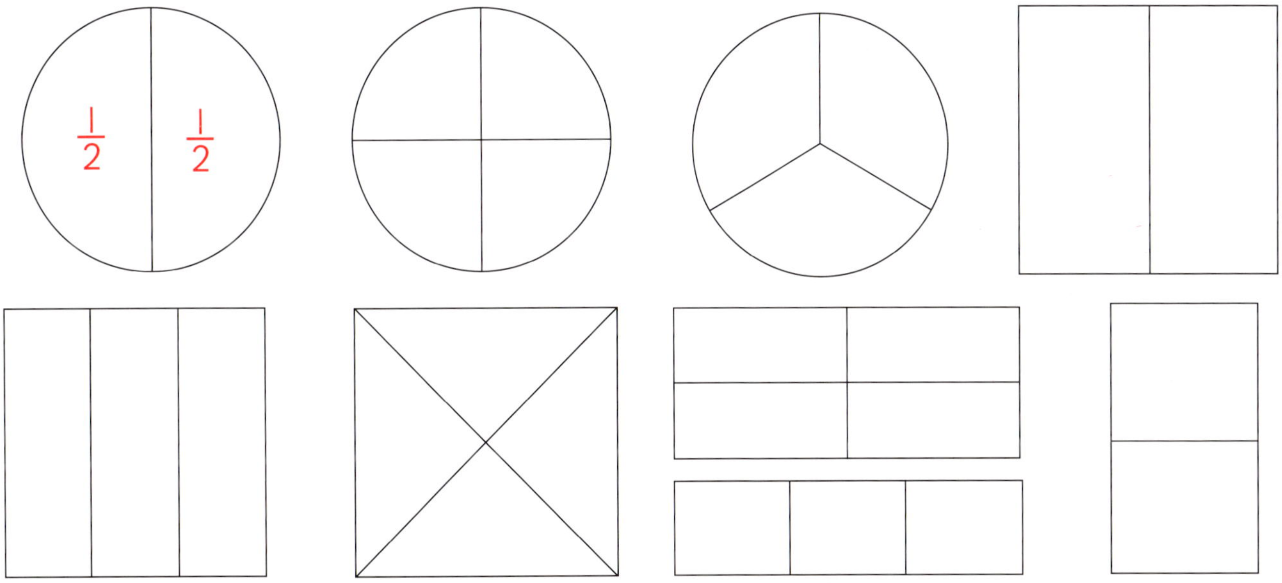

How many thirds in a whole?

How many fourths in a whole?

How many halves in a whole?

How many fourths in a half?

Money

You have only 3 coins in each purse. Draw the 3 coins that make the exact amount needed. You may use each coin more than once.

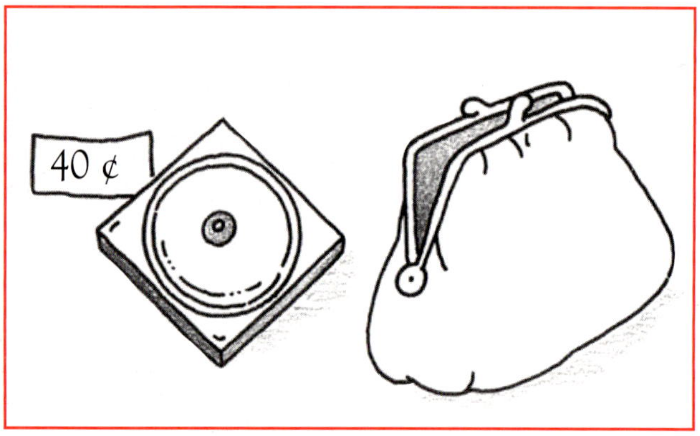

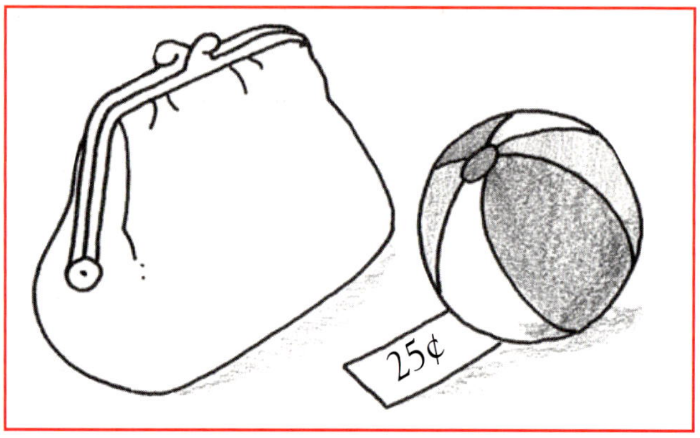

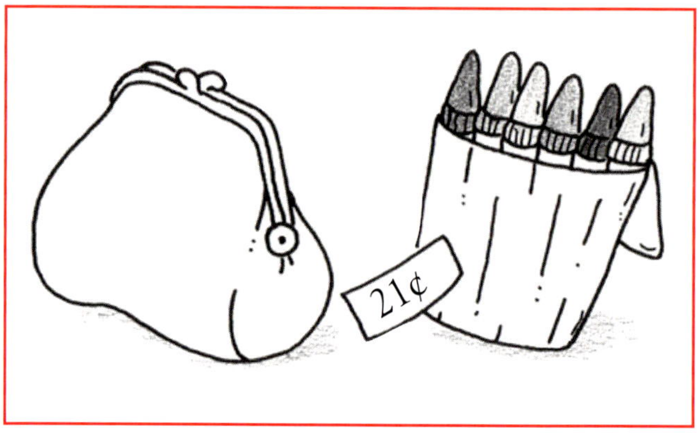

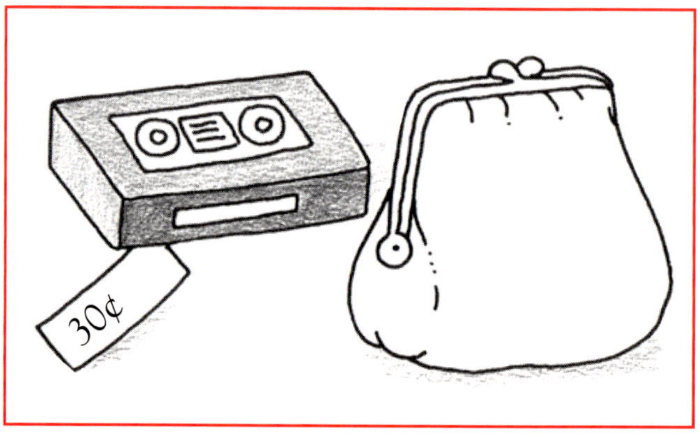

Fact families

Use the 3 numbers to write 4 different facts.

6 + 7 = 13	7 + 6 = 13	13 – 7 = 6	13 – 6 = 7
16 + 4 = 20	+ =	– =	– =
6 + 5 = 11			
7 + 8 = 15			
8 + 12 = 20			
10 + 8 = 18			
8 + 9 = 17			
9 + 7 = 16			
14 + 6 = 20			
11 + 8 = 19			

Adding money

Add the money. Write the totals in the right squares.

+	2¢	5¢	8¢	6¢
3¢				9¢
11¢				
29¢		34¢		
32¢				

+	2¢	4¢	6¢	9¢	3¢
17¢					
20¢				29¢	
33¢	35¢				
41¢					

Using doubles

Use the doubles to find the answers.

6 + 6 = 12	10 + 10 = 20
6 + 7 6 + 6 + 1 = 13	10 + 11 10 + 10 + 1 = 21
6 + 5 6 + 6 – 1 = 11	10 + 9 10 + 10 – 1 = 19

Use doubles to find the answers.

4 + 4 = ☐ 4 + 5 = ☐ + ☐ + 1 = ☐

4 + 3 = ☐ + ☐ – 1 = ☐

7 + 7 = ☐ 7 + 8 = ☐ + ☐ + 1 = ☐

7 + 6 = ☐ + ☐ – 1 = ☐

8 + 8 = ☐ 8 + 9 = ☐ + ☐ + 1 = ☐

8 + 7 = ☐ + ☐ – 1 = ☐

Double your doubles.

1	double it	2	double it	4	4	double it	☐	double it	☐
2	double it	☐	double it	☐	5	double it	☐	double it	☐
3	double it	☐	double it	☐	6	double it	☐	double it	☐

Adding up

Add the numbers on the sails. Write the totals on the boats.

Add the numbers. Write the totals.

3 + 4 + 10 = 17	9 + 0 + 20 =	2 + 40 + 3 =
5 + 40 + 2 =	20 + 7 + 2 =	4 + 5 + 20 =
30 + 4 + 3 =	1 + 30 + 7 =	40 + 8 + 1 =

$$\begin{array}{r} 30 \\ 1 \\ +\ 7 \\ \hline \end{array} \qquad \begin{array}{r} 10 \\ 2 \\ +\ 5 \\ \hline \end{array} \qquad \begin{array}{r} 20 \\ 2 \\ +\ 4 \\ \hline \end{array} \qquad \begin{array}{r} 40 \\ 5 \\ +\ 0 \\ \hline \end{array}$$

Count by 2s

Draw the pictures. Count by 2s. Write the totals.

Sasha has 4 hutches. There are 2 rabbits in each hutch.

8 rabbits

Joel has 3 boxes. There are 2 pencils in each box.

Mrs. Reaves has 6 flower pots. There are 2 flowers in each pot.

Mr. Hastings has 5 fish. Each fish has 2 eyes.

Draw the pictures, then write the answers.

There are 6 birds. There are 2 birds in each tree. How many trees are there?

There are 8 tarts. There are 2 tarts on each plate. How many plates are there?

Addition

Add to find each sum.

2	4	18
+ 13	+ 10	+ 11
15	14	29

Add to find each sum.

1	6	3	3
+ 3	+ 2	+ 1	+ 4
5	2	3	1
+ 1	+ 2	+ 5	+ 1
7	1	10	6
+ 2	+ 5	+ 9	+ 11
13	16	10	14
+ 2	+ 2	+ 4	+ 5
11	12	18	16
+ 3	+ 1	+ 11	+ 20

Addition

Add to find each sum.

5 + 1 6	14 + 24 38	50 + 10 60

Add to find each sum.

2 + 2	5 + 1	3 + 4	1 + 3
6 + 2	1 + 1	10 + 10	50 + 40
16 + 33	29 + 20	61 + 35	74 + 12

Michael has 21 fish. His dad gives him 7 more fish. How many fish does Michael have?

Sonia read 13 books one month. She read 6 books the next month. How many books did she read in all?

Addition and subtraction

Write the missing numbers.

? + 8 = 12	7 − ? = 1
4 + 8 = 12	7 − 6 = 1

Write the missing numbers.

15 − ☐ = 10	☐ + 3 = 6	8 − ☐ = 2
9 + ☐ = 11	☐ − 8 = 0	☐ + 5 = 14
☐ + 3 = 10	6 − ☐ = 2	☐ − 10 = 7
☐ − 4 = 1	2 + ☐ = 7	1 + ☐ = 4
14 − ☐ = 7	☐ + 1 = 9	3 + ☐ = 12
8 + ☐ = 14	☐ − 1 = 2	12 − ☐ = 6
18 − ☐ = 9	☐ + 6 = 11	☐ − 1 = 0
☐ − 7 = 4	4 + ☐ = 13	☐ + 5 = 8
☐ + 3 = 5	16 − ☐ = 10	8 + ☐ = 18
5 + ☐ = 12	☐ + 4 = 0	9 − ☐ = 6

Real-life problems

Look at the picture. Answer the questions.

What time is it ? ....

Today is Friday. What day was it yesterday? ....

How many cupcakes can each person have? ....

If half of the apples were eaten, how many would be left? ....

If each person had 2 drinks, how many drinks would there be altogether? ....

How many more sandwiches are there than apples? ....

If 13 candies were eaten, how many would be left? ....

Each package contains 2 presents. How many presents are there altogether? ....

What shape are the sandwiches? ....

Is there an odd or an even number of chairs? ....

Real-life problems

Complete the pictures, and then write the answers.

There were 12 biscuits. James ate 3. How many were left?

9

Share 9 marbles equally among 3 people. How many marbles will each have?

Susie has ten fish. She is given 11 more for her birthday. How many fish does she have altogether?

Joe had 5 boxes. He had 3 pencils in each box. How many pencils did he have altogether?

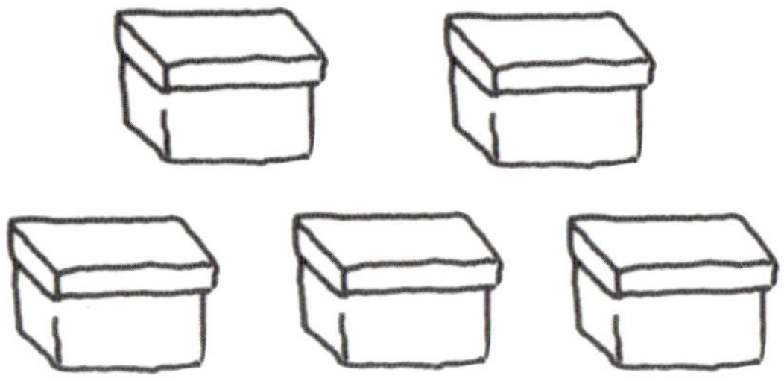

If you share 8 carrots equally among 4 rabbits, how many carrots will each have?

Mom had 16 cups, but she broke 9 of them. How many cups does she have left?

Addition

Find each sum.

40 + 30 = 70	80 + 80 = 160	20 + 50 =	20 + 30 =
10 + 10 =	40 + 50 =	40 + 40 =	50 + 30 =
10 + 80 =	50 + 40 =	20 + 10 =	30 + 20 =
10 + 70 =	20 + 40 =	10 + 40 =	10 + 30 =

Find each sum.

70 + 20 = 90	80 + 10 =	10 + 40 =
60 + 10 =	30 + 30 =	50 + 10 =
20 + 70 =	70 + 10 =	10 + 20 =
20 + 60 =	40 + 40 =	10 + 80 =

Clocks and watches

Write the times.

4 o'clock

half past 10

Puzzles

Read the clues and solve the puzzle.

I am a number between 20 and 30. If you count by fives, you will say my name. Who am I? 25

Read the clues and solve each puzzle.

I am an even number. I am between 6 and 9. Who am I?

7 + 7 is less than I am. 7 + 9 is greater than I am. Who am I?

I am a number less than 10. If you add me to myself, you will find a number greater than 16. Who am I?

16 – 10 is less than I am. 16 – 8 is greater than I am. Who am I?

I am a number between 7 and 12. If you count by threes, you will say my name. Who am I?

I am an odd number. I am between 11 and 14. Who am I?

If you subtract me from 14, you will find a number greater than 11. I am an odd number. Who am I?

If you add me to 50, you will find a number less than 70. If you count by tens you will say my name. Who am I?

If you add me to 1, you will find an odd number. I am less than 2. Who am I?

Tables

Water animals

	Has 4 legs	Eats insects	Has a furry coat	Lays eggs
Frog	yes	yes	no	yes
Newt	yes	yes	no	yes
Otter	yes	no	yes	no

Use the table to answer the questions.

What does the frog eat? insects

Who lays eggs? ....

Who has a furry coat? ....

Does the otter eat insects? ....

Who has a furry coat and does not lay eggs? ....

School friends

	Age	Hobby	Pet	Favourite colour
Dean	7	Computers	Rat	Black
Joe	6	Reading	Rabbit	Purple
Taif	7	Judo	Cat	Orange
Maddie	8	Computers	Parrot	Green

Use the table to answer the questions.

Whose favourite colour is black? Dean's

Who is the oldest? ....

Who has judo for a hobby? ....

What kind of pet does Joe have? ....

Who likes computers and has a parrot? ....

Who is seven and does not have a rat? ....

Venn diagrams

Things made with metal | Things made with plastic

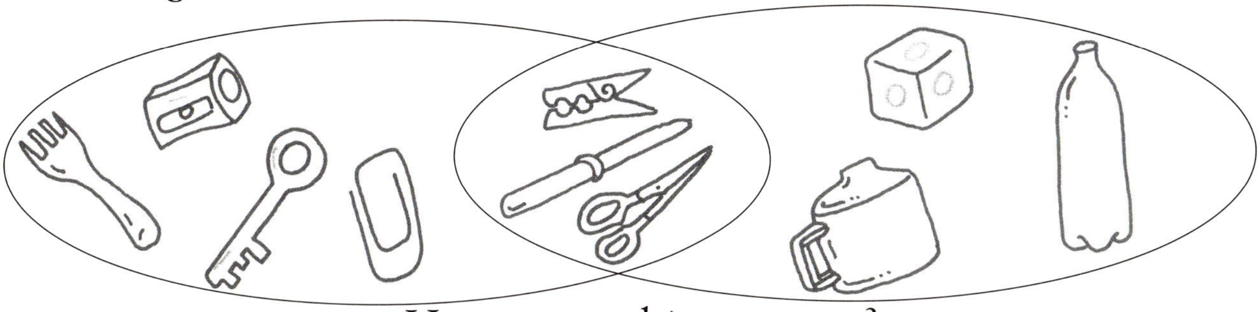

How many things are ...?

made with plastic?	6	made with metal?	7
made with metal and plastic?	3	not made with plastic?	4

Odd numbers | Numbers greater than 20

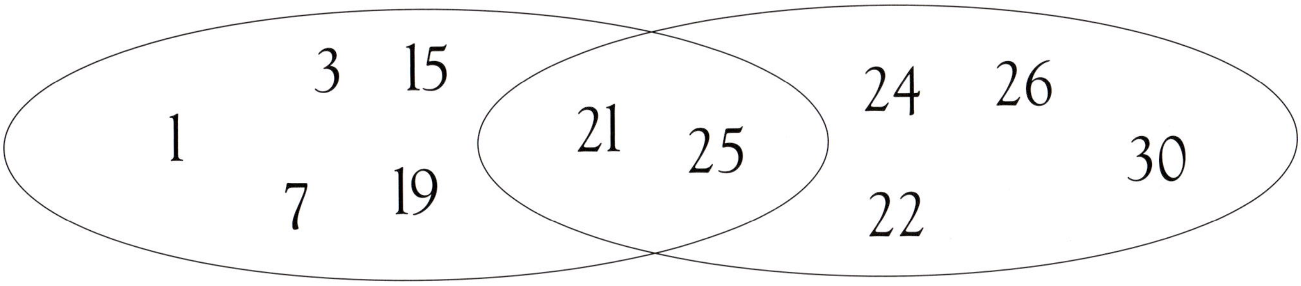

How many numbers are ...?

odd?		greater than 20?	
odd and greater than 20?		not odd?	

White things | Green things

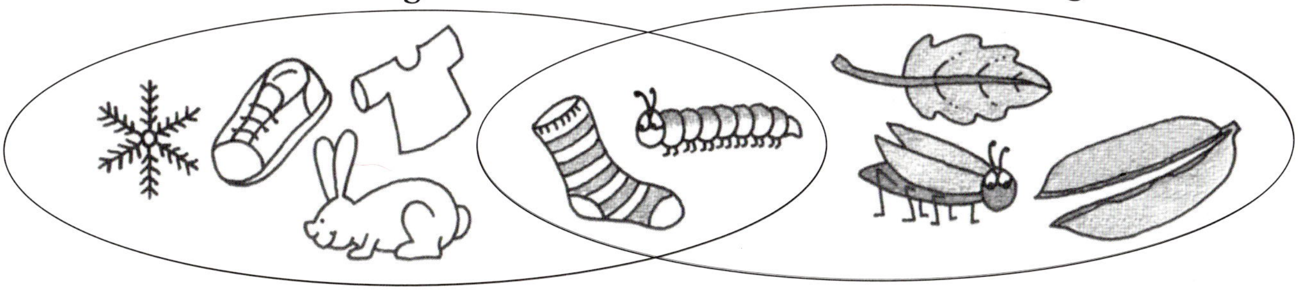

How many things are ...?

green?		white?	
green and white?		not green?	

Appropriate units of measure

Which unit would you use to measure the length of each item? Circle the answer.

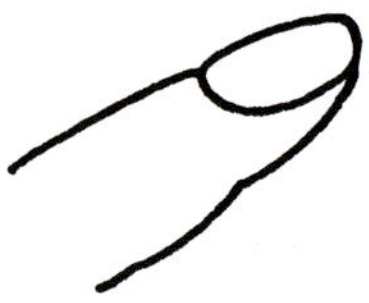	centimetres	kilometres	kilograms	litres
	kilometres	grams	kilograms	metres

Which unit would you use to measure the weight of each item? Circle the answer.

	centimetres	kilometres	kilograms	grams
	kilometres	kilograms	litres	grams

Which unit would you use to measure how much liquid each container holds? Circle the answer.

	tonnes	centimetres	millilitres	kilograms
	kilometres	centimetres	grams	litres

Symmetry

Draw a line of symmetry on each picture.

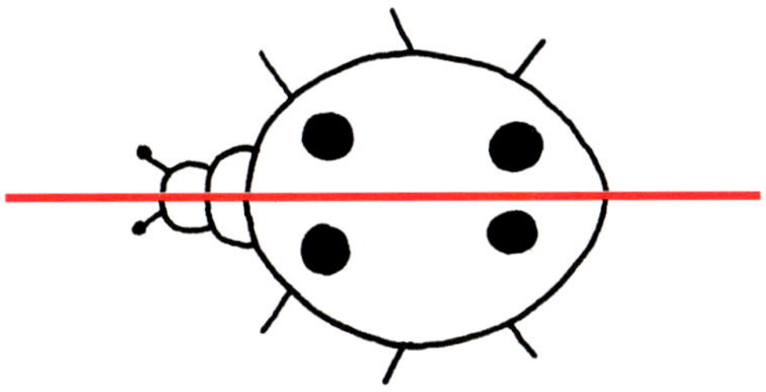
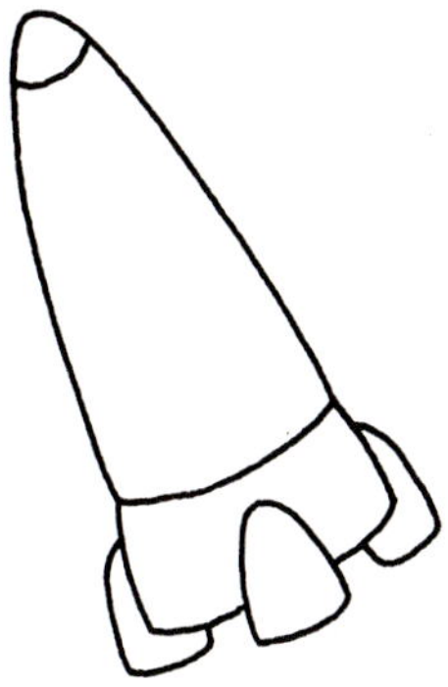

Draw lines of symmetry on these shapes.

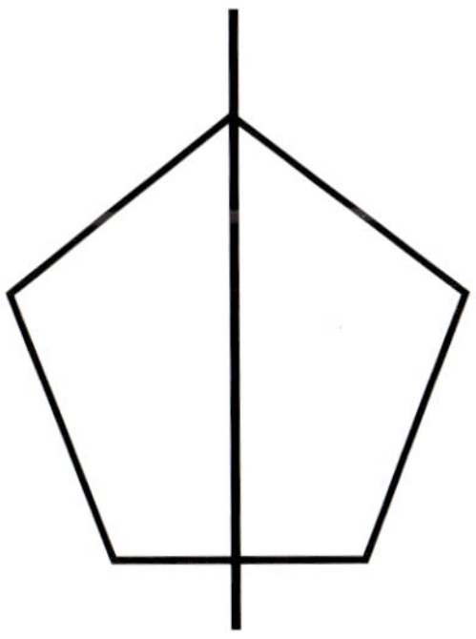
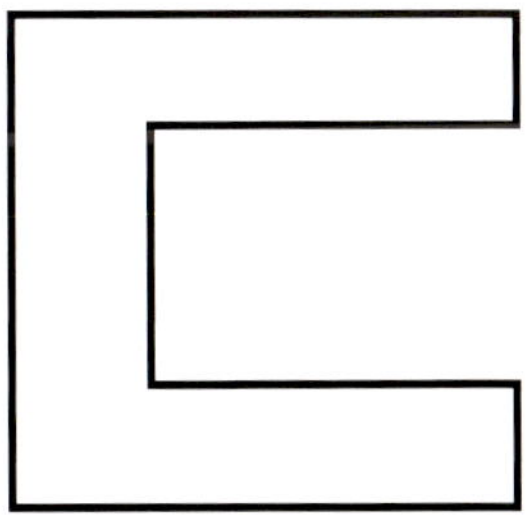
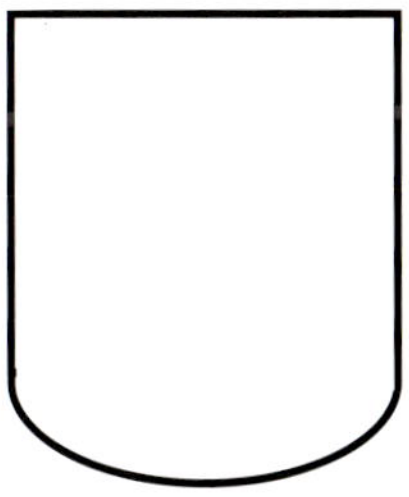
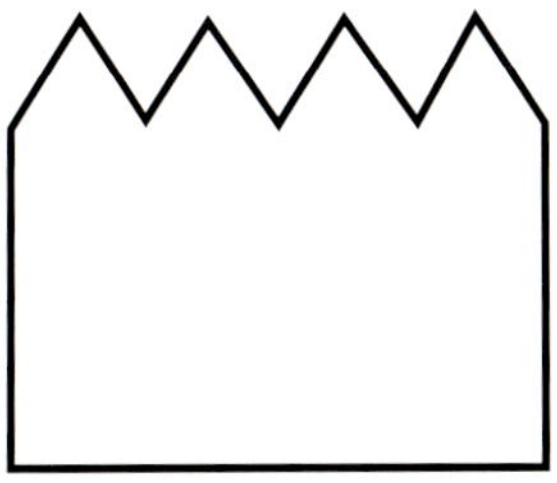
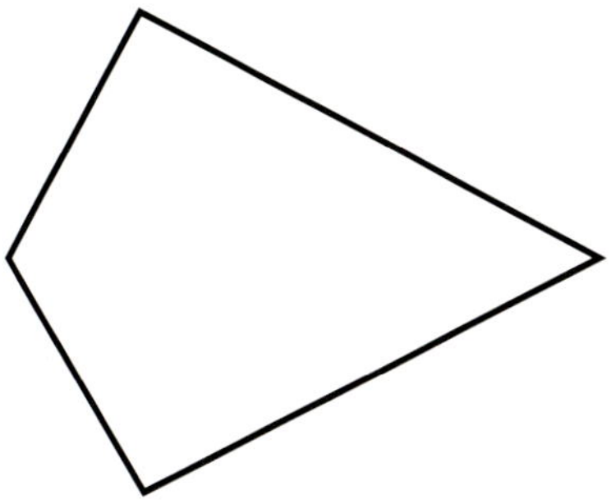

2-dimensional shapes

Write the name of the shape. Count the corners and sides.

Name hexagon

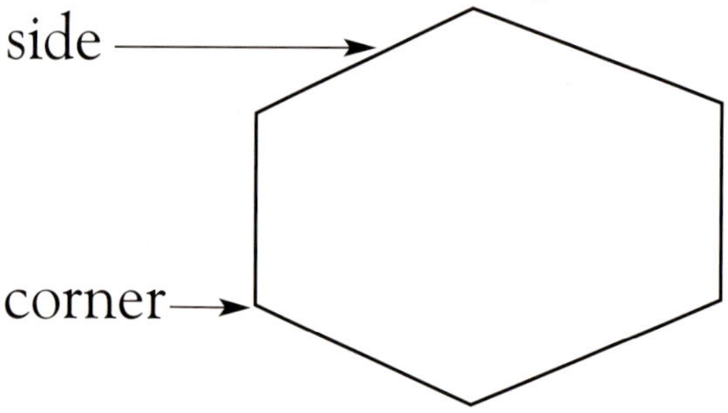

Sides 6

Corners 6

Name ....

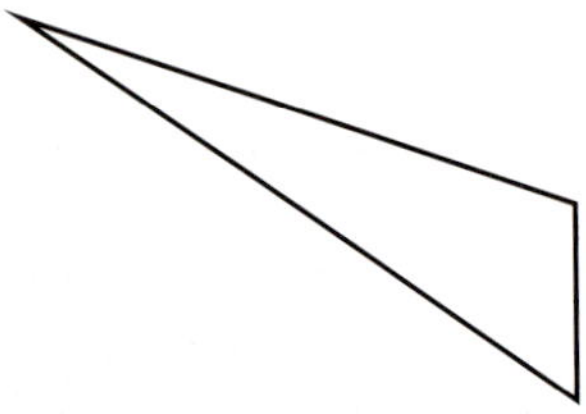

Sides ☐

Corners ☐

Name ....

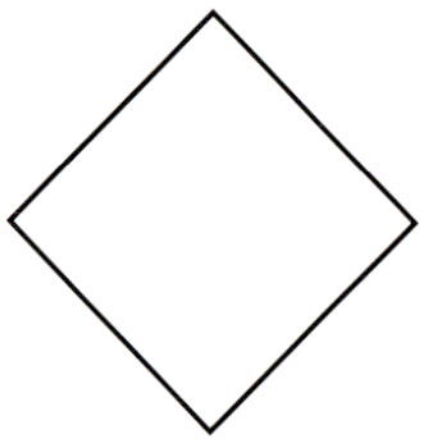

Sides ☐

Corners ☐

Name ....

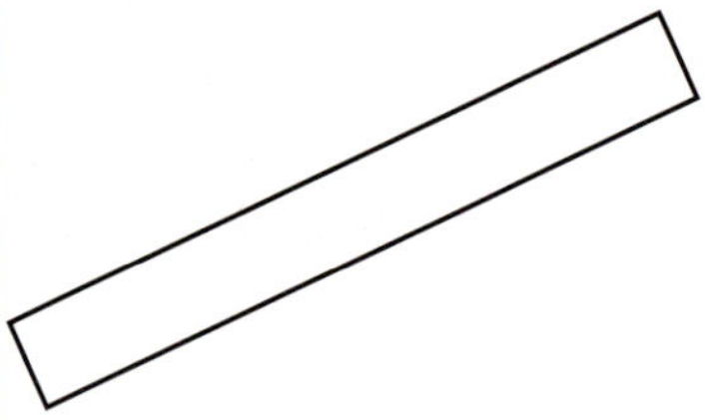

Sides ☐

Corners ☐

Name ....

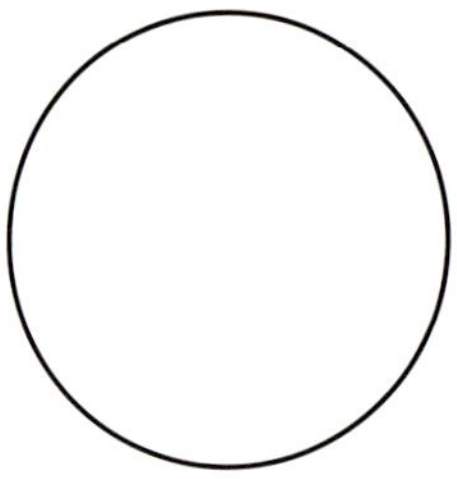

Sides ☐

Corners ☐

Name ....

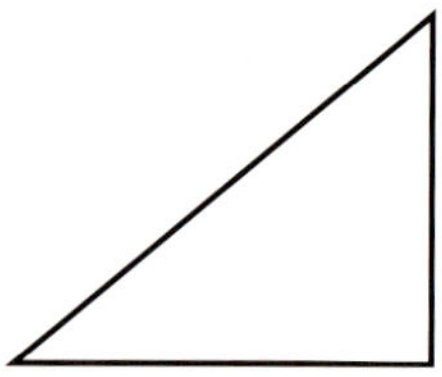

Sides ☐

Corners ☐

Name ....

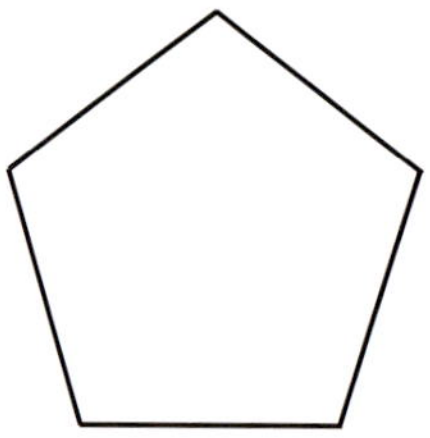

Sides ☐

Corners ☐

Name ....

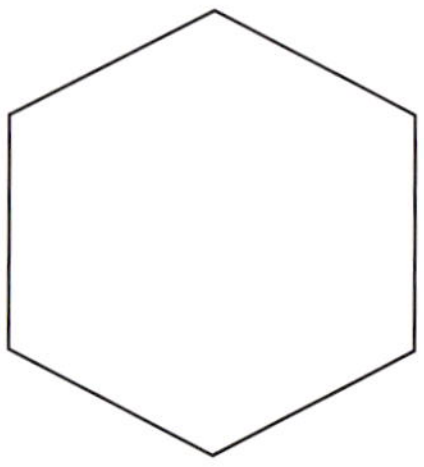

Sides ☐

Corners ☐

Name ....

Sides ☐

Corners ☐

Equal value

Circle the coins that add up to the amount shown.

7¢	6¢	15¢	8¢	20¢
5¢	1¢	1¢	10¢	10¢
1¢	1¢	1¢	5¢	10¢
1¢	1¢	1¢	1¢	5¢
1¢	1¢	1¢	1¢	1¢
1¢	1¢	5¢	1¢	1¢
1¢	1¢	10¢	1¢	1¢

Write the amounts. Tell if they are equal.

10¢ 5¢ — 15¢
5¢ 5¢ 5¢ — 15¢
equal

10¢ 1¢ 1¢ — ____
5¢ 5¢ 1¢ 1¢ — ____
____

1¢ 1¢ 1¢ 1¢ 1¢ 1¢ — ____
5¢ 1¢ 1¢ — ____
____

5¢ 5¢ — ____
5¢ 1¢ 1¢ 1¢ 1¢ — ____
____

1¢ 5¢ 10¢ — ____
5¢ 5¢ 5¢ 1¢ — ____
____

Shapes and places

Look at the shapes and answer the questions.

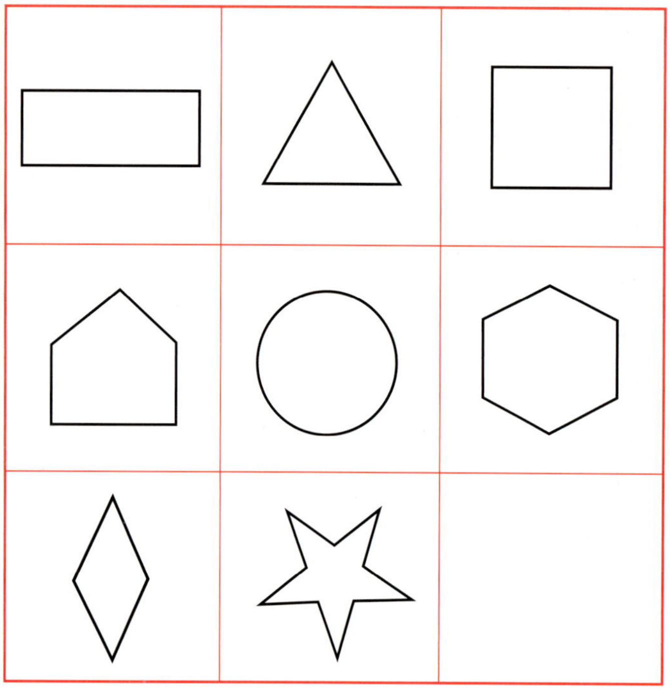

circle

hexagon

diamond

pentagon

rectangle

square

star

triangle

Which shape is ...

underneath the circle?

to the **left** of the triangle?

above the hexagon?

below the pentagon?

between the rectangle and the diamond?

diagonally above the empty space?

beside the diamond?

on top of the diamond?

between the triangle and the star?

on the **right-hand end** of the top row?

in the **centre** of the grid?

in the **top left-hand corner**?

Numbers

Which numbers are the snakes hiding?

1	2	3	4	5		7	8	9	
11	12	13		15			18	19	
21	22	23	24		26	27	28		
31				35	36		38	39	40
41				45		47	48	49	50
	52	53	54	55		57	58	59	60
61		63	64	65				69	70
		73	74		76	77	78	79	80
81	82		84				88		
		93		95	96		98		

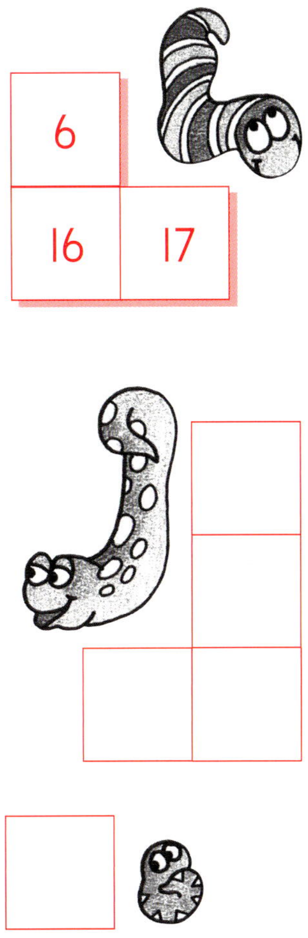

Counting by 1s and 10s

Finish each row.

Count by 1s.	24	25	26	27	28	29
Count by 10s.	31	41	51	61	71	81

Finish each row. Count by 1s.

17	18	19					
36	37	38					
69	70	71					
45	46	47					
85	86					91	

Finish each row. Count by 10s.

10	20	30					
12	22	32					
15	25	35					
16	26	36					
17	27		47				
19			49				

Finish each row. Count by 1s and 10s.

8	9	10					
18	28	38					
4	5	6					
14	24	34					
0	1						7

Counting by 2s

Count by 2s.	12	14	16	18	20	22
Count by 2s.	31	33	35	37	39	41

Finish each row. Count by 2s.

17	19	21					
36	38	40					
72	74	76					
43	45	47					
14	16					26	
39		43					53

Finish each row. Count by 2s.

20							34
75							89
44							58
69							83
31							45
88							102

Finish each row. Count by 2s.

				28			34
			53			59	
					87		91
	48		52				
					97	99	
		50			56		

Odd and even

Numbers ending in	0	2	4	6	8	are called even numbers.
Numbers ending in	1	3	5	7	9	are called odd numbers.

Circle the numbers that are even.

10 25 13 34
21 22
18 9 17
6

Circle the numbers that are odd.

50
49 48 16
21 32
23 35 44 37

Write the odd numbers between 30 and 50.

Write the even numbers between 21 and 41.

More and less

Which number is 1 more than 49?	50
Which number is 10 less than 64?	54

Write the number that is 1 more than each of these.

35		78		69		53		9		54	
41		24		67		40		36		73	

Write the number that is 1 less than each of these.

52		18		20		76		37		50	
40		54		23		100		31		83	

Write the number that is 10 more than each of these.

46		21		86		53		16	
18		29		39		38		90	
60		81		59		23		80	

Write the number that is 10 less than each of these.

56		75		86		18		23	
68		45		50		40		80	
60		90		60		70		10	

Write the number that is 10 more than each of these.

65		76	
90		60	

Write the number that is 10 less than each of these.

50		10	
80		75	

Fact families

Finish the fact family for each group of numbers.

9
5 4

5 + 4 = 9
4 + 5 = 9
9 − 4 = 5
9 − 5 = 4

Finish the fact family for each group of numbers.

7
4 3

4 + 3 =
3 + 4 =
7 − 3 =
7 − 4 =

8
3 5

3 + 5 =
5 + 3 =
8 − 5 =
8 − 3 =

7
6 1

6 + 1 =
1 + 6 =
7 − 1 =
7 − 6 =

6
2 4

2 + 4 =
4 + 2 =
6 − 4 =
6 − 2 =

9
2 7

2 + 7 =
7 + 2 =
9 − 2 =
9 − 7 =

3
2 5

3 + 2 =
2 + 3 =
5 − 2 =
5 − 3 =

3
1 4

3 + 1 =
1 + 3 =
4 − 1 =
4 − 3 =

8
10 2

2 + 8 =
8 + 2 =
10 − 2 =
10 − 8 =

10 5

5 + 5 =
10 − 5 =

4 8

4 + 4 =
8 − 4 =

3 6

3 + 3 =
6 − 3 =

4 2

2 + 2 =
4 − 2 =

Write the fact family for each group of numbers.

3
10 7

9
3 6

8
6 2

7
5 2

Fractions

Colour one-third ($\frac{1}{3}$) of each shape.

Colour one-half ($\frac{1}{2}$) of each shape.

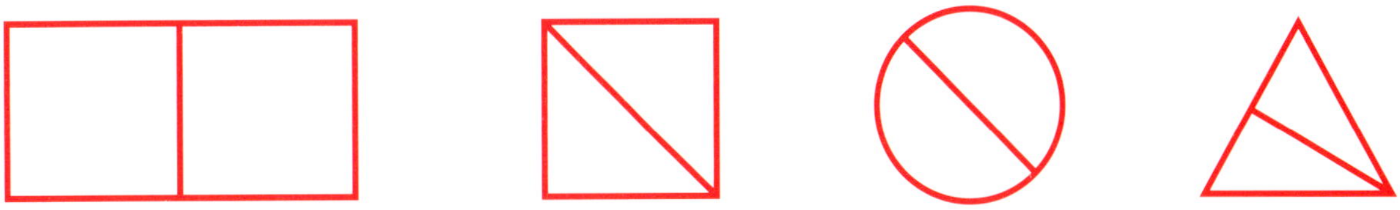

Colour one-fourth ($\frac{1}{4}$) of each shape.

Colour one-third ($\frac{1}{3}$) of each shape.

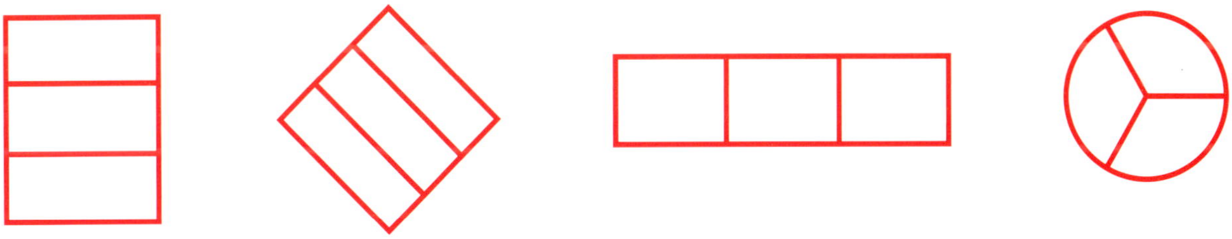

Colour one-eighth ($\frac{1}{8}$) of each shape.

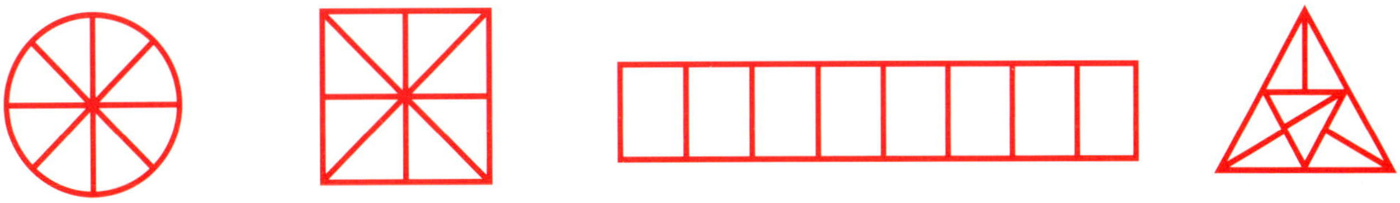

Colour one-tenth ($\frac{1}{10}$) of each shape.

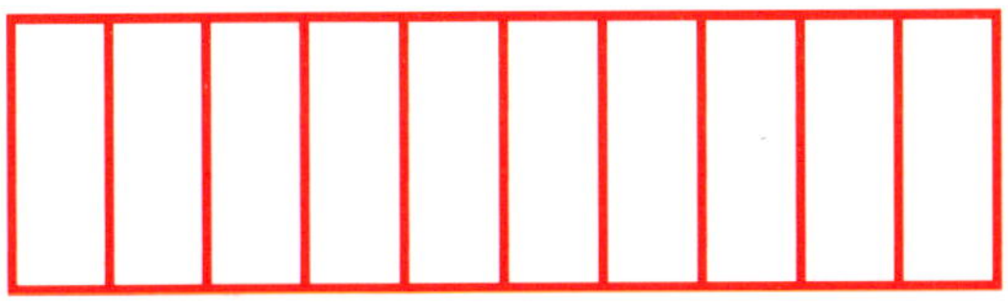

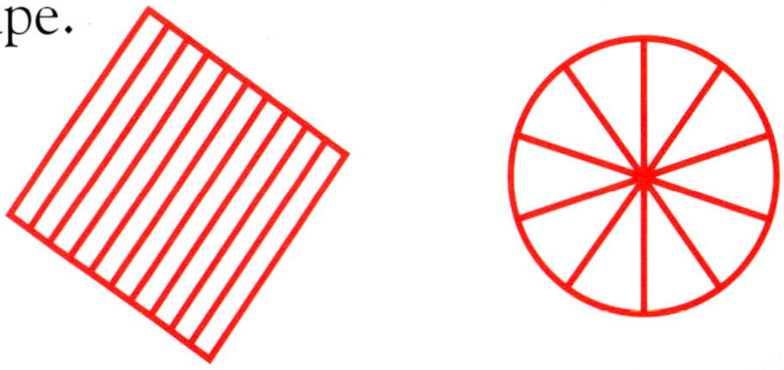

Adding

Write the answers between the lines.

13 +16 29	11 + 5 16	14 + 5 19

Write the answers between the lines.

4 + 9	3 + 6	1 + 7	4 + 5
3 + 7	2 + 5	4 + 7	8 + 8
6 +10	7 +11	13 +12	31 + 9

Write the answers between the lines.

2 2 + 2	3 3 + 3	2 2 + 6	4 4 + 4
12¢ 6¢ +10¢	12¢ 7¢ +10¢	8¢ 1¢ + 6¢	3¢ 9¢ + 6¢
20¢ 7¢ +10¢	15¢ 10¢ + 2¢	8¢ 10¢ + 4¢	10¢ 8¢ +10¢

Estimating length

Circle the longest string.

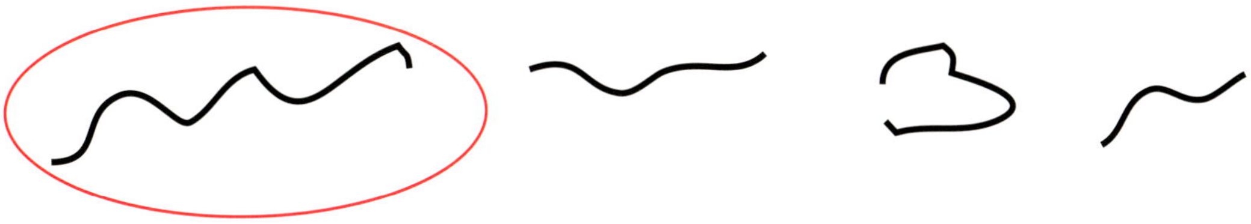

Circle the shortest string.

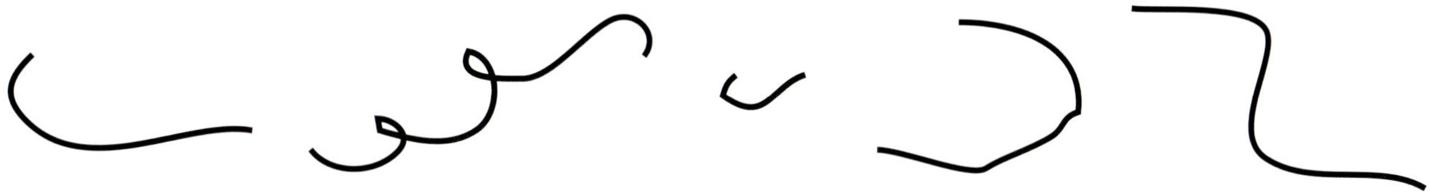

Circle the longest string.

Look at the ruler. Circle the closest measure.

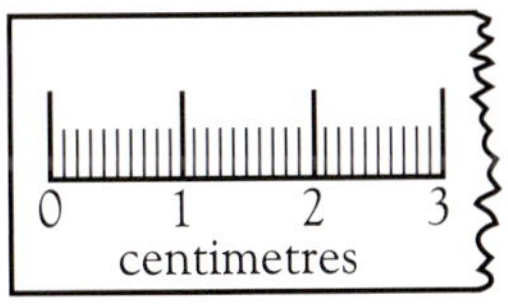

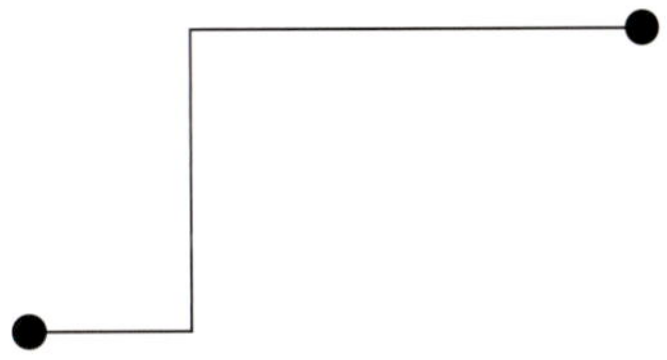

1 centimetres 2 centimetres 4 centimetres 8 centimetres

2 centimetres 4 centimetres 11 centimetres 30 centimetres

5 centimetres 10 centimetres 15 centimetres 20 centimetres

Subtracting

Write the answers between the lines.

28	$\overset{2\ 11}{\cancel{3}\cancel{1}}$	$\overset{3\ 10}{\cancel{4}\cancel{0}}$
− 16	− 14	− 17
12	17	23

Write the answers between the lines.

7 − 4	8 − 5	9 − 7	9 − 8
8 − 4	9 − 6	3 − 0	7 − 7
8 − 8	7 − 6	9 − 4	36 − 2
28¢ − 16¢	46¢ − 35¢	39¢ − 26¢	48¢ − 37¢
56¢ − 35¢	39¢ − 28¢	50¢ − 47¢	48¢ − 38¢
40¢ − 8¢	50¢ − 26¢	41¢ − 14¢	44¢ − 36¢

Simple tally charts and bar graphs

Look at the tally chart and then answer the question.

blue	𝍸 𝍸 𝍸 |||
red	𝍸 ||

How many votes did blue receive? 18

Look at the tally chart and then answer the questions.

Favourite ice cream flavours

vanilla	𝍸 𝍸 |
chocolate	𝍸 𝍸 𝍸 𝍸 ||||
strawberry	𝍸 𝍸 𝍸 |||

Which flavour had the most votes?

Which flavour had 11 votes?

What was the difference in votes between the most popular flavour and strawberry?

Look at the bar graph and then answer the questions.

Favourite sports

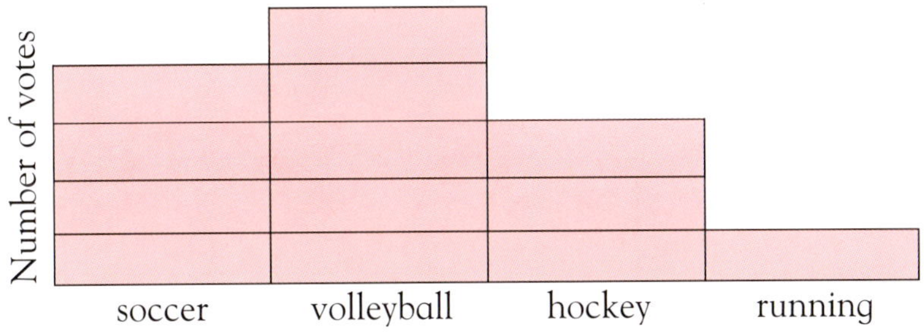

Which sport did four children vote for?

How many votes did volleyball receive?

Which was the least popular sport?

How many children voted altogether?

How many more voted for soccer than for hockey?

Addition properties

Circle the number that makes the sentence true.

___ + 7 = 7 — 1, (0), 14

43 + 21 = 21 + ___ — 22, 64, (43)

Circle the number that makes the sentence true.

___ + 3 = 3
0 3 6

15 + ___ = 15
30 0 5

___ + 23 = 23 + 16
16 23 46

25 + 41 = 41 + ___
16 66 25

___ + 45 = 45
45 0 1

50 + 0 = 0 + ___
50 0 500

Complete the number sentences.

☐ + 27 = 27 | 40 + 0 = ☐ | 13 + 28 = 28 + ☐

25 + 3 = ☐ + 25 | ☐ + 0 = 47 | 16 + 43 = 43 + ☐

2 + 28 = ☐ + 2 | ☐ + 12 = 12 | ☐ + 20 = 20 + 28

35 + ☐ = 35 | ☐ + 0 = 10 | 20 + 8 = 8 + ☐

☐ + 0 = 47 | 8 + 0 = ☐ | 34 + 11 = ☐ + 34

Equations

Circle the correct number sentence.

$7 + 3 = 10$ $4 + 3 = 7$ $4 - 3 = 1$

$2 + 4 = 6$ $2 + 3 = 5$ $5 - 3 = 2$

Circle the correct addition sentence.

$5 + 2 = 7$ $3 + 2 = 5$ $3 - 2 = 1$

$4 + 2 = 6$ $5 - 1 = 4$ $5 + 1 = 6$

Circle the correct subtraction sentence.

$3 + 3 = 6$ $3 - 3 = 0$ $6 - 3 = 3$

$6 - 2 = 4$ $6 + 2 = 8$ $4 - 2 = 2$

Circle the correct number sentence.

$9 - 3 = 6$ $5 - 3 = 2$ $6 - 3 = 3$

$5 - 2 = 3$ $2 + 5 = 7$ $7 - 5 = 2$

$6 - 4 = 2$ $4 + 2 = 6$ $6 + 2 = 8$

$5 - 1 = 4$ $4 + 5 = 9$ $9 - 4 = 5$

Picture graphs

Look at this picture graph. Then answer the questions.

Mina's marbles

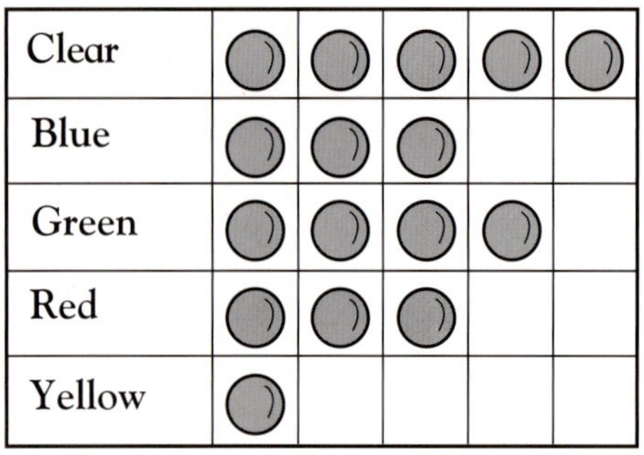

How many blue marbles does Mina have?

Does Mina have more green marbles or yellow marbles?

How many marbles does Mina have in all?

Look at this picture graph. Then answer the questions.

Books on Pablo's shelf

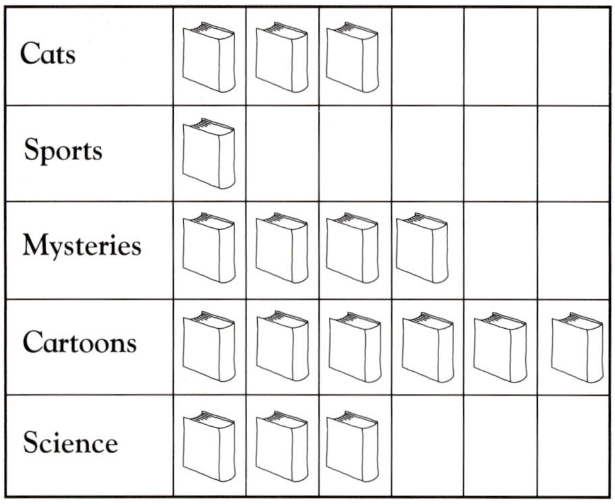

How many science books does Pablo have?

Does he have more books about cats than mysteries?

How many more cartoon books does he have than mysteries?

How many books about cats and science does he have?

Look at this picture graph. Then answer the questions.

Pets on Redmond Road

On Redmond Road, are there more cats or dogs?

How many more fish are there than dogs?

How many cats and dogs are there?

How many pets are there in all?

3-dimensional shapes

Write the name of each shape.

sphere

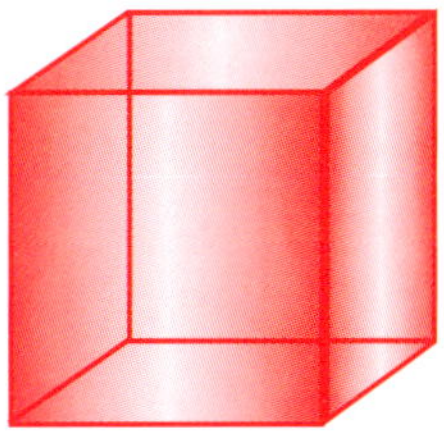

cube

Write the name of each shape. Use the words in the Word Box.

Word Box					
sphere	prism	cone	cube	cylinder	pyramid

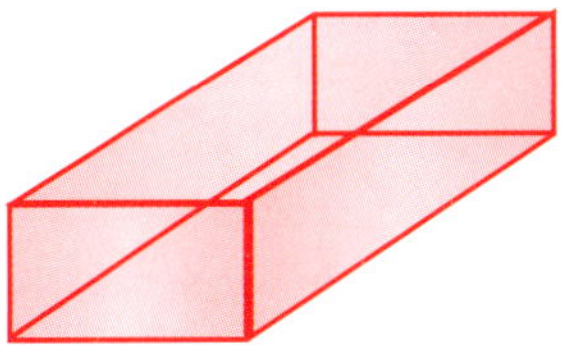

prism

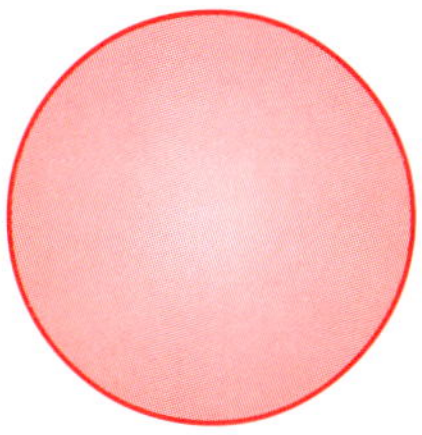

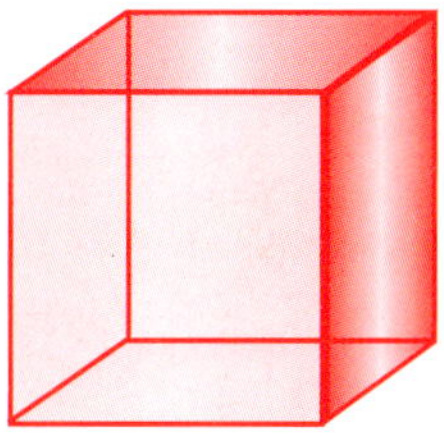

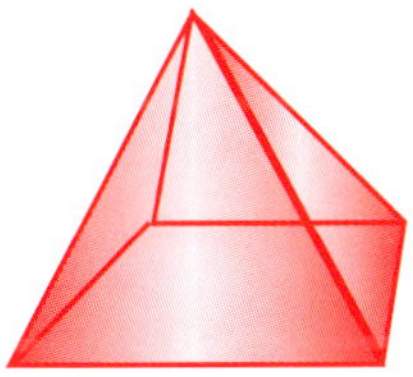

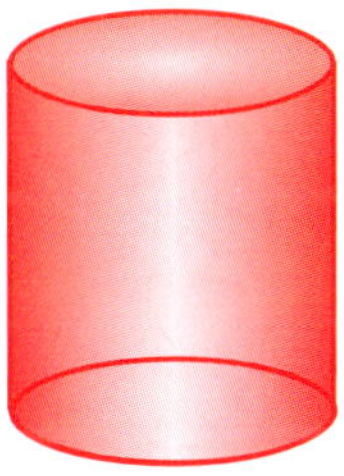

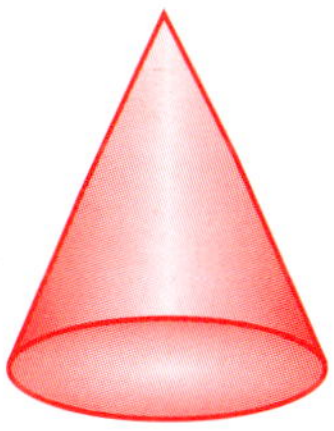

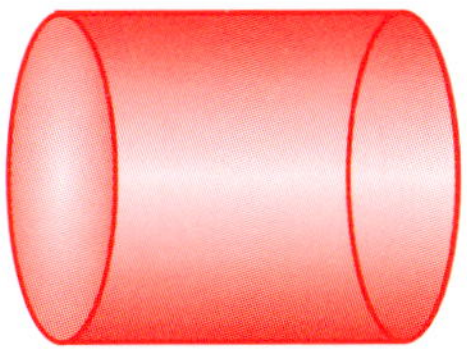

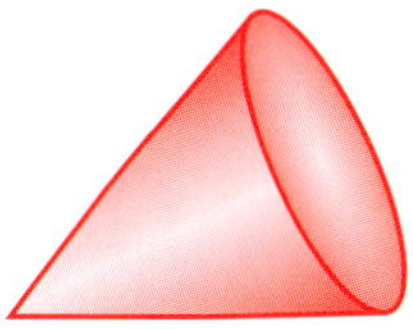

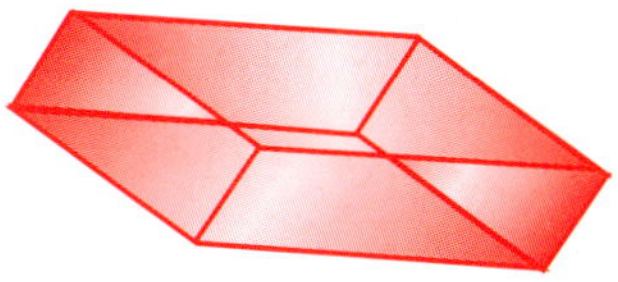

Missing addends

Write the missing addend.

6 + 7 = 13

Write the missing addend.

3 + ☐ = 9

5 + ☐ = 12

9 + ☐ = 11

8 + ☐ = 16

Write the missing addend.

3 + ☐ = 7	5 + ☐ = 14	9 + ☐ = 12	8 + ☐ = 10
7 + ☐ = 12	7 + ☐ = 15	7 + ☐ = 12	9 + ☐ = 17
7 + ☐ = 13	8 + ☐ = 14	10 + ☐ = 13	4 + ☐ = 13
4 + ☐ = 7	3 + ☐ = 9	2 + ☐ = 11	8 + ☐ = 13
6 + ☐ = 8	5 + ☐ = 9	7 + ☐ = 8	8 + ☐ = 12
8 + ☐ = 9	6 + ☐ = 13	8 + ☐ = 16	5 + ☐ = 11
4 + ☐ = 11	10 + ☐ = 15	8 + ☐ = 11	4 + ☐ = 10
7 + ☐ = 14	8 + ☐ = 15	9 + ☐ = 14	6 + ☐ = 15
9 + ☐ = 16	9 + ☐ = 18	3 + ☐ = 10	5 + ☐ = 9

Reading tables

Read the table. Then answer the questions.

Ages of cousins

NAME	AGE
Kinta	8
Paul	7
Clara	9
Meg	7
Lee	6

How old is Paul?

Who is older than Kinta?

Who is the same age as Meg?

Who is the youngest?

Read the table. Then answer the questions.

Favourite juice

Apple	6
Cranberry	2
Grape	3
Cherry	1
Orange	9

How many people chose orange juice?

Which juice did 2 people choose?

How many more people like orange juice than apple juice?

Did more people choose grape juice or cranberry juice?

Read the table. Then answer the questions.

Mass of dogs

NAME	Bear	Mike	Perry	Spike	Marca
KILOGRAMS	30	6	9	5	3

Which dog has a mass of more than 25 kilograms?

Which dog has a mass of less than 4 kilograms?

How much more mass does Perry have than Mike?

How much less mass does Spike have than Mike?

Adding

Write the answer in the box.

34 + 13 = 47	26 + 15 = 41	73 + 27 = 100

Write the answer in the box.

5 + 4	1 + 8	3 + 6	2 + 6
7 + 0	6 + 3	2 + 5	5 + 6
9 + 0	4 + 5	42 + 7	6 + 4
36 + 3	12 + 6	37 + 1	34 + 3
48 + 2	64 + 4	36 + 13	33 + 15
26 + 12	37 + 12	48 + 11	56 + 12
2 + 16	22 + 26	3 + 27	37 + 23
9 + 24	17 + 27	28 + 17	19 + 26
26 + 18	36 + 16	16 + 14	14 + 26

Reading a calendar

Look at this calendar. Then answer the questions.

September

S	M	T	W	T	F	S
	1	2	3	4	5	6
7	8	9	10	11	12	13
14	15	16	17	18	19	20
21	22	23	24	25	26	27
28	29	30				

What day of the week is the first day of September on this calendar?

What date is the last Tuesday in September?

Look at this calendar. Then answer the questions.

July

S	M	T	W	T	F	S
				1	2	3
4	5	6	7	8	9	10
11	12	13	14	15	16	17
18	19	20	21	22	23	24
25	26	27	28	29	30	31

How many days are in the month of July?

What day of the week is the last day of July on this calendar?

A camp starts on July 5 and ends on July 9. How many camp days are there?

The campers go swimming on Tuesday and Thursday. On which dates will they swim?

Look at this calendar. Then answer the questions.

November

S	M	T	W	T	F	S
						1
2	3	4	5	6	7	8
9	10	11	12	13	14	15
16	17	18	19	20	21	22
23	24	25	26	27	28	29
30						

What date is the first Sunday of November?

What day of the week is November 14?

How many Saturdays are shown in November?

Jenna's birthday is November 23. What day of the week is it?

Subtracting

Write the answer in the box.

6 13 ~~7~~~~3~~ − 48 25	3 15 ~~4~~~~5~~ − 26 19	6 12 ~~7~~~~2~~ − 36 36

Write the answer in the box.

27 − 6	16 − 4	25 − 2	38 − 5
39 − 7	28 − 6	36 − 4	19 − 7
26 − 6	43 − 3	37 − 17	18 − 17

Write the answer in the box.

48 cm − 18 cm	49 cm − 36 cm	47 cm − 27 cm	45 cm − 44 cm
49 cm − 47 cm	38 cm − 26 cm	39 cm − 4 cm	47 cm − 47 cm

Write the answer in the box.

43¢ − 17¢	41¢ − 24¢	43¢ − 36¢	51¢ − 46¢
50¢ − 44¢	51¢ − 37¢	53¢ − 46¢	54¢ − 44¢
50 cm − 34 cm	50 cm − 47 cm	36 cm − 18 cm	47 cm − 35 cm

Properties of polygons

Circle the polygon that has the same number of sides.

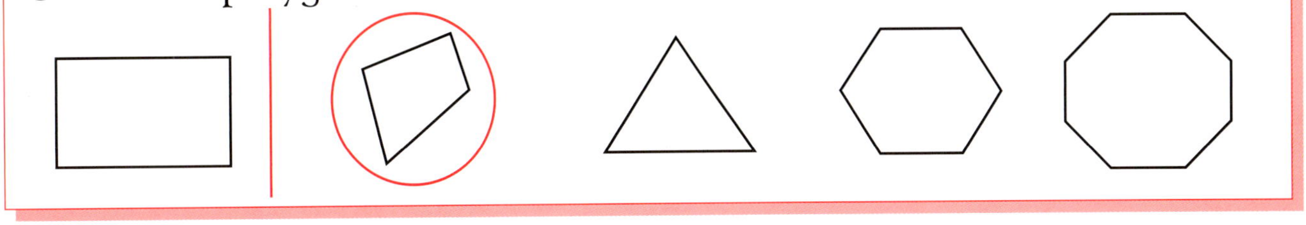

Circle the polygon that has the same number of sides.

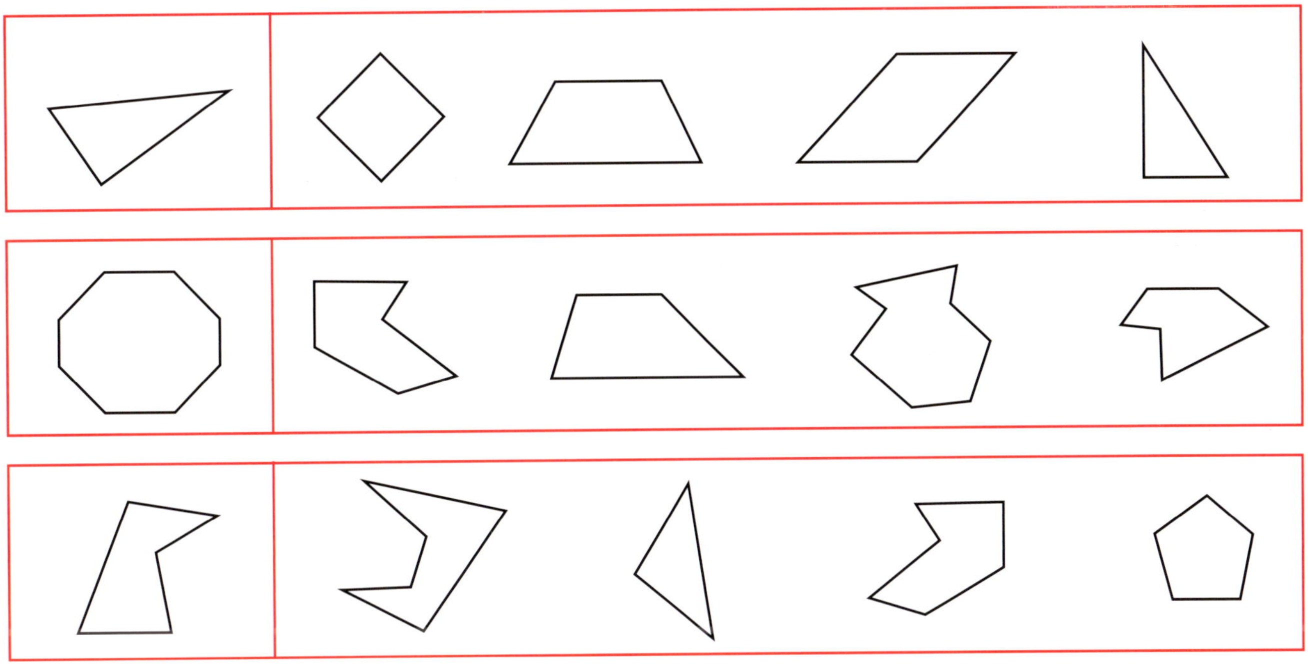

Circle the polygon that has a different number of sides.

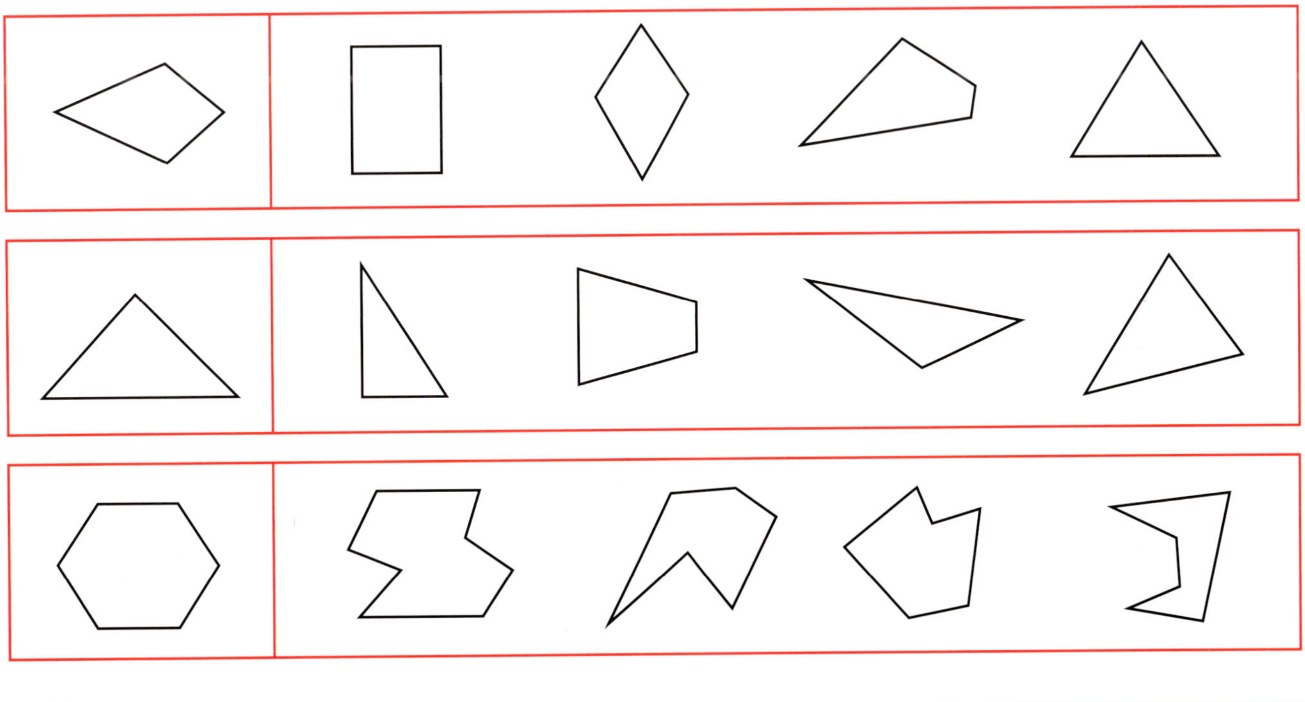

Venn diagrams

Read the clues to find the secret number.

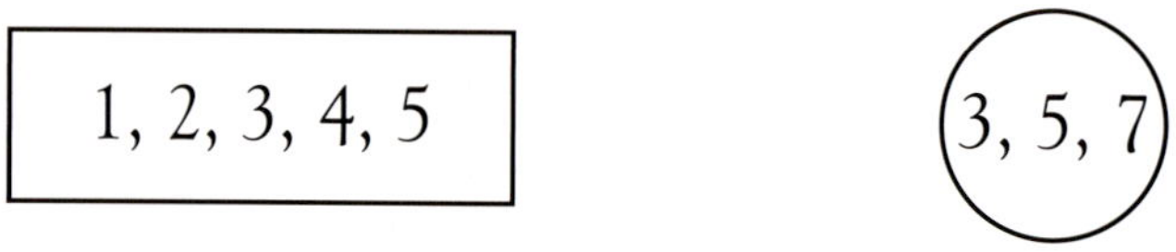

It is in both the rectangle and the circle.

It is greater than 3.

What number is it?

Read the clues to find the secret number.

It is not in the square.
It is an even number.
It is less than 12.

What number is it?

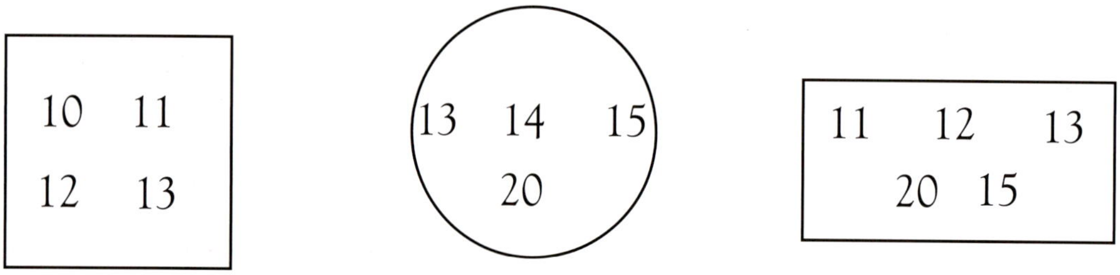

It is in the rectangle and the circle.
It is greater than 13 and less than 20.
It is an odd number.

What number is it?

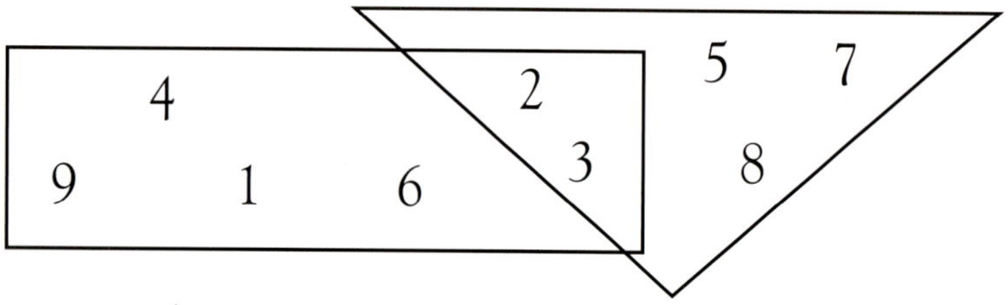

It is not an even number.
It is in the triangle.
It is in the rectangle.

What number is it?

Most likely/least likely

Look at the marbles. Then answer the questions.

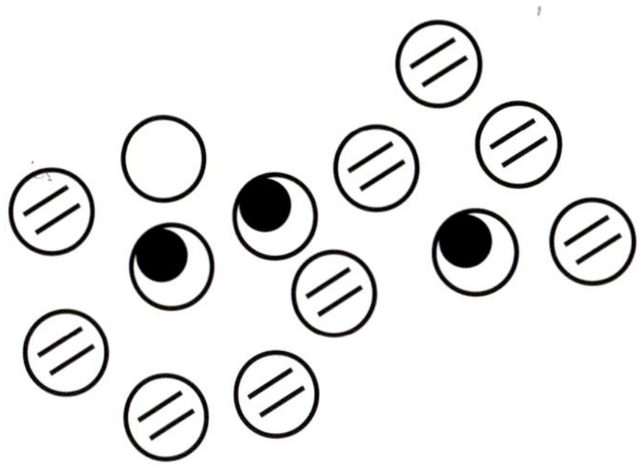

Which kind of marble would you be least likely to pick without looking?

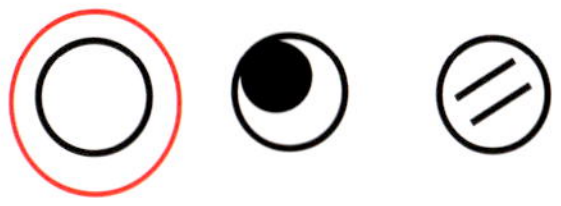

Which kind of marble would you be most likely to pick without looking?

Look at the spinner. Then answer the questions.

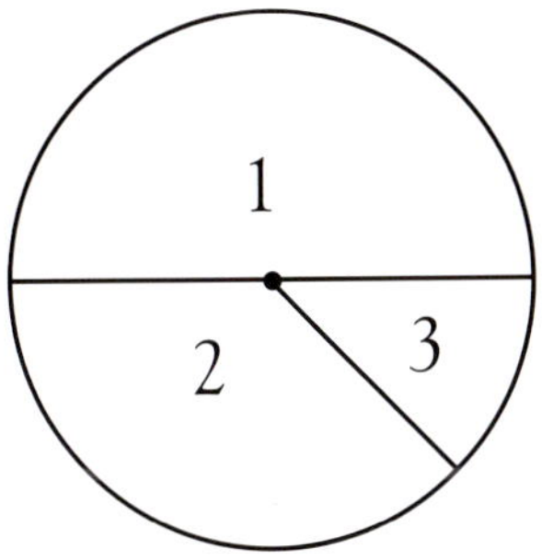

Is the spinner more likely to land on 1 or 2?

Is the spinner more likely to land on 2 or 3?

Which number is the spinner most likely to land on?

Which number is the spinner least likely to land on?

Look at the tally chart. Then answer the questions.

Imagine that each time you shake the bag, one coin falls out.

Tally of coins in the bag

COINS	TALLIES
Pennies	||||
Dimes	||
Nickels	卌 |||
Quarters	卌

Is a penny or a dime more likely to fall out?

Is a quarter or a nickel more likely to fall out?

Which coin is most likely to fall out?

Which coin is least likely to fall out?

3-dimensional shapes

Write the name of each shape.

Sphere

Cube

Write the name of each shape. Use the names in the Word Box.

Word Box

Sphere
Cube
Cylinder
Prism
Pyramid
Cone

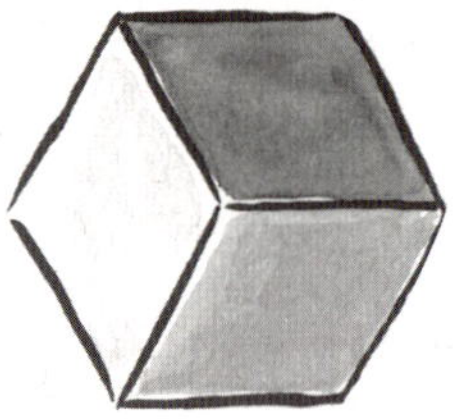

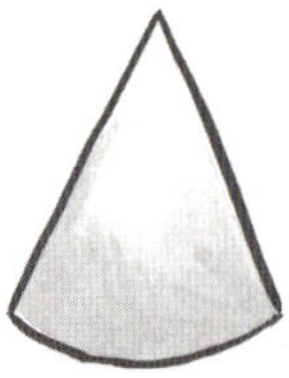

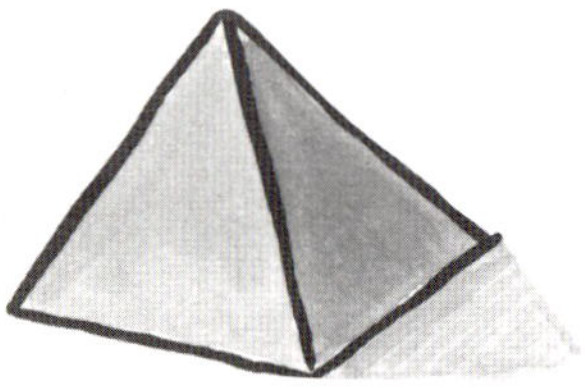

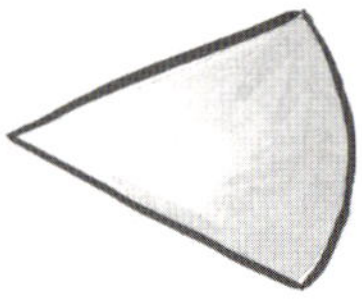

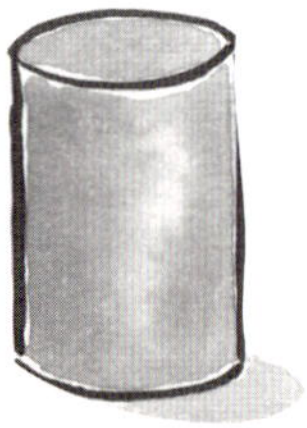

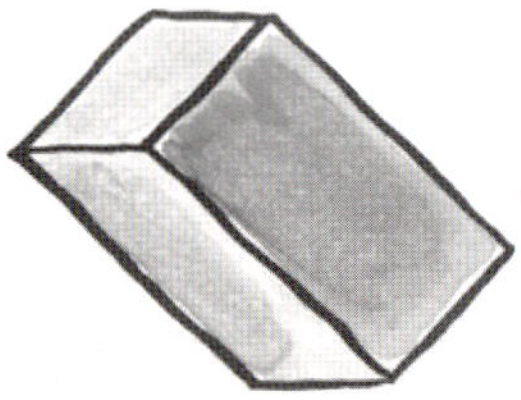

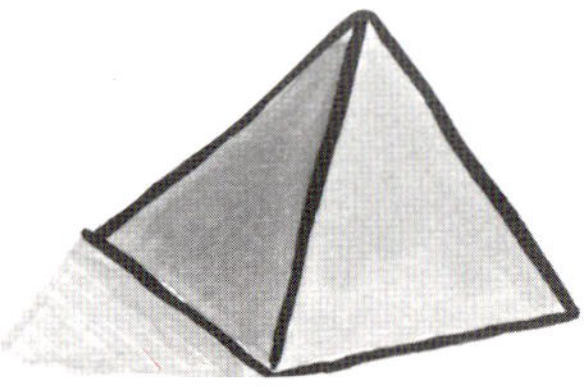

Counting

Write the missing number above each ↑.

23	24	25	26				30			33	34		
							↑			↑	↑		

Write the missing number above each ↑.

12		14											
					↑				↑		↑	↑	

5	6			9							16		
					↑				↑	↑			↑

						23	24			27			
↑	↑	↑											↑

31			34						40	41			
		↑		↑			↑						↑

17			20			23					28		
					↑		↑					↑	↑

						27		29					
↑	↑				↑							↑	

Finding patterns

Find the counting pattern. Write the missing numbers.

12	14	16	18	20	22	24	26	28	30

Find the counting pattern. Write the missing numbers.

5				25	30		40	45	
	6				18	21	24		30
11	15		23				39		47
21			27	29		33			39
19	20						26		28
6	12	18					48	54	
19	17	15			9	7			
	90			60	50			20	10
10	20	30		50			80		
	55					40	37	34	
50			35		25		15		5
	38		30			18	14		

Reading tally charts

Look at the tally chart. Then answer the questions.

Winners at Tag

Kelly	Mark	Sandy	Rita	Brad
𝍸𝍷𝍷	𝍷𝍷𝍷	𝍸𝍷	𝍸	𝍸𝍷𝍷𝍷𝍷

Who won the most games?

Who won more games, Sandy or Kelly?

How many more games did Rita win than Mark?

Look at the tally chart. Then answer the questions.

Colours of T-Shirts sold

Blue	𝍸𝍸𝍷
White	𝍸𝍷𝍷𝍷
Green	𝍸𝍷𝍷𝍷𝍷
Black	𝍸𝍸𝍷𝍷

Which colour shirt was sold most?

How many green shirts were sold?

Which colour sold more, blue or green?

How many black shirts were sold?

How many more green shirts were sold than white shirts?

How many more black shirts were sold than green shirts?

How many T-shirts were sold in all?

Look at the tally chart. Then answer the questions.

Snack choices

Chips	Cherries	Cheese	Cookie	Apple
𝍸𝍷𝍷𝍷𝍷	𝍸	𝍸𝍸𝍷	𝍸𝍷𝍷𝍷	𝍸𝍷𝍷

How many people chose chips?

Which snack did 7 people choose?

Did more people choose chips or cookies?

Which snack did the fewest people choose?

How many more people chose cheese than chips?

How many people chose apples and cherries?

Same shape and size

Which figure has same shape and size?

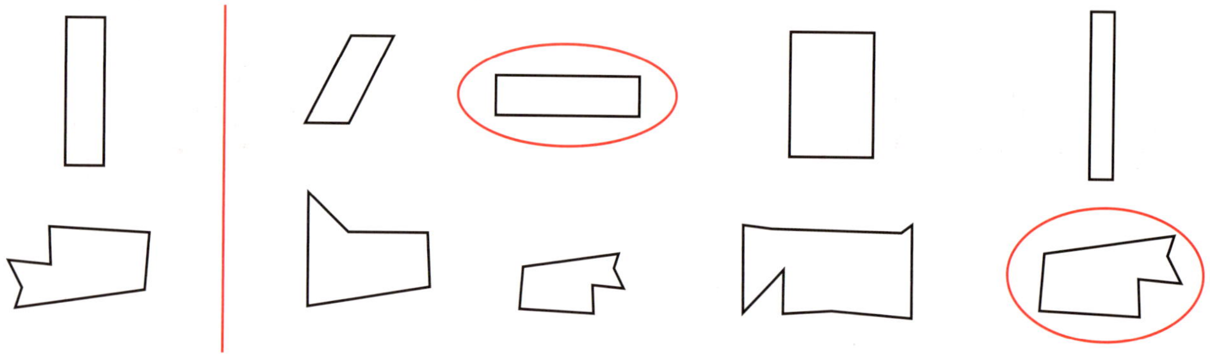

Circle the figure that has same shape and size.

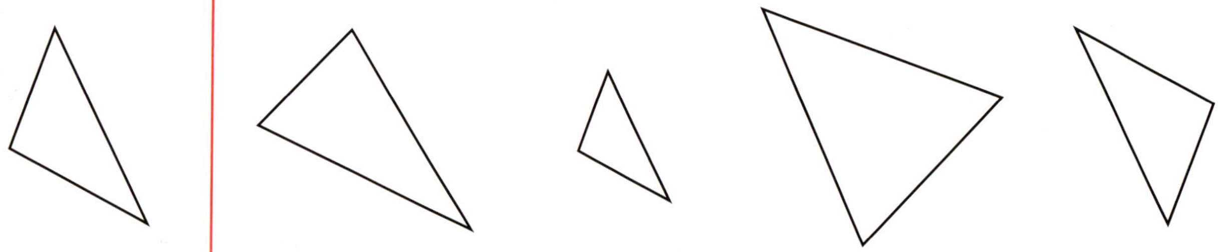

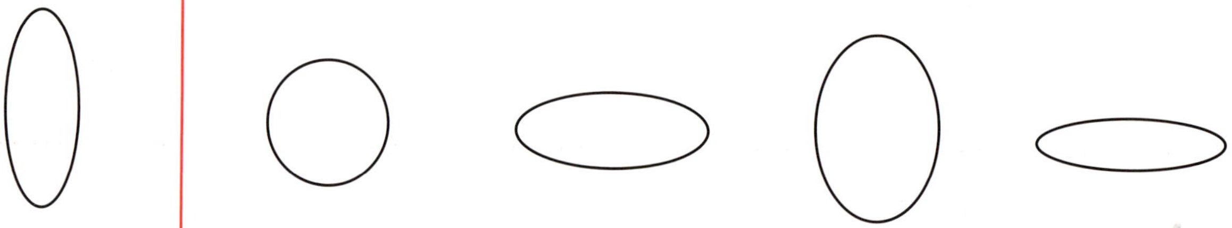

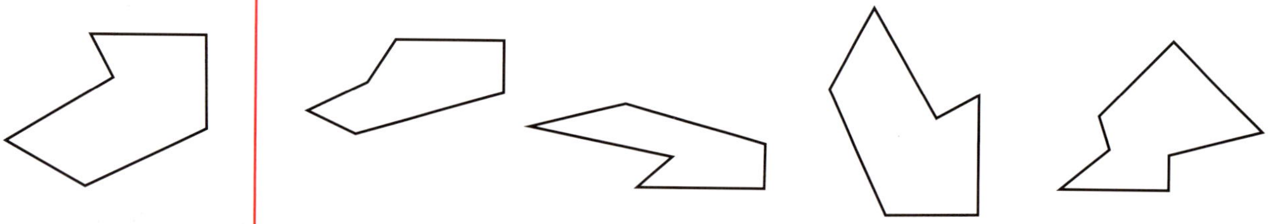

Parts of a set

Write the fraction that shows the red part of the set.
How many of the fish are red?

How many  ? 3

How many fish in all? 4

Write the fraction. $\frac{3}{4}$ part of the set / whole set

Circle the fraction that shows the shaded part of the set.

$\frac{1}{3}$ $\frac{2}{3}$ $\frac{3}{2}$

$\frac{2}{3}$ $\frac{3}{5}$ $\frac{2}{5}$

$\frac{1}{4}$ $\frac{3}{4}$ $\frac{2}{4}$

$\frac{4}{5}$ $\frac{1}{5}$ $\frac{1}{4}$

Write the fraction that shows the shaded part of the set.

$\frac{}{3}$

$\frac{}{5}$

$\frac{}{4}$

$\frac{}{5}$

$\frac{}{7}$

$\frac{}{8}$

$\frac{}{7}$

$\frac{}{8}$

$\frac{}{6}$

Symmetry

Hold a mirror along the dotted line. Does it show a line of symmetry?

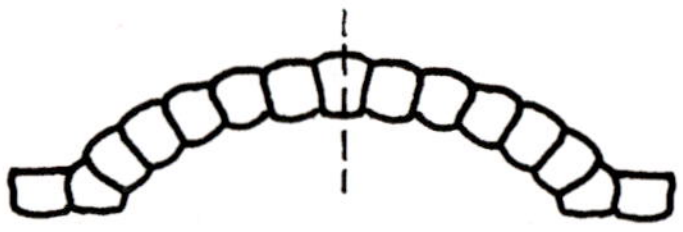
yes

no

yes

Does the dotted line show a line of symmetry? Write yes or no.

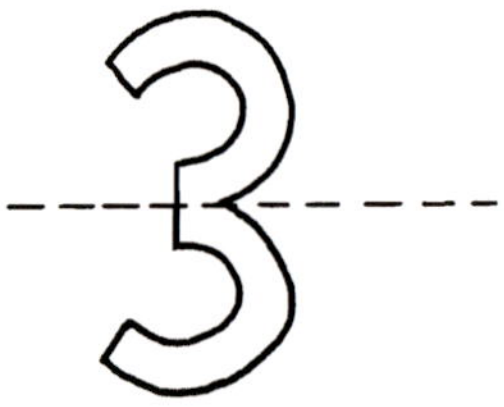

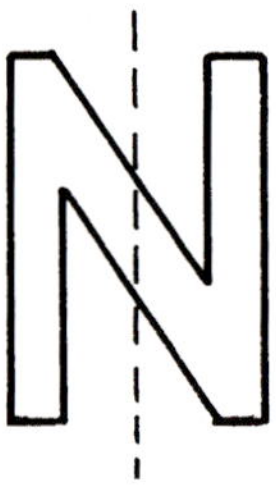

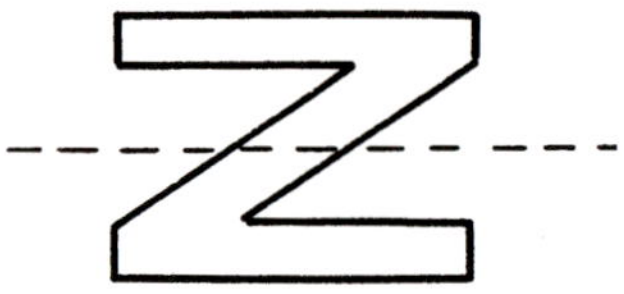

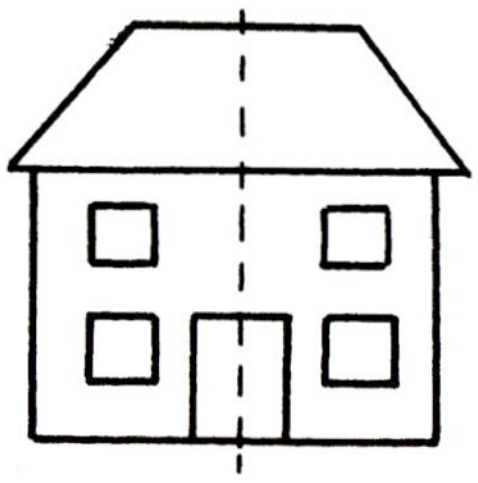

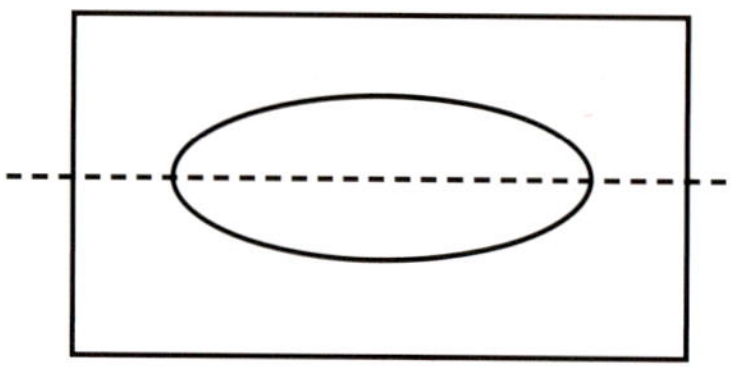

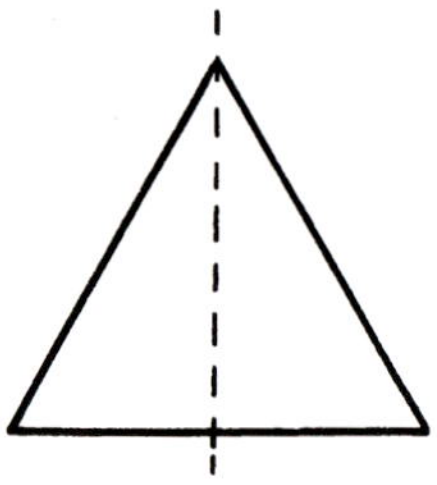

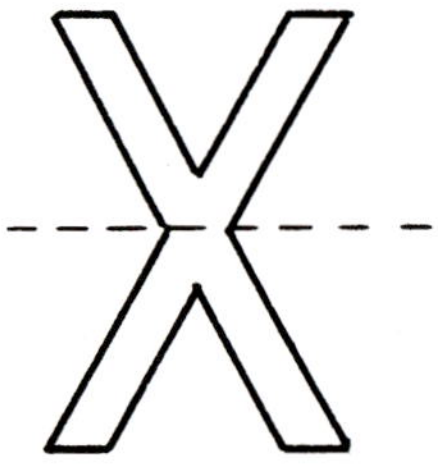

Measurement problems

Write the measurement shown by the arrow.

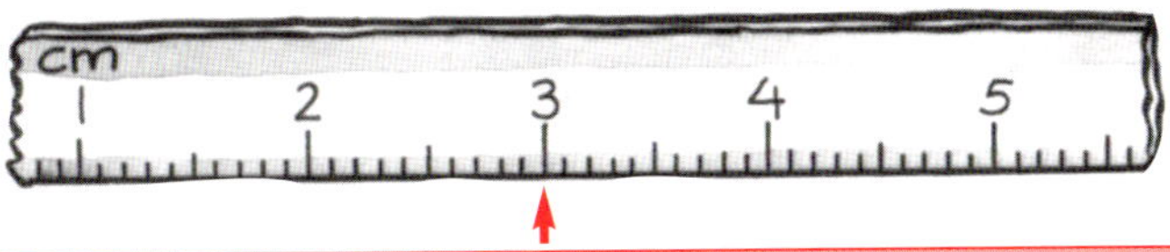

3 cm

Write the measurement shown by the arrow.

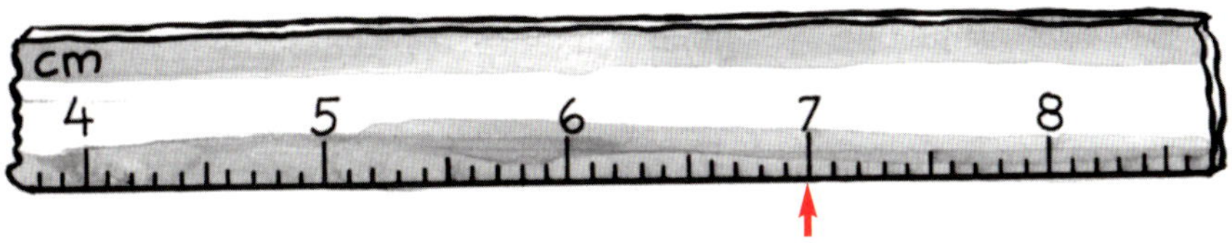

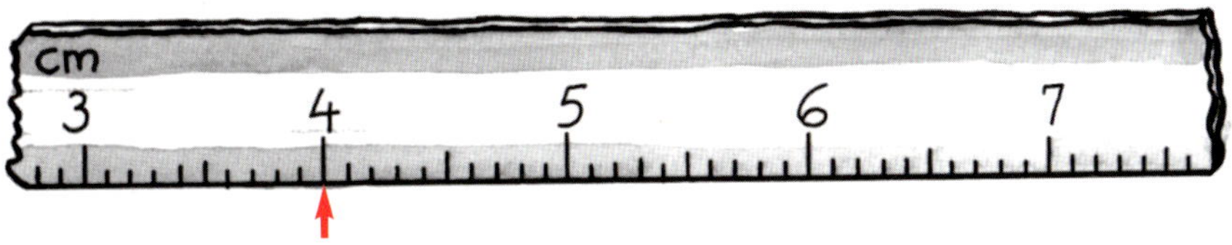

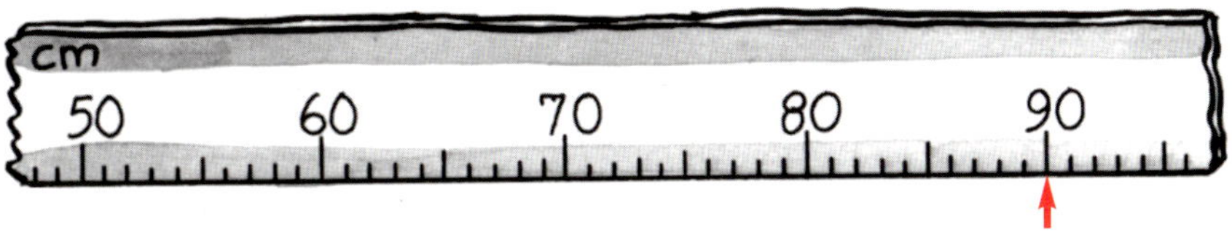

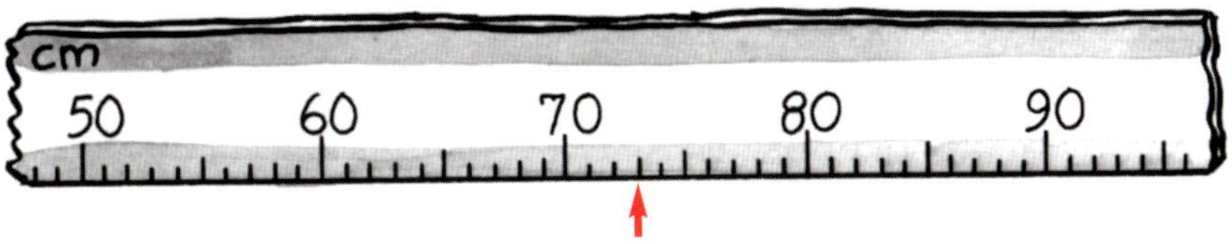

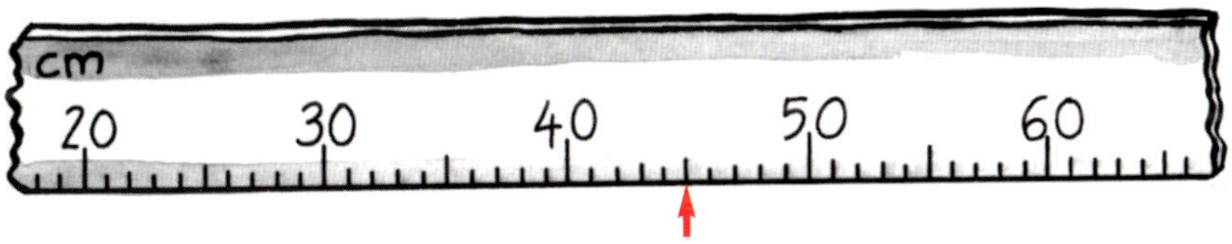

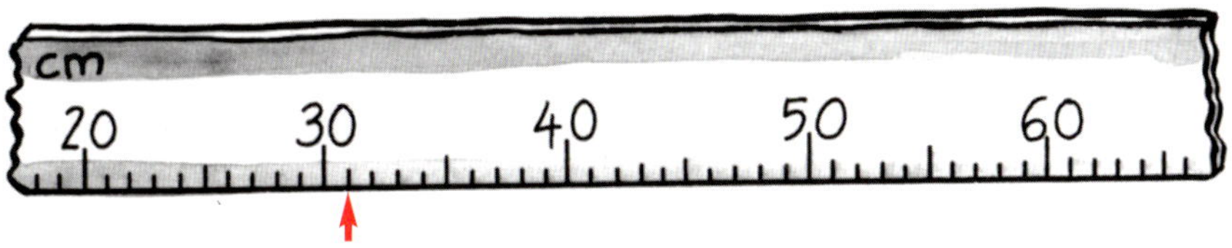

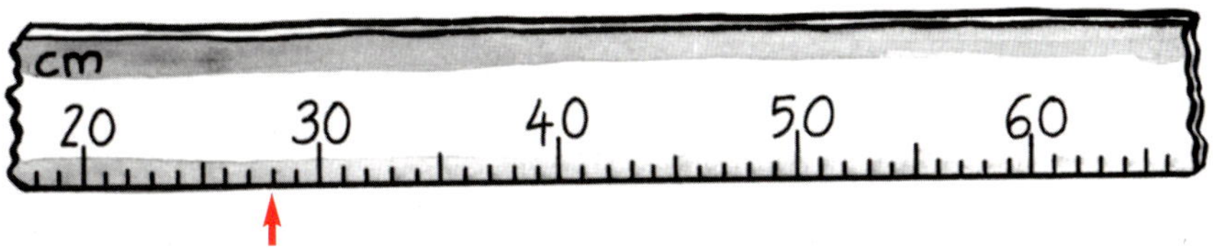

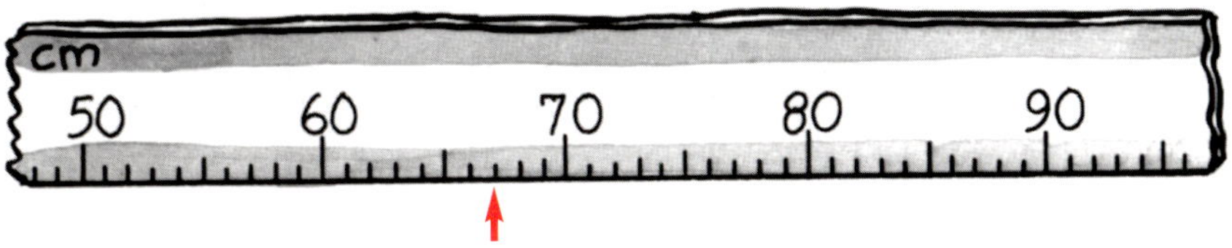

3-dimensional shapes

Write the name of each shape in the box.

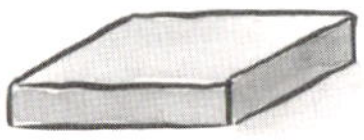

prism

sphere

Write the name of each shape in the box.

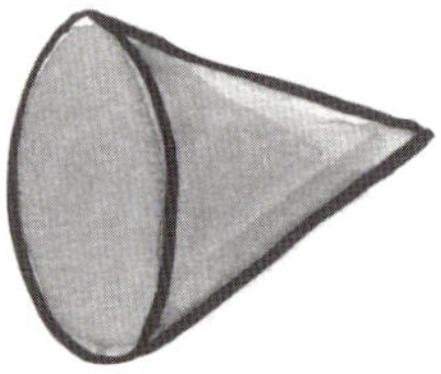

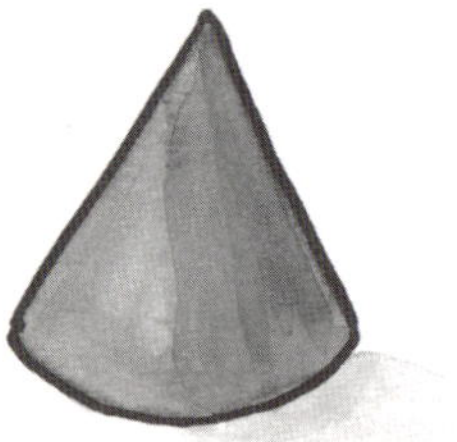

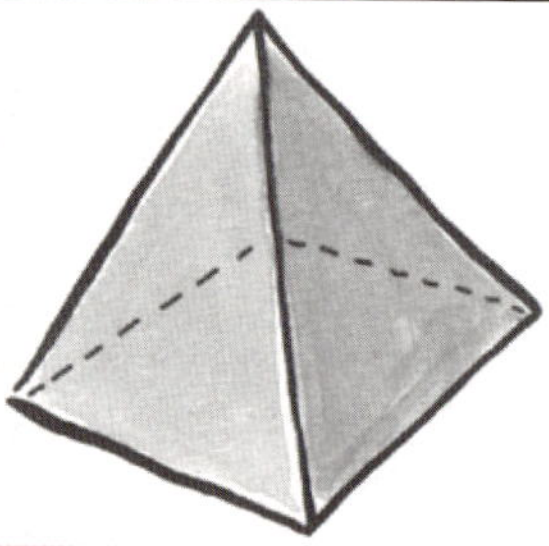

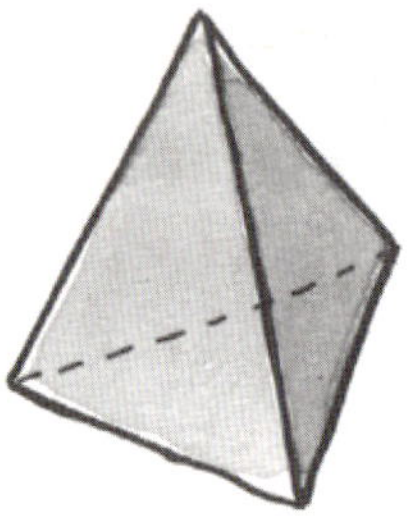

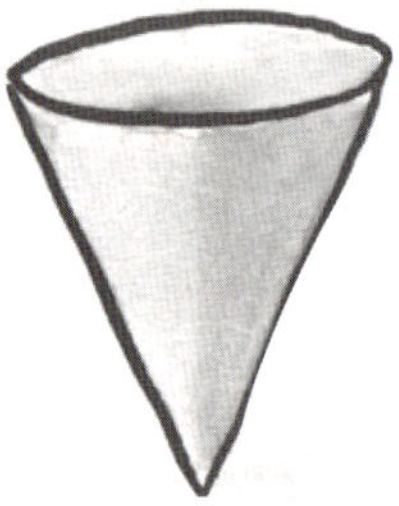

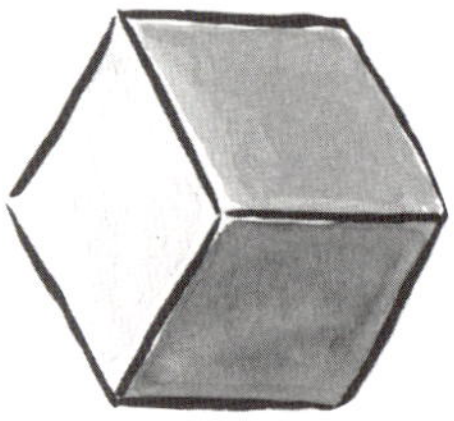

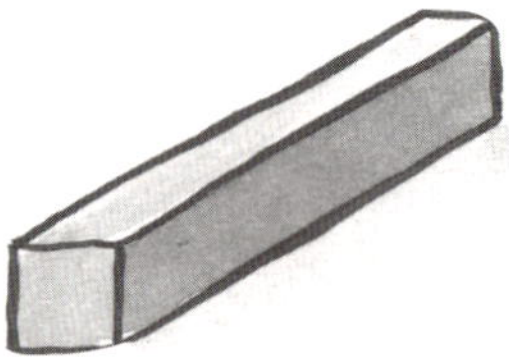

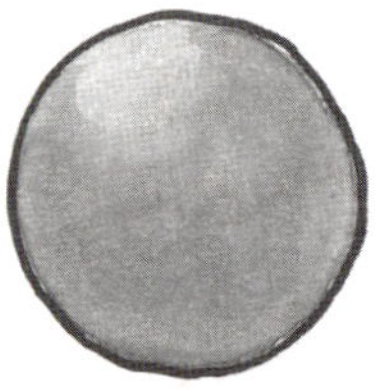

Answer Section with Parents' Notes

Grade 1
ages 6–7
Workbook

This section provides answers to all the activities in the book. These pages will enable you to mark your children's work, or they can be used by your children if they prefer to do their own marking.

The notes for each page help to explain common errors and problems and, where appropriate, indicate the kind of practice needed to ensure that your children understand where and how they have made errors.

2

Numbers

Trace the numbers.

0 1 2 3 4
5 6 7 8 9

Write the numbers.

0 0 0 0 0 0 0 0 0 0 0 0
1 1 1 1 1 1 1 1 1 1 1 1
2 2 2 2 2 2 2 2 2 2 2 2
3 3 3 3 3 3 3 3 3 3 3 3
4 4 4 4 4 4 4 4 4 4 4 4
5 5 5 5 5 5 5 5 5 5 5 5
6 6 6 6 6 6 6 6 6 6 6 6
7 7 7 7 7 7 7 7 7 7 7 7
8 8 8 8 8 8 8 8 8 8 8 8
9 9 9 9 9 9 9 9 9 9 9 9

Throughout Grade 1, children will need regular writing practice to reinforce the correct movement of the pencil. Watch out for numerals written backward and for any numeral written from the bottom up. All numerals should begin at the top.

3

Numbers and pictures

Count the animals, draw the dots, and write the number.

2 — (2 dots) — two

3 — (3 dots) — three

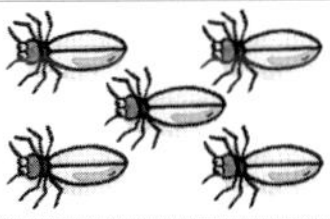
5 — (5 dots) — five

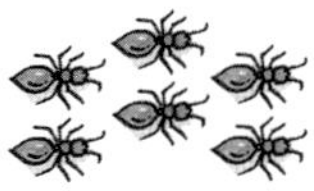
6 — (6 dots) — six

Draw your own examples.

1 — (1 dot) — one

4 — (4 dots) — four

At this stage, it is more important for children to be able to read the word for each number than to be able to spell it without help. Children can refer to the number line of the Progress Chart. Children can learn correct spellings gradually.

4

Counting

Connect each set to the correct number.

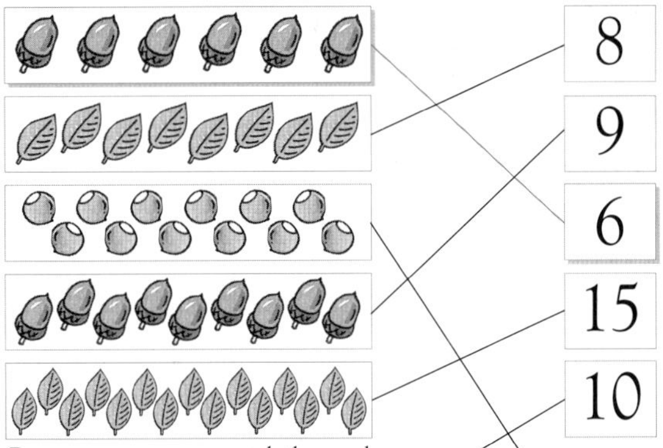

Draw your own set to match the number.

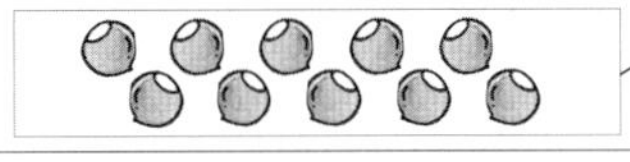

Count the beads.

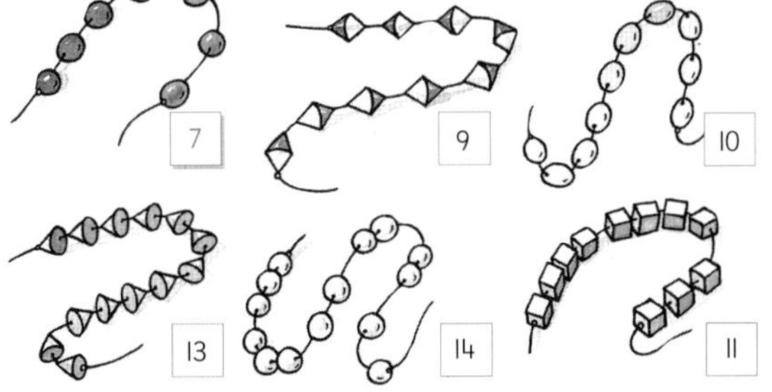

Counting and then re-counting to check an answer before writing anything down is a useful habit to develop. Some children will be able to count without pointing to the objects, but when re-counting, children may need to point to each item.

5

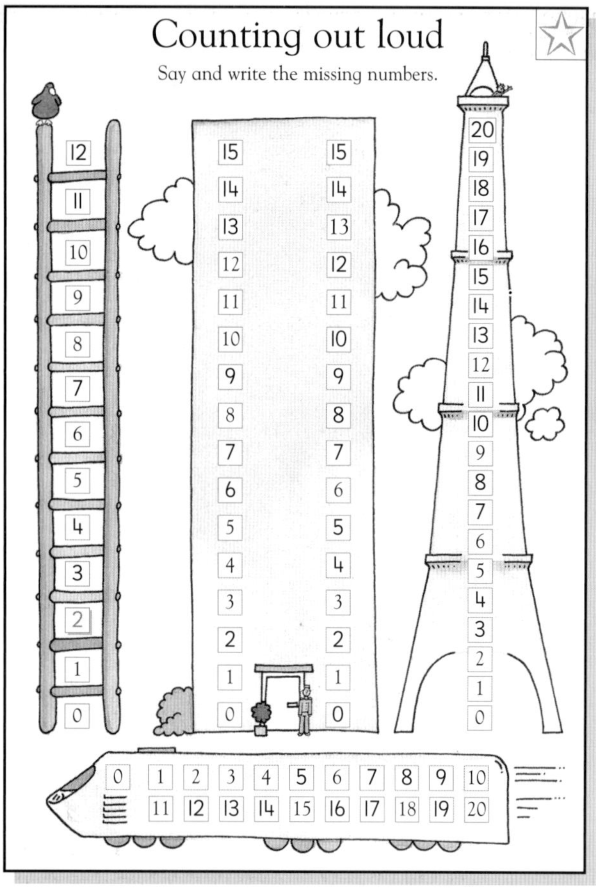

It is important that children say the numbers out loud while completing each picture to reinforce the pattern of sounds that the numbers make. This will help them acquire a sense of whether the sequence sounds right. Make sure that zero is included here.

6

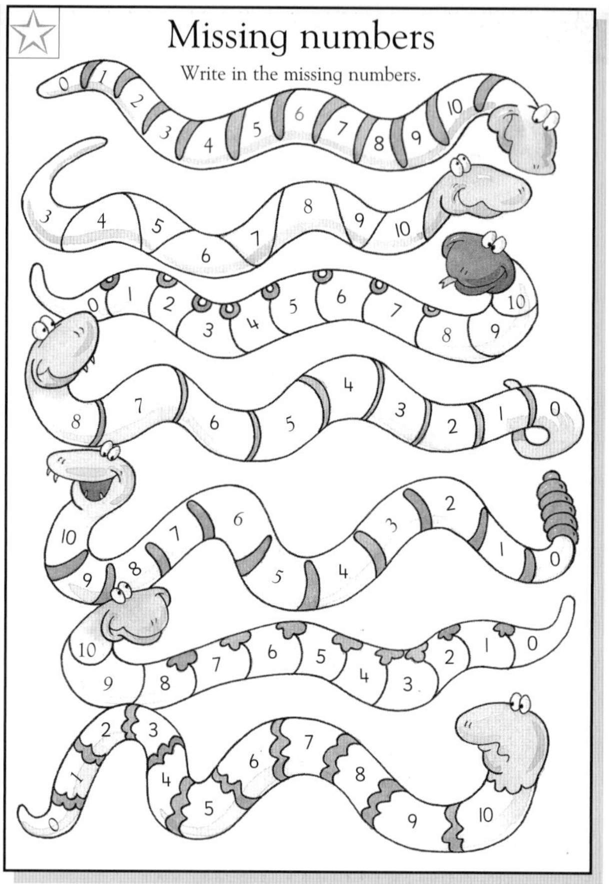

For snakes 4, 5, and 6, make sure that children write 0 (zero) as the number nearest the tail and not 1. It is essential to encourage the use of the term *zero* and not *O* (as in *only*) or *nothing*. Have children look at the number line if they have problems.

7

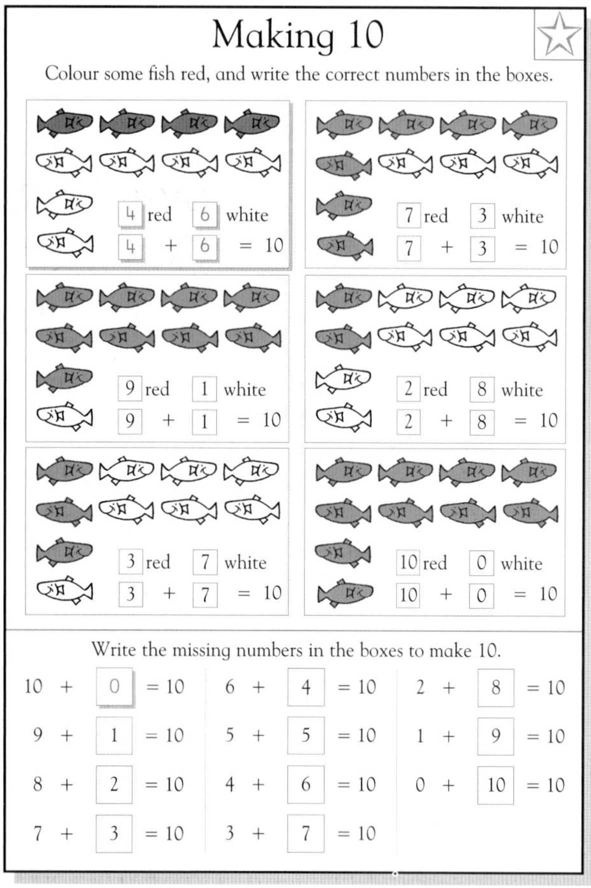

The number of items shaded and the number of items unshaded must match the numbers written in the answer boxes. For the bottom activity, find out whether children have noticed the pattern as it develops.

8

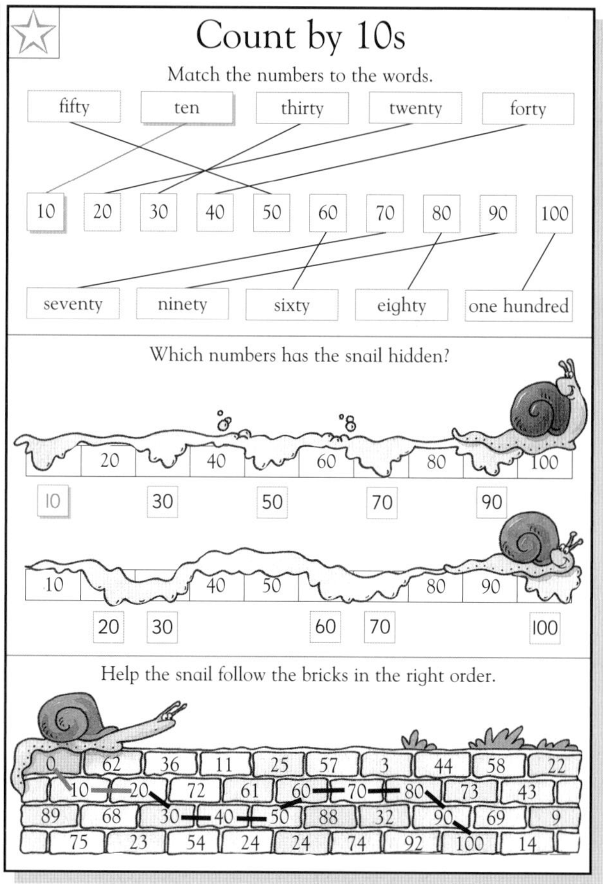

Help children recite the sequence and then say it in reverse, from 100 back down to 10.

9

Encourage children to read out loud the sequence of numbers they have found, e.g. 2, 4, 6, 8. For the grid activity (bottom left), make sure children notice the pattern. Point out that the shaded squares have even numbers and the others have odd numbers.

10

Encourage children to talk about their own patterns and to explain what they have done. Explain that a mathematical pattern must have elements that repeat or progress in a predictable way.

11

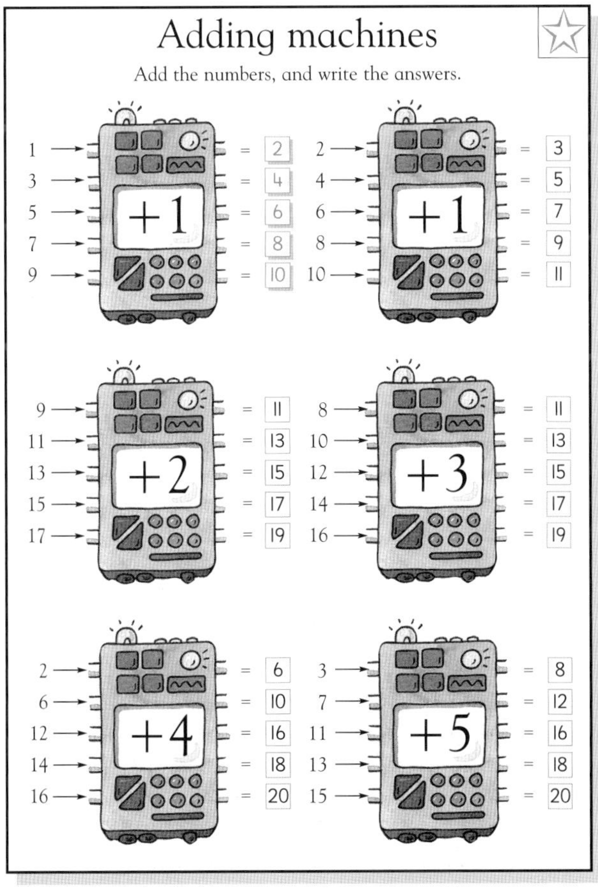

If children have difficulty with the exercises on the page, suggest to them that they use their fingers or counters to find the answers.

12

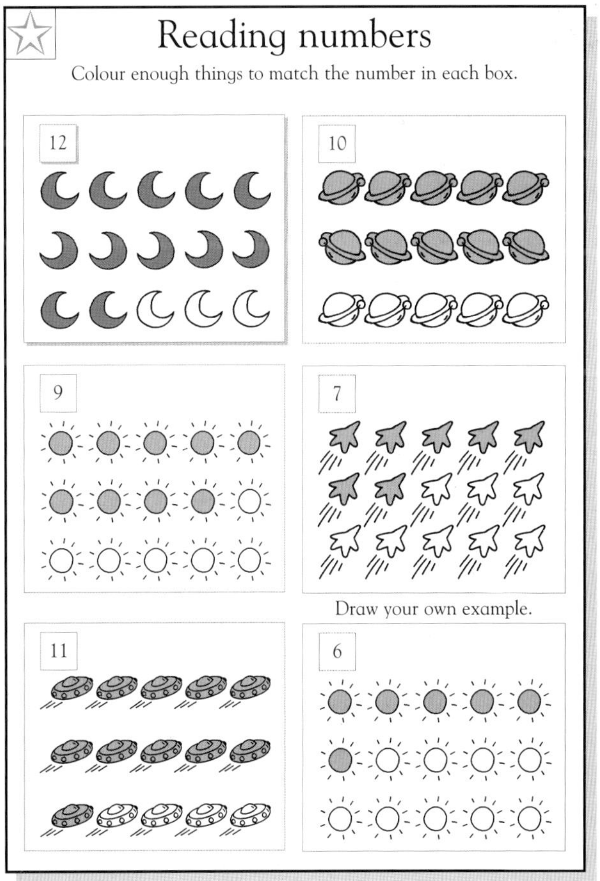

When checking the number of pictures children have coloured, encourage them to go back and re-count the pictures aloud. Children might find it helpful to point to each picture as they count it.

13

Finding 10s

Ring 10 items, and write the numbers.

12 = 10 + 2

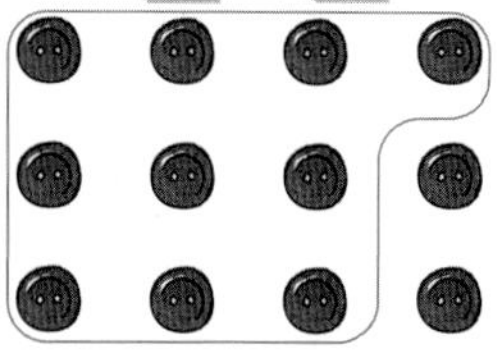

16 = 10 + 6

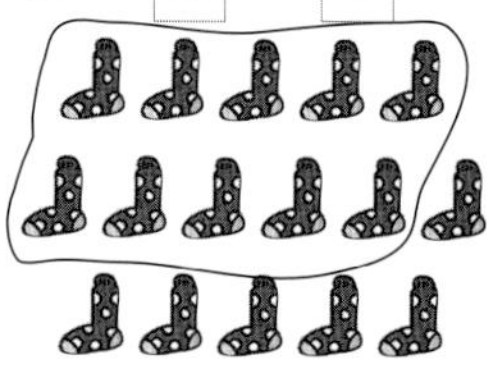

19 = 10 + 9

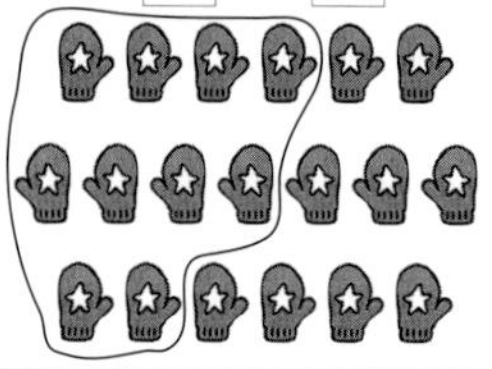

17 = 10 + 7

11 = 10 + 1

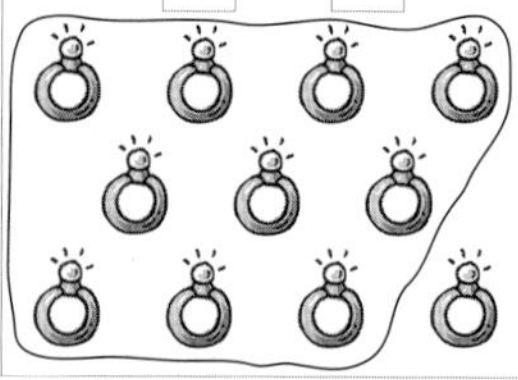

20 = 10 + 10

Make sure that each drawn ring does actually enclose 10 objects. If children ring any number of objects other than 10, they will arrive at an incorrect answer.

14

Tens and ones

How many tens and ones do you see?

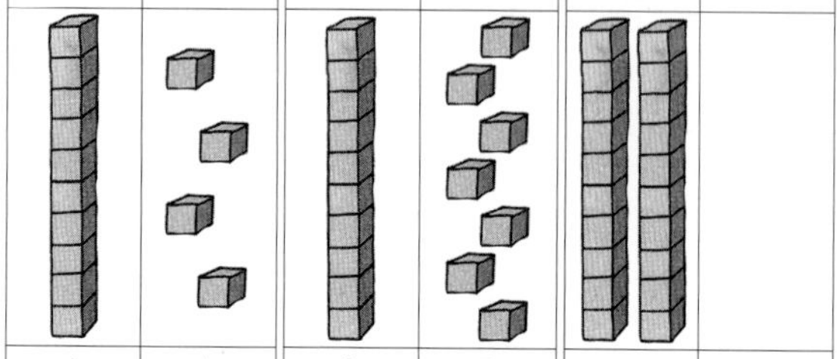

tens	ones	tens	ones	tens	ones
1	4	1	7	2	0

14 17 20

Draw the tens and ones.

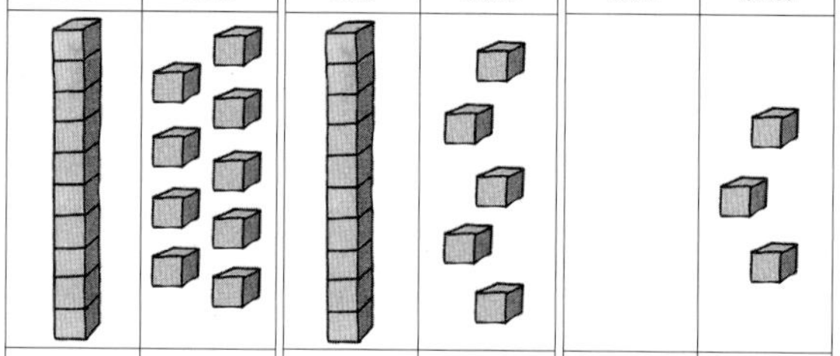

tens	ones	tens	ones	tens	ones
1	9	1	5		3

19 15 3

Make sure that children understand that the *1* in *14* stands for 1 ten, but the *1* in 41 represents 1 one.

15

One more or one less?

Write one less and one more than the numbers shown in the boxes.

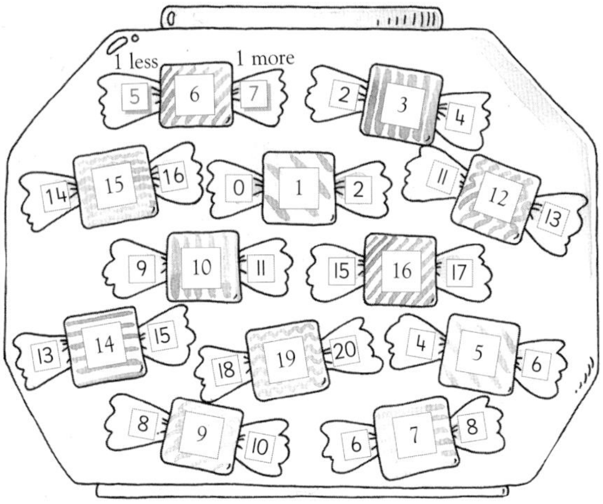

Draw one more or one less, and write the new number.

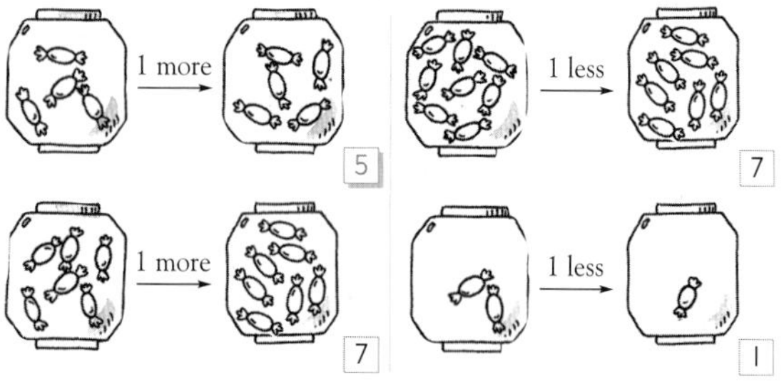

Children might benefit from making up their own number stories about the candies. For example, Rebecca had 3 candies, but her mother said she could have 1 more. Rebecca has 4 candies now.

16

Ordering

Colour the prize ribbons.

4th= purple 3rd= yellow 1st= green 6th= red 2nd= blue 5th= orange

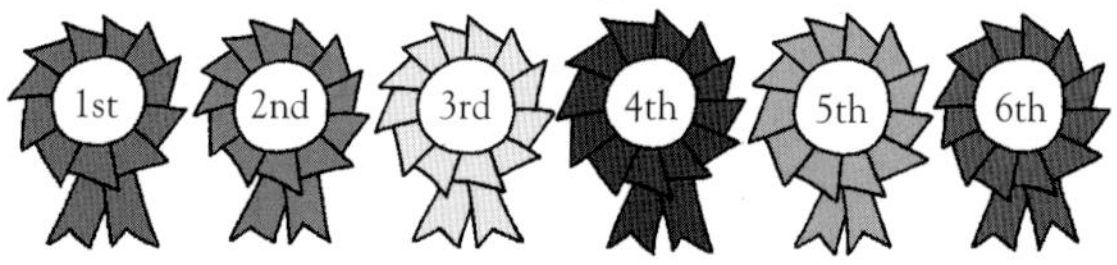

Which rabbit is 1st, 2nd, 3rd ...?

Which shape comes 1st, 2nd, 3rd ...?

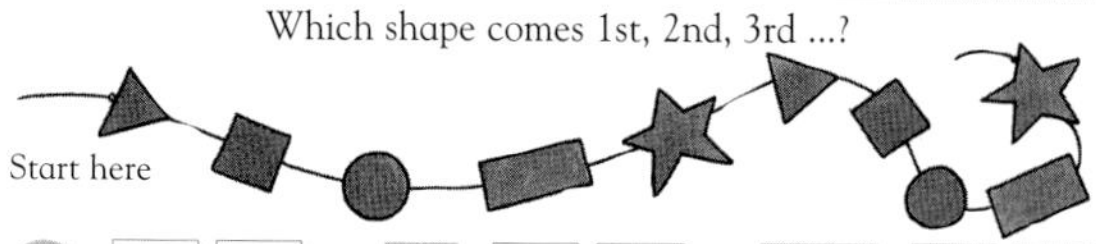

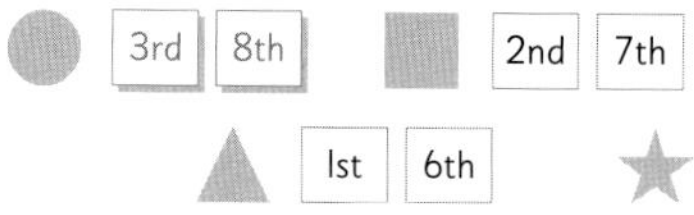

Make sure that children understand the relationship between the numbers and the ordinals, that position 3 is 3rd, position 10 is 10th, and so on.

17

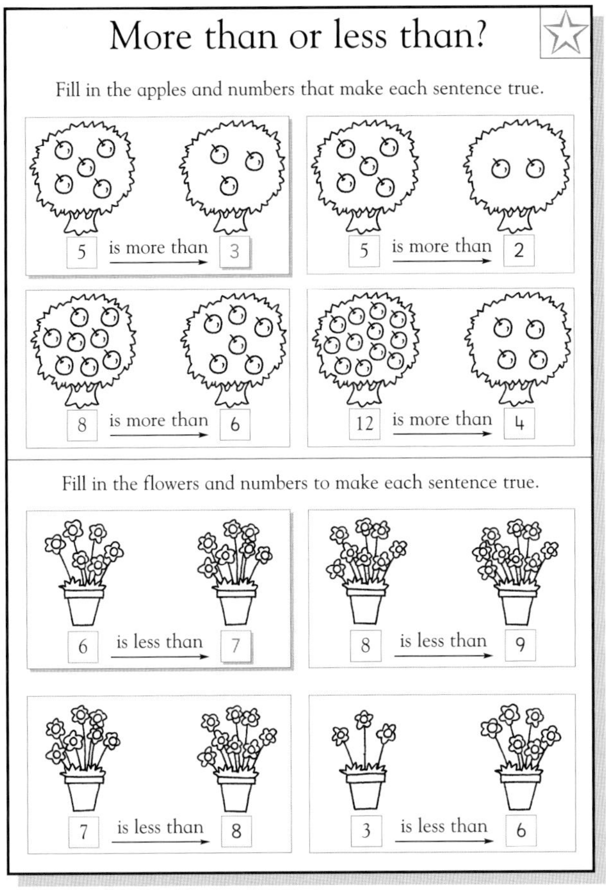

Children's answers will vary. Make sure that the number of objects drawn matches the numeral written in the box and that the number sentence is valid.

18

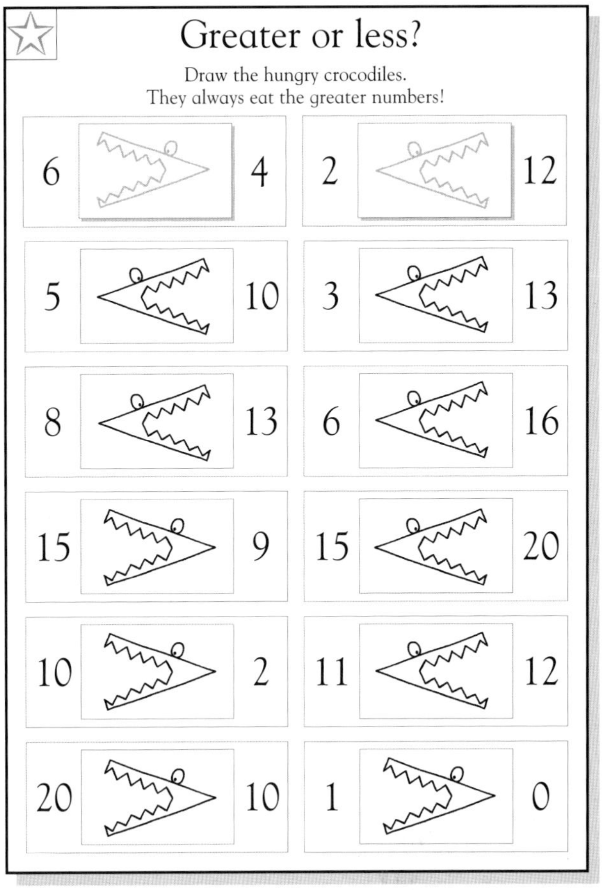

Make sure that children understand that the word *greater* means that one number is larger or higher in value than another. Make sure that children understand that even though 1 is a small number, it is greater than 0.

19

Make sure that children understand the kind of relationship among the three items that the comparative word describes.

20

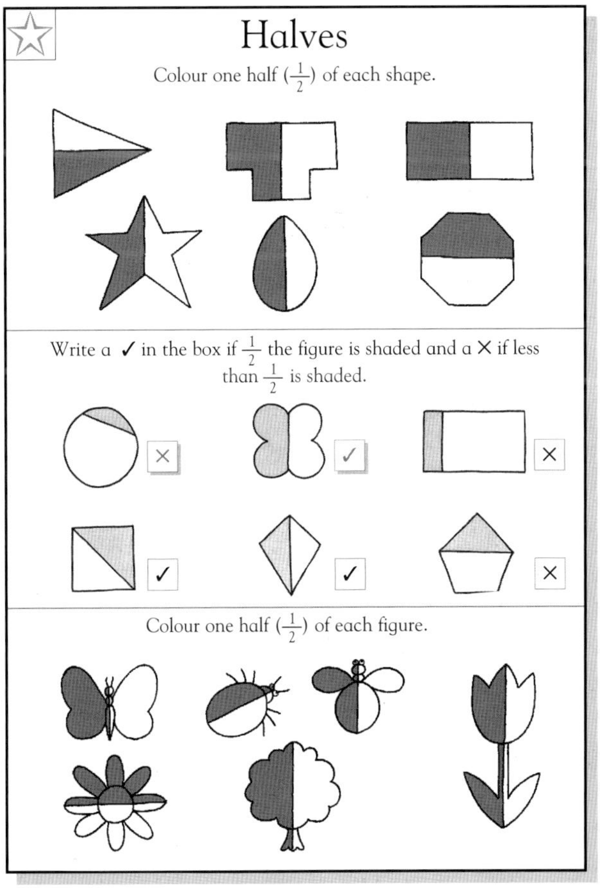

Make sure that children understand that the two halves of something must be exactly the same size.

21 Quarters

Colour one quarter ($\frac{1}{4}$) of each shape.

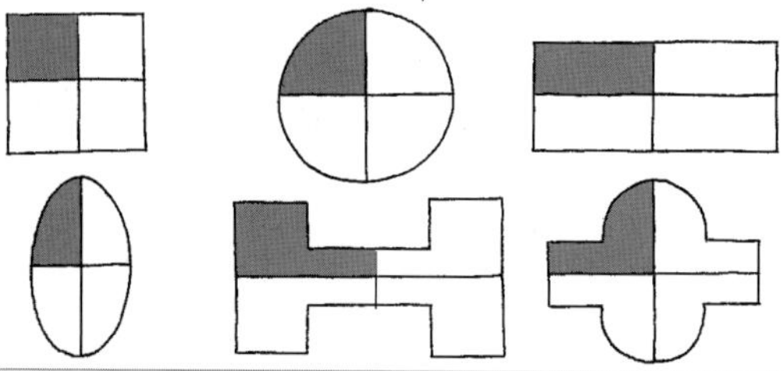

Write a ✓ in the box if $\frac{1}{4}$ of the figure is shaded and a ✗ if less than $\frac{1}{4}$ is shaded.

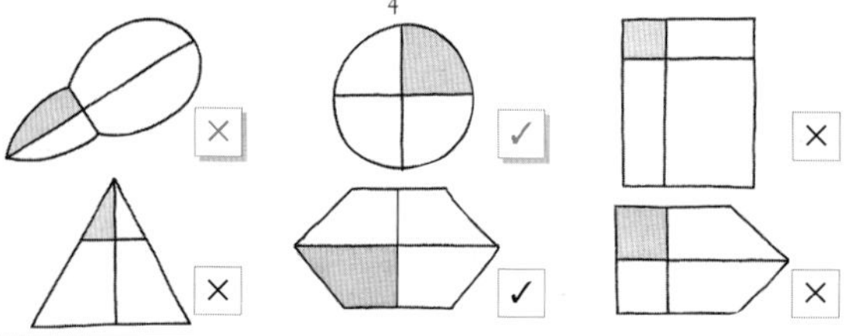

Colour one quarter ($\frac{1}{4}$) of each picture.

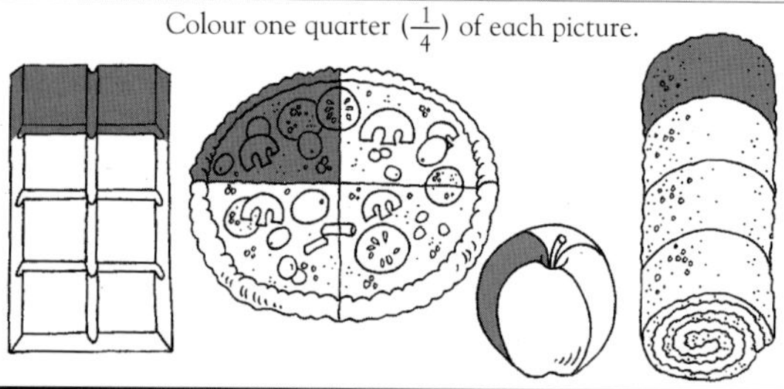

Make sure children understand that the four quarters of something must be exactly the same size.

22 Adding up

Fill in the missing numbers, and add.

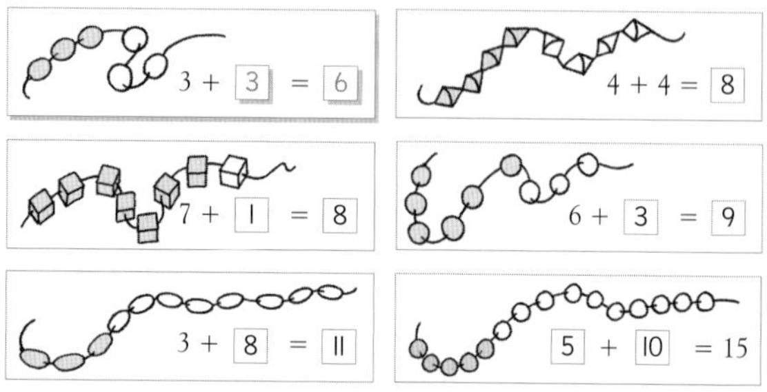

Count on to find out on which step the rabbit stops.

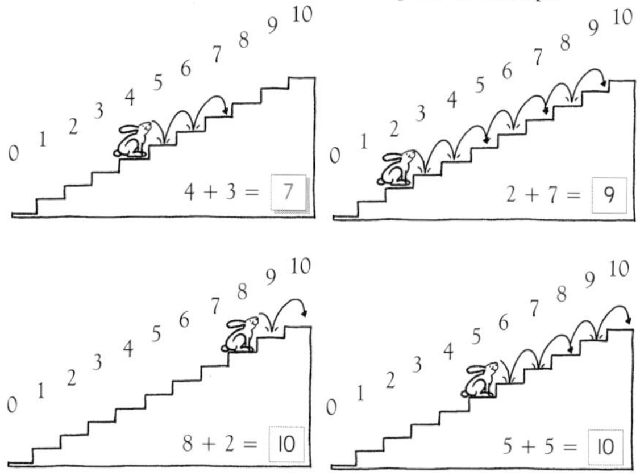

In the activity on top, the two numbers written must match the numbers of beads shaded and unshaded. In the last example, any one of a number of combinations could be correct. For the second activity, encourage your child to count mentally.

23 Adding animals

Count and add the animals, and then write the new number.

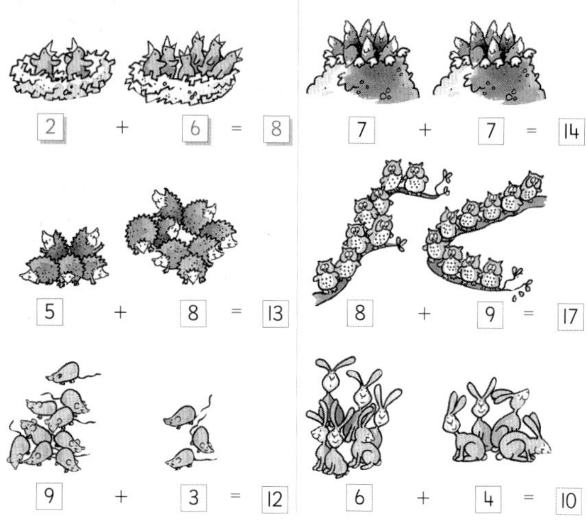

Fill in the missing numbers in the equations.

7 + 4 = 11	3 + 9 = 12	6 + 6 = 12
9 + 5 = 14	2 + 8 = 10	3 + 11 = 14
9 + 3 = 12	6 + 4 = 10	13 + 4 = 17
2 + 3 = 5	16 + 0 = 16	15 + 4 = 19

Children can solve these problems by counting on. They might also find it helpful to check their answers by using a number line.

24 Subtracting

Cross out the correct number of animals, and fill in the answers.

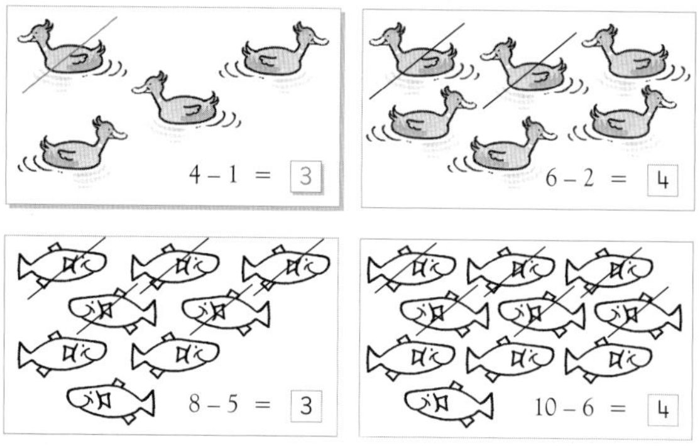

Cross out the correct number of fruits, and fill in the answers.

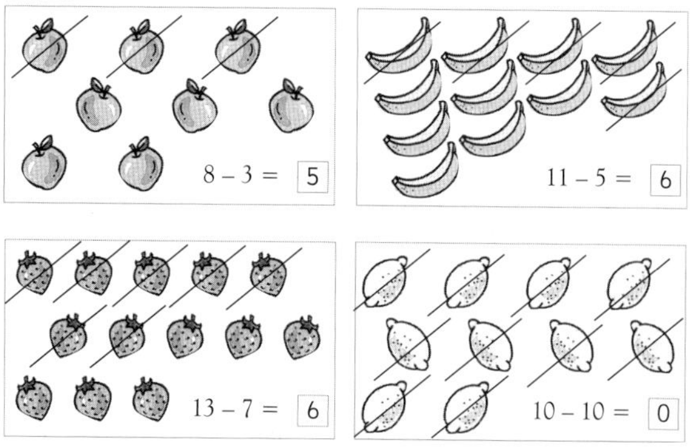

Make sure children understand the terms *cross out* and *left*. Guide children to see that crossing out a picture is a way of "taking away."

25

Counting back

Count back to find out on which step the frog stops.

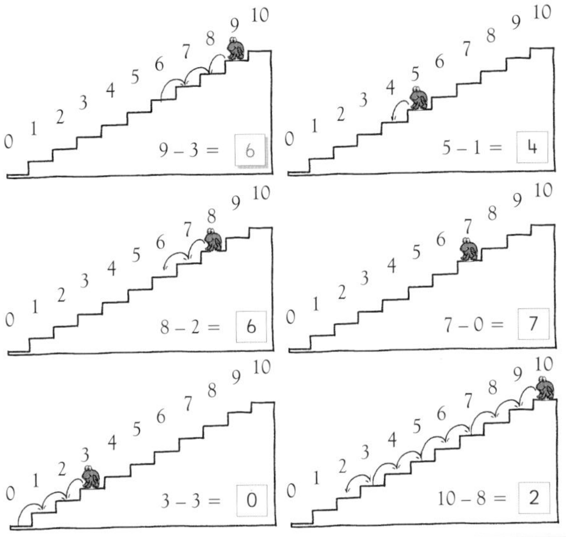

Write the missing numbers in the boxes.

3 – 3 = 0	20 – 10 = 10	9 – 3 = 6	15 – 10 = 5
5 – 4 = 1	8 – 8 = 0	5 – 5 = 0	20 – 16 = 4
15 – 4 = 11	19 – 9 = 10	6 – 4 = 2	18 – 7 = 11
10 – 9 = 1	16 – 9 = 7	10 – 6 = 4	13 – 3 = 10

Make sure children understand that counting back is simply the reverse of counting on. Some children might find it helpful to use a number line to check the answers.

26

Sets

Write the missing numbers in the boxes.

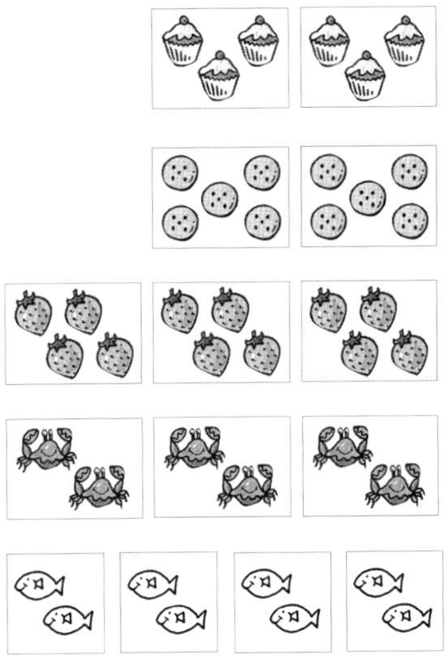

2 sets of 3 = 6

2 sets of 5 = 10

3 sets of 4 = 12

3 sets of 2 = 6

4 sets of 2 = 8

Draw pictures in the boxes to match the equations.

3 sets of 3 = 9

2 sets of 4 = 8

Talk with children about the pictures and what they show. If children have difficulties, make sure they haven't simply added the two numbers given beside the sets, e.g. 2 sets of 3 added together to make 5.

27

Money

Which coin?

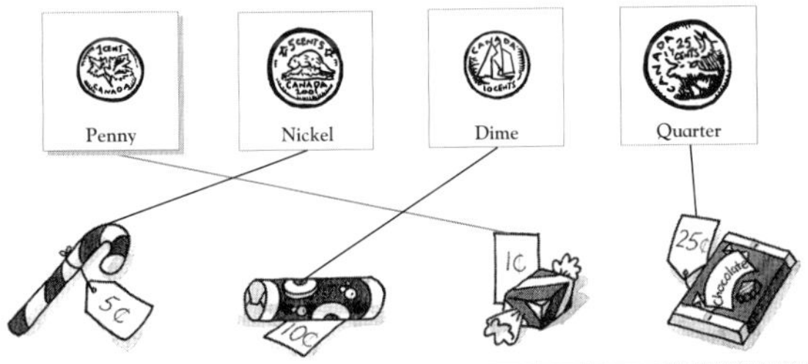

How much?

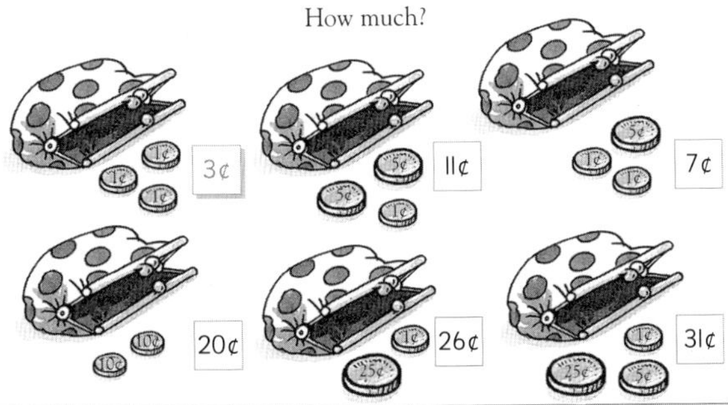

Put the correct change in the piggy bank.

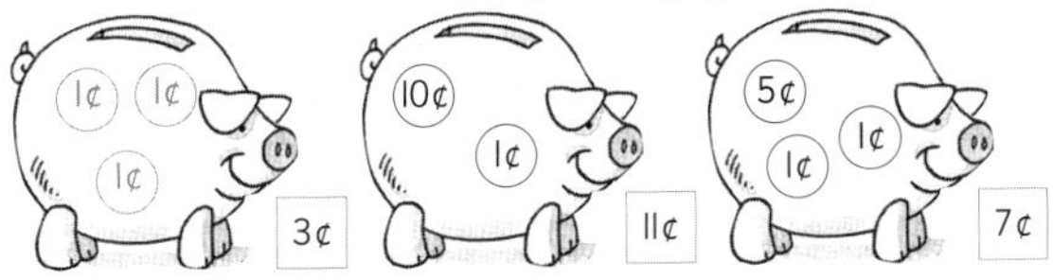

In the last activity, a number of combinations could be correct, and it might be helpful to re-count the amounts with children. For example: 1¢ 1¢ 1¢ 1¢ 1¢ 1¢ 1¢ or 5¢ 1¢ 1¢. Encourage children to use fewer coins when possible.

28

Ordering stories

Which happens 1st, 2nd, and 3rd?

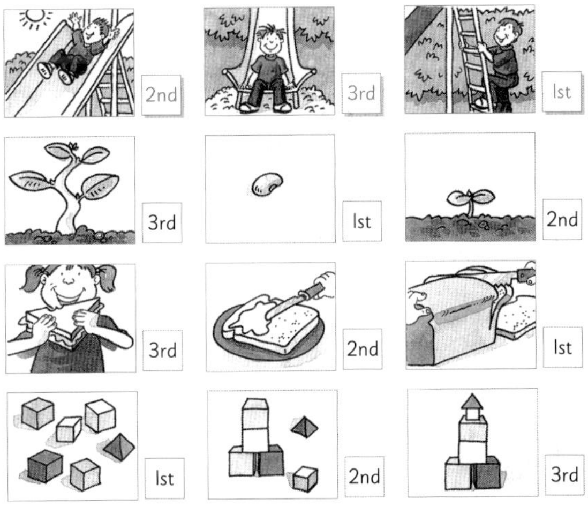

Match the pictures to the order in which they happened.

Ask children to explain their reasons for each set of pictures in a particular way. If children have difficulty with the last set of pictures, point out that the girl's hair is dry when she is standing on the ladder into the pool.

29

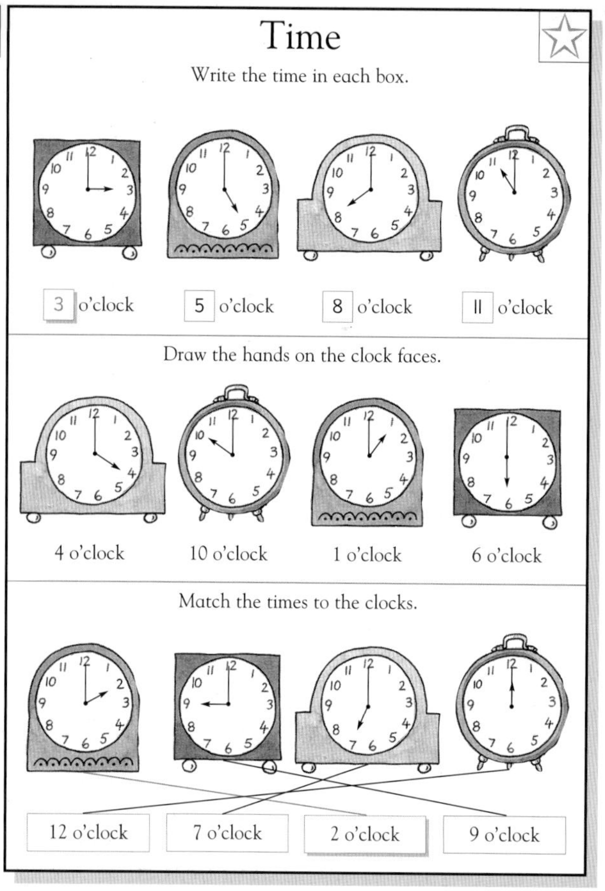

Explain to children that when the hour hand (the short hand) points exactly to an hour, the minute hand (the long hand) should point exactly to 12 on the clock face.

30

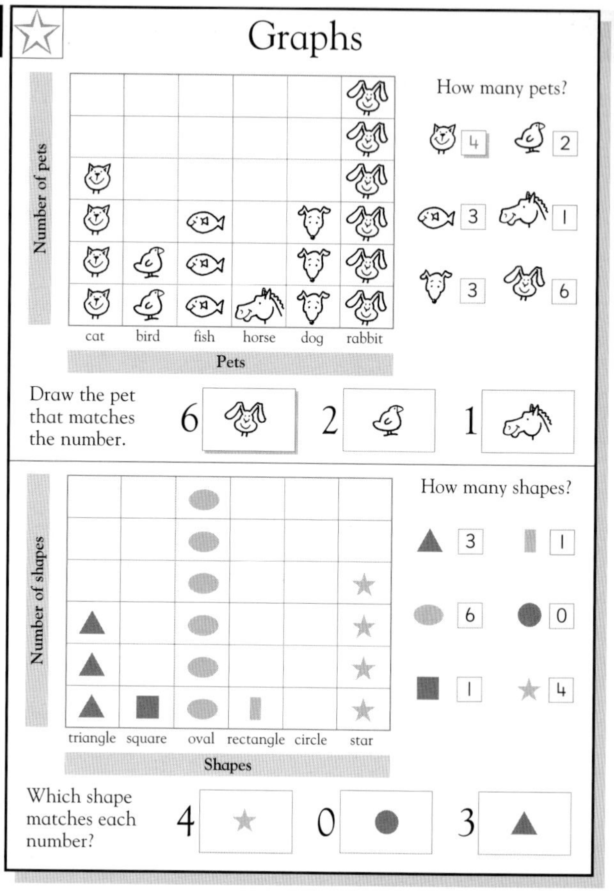

Talk with children about the graphs and what they show. Discuss the numbers and labels on the graphs and what they mean. Explain that graphs show information that can be used to solve problems.

31

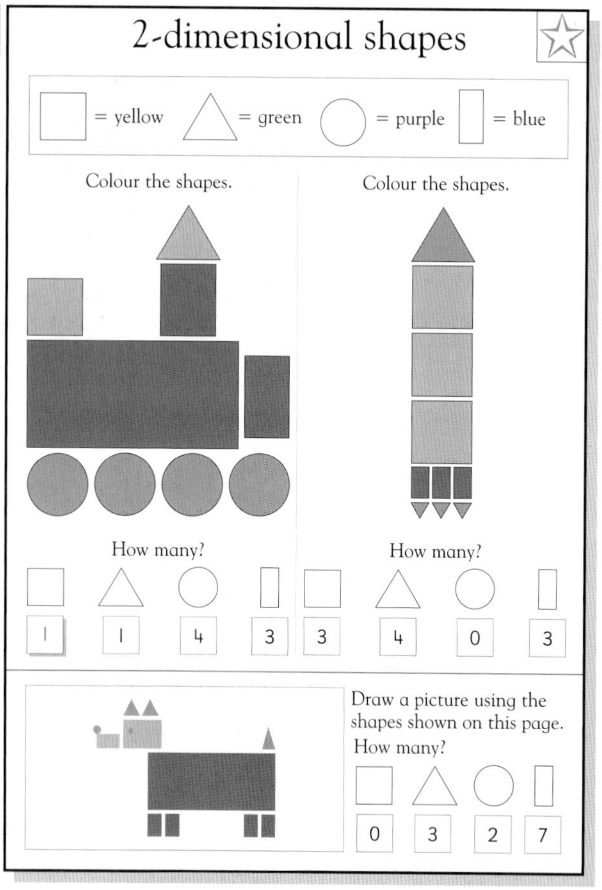

For the last activity, talk to children about their pictures. Encourage them to name each shape used and to state how many of each shape they used.

32

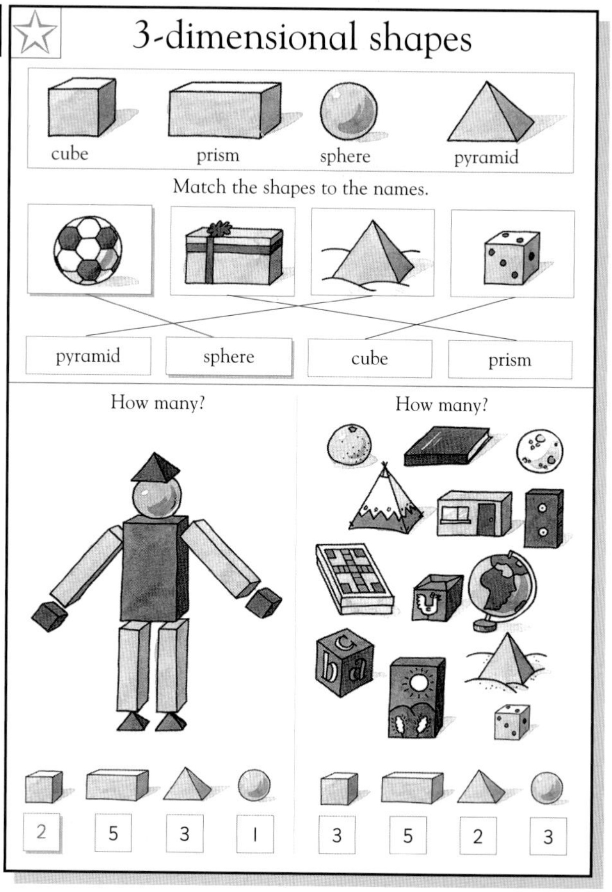

Make sure that children recognize the same shapes when they are positioned differently. For example, they should recognize an upside-down pyramid.

33

Make sure that children understand they are to write the *number* of letters in the names and spell out the numbers. Praise their attempts if they are able to recognize letter patterns such as *teen* and use them to spell numbers such as *fourteen*, etc.

34

Some children may find it difficult to "cross over" a ten, e.g., from *19* to *20*, *21* and so on. Encourage them to see that after a number ends in *9*, the next number ends in *0*, and then the counting sequence begins again.

35

Talk with children about the difference between Elizabeth Even's hops and Oliver Odd's hops. Tell them that counting by 2s is the same as counting every other number. Have children recite the sequences to become familiar with them.

36

Children might need to count each set individually to find out which of three sets of items has the most or the least. Children can use counters, if necessary.

37

Counting by 10s

Use this number line to help you.

0	10	20	30	40	50	60	70	80	90	100
zero	ten	twenty	thirty	forty	fifty	sixty	seventy	eighty	ninety	one hundred

How many candies? Count, say, and write.

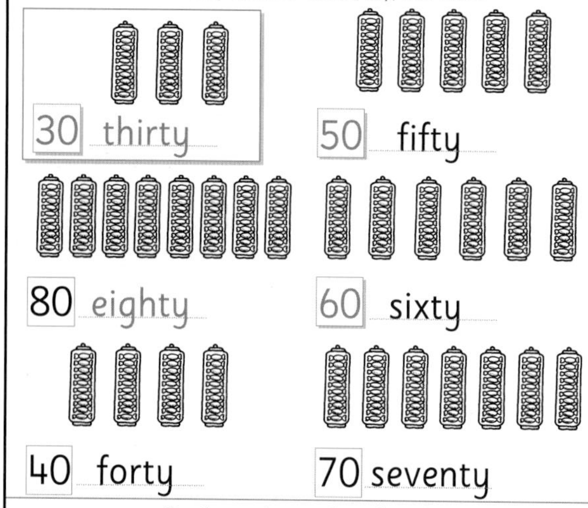

Put the numbers in the right order.

~~10~~ ~~60~~ ~~100~~ ~~50~~ ~~20~~ ~~70~~ ~~90~~ ~~30~~ ~~40~~ ~~80~~

10 20 30 40 50 60 70 80 90 100

Greatest first

100 90 80 70 60 50 40 30 20 10

Point out the link between the sounds of some numbers, such as six and sixty, but also point out the exceptions. Check the spelling of *forty* (not *fourty*). Also point out that 100 is *one hundred*, not *ten-ty*, and 20 is *twenty*, not *two-ty*.

38

Counting forward or back

Draw pathways by writing the missing numbers.

If children have difficulty, let them work with a number line, using both hands. Tell them to keep one finger on the number they are starting from and to use the other hand to count. This way, they will not count the starting number.

39

Reading numbers

Connect the numbers, and complete the drawings.

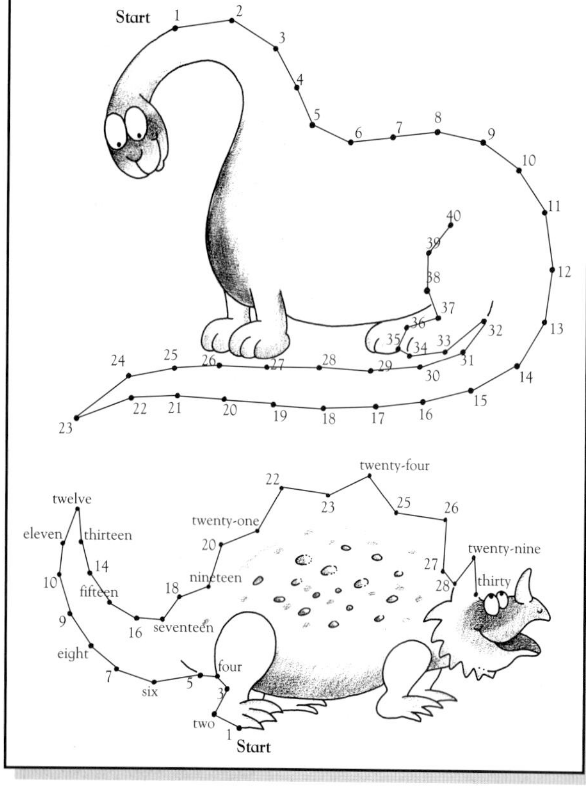

Encourage children to use the counting sequence to help them connect the numbers. For the second picture, help students to see that the counting sequence is the same, but some of the numbers are words.

40

Tens and ones

Write the tens and ones.

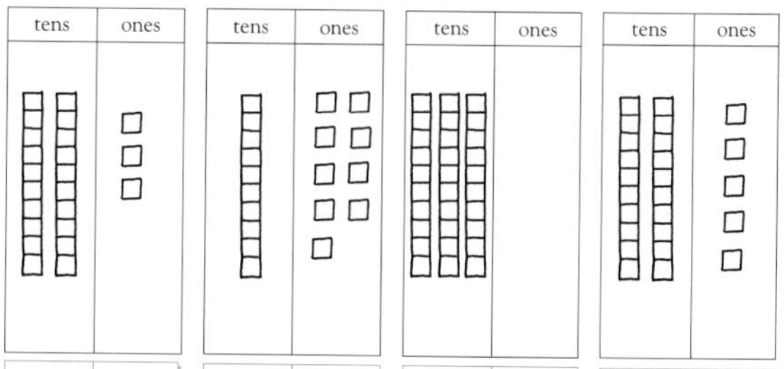

tens	ones	tens	ones	tens	ones	tens	ones
2	3	1	9	3	0	2	5
23		19		30		25	

Draw and write the tens and ones.

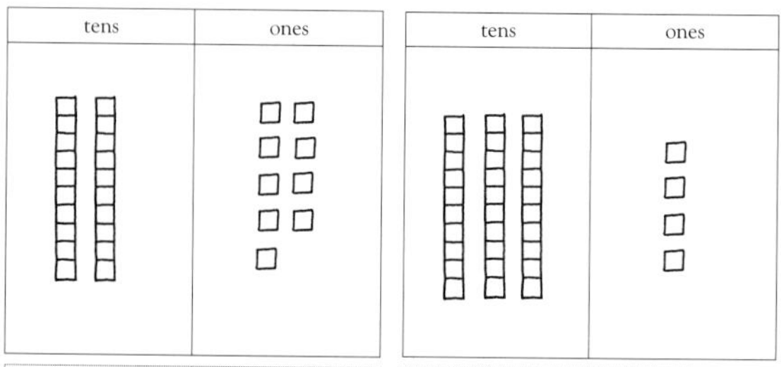

tens	ones	tens	ones
2	9	3	4
29		34	

Breaking large numbers into parts makes adding them easier. So, 22 + 14 becomes 20 + 2 + 10 + 4. Adding the ones first gives 2 + 4 = 6 and the tens next gives 20 + 10 = 30. The two partial answers can then be combined to give 30 + 6 = 36.

41

Comparisons

Add the values, and write *is greater than* or *is less than*.

16 is greater than 9

12 is less than 14

16 is less than 17

16 is greater than 13

Write the numbers that are 1 more, 1 less, or between.

1 less	between	1 more
20	21	22

1 less	number	1 more
25	26	27

number	between	number
19	20	21

1 less	number	1 more
28	29	30

1 less	number	1 more
10	11	12

number	between	number
30	31	32

Children should make use of addition facts to determine totals. If they manage the greater-than and less-than part of the page well, they could then find out how much greater or less one number is than another.

42

Comparing money

Colour the one who has the most money.

Draw some coins in the purses.

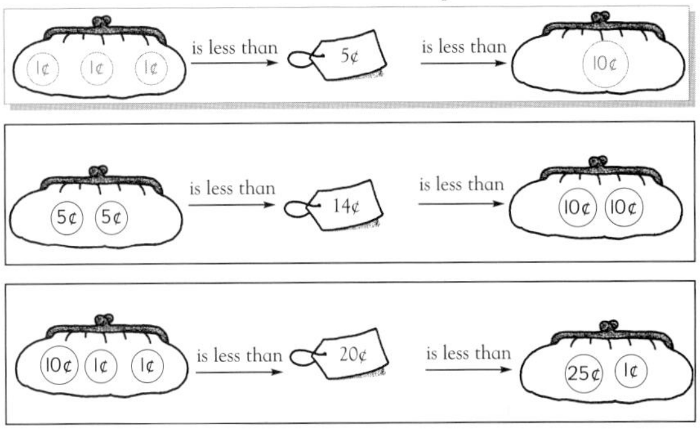

Answers for the lower activity will vary. Make sure that the amount children assign to the first purse is less than the amount on the tag and that the amount children assign to the second purse is greater than that on the tag.

43

Spot the doubles

Draw the missing spots and write the numbers.

3 + 3 = 6
double 3 is 6

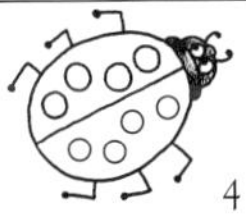

4 + 4 = 8
double 4 is 8

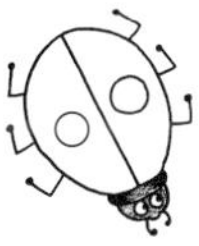

1 + 1 = 2
double 1 is 2

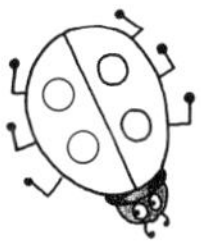

2 + 2 = 4
double 2 is 4

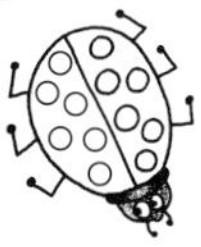

6 + 6 = 12
double 6 is 12

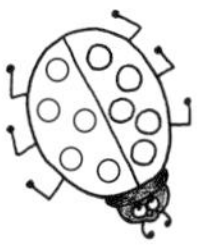

5 + 5 = 10
double 5 is 10

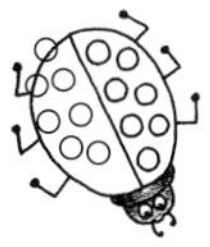

7 + 7 = 14
double 7 is 14

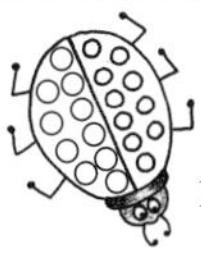

10 + 10 = 20
double 10 is 20

Encourage children to become familiar with doubles. These facts can then be used in other situations, such as "doubles plus 1."

44

10 more or 10 less

Draw a line to add 10 to each number on the rocket.

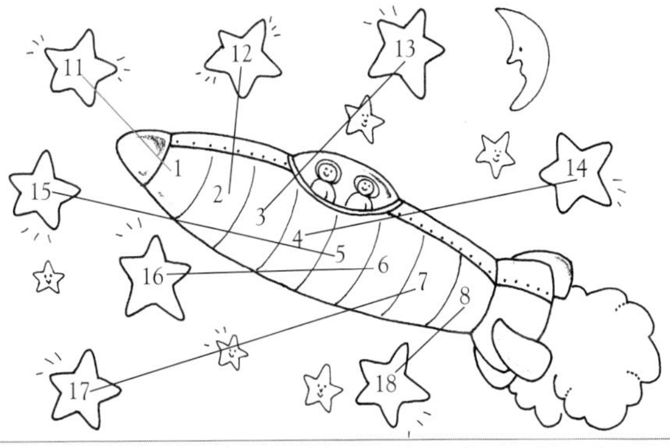

Draw a line to subtract 10 from each number on the rocket.

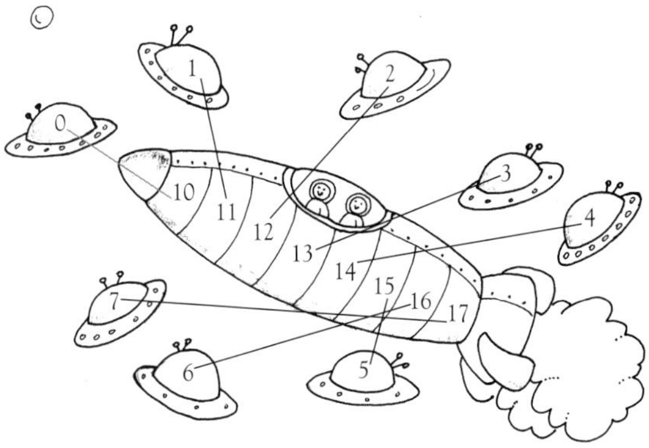

Familiarity with "10 more" and "10 less" will help to develop the ability to do mental math.

45 Ordinals

Colour the beads.

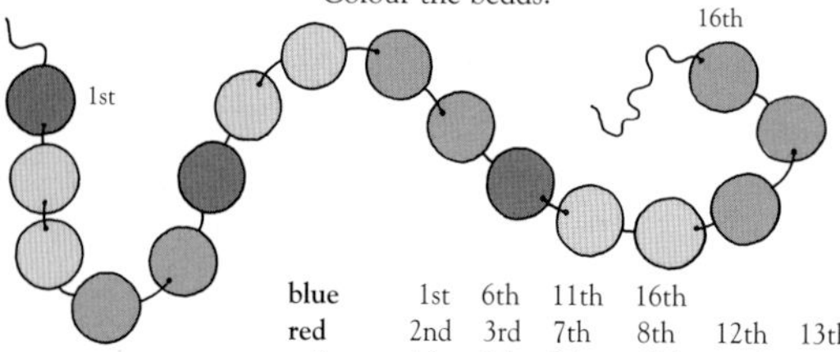

blue	1st	6th	11th	16th		
red	2nd	3rd	7th	8th	12th	13th
yellow	4th	5th	9th	10th	14th	15th

Write the positions.

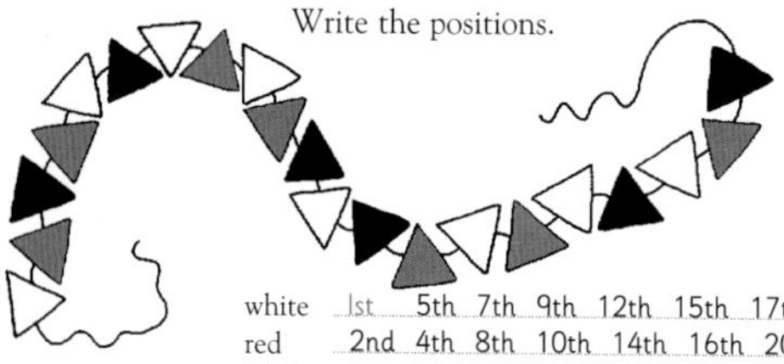

white 1st 5th 7th 9th 12th 15th 17th 19th

red 2nd 4th 8th 10th 14th 16th 20th

black 3rd 6th 11th 13th 18th 21st

Choose 3 colours. Make your own pattern. Write the positions.

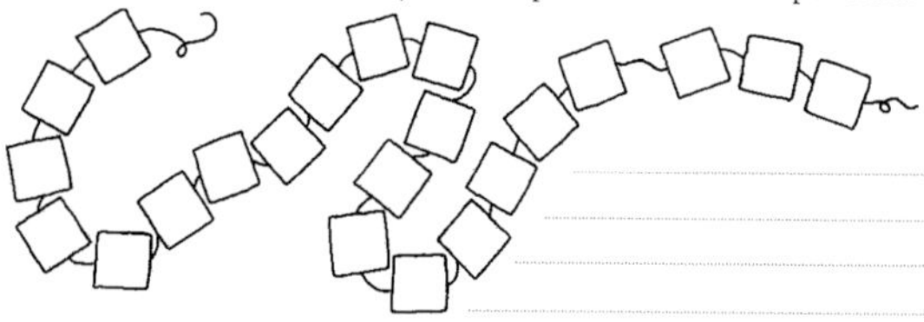

Make sure children understand that the sequence of ordinals is the same as the basic counting sequence.

46 Ordering

Look for a pattern. Write the numbers in order.

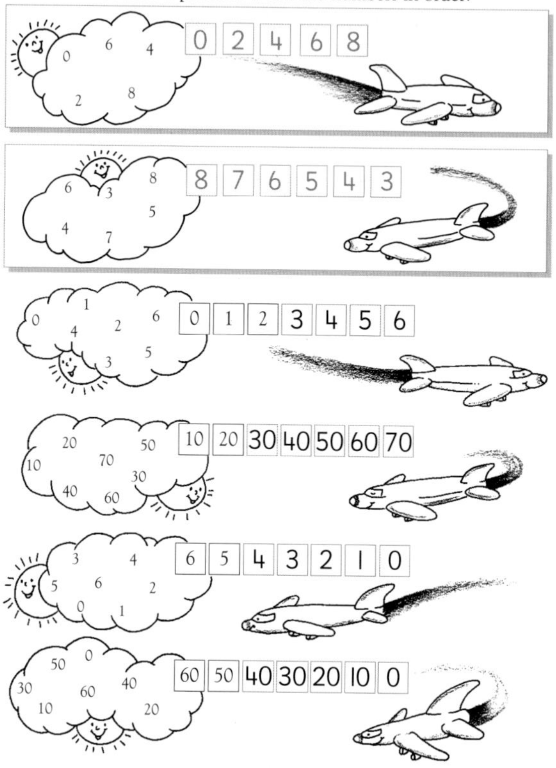

0 2 4 6 8

8 7 6 5 4 3

0 1 2 3 4 5 6

10 20 30 40 50 60 70

6 5 4 3 2 1 0

60 50 40 30 20 10 0

Make sure children understand that some of the patterns require counting on and some require counting back. Children should see that some patterns are familiar, such as counting by 2s, counting by 10s, and the basic counting sequence.

47 Halves and fourths

For each shape colour one half red or one fourth yellow.

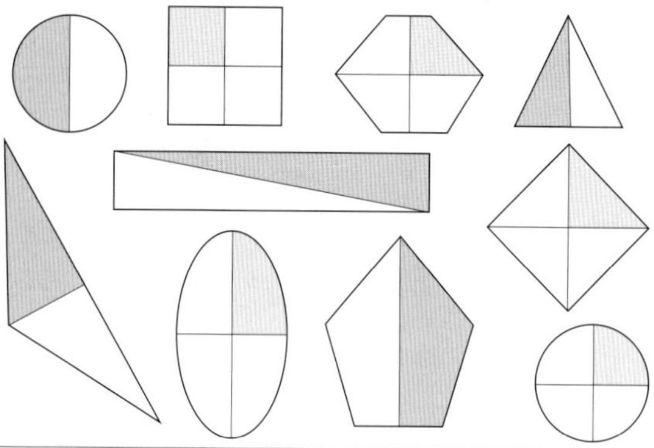

Halves or fourths?

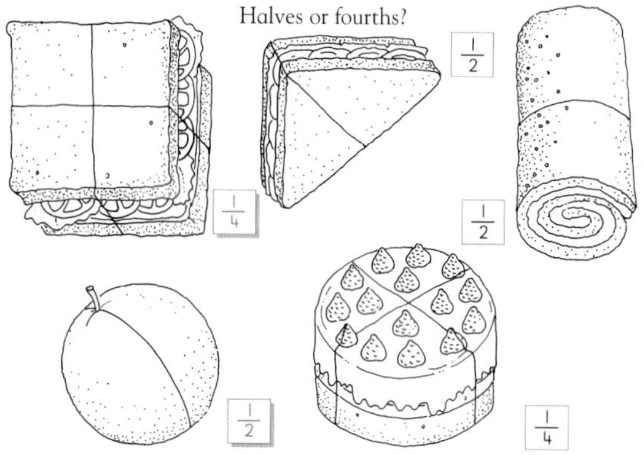

Make sure that children understand that halves must be two exactly equal parts and that fourths must be four exactly equal parts. Encourage children to see that two fourths are the same as one half.

48 Place value

What is in the ones place in each number?

24	61	87	19
4	1	7	9
65	68	13	42
5	8	3	2

What is in the tens place in each number?

30	94	10	69
3	9	1	6
27	81	18	50
2	8	1	5

What is in the tens place in each number?

12	90	43	58
1	9	4	5

Circle the number that has a 7 in the tens place.

57 (79) (70)

Circle the number that has a 3 in the ones place.

34 (93) 30

Circle the number that has a 1 in the tens place.

(10) 61 21

Make sure children understand that the ones are at the right of a number. Children should then see that the tens are just to the left of the ones.

49

Expanded form

Write each number as a sum of tens and ones.

54 = 50 + 4 | 12 = 10 + 2 | 88 = 80 + 8
47 = 40 + 7 | 29 = 20 + 9 | 11 = 10 + 1
75 = 70 + 5 | 51 = 50 + 1 | 44 = 40 + 4
62 = 60 + 2 | 93 = 90 + 3 | 19 = 10 + 9
25 = 20 + 5 | 74 = 70 + 4 | 36 = 30 + 6

Write the missing number.

80 + 6 = 86 | 90 + 7 = 97
30 + 3 = 33 | 60 + 1 = 61
10 + 5 = 15 | 50 + 8 = 58
20 + 2 = 22 | 70 + 9 = 79
40 + 3 = 43 | 90 + 4 = 94

Children should be able to apply what they know about place value to help them to understand expanded form. Make sure that children correctly break numbers apart into tens and ones.

50

Adding dice

Count the dots on the dice.

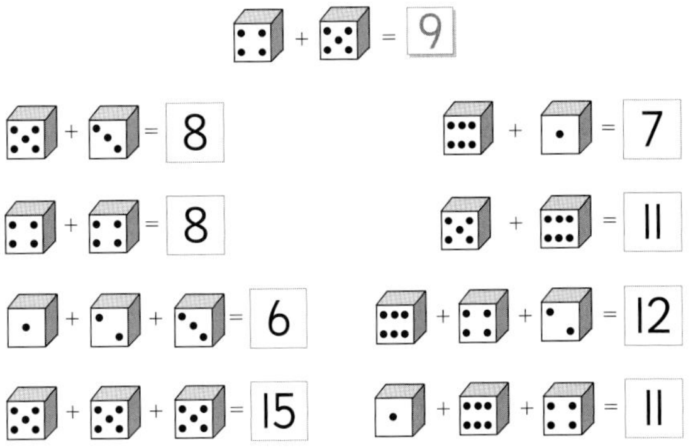

Make your own dice problems. You can roll real dice to help.

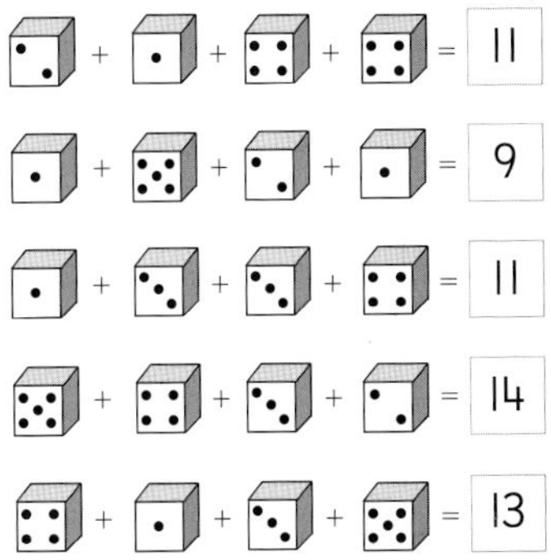

Children can use addition facts to find the answers for the first section. Their answers will vary for the second section. Possible answers are given.

51

Adding

Add up the numbers on the socks.

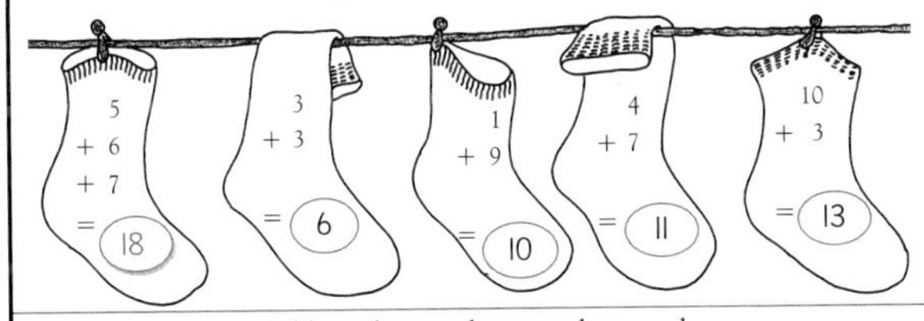

Add up the numbers on the towels.

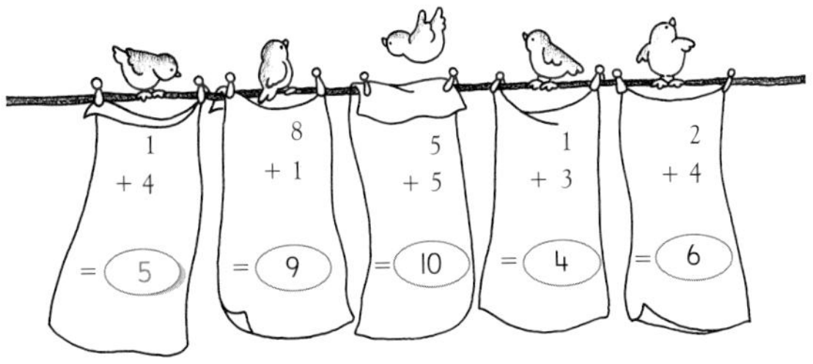

Make up your own number towels.

Encourage children to use addition facts to help them to find the totals.

52

Crossing out

Cross out one type of shape in each box.

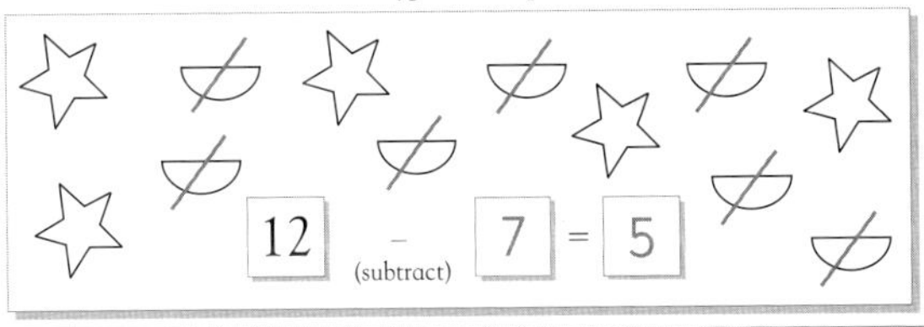

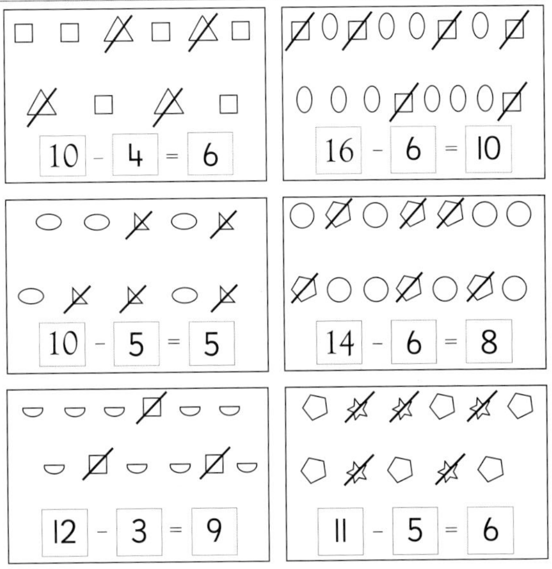

It doesn't matter which set of shapes children choose to cross out. Point out that crossing out pictures is like subtracting these objects. Answers will vary, depending on which set of shapes children cross out.

53 Subtraction

Say and count as you write.

10 altogether. How many in the tent? 4

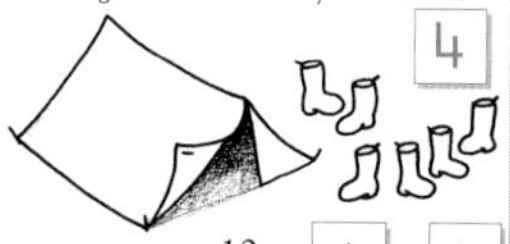

10 − 6 = 4

18 altogether. How many in the tent? 10

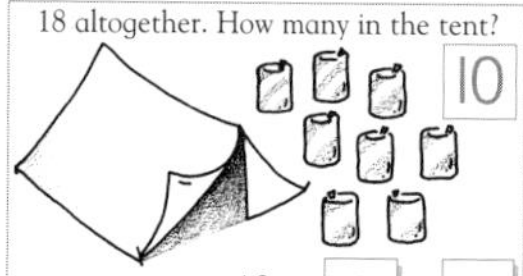

18 − 8 = 10

9 altogether. How many in the tent? 3

9 − 6 = 3

8 altogether. How many in the tent? 3

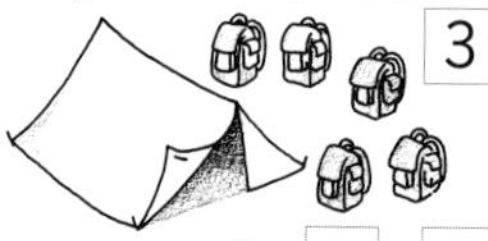

8 − 5 = 3

Say as you write.

16 − 4 = 12	18 − 11 = 7	12 − 10 = 2
15 − 1 = 14	19 − 14 = 5	15 − 6 = 9
9 − 5 = 4	17 − 6 = 11	11 − 1 = 10

Say as you write.

15 − 5 = 10	10 − 10 = 0	16 − 0 = 16
13 − 10 = 3	20 − 20 = 0	8 − 8 = 0

Have children recall fact families for help in solving problems such as 18 – 8 = 10 and 18 – 10 = 8. Remind children that a number subtracted from itself gives a difference of zero.

54 Sets of

Say and count as you write.

4 + 4 + 4 = 12 legs

3 sets of 4 → 12

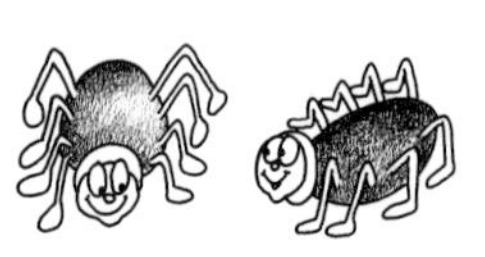

8 + 8 = 16 legs

2 sets of 8 → 16

5 + 5 + 5 + 5 = 20 legs

4 sets of 5 → 20

3 + 3 + 3 + 3 = 12 legs

4 sets of 3 → 12

2 + 2 + 2 = 6 legs

3 sets of 2 → 6

10 + 10 = 20 legs

2 sets of 10 → 20

Talk with children about the pictures and what they show. If children have difficulty, make sure that they haven't simply added the two numbers given below the sets: for example, 3 sets of 4 added together to make 7.

55 Sharing

Share the food equally.

How many each? 2

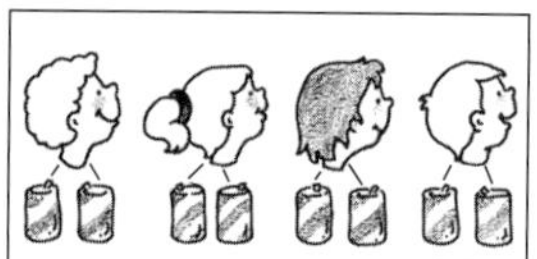

How many each? 2

How many each? 3

How many each? 4

Draw lines to share the picnic.

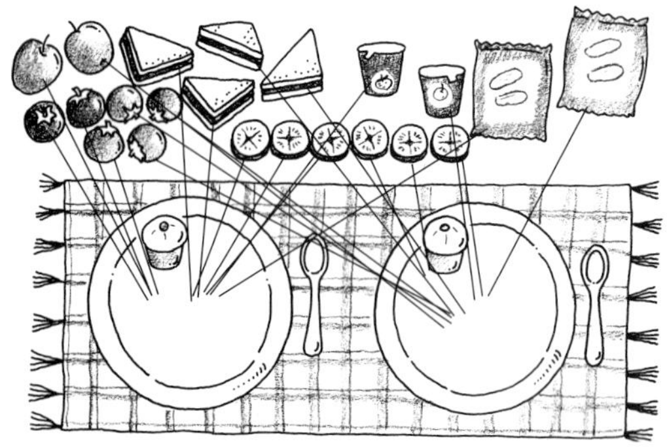

Encourage the use of the word *sharing*. Lead children to understand that sharing means separating a group of items into smaller, equal-size groups. For example, 3 dogs sharing 9 bones gives 3 bones to each dog.

56 Addition properties

Write the missing number.

6 + 0 = 6	0 + 6 = 6
10 + 7 = 17	7 + 10 = 17
11 + 0 = 11	0 + 11 = 11
4 + 8 = 12	8 + 4 = 12
13 + 6 = 19	6 + 13 = 19
0 + 3 = 3	3 + 0 = 3

Circle the addition fact that has the same sum as 2 + 3.

1 + 5   (3 + 2)   4 + 2

Circle the addition fact that has the same sum as 5 + 8.

(8 + 5)   6 + 6   3 + 9

Circle the addition fact that has the same sum as 1 + 7.

8 + 2   2 + 5   (7 + 1)

Circle the addition fact that has the same sum as 10 + 6.

7 + 4   9 + 9   (6 + 10)

Circle the addition fact that has the same sum as 4 + 2.

1 + 6   (2 + 4)   3 + 2

Circle the addition fact that has the same sum as 9 + 5.

(5 + 9)   7 + 6   10 + 5

Guide children to understand that the sum of zero and any number is that number. Also, the sum of any two numbers is the same, no matter which of the numbers comes first.

57

Most and least likely

What are you most likely to pick out of each bag? Circle the answer.

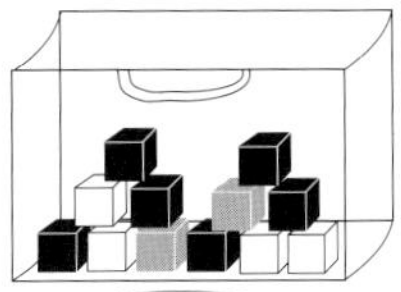

a black cube (circled)
a grey cube
a white cube

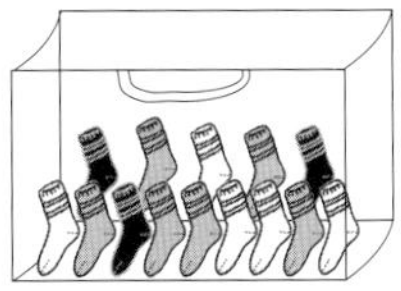

a black sock
a grey sock (circled)
a white sock

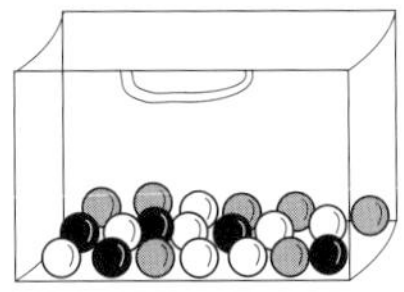

a black marble (circled)
a grey marble
a white marble (circled)

What are you least likely to pick out of each bag? Circle the answer.

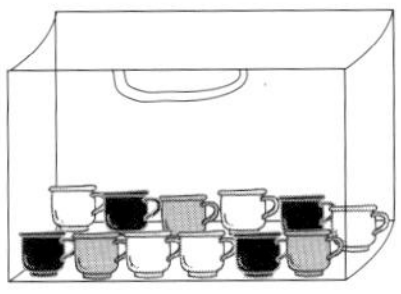

a black tea cup
a grey tea cup (circled)
a white tea cup

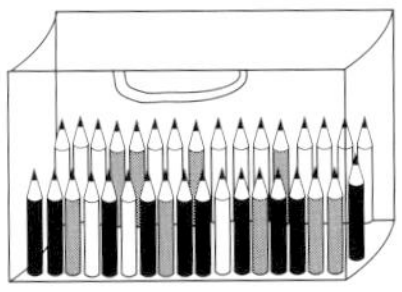

a black pencil
a grey pencil (circled)
a white pencil

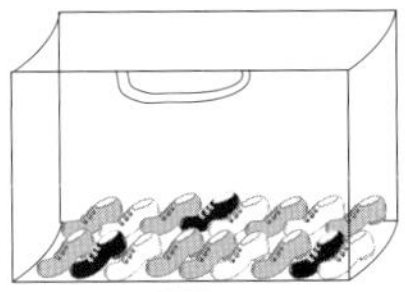

a black boot (circled)
a grey boot
a white boot

Children should understand that the most likely item is the item of which there are the most and that the least likely item is the item of which there are the fewest.

58

Days and seasons

Days of the week

Can you write them in order?

Monday Tuesday Wednesday Thursday Friday Saturday Sunday

Wednesday Thursday Friday Saturday Sunday Monday Tuesday

Saturday Sunday Monday Tuesday Wednesday Thursday Friday

Thursday Friday Saturday Sunday Monday Tuesday Wednesday

Yesterday and tomorrow

yesterday	today	tomorrow
Tuesday	Wednesday	Thursday
Sunday	Monday	Tuesday
Wednesday	Thursday	Friday
Saturday	Sunday	Monday

Seasons of the year

Draw lines to connect each picture to a season.

Children need to know the order of the days. They should also know that the name of each day begins with a capital letter. Ask children to explain their reasons for connecting the season pictures the way they did.

59

Using clocks

Write the time.

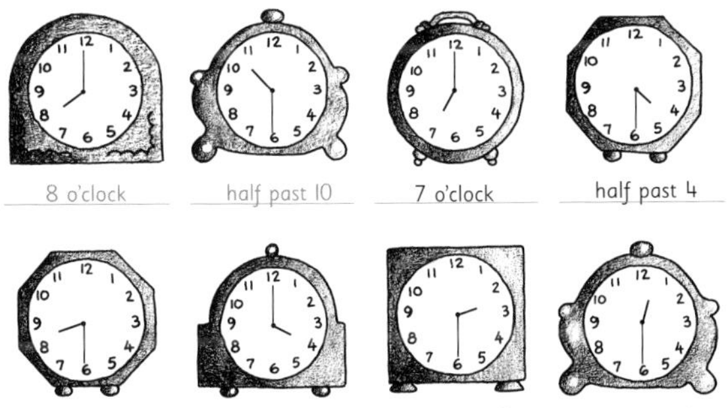

8 o'clock | half past 10 | 7 o'clock | half past 4

half past 8 | 4 o'clock | half past 2 | half past 12

Draw the hands.

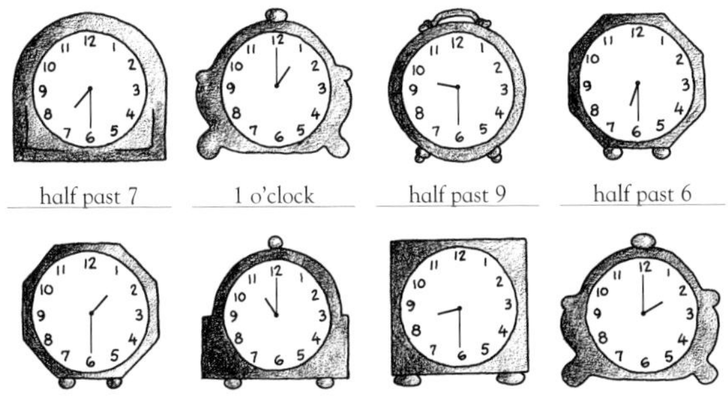

half past 7 | 1 o'clock | half past 9 | half past 6

half past 1 | 11 o'clock | half past 8 | 2 o'clock

Children should understand that at half past the hour, the long hand (the minute hand) must point to the 6 on the clock face.

60

Favourite fruits

This table shows the favourite fruits of a class of children.

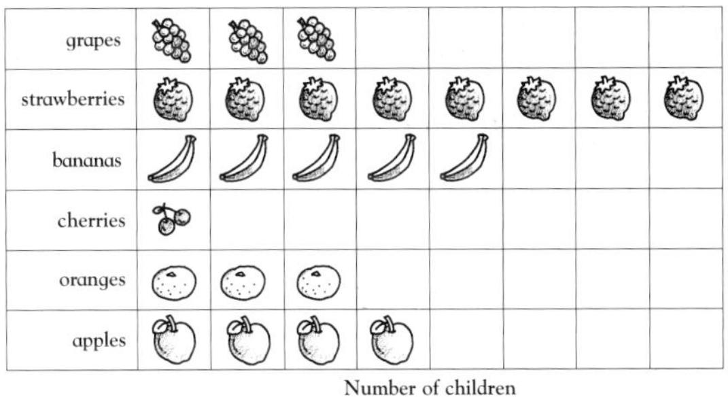

How many preferred each fruit?

3 8 5 1 3 4

Which fruit? Draw.

5 8 1 3

Say and draw.

The fruit chosen most often is .

The fruit chosen least often is .

More children chose than .

My favourite is .

Children should be able to give reasons for their choices. Make sure they understand that each individual drawing of a fruit or a bunch of fruit on the table stands for one child in the class.

61

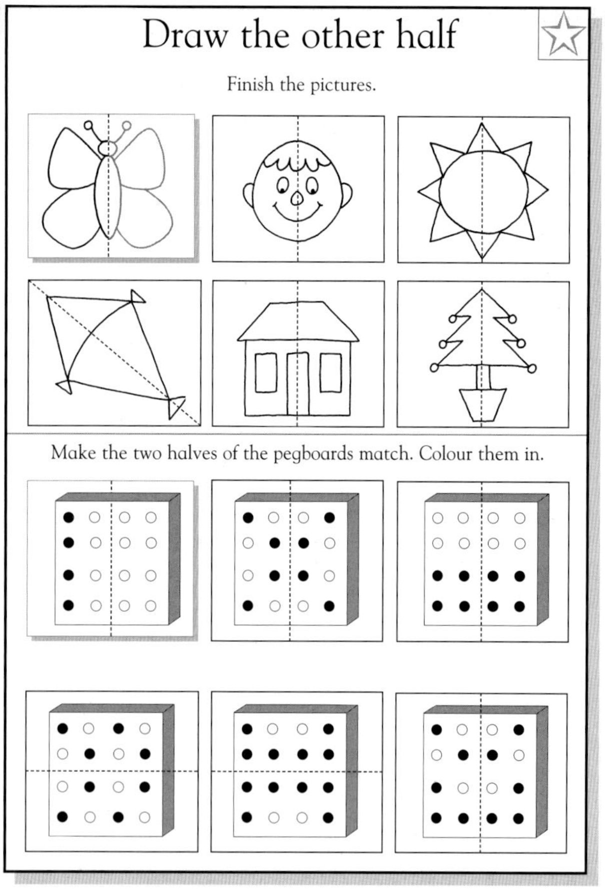

Placing a small mirror along the line of symmetry will enable children to see the complete image. For the second activity, it is important to understand that the unmarked half should be a mirror image of the marked half.

62

Read the words with children before they do the page. Point out that sometimes more than one term may describe similar positions. For example, *above* can sometimes be used in place of *on top*.

63

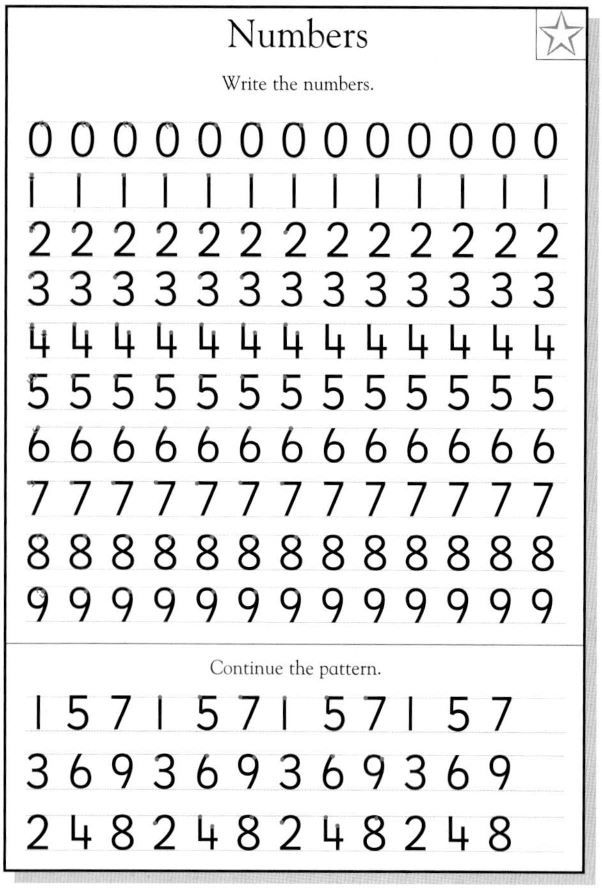

Children need to practise writing numbers correctly. Explain to children that they should write each number beginning from the top of the number.

64

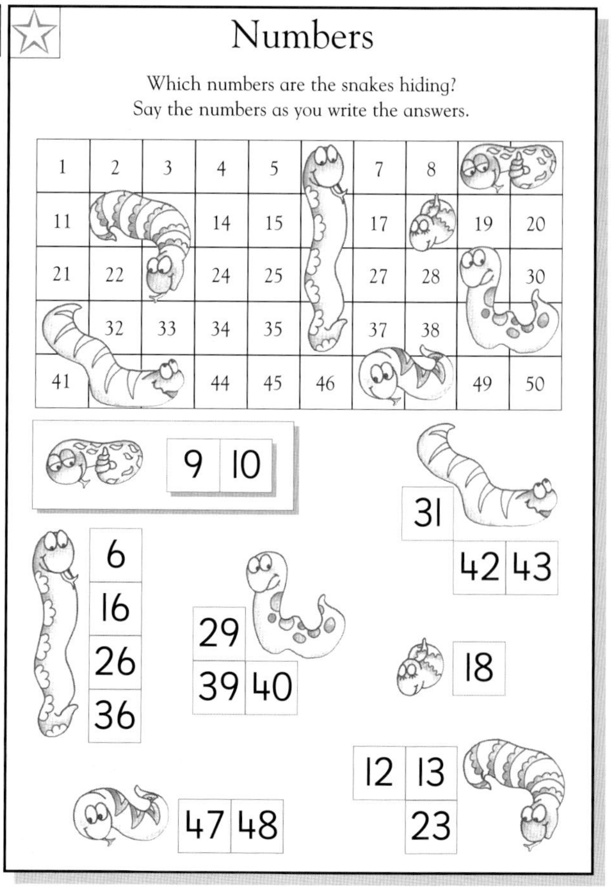

Encourage children to look at the patterns in the numbers as they read down columns. They should also know the basic counting sequence. Make sure children understand that a snake can hide numbers that do not form a sequence.

65

Addition

How many are there in all? Colour them in.

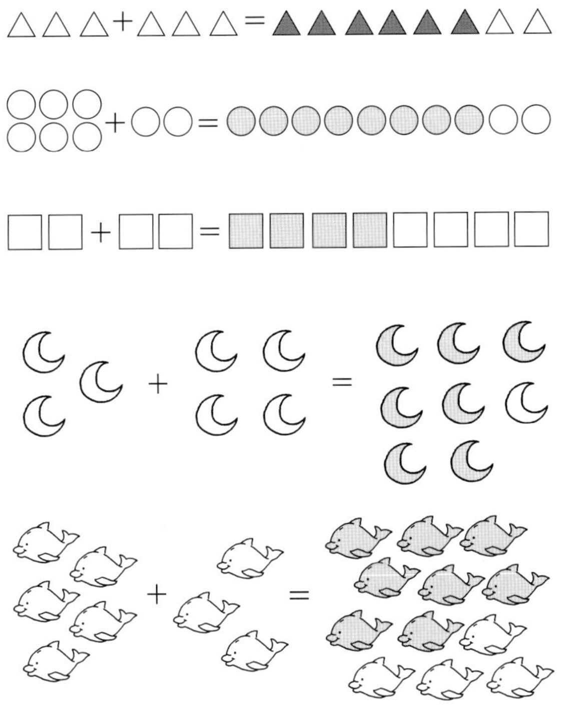

Children may either count to find the total or determine the number of items on either side of the addition symbol and add the two numbers to find the total.

66

1 less or 1 more

Count, draw, and write.

Children should understand that *1 less* means that they should subtract 1 and that *1 more* means that they should add 1. Help them, if necessary, to cross tens, such as adding 1 more to 19.

67

Tallies

Which tally marks show 13?

Which tally marks show 15?

Which tally marks show 17?

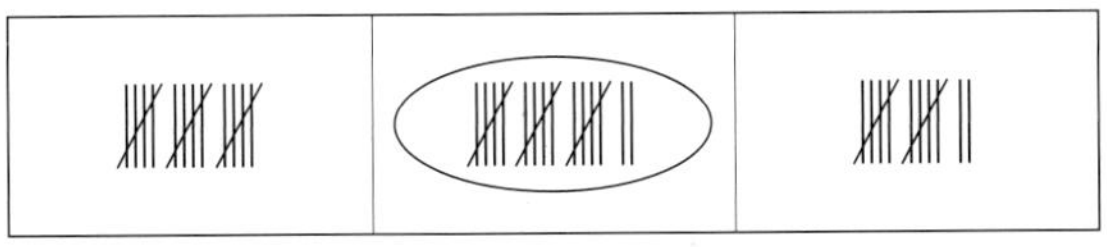

Which tally marks show 23?

Make sure children understand that each complete tally-mark set represents 5. Children can then determine totals by counting by 5s and then counting on.

68

Using a table

Use the table to answer the questions.
Circle the correct answer.

Glasses of water

Name	Saturday	Sunday
Sasha	4	6
William	6	4
Anita	6	8
Nabi	5	7

Who drank less water on Saturday? (Sasha) Nabi

How many glasses of water did Anita drink on Sunday? 4 (8) 7

Who drank 7 glasses of water on Sunday? (Nabi) Anita

Who drank a total of 10 glasses of water? Nabi (William)

Who drank the most glasses of water? Nabi (Anita)

Who drank less water on Sunday? Anita (Nabi)

How many glasses of water did Sasha and William together drink on Saturday? (10) 12

If children have difficulty reading the names in the table, point out to them that they can identify the names in the questions by matching them with the spellings of the names in the table.

69

Patterns of 2, 5, and 10

Count, colour, and find a pattern.

Count by 2s and colour them red.

1	2	3	4	5	6	7	8	9	10
11	12	13	14	15	16	17	18	19	20
21	22	23	24	25	26	27	28	29	30
31	32	33	34	35	36	37	38	39	40
41	42	43	44	45	46	47	48	49	50

Count by 5s and colour them purple.

1	2	3	4	5	6	7	8	9	10
11	12	13	14	15	16	17	18	19	20
21	22	23	24	25	26	27	28	29	30
31	32	33	34	35	36	37	38	39	40
41	42	43	44	45	46	47	48	49	50

Count by 10s and colour them yellow.

1	2	3	4	5	6	7	8	9	10
11	12	13	14	15	16	17	18	19	20
21	22	23	24	25	26	27	28	29	30
31	32	33	34	35	36	37	38	39	40
41	42	43	44	45	46	47	48	49	50

Discuss the patterns made. Ask children to look for any numbers that are coloured in all the patterns. (The 10s will be.) Guide children to see that all the numbers in the pattern formed by counting by 5s end in a 5 or a 0.

70

More or less

Connect the spaceships to the planets and the rockets to the stars.

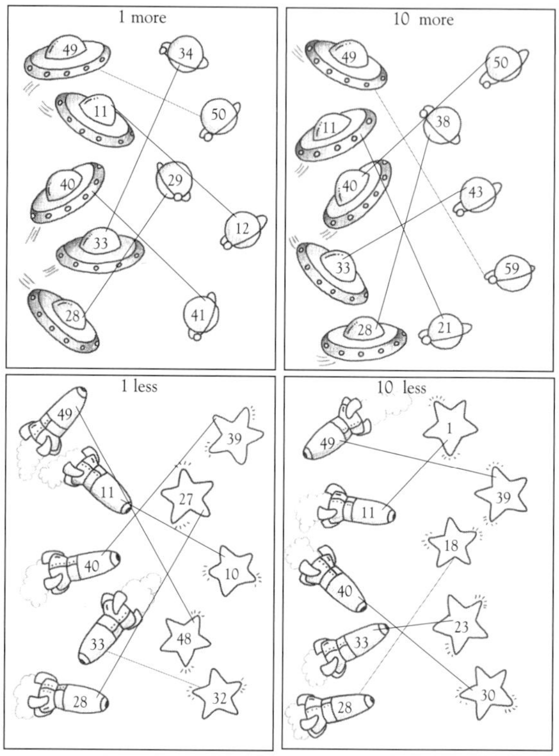

Discuss the changes for each set of numbers. Point out to children that, in some cases, both the tens digit and the ones digit change. Remind children that *more* means they must add and that *less* means they must subtract.

71

Ordering

Write the numbers in order.

smallest first

7 | 16 | 26 | 30 | 39 | 45

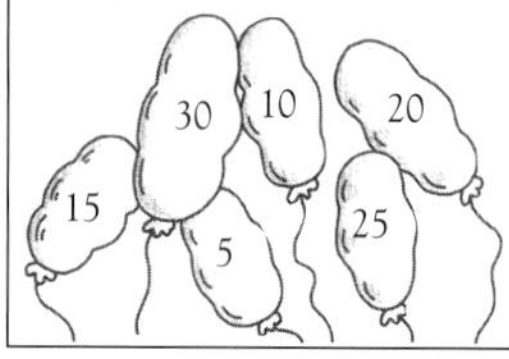

greatest first

30 | 25 | 20 | 15 | 10 | 5

smallest first

3 | 12 | 21 | 23 | 32 | 41

greatest first

50 | 40 | 30 | 20 | 10 | 0

Watch out for possible reversals such as reading 16 as 61. In the third section, 23, 32, 12, and 21 have been included to deal with such reversals. Ask children to identify the place values of the digits in 23 and 32.

72

Fractions of shapes

Colour one third($\frac{1}{3}$).

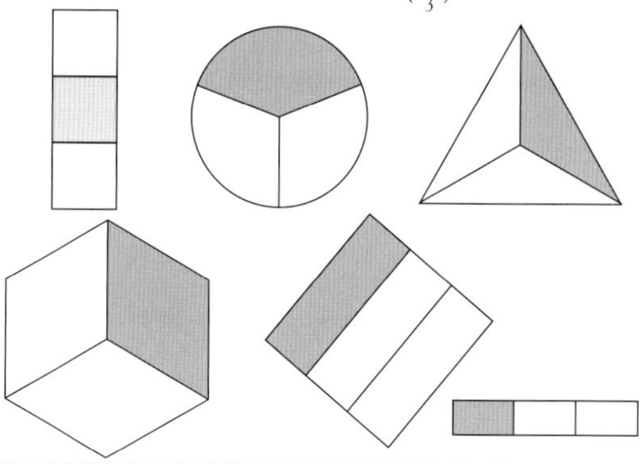

Is it $\frac{1}{3}$? Yes or no.

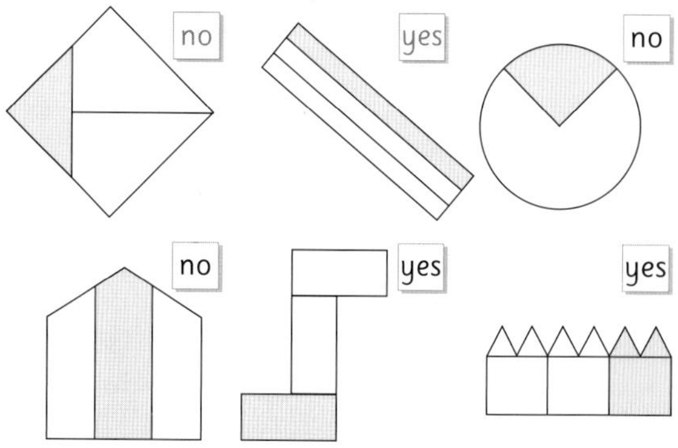

Explain why some of the pictures in the second section do not show one third, even though each shape is cut into three pieces. (The pieces are not all of equal size.)

73

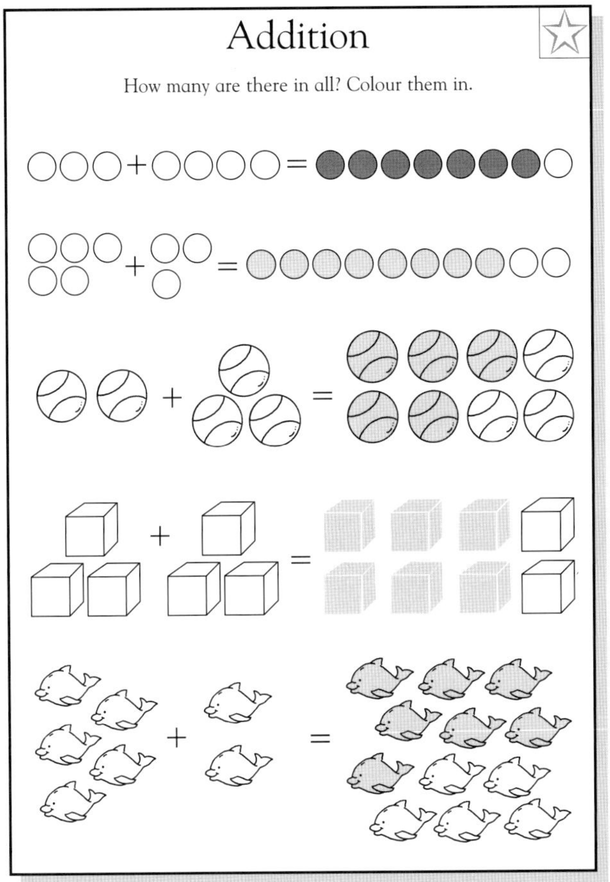

Suggest to children that they write the number of items below each group on either side of the addition symbol. When they find the total, they can write that number under the items they have coloured in.

74

Encourage children to keep track of the different combinations of coins that they use. In this way, they can avoid repeating combinations.

75

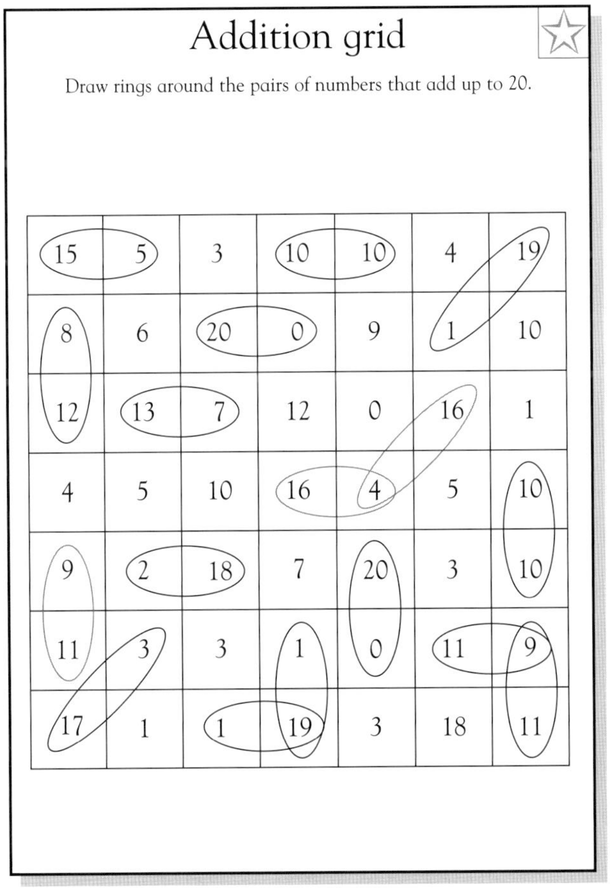

Addition grid

Draw rings around the pairs of numbers that add up to 20.

15	5	3	10	10	4	19
8	6	20	0	9	1	10
12	13	7	12	0	16	1
4	5	10	16	4	5	10
9	2	18	7	20	3	10
11	3	3	1	0	11	9
17	1	1	19	3	18	11

If children find this page difficult, encourage them to find 20 objects, such as counters or pennies and find different ways of separating them into 2 groups, such as 2 and 18, 15 and 5. Children can then look for these pairs of numbers.

76

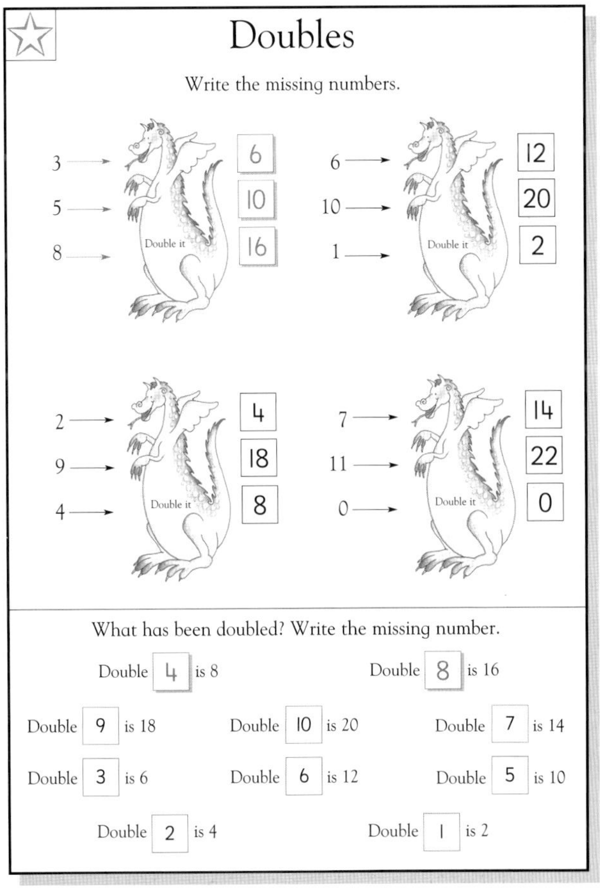

Explain that doubling is the same as adding two sets of the same number. If children cannot yet double in their heads, use counters to make two sets of the number, and add them.

77

Fact families

Complete each fact family.

4, 5, 9				
4	+	5	=	9
5	+	4	=	9
9	−	4	=	5
9	−	5	=	4

3, 4, 7				
3	+	4	=	7
4	+	3	=	7
7	−	3	=	4
7	−	4	=	3

2, 4, 6				
2	+	4	=	6
4	+	2	=	6
6	−	4	=	2
6	−	2	=	4

3, 5, 8				
3	+	5	=	8
5	+	3	=	8
8	−	3	=	5
8	−	5	=	3

Make sure children understand that a fact family consists of four number sentences: two are addition sentences, and two are subtraction sentences. Encourage students to see the inverse relationship between addition and subtraction with these facts.

78

Addition

Add to find each sum.

13 + 4 = 17

Add to find each sum.

8 + 1 = 9	3 + 4 = 7	2 + 6 = 8	0 + 5 = 5
10 + 9 = 19	10 + 3 = 13	10 + 4 = 14	10 + 2 = 12
12 + 3 = 15	16 + 3 = 19	14 + 3 = 17	12 + 5 = 17
17 + 1 = 18	12 + 4 = 16	10 + 7 = 17	11 + 7 = 18

If children have difficulty with these exercises, make sure that they are adding in the correct order. In other words, they should add the ones first and then add the tens.

79

Subtraction

Subtract to find the difference.

14 − 3 = 11

Subtract to find each difference.

8 − 1 = 7	5 − 2 = 3	6 − 2 = 4	5 − 4 = 1
19 − 7 = 12	13 − 2 = 11	14 − 4 = 10	19 − 3 = 16
16 − 3 = 13	16 − 5 = 11	18 − 7 = 11	17 − 5 = 12
17 − 1 = 16	14 − 2 = 12	17 − 4 = 13	17 − 1 = 16

Make sure children begin by subtracting the ones. If children have difficulty, point out to them that they have no tens to subtract, so they can write the tens value in the answer.

80

Subtraction

Subtract to find the difference.

80 − 30 = 50

Subtract to find each difference.

30 − 20 = 10	50 − 30 = 20	40 − 20 = 20	20 − 10 = 10
40 − 30 = 10	50 − 20 = 30	60 − 40 = 20	90 − 30 = 60
70 − 30 = 40	90 − 40 = 50	40 − 10 = 30	50 − 40 = 10
90 − 70 = 20	80 − 10 = 70	60 − 50 = 10	40 − 40 = 0

Point out to children that although they are subtracting two-digit numbers, the ones digit in each number is zero, so each answer will have a zero in the ones place. Children should understand that subtracting any number from itself leaves zero.

81

Subtraction

Subtract to find the difference.

$$\begin{array}{r} 87 \\ -34 \\ \hline 53 \end{array}$$

Subtract to find each difference.

$$\begin{array}{r} 39 \\ -27 \\ \hline 12 \end{array} \quad \begin{array}{r} 58 \\ -32 \\ \hline 26 \end{array} \quad \begin{array}{r} 44 \\ -11 \\ \hline 33 \end{array} \quad \begin{array}{r} 27 \\ -17 \\ \hline 10 \end{array}$$

$$\begin{array}{r} 46 \\ -33 \\ \hline 13 \end{array} \quad \begin{array}{r} 59 \\ -46 \\ \hline 13 \end{array} \quad \begin{array}{r} 75 \\ -31 \\ \hline 44 \end{array} \quad \begin{array}{r} 88 \\ -14 \\ \hline 74 \end{array}$$

$$\begin{array}{r} 77 \\ -33 \\ \hline 44 \end{array} \quad \begin{array}{r} 93 \\ -22 \\ \hline 71 \end{array} \quad \begin{array}{r} 67 \\ -53 \\ \hline 14 \end{array} \quad \begin{array}{r} 38 \\ -22 \\ \hline 16 \end{array}$$

$$\begin{array}{r} 99 \\ -79 \\ \hline 20 \end{array} \quad \begin{array}{r} 82 \\ -70 \\ \hline 12 \end{array} \quad \begin{array}{r} 69 \\ -69 \\ \hline 0 \end{array} \quad \begin{array}{r} 47 \\ -46 \\ \hline 1 \end{array}$$

This page presents straightforward subtraction with two-digit numbers, with no regrouping. Make sure that children subtract in the correct order, that is, they should subtract the ones first and then the tens.

82

Real-life problems

All the piggy banks need 30¢. Draw different coins in each one. You can use any coin more than once.

Explain that to make 5¢, five 1¢ coins or a 5¢ coin can be used. So, 10¢ can be made with any of these combinations plus a 5¢ coin. Then another 10¢ coin will make 20¢.

83

Real-life problems

6¢ 5¢ 4¢ 2¢ 1¢

Draw the stamps on the letters. You can use any stamp more than once.

6¢ 4¢ 2¢

Ms. Heather Hedgehog
1 The Leaf Pile
Snowdrop Corner
Garden City

12¢

5¢ 5¢ 5¢ 5¢

Doctor Dilly Dinosaur
6 The Swamp
Mud Town

20¢

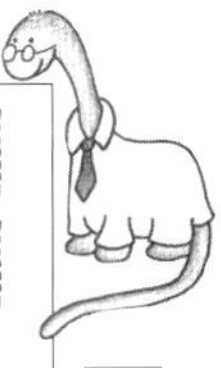

2¢ 2¢ 2¢ 2¢ 2¢

Rachel Robot
999 Mechanical Mansion
Metalville

10¢

6¢ 6¢ 6¢

Cheeky Charlie Chimp
100 Banana Court
Giggleton
Apeland

18¢

6¢ 5¢

Mr. Bertie Bear
The Toy Box
Betty's Bedroom
The Big House

11¢

2¢ 1¢ 1¢ 1¢ 1¢

Samuel Spider
Wonder Web
Grandpa's Greenhouse
South Central Garden

6¢

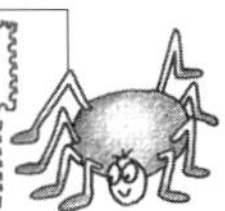

Children may use different stamp combinations to reach the totals. In real-life situations, most people would use as few stamps as possible. For 6¢ postage, a 5¢ stamp and a 1¢ stamp would be better than six 1¢ stamps.

84

Subtraction tables

Finish each table.

–	2	3	5	10
11	9	8	6	1
15	13	12	10	5
20	18	17	15	10

–	1	6	8	9
14	13	8	6	5
19	18	13	11	10
20	19	14	12	11

–	0	4	7	11
12	12	8	5	1
28	28	24	21	17
18	18	14	11	7

Ask children to point out on the table where the information is and where the answers should go. If they need help, tell them to subtract each number in the top row from each number in the left-hand column.

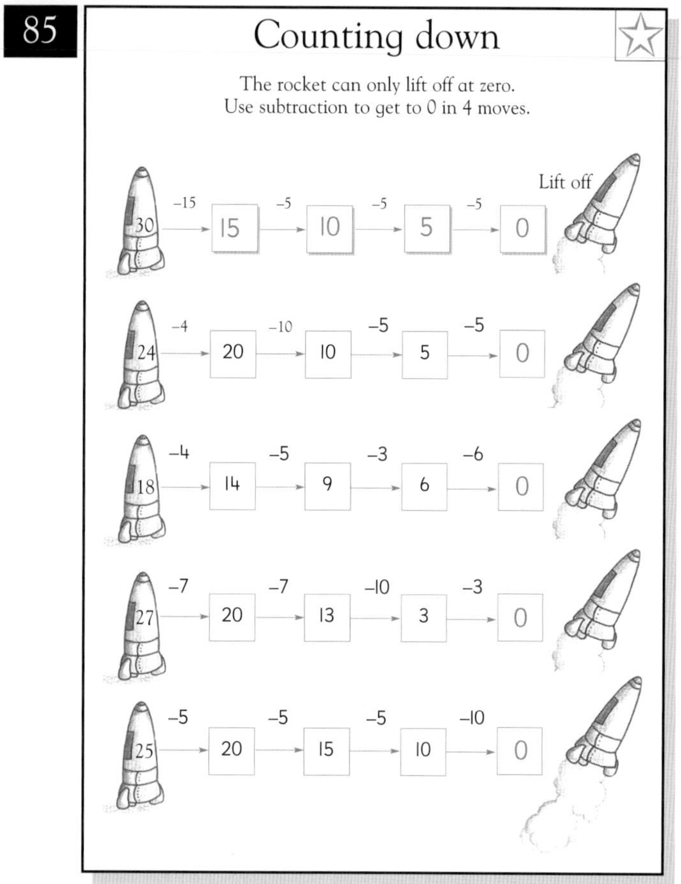
85

Counting down

The rocket can only lift off at zero.
Use subtraction to get to 0 in 4 moves.

Lift off

Start								
30	−15	15	−5	10	−5	5	−5	0
24	−4	20	−10	10	−5	5	−5	0
18	−4	14	−5	9	−3	6	−6	0
27	−7	20	−7	13	−10	3	−3	0
25	−5	20	−5	15	−5	10	−10	0

Answers will vary. If children reach zero too soon, they can look for ways to use smaller numbers. If they don't reach zero, they can look for larger numbers to subtract.

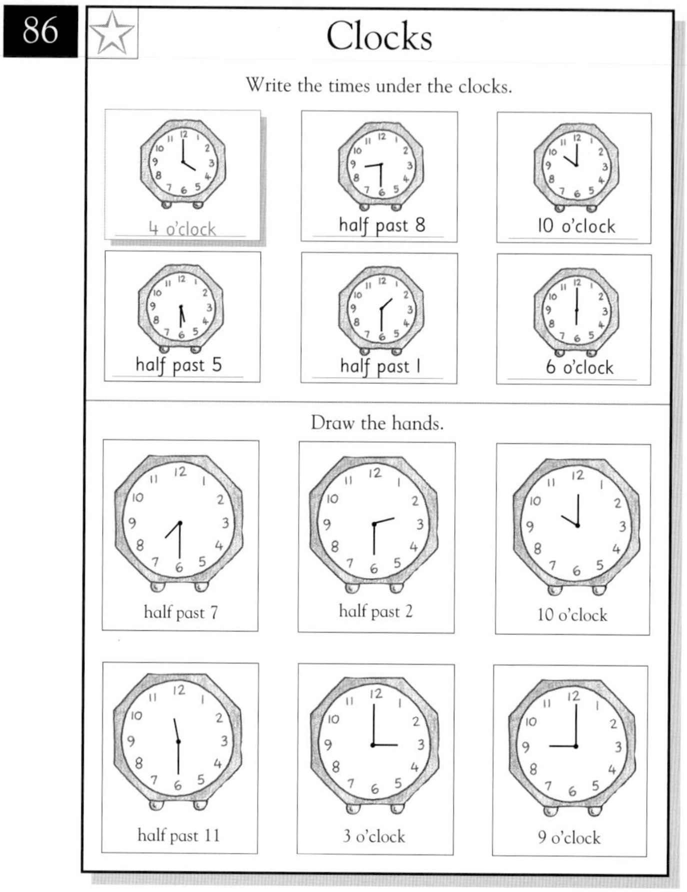
86

Clocks

Write the times under the clocks.

4 o'clock | half past 8 | 10 o'clock

half past 5 | half past 1 | 6 o'clock

Draw the hands.

half past 7 | half past 2 | 10 o'clock

half past 11 | 3 o'clock | 9 o'clock

The lengths of the clock hands show that times such as half past 12 and 6 o'clock are different. Remind children that the long hand is the minute hand and the short hand is the hour hand.

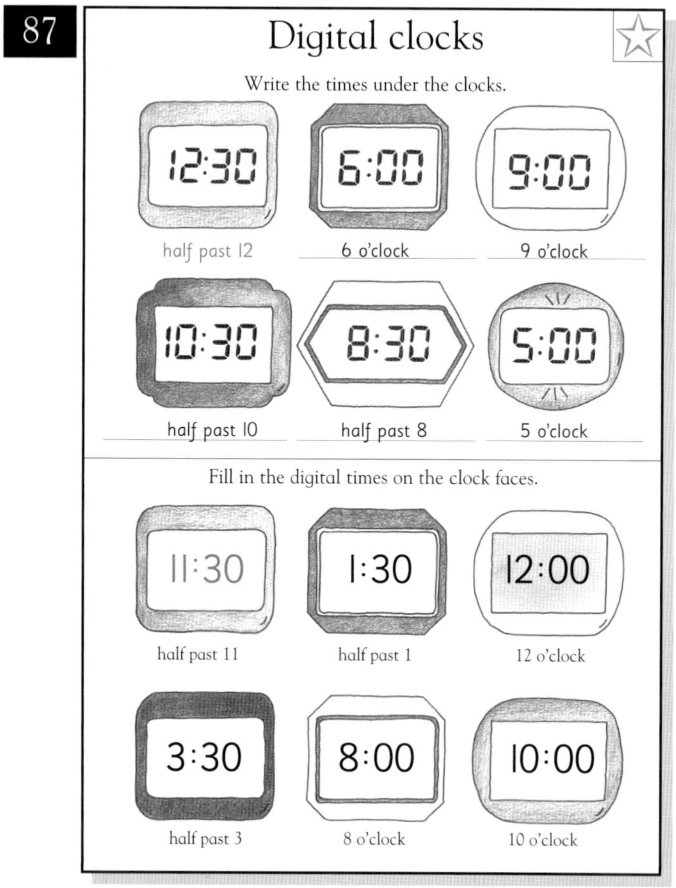
87

Digital clocks

Write the times under the clocks.

12:30 half past 12 | 6:00 6 o'clock | 9:00 9 o'clock

10:30 half past 10 | 8:30 half past 8 | 5:00 5 o'clock

Fill in the digital times on the clock faces.

11:30 half past 11 | 1:30 half past 1 | 12:00 12 o'clock

3:30 half past 3 | 8:00 8 o'clock | 10:00 10 o'clock

Watch out for confusion between the digital versions of 5 and 2. Point out to children that the start positions of both digital and regular numbers are the same.

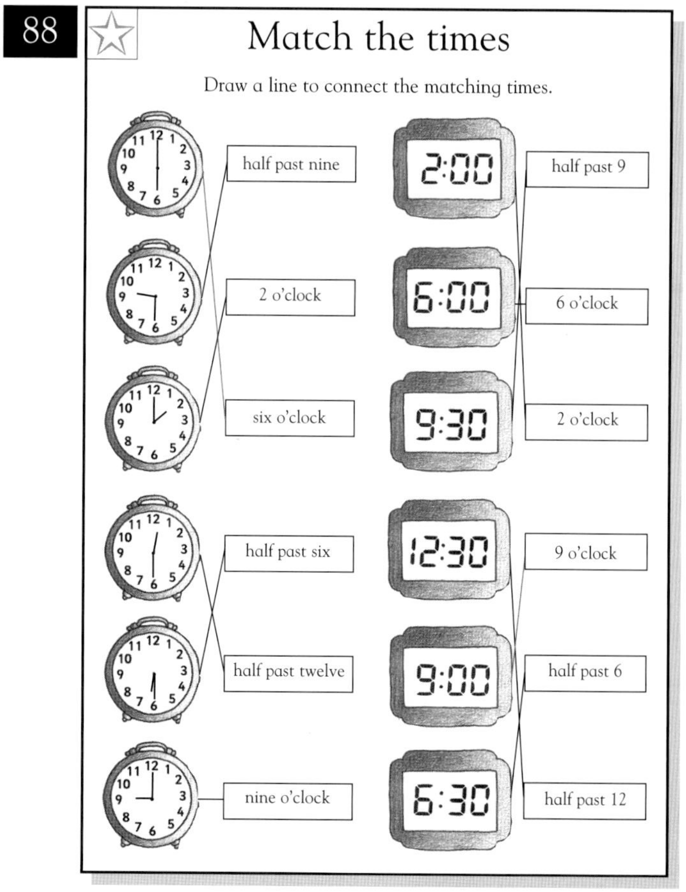
88

Match the times

Draw a line to connect the matching times.

half past nine | 2:00 | half past 9

2 o'clock | 6:00 | 6 o'clock

six o'clock | 9:30 | 2 o'clock

half past six | 12:30 | 9 o'clock

half past twelve | 9:00 | half past 6

nine o'clock | 6:30 | half past 12

Ask children to talk about digital times, as compared with times shown on analog clock faces. Ask them which they find easier to read.

89

These numbers are all facts that have to be learned rather than developed. Children can learn the rhyme and then have fun answering questions about the number of days in the month in which there is a certain holiday.

90

Make sure children understand that two shapes can match each other exactly even if they are not oriented in the same way. Make sure they understand the difference between shapes that have straight edges and shapes that are curved.

91

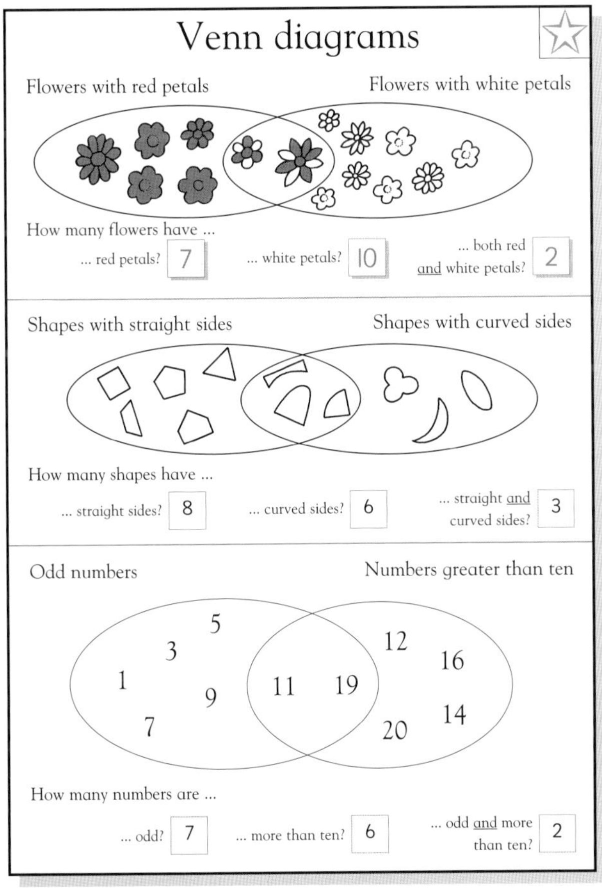

Make sure children understand that the items in the part of the diagram where the two ovals intersect are a part of both sets of items. They must be included when counting either of the main sets.

92

Children might need help in grasping the idea of same shape, different size. Remind children to eliminate obviously incorrect choices first.

93 2-dimensional shapes

Add the costs to find the cost of each picture.

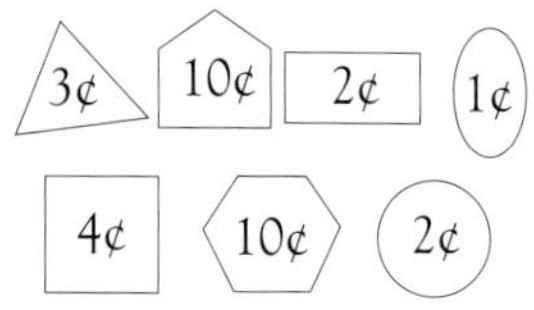

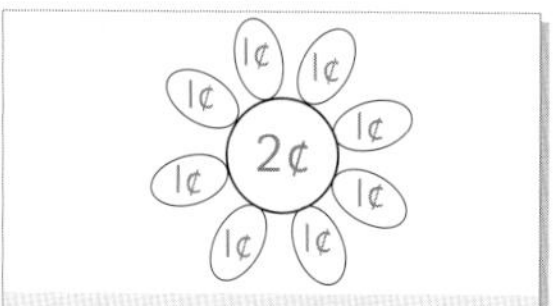

2¢ + 1¢ + 1¢ + 1¢ + 1¢ + 1¢ + 1¢ + 1¢ + 1¢ = 10¢

House

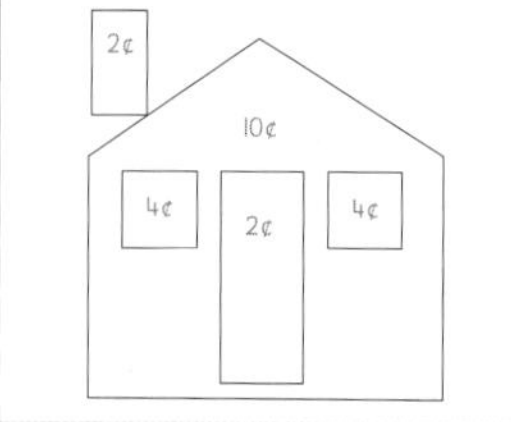

10¢ + 2¢ + 4¢ + 2¢ + 4¢ = 22¢

Bee and honeycomb

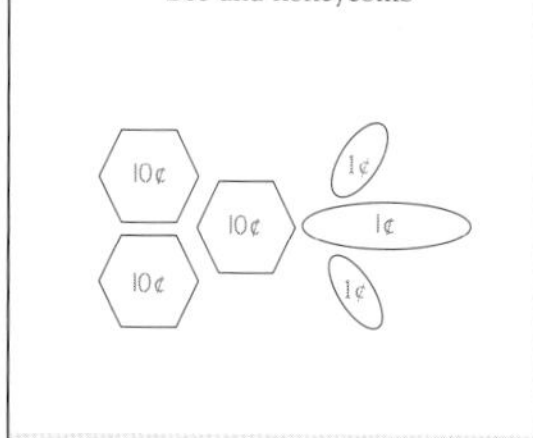

10¢ + 10¢ + 10¢ + 1¢ + 1¢ + 1¢= 33¢

Teddy bear

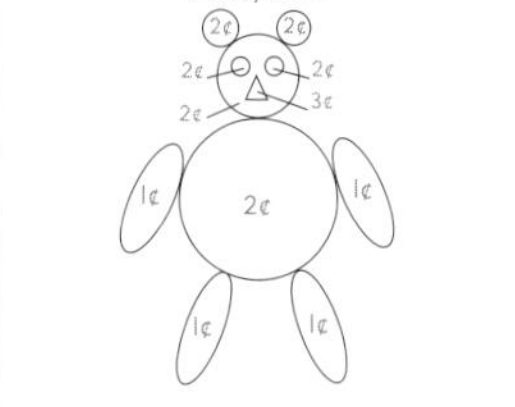

2¢ + 2¢ + 2¢ + 2¢ + 2¢ + 3¢ + 1¢ + 1¢ + 1¢ + 1¢ + 2¢ = 19¢

Crown

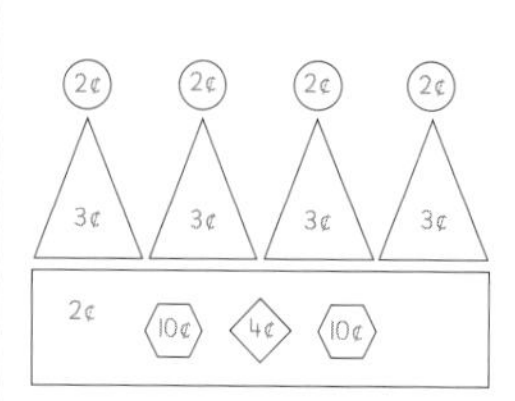

2¢ + 2¢ + 2¢ + 2¢ + 3¢ + 3¢ + 3¢ + 3¢ + 2¢ + 10¢ + 4¢ + 10¢ = 46¢

Encourage children to find their own ways of making the addition simpler. If children find adding difficult, help them to use counters to count out the individual amounts and then find the total.

94 3-dimensional shapes

Label the 3-D shapes.
(cone, cylinder, pyramid, cube, sphere, rectangular prism)

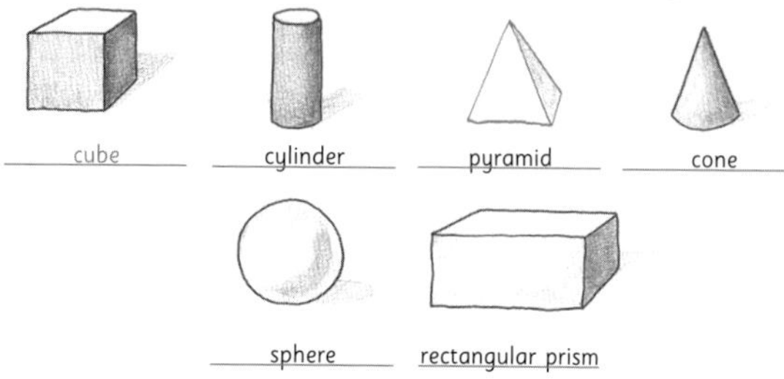

How many of each 3-D shape?

cube 3 rectangular prism 3 cone 4 cylinder 4

pyramid 2 sphere 2

Have children describe the differences between a cube and a prism or between a cone and a cylinder. Children should begin to use appropriate mathematical language such as *curved*, *straight*, *corners*, *sides*, and so on.

95 Read, write, and draw

Write the numbers and draw the pictures.

16 sixteen 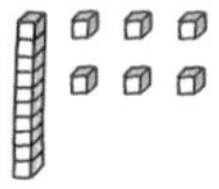

19 nineteen 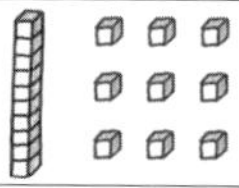

10 ten 

12 twelve 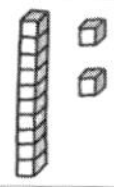

21 twenty-one 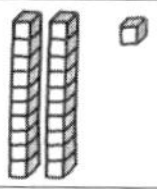

7 seven 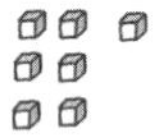

50 fifty 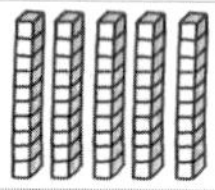

Children should use their knowledge of place value for this page. For example, in 16, the 1 means one ten, and the 6 means six ones.

96 Counting

Count on forward or backward by 10s.
Write the missing numbers.

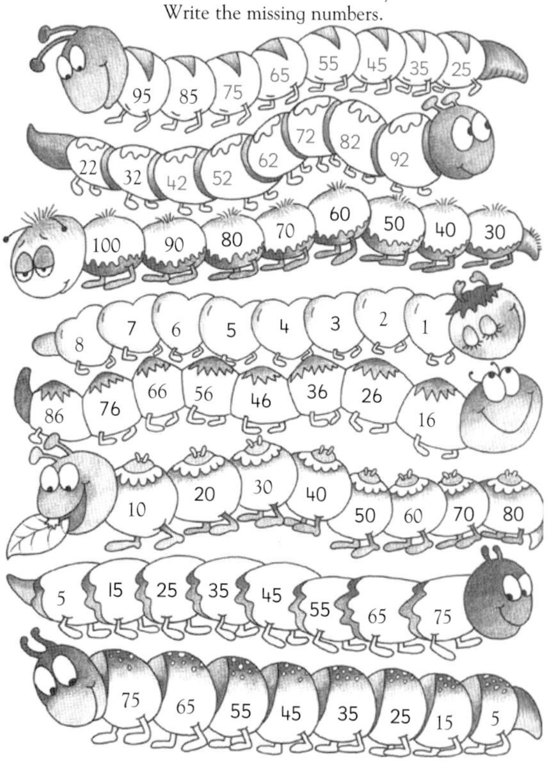

Children should determine whether the numbers are increasing or decreasing. They can then decide whether to count on or to count back. Children should see that the ones digits remain unchanged and the tens digits increase or decrease.

Bar graphs

Fruit

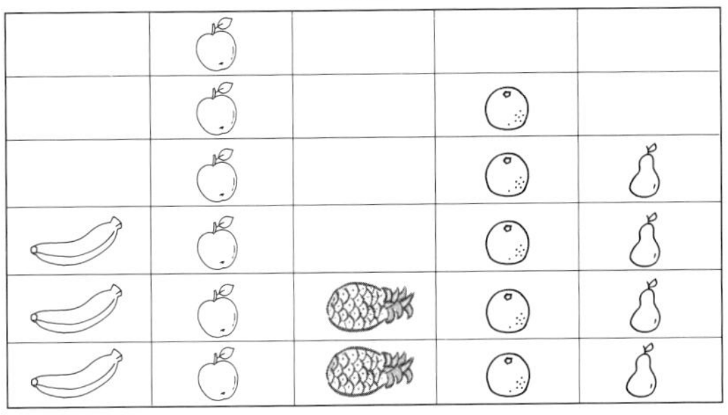

How many pears are there? 4 How many bananas are there? 3

The graph shows 6 apples . The graph shows 2 pineapples .

How many more oranges are there than bananas? 2

How many apples and pears are there altogether? 10

Ellen's marbles

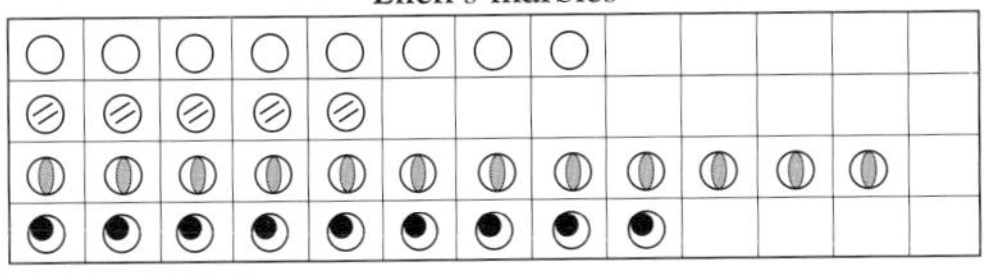

How many ⊘ does Ellen have? 5 How many ◍ does Ellen have? 12

How many fewer ● than ◍ does she have? 3

How many ○ and ⊘ does she have altogether? 13

Discuss with children what the bar graphs show, what the labels mean, and what the drawings or symbols mean. Guide children to compare the heights of the columns or the lengths of the rows to make quick comparisons of amounts.

Subtraction

If each child eats 1 slice, how many slices will be left? 5

If the children eat 6 slices, how many slices will be left? 2

If the children eat 8 slices, how many slices will be left? 0

If each child reads 1 book, how many books will be left? 8

How many books will be left if the children take 6 books altogether? 6

How many books will be left if the children take 9 books? 3

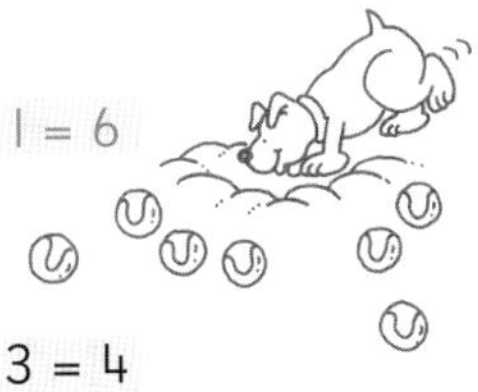

If the dog buries 1 ball, how many balls are left? 6

Write a subtraction sentence. 7 – 1 = 6

If the dog buries 3 balls, how many balls are left? 4

Write a subtraction sentence. 7 – 3 = 4

Guide children to see that when they take something away from a set of things or a whole, something is left behind. What is left behind is less than or smaller than what was there originally. This procedure is called subtraction.

2s, 5s, and 10s

Count by 2s, 5s and 10s to help you connect the dots.

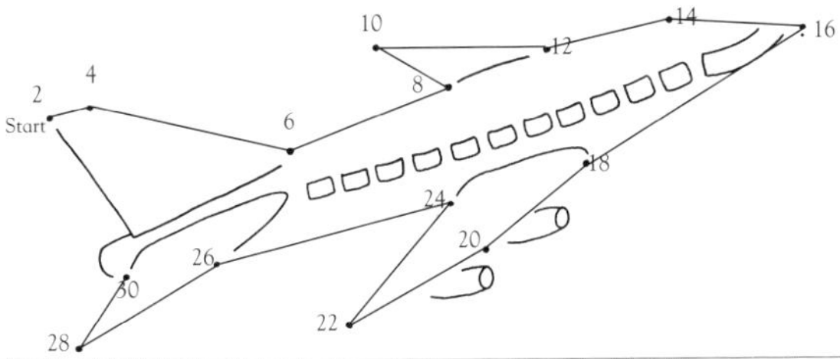

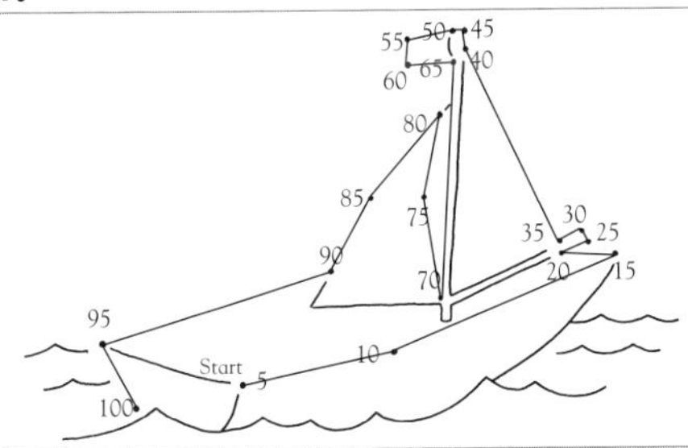

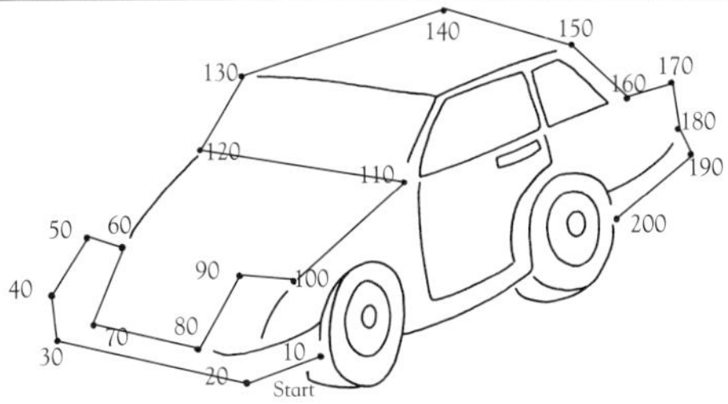

Make sure that children understand the patterns in the number sequences. Have them practise counting by 2s, 5s, and 10s before connecting the dots.

Comparing

Complete the boxes.

2 less	number	2 more
51	53	55

number	between	number
96	97 98	99

number	between	number
20	21 22 23	24

3 less	number	3 more
27	30	33

2 less	number	2 more
27	29	31

number	between	number
18	19 20 21	22

number	between	number
31	32 33	34

10 less	number	10 more
9	19	29

5 less	number	5 more
20	25	30

number	between	number
40	41, 42, 43, 44	45

number	between	number
39	40 41	42

5 less	number	5 more
10	15	20

Make sure children understand the meaning of *more*, *less*, and *between*. Have them give examples such as 3 more or 3 less than 10. Children should see that they must fill in the sequence of numbers that lie between two numbers.

101

Ordering

Find the totals.

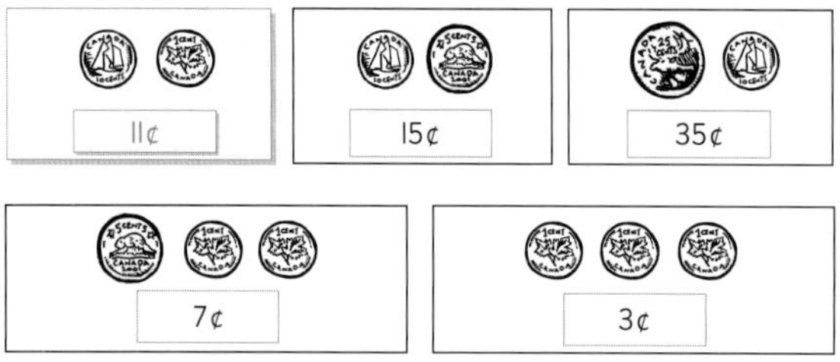

Write the totals in order, greatest first.

1st	2nd	3rd	4th	5th
35¢	15¢	11¢	7¢	3¢

Find the totals.

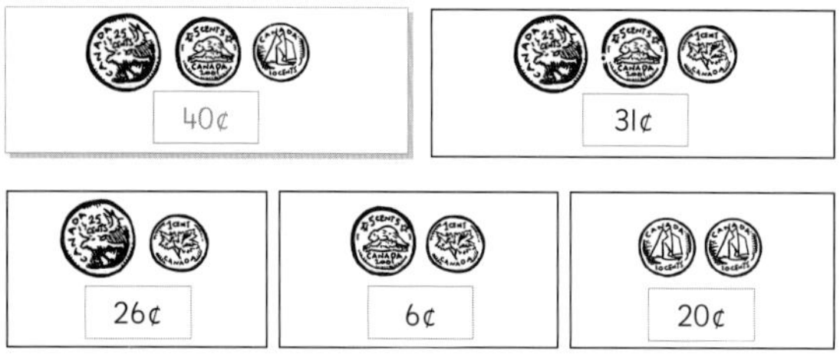

Write the totals in order, smallest first.

1st	2nd	3rd	4th	5th
6¢	20¢	26¢	31¢	40¢

Have children practice writing amounts of money, using the symbol for cents (¢). Discuss strategies for adding money, such as adding the coins of greater value first.

102

Subtraction

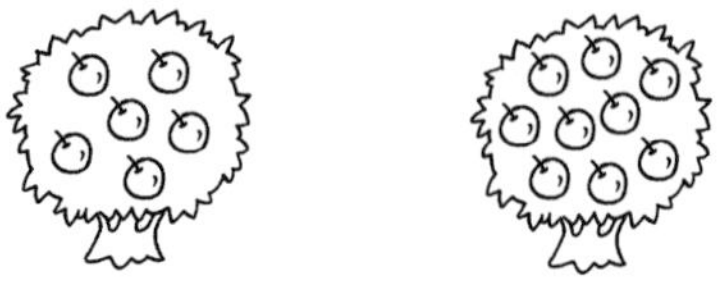

How many fewer apples are on the left tree than on the right tree? 3

Write the subtraction sentence. 9 – 6 = 3

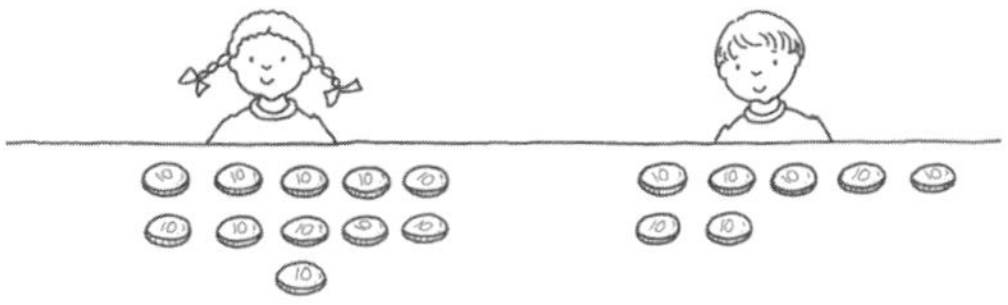

How many more dimes does Tasha have than Juan? 4

What is the subtraction sentence? 11 – 7 = 4

How many fewer bricks are in the left stack than in the right stack? 5

What is the subtraction sentence? 15 – 10 = 5

Guide children to understand that they can use subtraction to compare quantities. By subtracting, children can find out how much more or how much less or how many more or how many fewer one quantity is than another.

103

Matching fractions

Colour all the matching squares.

Use yellow for halves.
Use orange for thirds.
Use green for fourths.

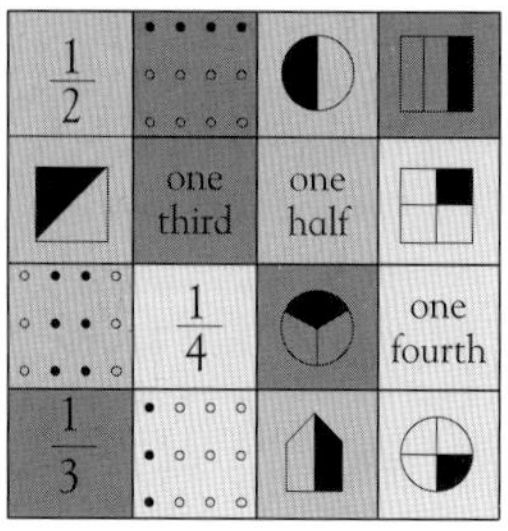

Label each part.

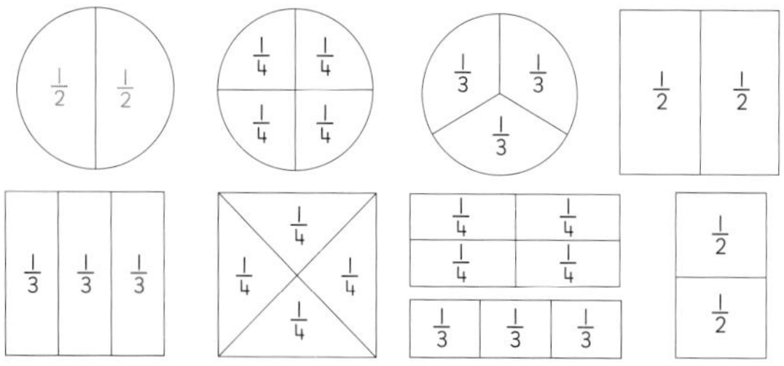

How many thirds in a whole? 3

How many fourths in a whole? 4

How many halves in a whole? 2

How many fourths in a half? 2

Children can look back at the drawings they labeled for help in answering the questions in the last section on the page.

104

Money

You have only 3 coins in each purse. Draw the 3 coins that make the exact amount needed. You may use each coin more than once.

Limiting the number of coins causes children to think more carefully about which coins they should use. Children may need help realizing that it would help to begin with the largest coin.

105

Fact families

Use the 3 numbers to write 4 different facts.

6 + 7 = 13	7 + 6 = 13	13 – 7 = 6	13 – 6 = 7
16 + 4 = 20	4 + 16 = 20	20 – 4 = 16	20 – 16 = 4
6 + 5 = 11	5 + 6 = 11	11 – 5 = 6	11 – 6 = 5
7 + 8 = 15	8 + 7 = 15	15 – 7 = 8	15 – 8 = 7
8 + 12 = 20	12 + 8 = 20	20 – 8 = 12	20 – 12 = 8
10 + 8 = 18	8 + 10 = 18	18 – 10 = 8	18 – 8 = 10
8 + 9 = 17	9 + 8 = 17	17 – 9 = 8	17 – 8 = 9
9 + 7 = 16	7 + 9 = 16	16 – 9 = 7	16 – 7 = 9
14 + 6 = 20	6 + 14 = 20	20 – 14 = 6	20 – 6 = 14
11 + 8 = 19	8 + 11 = 19	19 – 11 = 8	19 – 8 = 11

Help children to understand that if they know one addition fact, they can form three other facts: one more addition fact and two subtraction facts. For example, 6 + 7 = 13 allows the formation of 7 + 6 = 13, 13 – 6 = 7, and 13 – 7 = 6.

106

Adding money

Add the money. Write the totals in the right squares.

+	2¢	5¢	8¢	6¢
3¢	5¢	8¢	11¢	9¢
11¢	13¢	16¢	19¢	17¢
29¢	31¢	34¢	37¢	35¢
32¢	34¢	37¢	40¢	38¢

+	2¢	4¢	6¢	9¢	3¢
17¢	19¢	21¢	23¢	26¢	20¢
20¢	22¢	24¢	26¢	29¢	23¢
33¢	35¢	37¢	39¢	42¢	36¢
41¢	43¢	45¢	47¢	50¢	44¢

Have children practice writing amounts of money, using the symbol for cents (¢). Discuss strategies for adding money, such as adding the coins of greater value first.

107

Using doubles

Use the doubles to find the answers.

6 + 6 = 12	10 + 10 = 20
6 + 7 6 + 6 + 1 = 13	10 + 11 10 + 10 + 1 = 21
6 + 5 6 + 6 – 1 = 11	10 + 9 10 + 10 – 1 = 19

Use doubles to find the answers.

4 + 4 = 8   4 + 5 = 4 + 4 + 1 = 9

4 + 3 = 4 + 4 – 1 = 7

7 + 7 = 14   7 + 8 = 7 + 7 + 1 = 15

7 + 6 = 7 + 7 – 1 = 13

8 + 8 = 16   8 + 9 = 8 + 8 + 1 = 17

8 + 7 = 8 + 8 – 1 = 15

Double your doubles.

1 double it 2 double it 4   4 double it 8 double it 16

2 double it 4 double it 8   5 double it 10 double it 20

3 double it 6 double it 12   6 double it 12 double it 24

Guide children to see that doubles, doubles plus 1, and doubles minus 1 can be useful strategies for solving addition problems.

108

Adding up

Add the numbers on the sails. Write the totals on the boats.

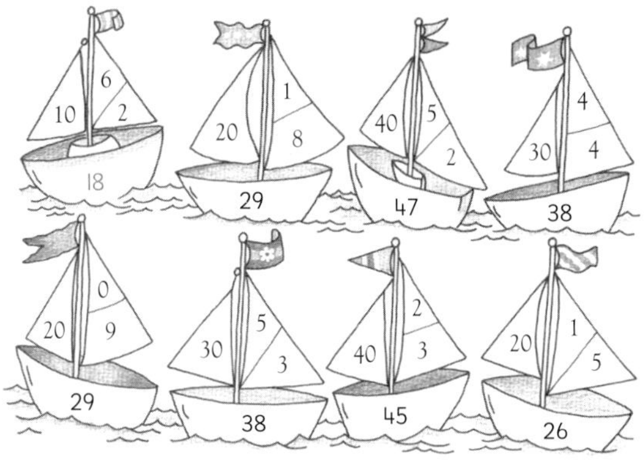

Add the numbers. Write the totals.

3 + 4 + 10 = 17   9 + 0 + 20 = 29   2 + 40 + 3 = 45

5 + 40 + 2 = 47   20 + 7 + 2 = 29   4 + 5 + 20 = 29

30 + 4 + 3 = 37   1 + 30 + 7 = 38   40 + 8 + 1 = 49

30	10	20	40
1	2	2	5
+ 7	+ 5	+ 4	+ 0
38	17	26	45

Help children to identify ways to make the addition problems simpler. Children can use what they know about addition facts and about adding 10s.

109

Count by 2s

Draw the pictures. Count by 2s. Write the totals.

Sasha has 4 hutches. There are 2 rabbits in each hutch.

8 rabbits

Joel has 3 boxes. There are 2 pencils in each box.

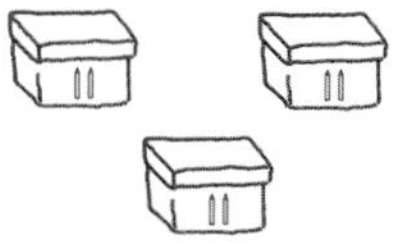

6 pencils

Mrs. Reaves has 6 flower pots. There are 2 flowers in each pot.

12 flowers

Mr. Hastings has 5 fish. Each fish has 2 eyes.

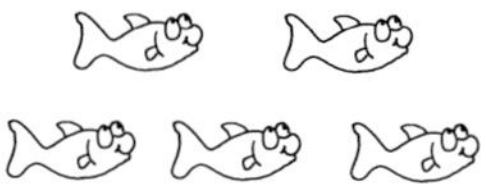

10 eyes

Draw the pictures, then write the answers.

There are 6 birds. There are 2 birds in each tree. How many trees are there?

3 trees

There are 8 tarts. There are 2 tarts on each plate. How many plates are there?

4 plates

Children should by now be comfortable with this counting sequence. For the last two exercises, help them to find the number of groups of 2 that make up the greater number.

110

Addition

Add to find each sum.

2 + 13 = 15	4 + 10 = 14	18 + 11 = 29

Add to find each sum.

1 + 3 = 4	6 + 2 = 8	3 + 1 = 4	3 + 4 = 7
5 + 1 = 6	2 + 2 = 4	3 + 5 = 8	1 + 1 = 2
7 + 2 = 9	1 + 5 = 6	10 + 9 = 19	6 + 11 = 17
13 + 2 = 15	16 + 2 = 18	10 + 4 = 14	14 + 5 = 19
11 + 3 = 14	12 + 1 = 13	18 + 11 = 29	16 + 20 = 36

This page presents straightforward addition of two-digit numbers, with no regrouping. Make sure that children add in the correct order, that is, they should add the ones first and then add the tens.

111

Addition

Add to find each sum.

5 + 1 = 6	14 + 24 = 38	50 + 10 = 60

Add to find each sum.

2 + 2 = 4	5 + 1 = 6	3 + 4 = 7	1 + 3 = 4
6 + 2 = 8	1 + 1 = 2	10 + 10 = 20	50 + 40 = 90
16 + 33 = 49	29 + 20 = 49	61 + 35 = 96	74 + 12 = 86

Michael has 21 fish. His dad gives him 7 more fish. How many fish does Michael have?

28

21 + 7 = 28

Sonia read 13 books one month. She read 6 books the next month. How many books did she read in all?

19

13 + 6 = 19

This page also presents straightforward addition of some two-digit numbers, with no regrouping. Once again, make sure that children add the ones first and then the tens.

112

Addition and subtraction

Write the missing numbers.

? + 8 = 12	7 − ? = 1
4 + 8 = 12	7 − 6 = 1

Write the missing numbers.

15 − 5 = 10	3 + 3 = 6	8 − 6 = 2
9 + 2 = 11	8 − 8 = 0	9 + 5 = 14
7 + 3 = 10	6 − 4 = 2	17 − 10 = 7
5 − 4 = 1	2 + 5 = 7	1 + 3 = 4
14 − 7 = 7	8 + 1 = 9	3 + 9 = 12
8 + 6 = 14	3 − 1 = 2	12 − 6 = 6
18 − 9 = 9	5 + 6 = 11	1 − 1 = 0
11 − 7 = 4	4 + 9 = 13	3 + 5 = 8
2 + 3 = 5	16 − 6 = 10	8 + 10 = 18
5 + 7 = 12	4 + 4 = 0	9 − 3 = 6

Children should use their knowledge of fact families to solve the problems on this page. If they need help, remind them that fact families are made up of two addition facts and two subtraction facts.

113

Real-life problems

Look at the picture. Answer the questions.

What time is it ? 4:30

Today is Friday. What day was it yesterday? Thursday

How many cupcakes can each person have? two

If half of the apples were eaten, how many would be left? three

If each person had 2 drinks, how many drinks would there be altogether? eight

How many more sandwiches are there than apples? four

If 13 candies were eaten, how many would be left? seven

Each package contains 2 presents. How many presents are there altogether? six

What shape are the sandwiches? triangular

Is there an odd or an even number of chairs? even

Children have to decide what each question is asking for and then find a way of arriving at each answer. For example, they recognize that the fifth question can be answered by counting by 2s.

114

Real-life problems

Complete the pictures, and then write the answers.

There were 12 biscuits. James ate 3. How many were left?

9

Share 9 marbles equally among 3 people. How many marbles will each have?

3

Susie has ten fish. She is given 11 more for her birthday. How many fish does she have altogether?

21

Joe had 5 boxes. He had 3 pencils in each box. How many pencils did he have altogether?

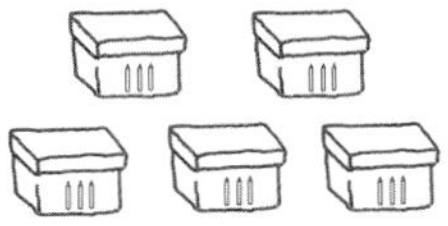

15

If you share 8 carrots equally among 4 rabbits, how many carrots will each have?

2

Mom had 16 cups, but she broke 9 of them. How many cups does she have left?

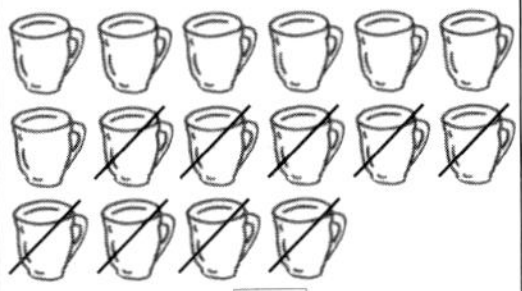

7

Children have to decide which operation to use and what kind of answer each question calls for. Call their attention to the words *altogether* and *left*. Point out that these words are clues whether to add or subtract.

115

Addition

Find each sum.

40 +30 70	80 +80 160	20 +50 70	20 +30 50
10 +10 20	40 +50 90	40 +40 80	50 +30 80
10 +80 90	50 +40 90	20 +10 30	30 +20 50
10 +70 80	20 +40 60	10 +40 50	10 +30 40

Find each sum.

70 + 20 = 90	80 + 10 = 90	10 + 40 = 50
60 + 10 = 70	30 + 30 = 60	50 + 10 = 60
20 + 70 = 90	70 + 10 = 80	10 + 20 = 30
20 + 60 = 80	40 + 40 = 80	10 + 80 = 90

Point out to children that even though they are adding two-digit numbers, they can write a zero in the ones place in each answer, because they are adding 10s.

116

Clocks and watches

Write the times.

4 o'clock

half past 10

9 o'clock

half past 5

11 o'clock

half past 2

half past 1

12 o'clock

half past 7

10 o'clock

half past 3

Encourage children to express times both as digital numbers and on analog clock faces.

117 Puzzles

Read the clues and solve the puzzle.

I am a number between 20 and 30. If you count by fives, you will say my name. Who am I? 25

Read the clues and solve each puzzle.

I am an even number. I am between 6 and 9. Who am I? 8

7 + 7 is less than I am. 7 + 9 is greater than I am. Who am I? 15

I am a number less than 10. If you add me to myself, you will find a number greater than 16. Who am I? 9

16 – 10 is less than I am. 16 – 8 is greater than I am. Who am I? 7

I am a number between 7 and 12. If you count by threes, you will say my name. Who am I? 9

I am an odd number. I am between 11 and 14. Who am I? 13

If you subtract me from 14, you will find a number greater than 11. I am an odd number. Who am I? 1

If you add me to 50, you will find a number less than 70. If you count by tens you will say my name. Who am I? 10

If you add me to 1, you will find an odd number. I am less than 2. Who am I? 0

Encourage children to use their knowledge of counting sequences, and addition and subtraction facts to solve the puzzles. If necessary, read the clues together.

118 Tables

Water animals

	Has 4 legs	Eats insects	Has a furry coat	Lays eggs
Frog	yes	yes	no	yes
Newt	yes	yes	no	yes
Otter	yes	no	yes	no

Use the table to answer the questions.

What does the frog eat? insects

Who lays eggs? frog, newt

Who has a furry coat? otter

Does the otter eat insects? no

Who has a furry coat and does not lay eggs? otter

School friends

	Age	Hobby	Pet	Favourite colour
Dean	7	Computers	Rat	Black
Joe	6	Reading	Rabbit	Purple
Taif	7	Judo	Cat	Orange
Maddie	8	Computers	Parrot	Green

Use the table to answer the questions.

Whose favourite colour is black? Dean's

Who is the oldest? Maddie

Who has judo for a hobby? Taif

What kind of pet does Joe have? rabbit

Who likes computers and has a parrot? Maddie

Who is seven and does not have a rat? Taif

Guide children to see that the first column in the table on top lists the animals and the next four columns describe them. Help them to see that the second table is the same but describes friends.

119 Venn diagrams

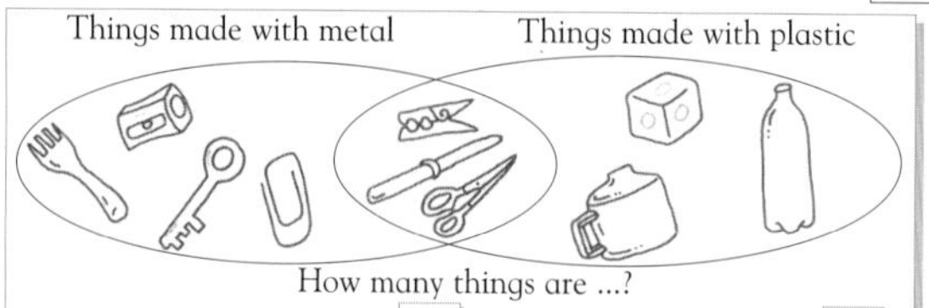

How many things are ...?

made with plastic? 6

made with metal? 7

made with metal and plastic? 3

not made with plastic? 4

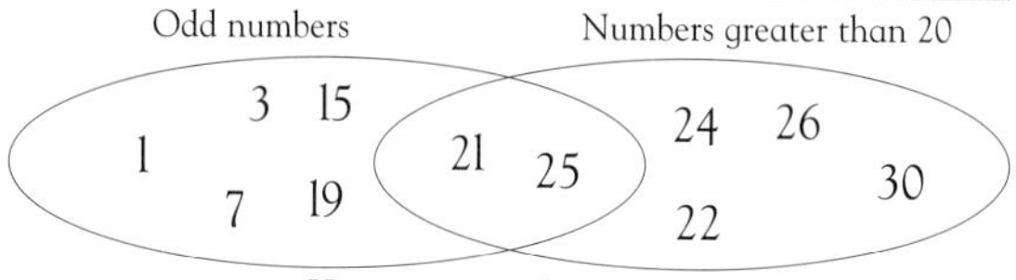

How many numbers are ...?

odd? 7

greater than 20? 6

odd and greater than 20? 2

not odd? 4

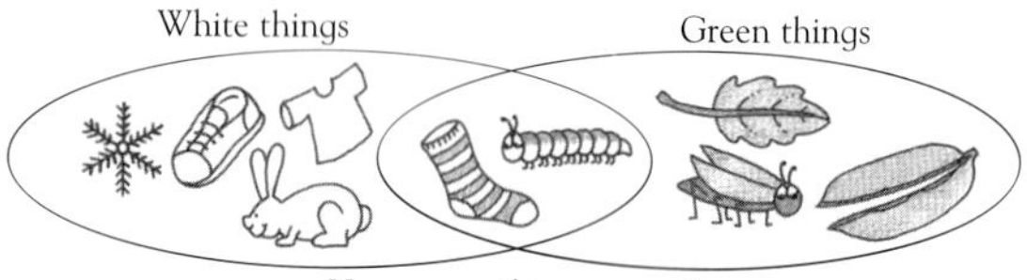

How many things are ...?

green? 5

white? 6

green and white? 2

not green? 4

Make sure children understand that the items in the part of the diagram where the two ovals intersect are a part of both sets of items. They must be included when counting either of the main sets.

120 Appropriate units of measure

Which unit would you use to measure the length of each item? Circle the answer.

	(centimetres) kilometres kilograms litres
	kilometres grams kilograms (metres)

Which unit would you use to measure the weight of each item? Circle the answer.

	centimetres kilometres kilograms (grams)
	kilometres (kilograms) litres grams

Which unit would you use to measure how much liquid each container holds? Circle the answer.

	tonnes centimetres (millilitres) kilograms
	kilometres centimetres grams (litres)

Discuss with children the relative magnitudes of various units of measure. Lead them to see that smaller units of measure should be used for smaller items, and larger units for larger items.

121

Symmetry

Draw a line of symmetry on each picture.

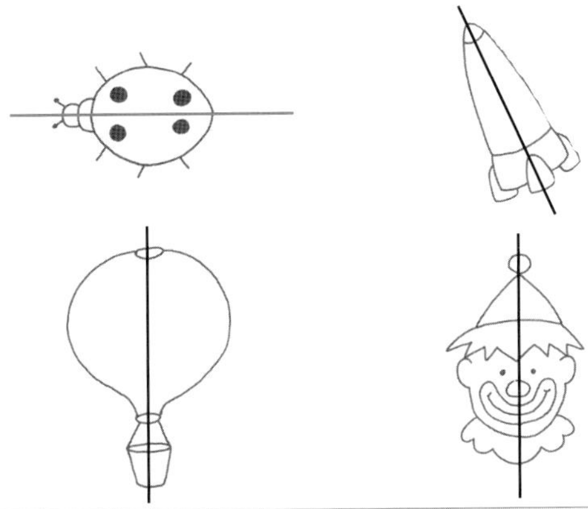

Draw lines of symmetry on these shapes.

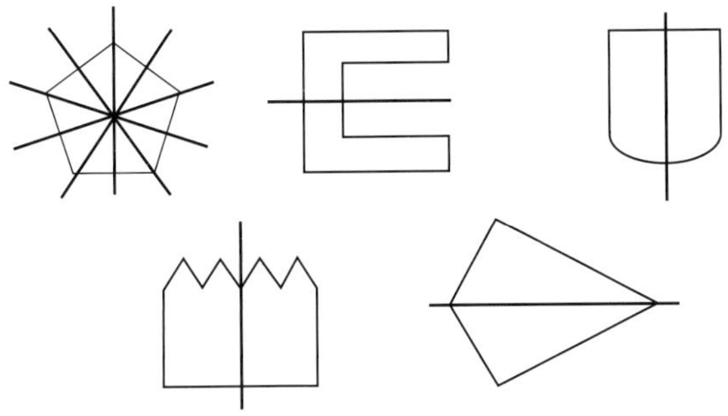

Explain to children that a line of symmetry separates something into two halves that are mirror images of each other. If children have difficulty, suggest that they look at the items from different angles.

122

2-dimensional shapes

Write the name of the shape. Count the corners and sides.

Name hexagon

side

corner

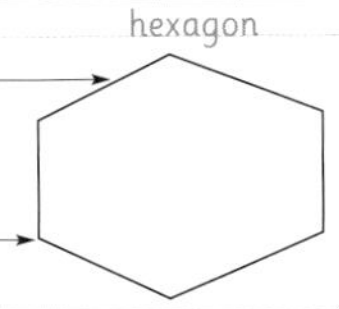

Sides 6

Corners 6

Name triangle

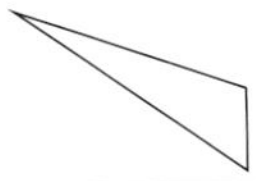

Sides 3

Corners 3

Name square

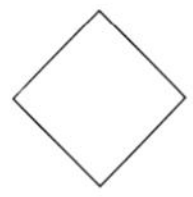

Sides 4

Corners 4

Name rectangle

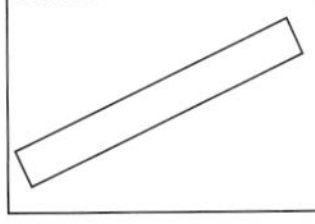

Sides 4

Corners 4

Name circle

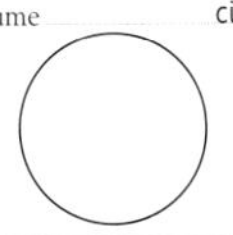

Sides 0

Corners 0

Name triangle

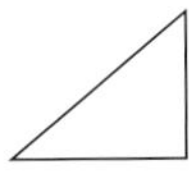

Sides 3

Corners 3

Name pentagon

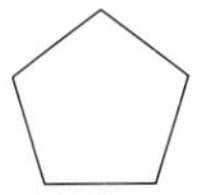

Sides 5

Corners 5

Name hexagon

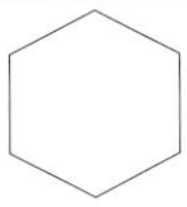

Sides 6

Corners 6

Name rectangle

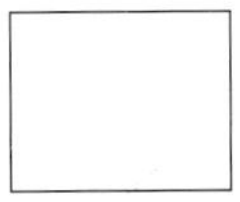

Sides 4

Corners 4

The second figure, although partially rotated, is still a square, not a diamond. Children should be able to identify the shapes by counting the number of sides and corners of each shape.

123

Equal value

Circle the coins that add up to the amount shown.

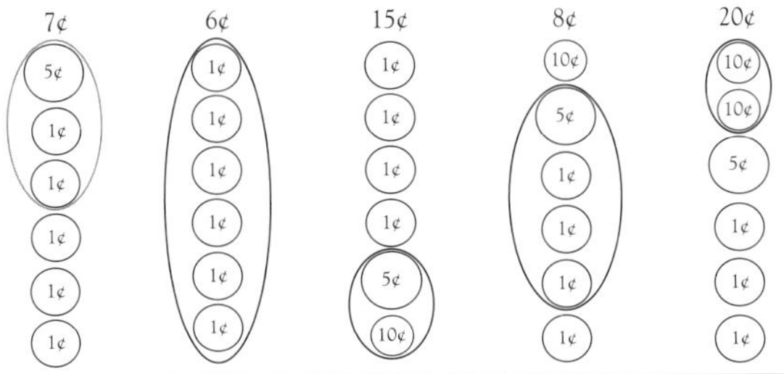

Write the amounts. Tell if they are equal.

10¢ 5¢	15¢	equal
5¢ 5¢ 5¢	15¢	
10¢ 1¢ 1¢	12¢	equal
5¢ 5¢ 1¢ 1¢	12¢	
1¢ 1¢ 1¢ 1¢ 1¢ 1¢	6¢	not equal
5¢ 1¢ 1¢	7¢	
5¢ 5¢	10¢	not equal
5¢ 1¢ 1¢ 1¢ 1¢	9¢	
1¢ 5¢ 10¢	16¢	equal
5¢ 5¢ 5¢ 1¢	16¢	

Encourage children to begin with the largest coin possible when they are deciding which coins to use to make the desired amount.

124

Shapes and places

Look at the shapes and answer the questions.

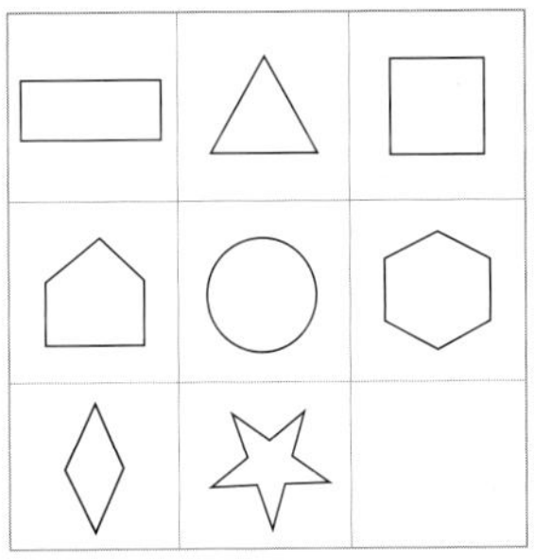

circle
hexagon
diamond
pentagon
rectangle
square
star
triangle

Which shape is ...

underneath the circle? star

to the **left** of the triangle? rectangle

above the hexagon? square

below the pentagon? diamond

between the rectangle and the diamond? pentagon

diagonally above the empty space? circle

beside the diamond? star

on top of the diamond? pentagon

between the triangle and the star? circle

on the **right-hand end** of the top row? square

in the **centre** of the grid? circle

in the **top left-hand corner**? rectangle

This page gives children practice with words that specify position or location. Help them with the questions, if necessary.

125 Numbers

Which numbers are the snakes hiding?

Ask children to explain how they can tell which numbers are hidden. Encourage them to use their knowledge of counting sequences, 5s and 10s and to look at both columns and rows.

126 Counting by 1s and 10s

Finish each row.

Count by 1s.	24	25	26	27	28	29
Count by 10s.	31	41	51	61	71	81

Finish each row. Count by 1s.

17	18	19	20	21	22	23	24
36	37	38	39	40	41	42	43
69	70	71	72	73	74	75	76
45	46	47	48	49	50	51	52
85	86	87	88	89	90	91	92

Finish each row. Count by 10s.

10	20	30	40	50	60	70	80
12	22	32	42	52	62	72	82
15	25	35	45	55	65	75	85
16	26	36	46	56	66	76	86
17	27	37	47	57	67	77	87
19	29	39	49	59	69	79	89

Finish each row. Count by 1s and 10s.

8	9	10	11	12	13	14	15
18	28	38	48	58	68	78	88
4	5	6	7	8	9	10	11
14	24	34	44	54	64	74	84
0	1	2	3	4	5	6	7

Children should realize that they need only increase the digit in the appropriate place value by 1. If they have difficulty with numbers such as 20 or 45, show them that the appropriate digit increases by 1, just as in counting by 1s.

127 Counting by 2s

Count by 2s.	12	14	16	18	20	22
Count by 2s.	31	33	35	37	39	41

Finish each row. Count by 2s.

17	19	21	23	25	27	29	31
36	38	40	42	44	46	48	50
72	74	76	78	80	82	84	86
43	45	47	49	51	53	55	57
14	16	18	19	21	22	23	25
39	41	43	45	47	49	51	53

Finish each row. Count by 2s.

20	22	24	26	28	30	32	34
75	77	79	81	83	85	86	89
44	46	48	50	52	54	56	58
69	71	73	75	77	79	81	83
31	33	35	37	39	41	43	45
88	90	92	94	96	98	100	102

Finish each row. Count by 2s.

20	22	24	26	28	30	32	34
47	49	51	53	55	57	59	61
77	79	81	83	85	87	89	91
46	48	50	52	54	56	58	60
87	89	91	93	95	97	99	101
46	48	50	52	54	56	58	60

Some children will need help crossing a tens or hundreds "border." Show them counting by 2s by counting by 1 two times.

128 Odd and even

Numbers ending in	0	2	4	6	8	are called even numbers.
Numbers ending in	1	3	5	7	9	are called odd numbers.

Circle the numbers that are even.

(10) 25 13 (34) 21 (22) (18) 9 (6) 17

Circle the numbers that are odd.

50 (49) 48 16 (21) 32 (23) (35) 44 (37)

Write the odd numbers between 30 and 50.

31 33 35 37 39 41 43 45 47 49

Write the even numbers between 21 and 41.

22 24 26 28 30 32 34 36 38 40

Children should realize that even numbers are all multiples of 2 and that all even numbers can be divided by 2 and give a whole-number quotient. Odd numbers cannot be divided by 2. If they are unsure, let them use counters and try to share them equally.

129

More and less

Which number is 1 more than 49? 50

Which number is 10 less than 64? 54

Write the number that is 1 more than each of these.

35	36	78	79	69	70	53	54	9	10	54	55
41	42	24	25	67	68	40	41	36	37	73	74

Write the number that is 1 less than each of these.

52	51	18	17	20	19	76	75	37	36	50	49
40	39	54	53	23	22	100	99	31	30	83	82

Write the number that is 10 more than each of these.

46	56	21	31	86	96	53	63	16	26
18	28	29	39	39	49	38	48	90	100
60	70	81	91	59	69	23	33	80	90

Write the number that is 10 less than each of these.

56	46	75	65	86	76	18	8	23	13
68	58	45	35	50	40	40	30	80	70
60	50	90	80	60	50	70	60	10	0

Write the number that is 10 more than each of these.

65	75	76	86
90	100	60	70

Write the number that is 10 less than each of these.

50	40	10	0
80	70	75	65

Children may be uncertain when addition or subtraction takes them over a tens "border," for example, where the child is asked to write 10 more than 90.

130

Fact families

Finish the fact family for each group of numbers.

9, 5, 4

5 + 4 = 9
4 + 5 = 9
9 − 4 = 5
9 − 5 = 4

Finish the fact family for each group of numbers.

7, 4, 3	8, 3, 5	7, 6, 1	6, 2, 4
4 + 3 = 7	3 + 5 = 8	6 + 1 = 7	2 + 4 = 6
3 + 4 = 7	5 + 3 = 8	1 + 6 = 7	4 + 2 = 6
7 − 3 = 4	8 − 5 = 3	7 − 1 = 6	6 − 4 = 2
7 − 4 = 3	8 − 3 = 5	7 − 6 = 1	6 − 2 = 4

9, 2, 7	3, 2, 5	3, 1, 4	8, 10, 2
2 + 7 = 9	3 + 2 = 5	3 + 1 = 4	2 + 8 = 10
7 + 2 = 9	2 + 3 = 5	1 + 3 = 4	8 + 2 = 10
9 − 2 = 7	5 − 2 = 3	4 − 1 = 3	10 − 2 = 8
9 − 7 = 2	5 − 3 = 2	4 − 3 = 1	10 − 8 = 2

10, 5	4, 8	3, 6	4, 2
5 + 5 = 10	4 + 4 = 8	3 + 3 = 6	2 + 2 = 4
10 − 5 = 5	8 − 4 = 4	6 − 3 = 3	4 − 2 = 2

Write the fact family for each group of numbers.

3, 10, 7	9, 3, 6	8, 6, 2	7, 5, 2
7 + 3 = 10	3 + 6 = 9	6 + 2 = 8	5 + 2 = 7
3 + 7 = 10	6 + 3 = 9	2 + 6 = 8	2 + 5 = 7
10 − 3 = 7	9 − 3 = 6	8 − 2 = 6	7 − 2 = 5
10 − 7 = 3	9 − 6 = 3	8 − 6 = 2	7 − 5 = 2

Children should understand that subtraction "undoes" addition. You may want to use counters to show the addition fact families.

131

Fractions

Colour one-third ($\frac{1}{3}$) of each shape.

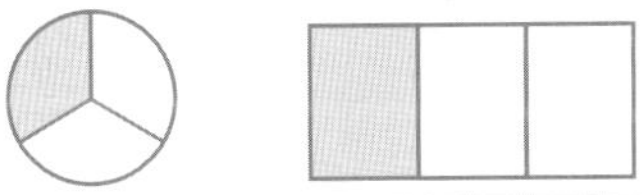

Colour one-half ($\frac{1}{2}$) of each shape.

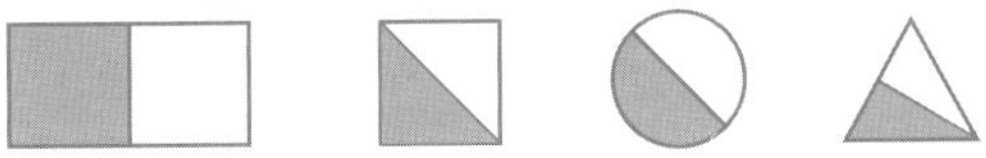

Colour one-fourth ($\frac{1}{4}$) of each shape.

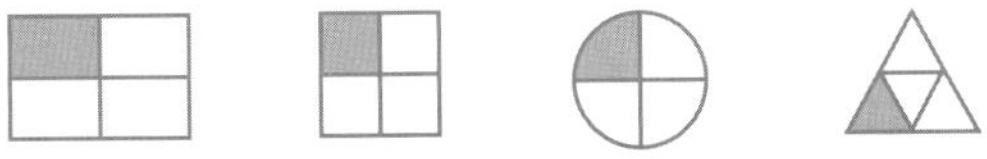

Colour one-third ($\frac{1}{3}$) of each shape.

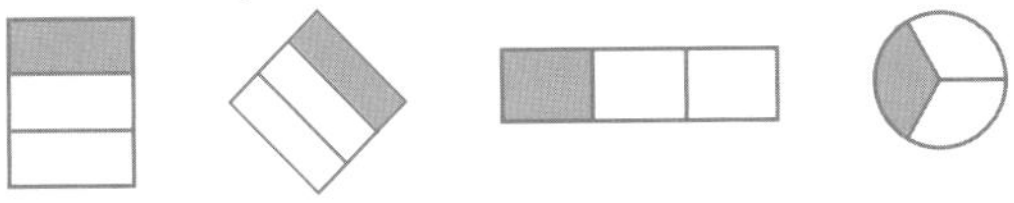

Colour one-eighth ($\frac{1}{8}$) of each shape.

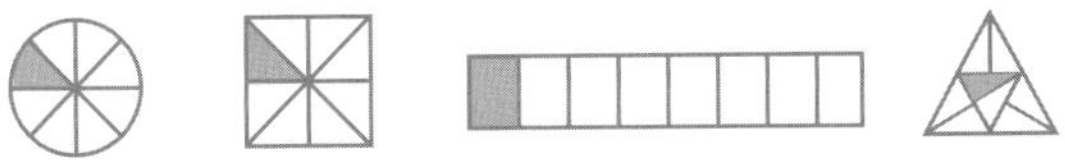

Colour one-tenth ($\frac{1}{10}$) of each shape.

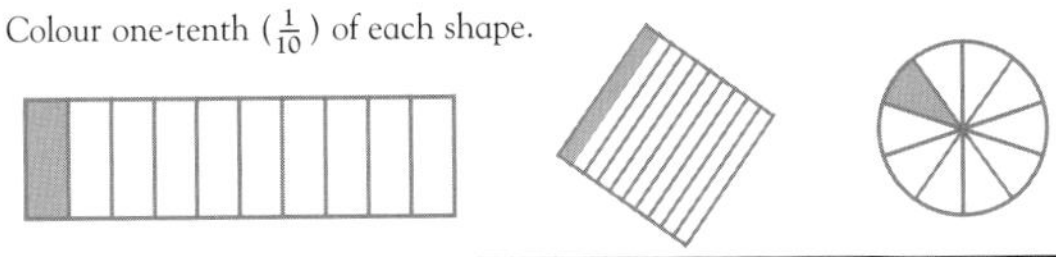

Sections other than those shown above may be coloured, but children must only colour one section in each shape. It is important for them to realize that the bottom number represents how many parts the whole has been divided into.

132

Adding

Write the answers between the lines.

13 + 16 = 29 | 11 + 5 = 16 | 14 + 5 = 19

Write the answers between the lines.

4 + 9 = 13	3 + 6 = 9	1 + 7 = 8	4 + 5 = 9
3 + 7 = 10	2 + 5 = 7	4 + 7 = 11	8 + 8 = 16
6 + 10 = 16	7 + 11 = 18	13 + 12 = 25	31 + 9 = 40

Write the answers between the lines.

2 + 2 + 2 = 8	3 + 3 + 3 = 9	2 + 2 + 6 = 10	4 + 4 + 4 = 12
12¢ + 6¢ + 10¢ = 28¢	12¢ + 7¢ + 10¢ = 29¢	8¢ + 1¢ + 6¢ = 15¢	3¢ + 9¢ + 6¢ = 18¢
20¢ + 7¢ + 10¢ = 37¢	15¢ + 10¢ + 2¢ = 27¢	8¢ + 10¢ + 4¢ = 22¢	10¢ + 8¢ + 10¢ = 28¢

For a few of these exercises, make sure that children do not neglect to regroup. For the final two rows of the second section, children should add all of the ones column first.

133

Estimating length

Circle the longest string.

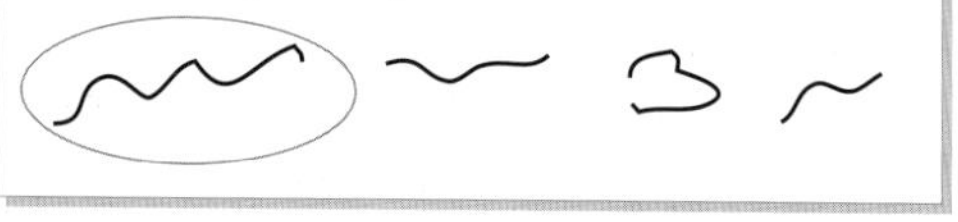

Circle the shortest string.

Circle the longest string.

Look at the ruler. Circle the closest measure.

1 centimetres   2 centimetres   (4 centimetres)   8 centimetres

2 centimetres   4 centimetres   (11 centimetres)   30 centimetres

5 centimetres   10 centimetres   15 centimetres   (20 centimetres)

Children should be able to compare the lengths by sight. For the last section of the page, allow them to use a benchmark (such as the length of one joint of a finger) to estimate length.

134

Subtracting

Write the answers between the lines.

28	${}^{2}3{}^{11}1$	${}^{3}4{}^{10}0$
− 16	− 14	− 17
12	17	23

Write the answers between the lines.

7	8	9	9
− 4	− 5	− 7	− 8
3	3	2	1
8	9	3	7
− 4	− 6	− 0	− 7
4	3	3	0
8	7	9	36
− 8	− 6	− 4	− 2
0	1	5	34
28¢	46¢	39¢	48¢
− 16¢	− 35¢	− 26¢	− 37¢
12¢	12¢	13¢	11¢
56¢	39¢	50¢	48¢
− 35¢	− 28¢	− 47¢	− 38¢
21¢	11¢	3¢	10¢
40¢	50¢	41¢	44¢
− 8¢	− 26¢	− 14¢	− 36¢
32¢	24¢	27¢	8¢

In some of these exercises, children may incorrectly subtract the larger digit from the smaller one, when they should be subtracting the smaller digit from the larger one. In such cases, point out that children should regroup.

135

Simple tally charts and bar graphs

Look at the tally chart and then answer the question.

blue	𝍸 𝍸 𝍸 III
red	𝍸 II

How many votes did blue receive? 18

Look at the tally chart and then answer the questions.

Favourite ice cream flavours

vanilla	𝍸 𝍸 I
chocolate	𝍸 𝍸 𝍸 𝍸 IIII
strawberry	𝍸 𝍸 𝍸 III

Which flavour had the most votes? chocolate

Which flavour had 11 votes? vanilla

What was the difference in votes between the most popular flavour and strawberry? 6

Look at the bar graph and then answer the questions.

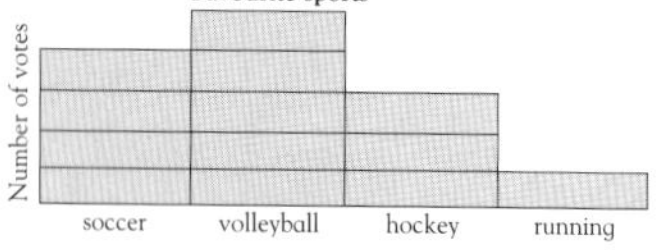

Which sport did four children vote for? soccer

How many votes did volleyball receive? 5

Which was the least popular sport? running

How many children voted altogether? 13

How many more voted for soccer than for hockey? 1

Children usually accept the concept of tally marks very quickly. They can count on by 5s for completed tallies.

136

Addition properties

Circle the number that makes the sentence true.

___ + 7 = 7   1 (0) 14

43 + 21 = 21 + ___   22 64 (43)

Circle the number that makes the sentence true.

___ + 3 = 3   (0) 3 6

15 + ___ = 15   30 (0) 5

___ + 23 = 23 + 16   (16) 23 46

25 + 41 = 41 + ___   16 66 (25)

___ + 45 = 45   45 (0) 1

50 + 0 = 0 + ___   (50) 0 500

Complete the number sentences.

0 + 27 = 27	40 + 0 = 40	13 + 28 = 28 + 13
25 + 3 = 3 + 25	47 + 0 = 47	16 + 43 = 43 + 16
2 + 28 = 28 + 2	0 + 12 = 12	28 + 20 = 20 + 28
35 + 0 = 35	10 + 0 = 10	20 + 8 = 8 + 20
47 + 0 = 47	8 + 0 = 8	34 + 11 = 11 + 34

This page tests children's understanding of the zero property and the commutative property of addition. Make sure that they understand that the order of addends does not affect the answer.

137

Equations

Circle the correct number sentence.

7 + 3 = 10 (4 + 3 = 7) 4 – 3 = 1 | 2 + 4 = 6 2 + 3 = 5 (5 – 3 = 2)

Circle the correct addition sentence.

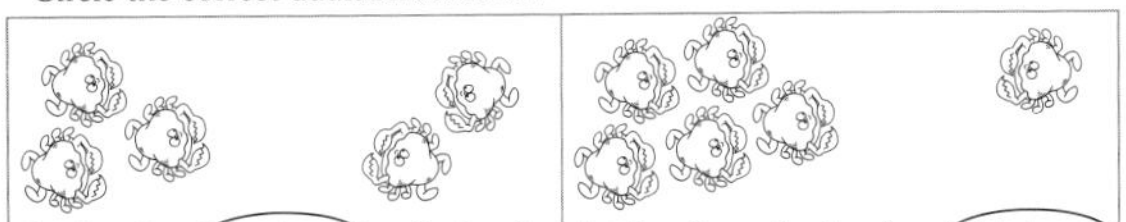

5 + 2 = 7 (3 + 2 = 5) 3 – 2 = 1 | 4 + 2 = 6 5 – 1 = 4 (5 + 1 = 6)

Circle the correct subtraction sentence.

3 + 3 = 6 3 – 3 = 0 (6 – 3 = 3) | (6 – 2 = 4) 6 + 2 = 8 4 – 2 = 2

Circle the correct number sentence.

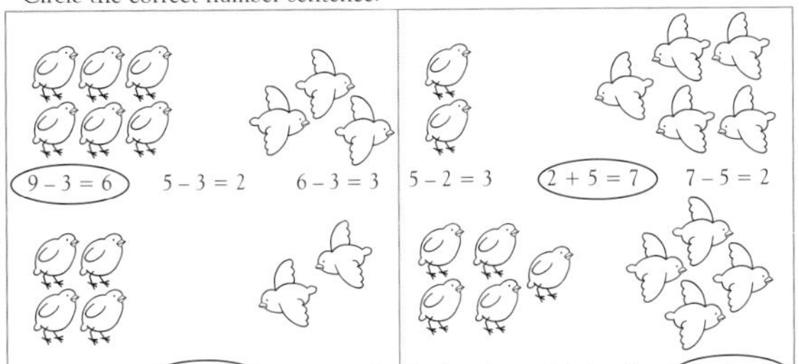

(9 – 3 = 6) 5 – 3 = 2 6 – 3 = 3 | 5 – 2 = 3 (2 + 5 = 7) 7 – 5 = 2

6 – 4 = 2 (4 + 2 = 6) 6 + 2 = 8 | 5 – 1 = 4 4 + 5 = 9 (9 – 4 = 5)

For the final section, make sure that children understand that animals approaching each other represent addition and animals moving away from each other represent subtraction.

138

Picture graphs

Look at this picture graph. Then answer the questions.

Mina's marbles

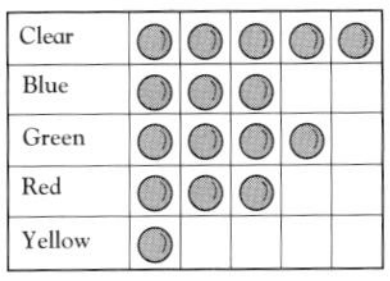

How many blue marbles does Mina have? 3

Does Mina have more green marbles or yellow marbles? green

How many marbles does Mina have in all? 16

Look at this picture graph. Then answer the questions.

Books on Pablo's shelf

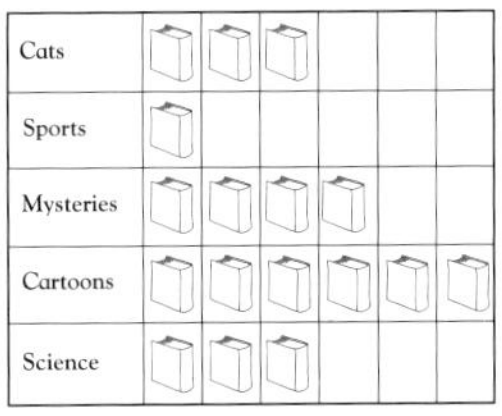

How many science books does Pablo have? 3

Does he have more books about cats than mysteries? no

How many more cartoon books does he have than mysteries? 2

How many books about cats and science does he have? 6

Look at this picture graph. Then answer the questions.

Pets on Redmond Road

On Redmond Road, are there more cats or dogs? dogs

How many more fish are there than dogs? 2 more

How many cats and dogs are there? 9

How many pets are there in all? 19

Children need to count the items for each category, and then add, subtract, and compare data.

139

3-dimensional shapes

Write the name of each shape.

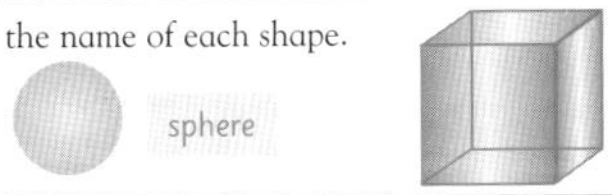

sphere cube

Write the name of each shape. Use the words in the word box.

Word Box

sphere prism cone cube cylinder pyramid

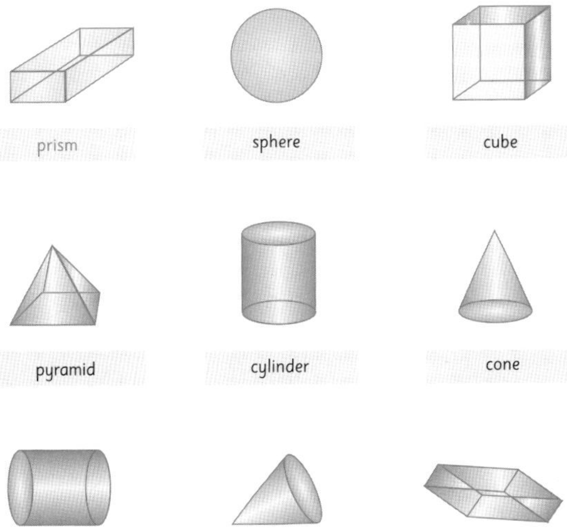

prism sphere cube

pyramid cylinder cone

cylinder cone prism

If children have difficulty, help them identify each shape and learn its name.

140

Missing addends

Write the missing addend.

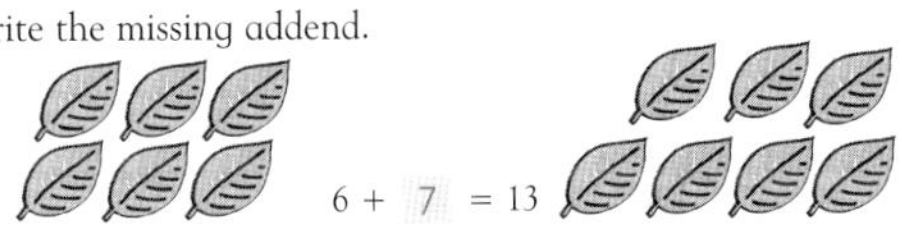

6 + 7 = 13

Write the missing addend.

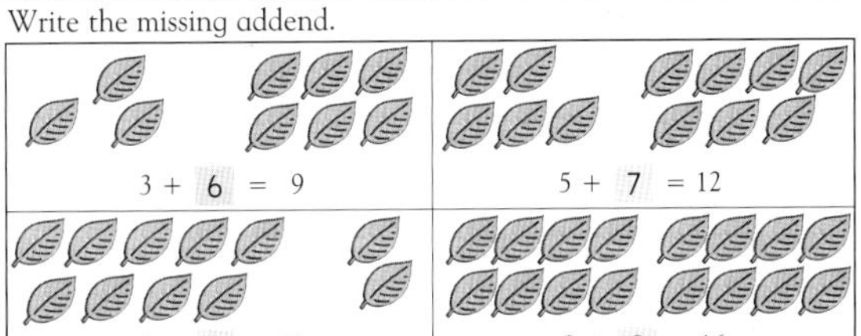

3 + 6 = 9 | 5 + 7 = 12

9 + 2 = 11 | 8 + 8 = 16

Write the missing addend.

3 + 4 = 7	5 + 9 = 14	9 + 3 = 12	8 + 2 = 10
7 + 6 = 12	7 + 8 = 15	7 + 5 = 12	9 + 8 = 17
7 + 6 = 13	8 + 6 = 14	10 + 3 = 13	4 + 9 = 13
4 + 3 = 7	3 + 6 = 9	2 + 9 = 11	8 + 5 = 13
6 + 2 = 8	5 + 4 = 9	7 + 1 = 8	8 + 4 = 12
8 + 1 = 9	6 + 7 = 13	8 + 8 = 16	5 + 6 = 11
4 + 7 = 11	10 + 5 = 15	8 + 3 = 11	4 + 6 = 10
7 + 7 = 14	8 + 7 = 15	9 + 5 = 14	6 + 9 = 15
9 + 7 = 16	9 + 9 = 18	3 + 7 = 10	5 + 4 = 9

Children can use any method they wish to answer these problems—using related subtraction facts, counting, or number sense. They should be able to complete the page using mental math.

141

Reading tables

Read the table. Then answer the questions.

Ages of cousins

NAME	AGE
Kinta	8
Paul	7
Clara	9
Meg	7
Lee	6

How old is Paul? 7

Who is older than Kinta? Clara

Who is the same age as Meg? Paul

Who is the youngest? Lee

Read the table. Then answer the questions.

Favourite juice

Apple	6
Cranberry	2
Grape	3
Cherry	1
Orange	9

How many people chose orange juice? 9

Which juice did 2 people choose? Cranberry

How many more people like orange juice than apple juice? 3 more

Did more people choose grape juice or cranberry juice? Grape juice

Read the table. Then answer the questions.

Mass of dogs

NAME	Bear	Mike	Perry	Spike	Marca
KILOGRAMS	30	6	9	5	3

Which dog has a mass of more than 25 kilograms? Bear

Which dog has a mass of less than 4 kilograms? Marca

How much more mass does Perry have than Mike? 3 kilograms

How much less mass does Spike have than Mike? 1 kilogram

If children have difficulty reading the information in the last table, help them with one question, reading across the appropriate row and down the appropriate column, showing them the intersection of the two.

142

Adding

Write the answer in the box.

34 + 13 = 47

26 + 15 = 41

73 + 27 = 100

Write the answer in the box.

5 + 4 = 9	1 + 8 = 9	3 + 6 = 9	2 + 6 = 8
7 + 0 = 7	6 + 3 = 9	2 + 5 = 7	5 + 6 = 11
9 + 0 = 9	4 + 5 = 9	42 + 7 = 49	6 + 4 = 10
36 + 3 = 39	12 + 6 = 18	37 + 1 = 38	34 + 3 = 37
48 + 2 = 50	64 + 4 = 68	36 + 13 = 49	33 + 15 = 48
26 + 12 = 38	37 + 12 = 49	48 + 11 = 59	56 + 12 = 68
2 + 16 = 18	22 + 26 = 48	3 + 27 = 30	37 + 23 = 60
9 + 24 = 33	17 + 27 = 44	28 + 17 = 45	19 + 26 = 45
26 + 18 = 44	36 + 16 = 52	16 + 14 = 30	14 + 26 = 40

Most of the sums require regrouping. Make sure that children do not neglect to add 10 to the tens column when they regroup.

143

Reading a calendar

Look at this calendar. Then answer the questions.

September

S	M	T	W	T	F	S
	1	2	3	4	5	6
7	8	9	10	11	12	13
14	15	16	17	18	19	20
21	22	23	24	25	26	27
28	29	30				

What day of the week is the first day of September on this calendar? Monday

What date is the last Tuesday in September? September 30

Look at this calendar. Then answer the questions.

July

S	M	T	W	T	F	S
				1	2	3
4	5	6	7	8	9	10
11	12	13	14	15	16	17
18	19	20	21	22	23	24
25	26	27	28	29	30	31

How many days are in the month of July? 31 days

What day of the week is the last day of July on this calendar? Saturday

A camp starts on July 5 and ends on July 9. How many camp days are there? 5 days

The campers go swimming on Tuesday and Thursday. On which dates will they swim? July 6 and July 8

Look at this calendar. Then answer the questions.

November

S	M	T	W	T	F	S
						1
2	3	4	5	6	7	8
9	10	11	12	13	14	15
16	17	18	19	20	21	22
23	24	25	26	27	28	29
30						

What date is the first Sunday of November? November 2

What day of the week is November 14? Friday

How many Saturdays are shown in November? 5

Jenna's birthday is November 23. What day of the week is it? Sunday

If children have difficulties, make sure they understand the abbreviations used in the calendars, and are able to read the calendars accurately.

144

Subtracting

Write the answer in the box.

73 − 48 = 25

45 − 26 = 19

72 − 36 = 36

Write the answer in the box.

27 − 6 = 21	16 − 4 = 12	25 − 2 = 23	38 − 5 = 33
39 − 7 = 32	28 − 6 = 22	36 − 4 = 32	19 − 7 = 12
26 − 6 = 20	43 − 3 = 40	37 − 17 = 20	18 − 17 = 1

Write the answer in the box.

48 cm − 18 cm = 30 cm	49 cm − 36 cm = 13 cm	47 cm − 27 cm = 20 cm	45 cm − 44 cm = 1 cm
49 cm − 47 cm = 2 cm	38 cm − 26 cm = 12 cm	39 cm − 4 cm = 35 cm	47 cm − 47 cm = 0 cm

Write the answer in the box.

43¢ − 17¢ = 26¢	41¢ − 24¢ = 17¢	43¢ − 36¢ = 7¢	51¢ − 46¢ = 5¢
50¢ − 44¢ = 6¢	51¢ − 37¢ = 14¢	53¢ − 46¢ = 7¢	54¢ − 44¢ = 10¢
50 cm − 34 cm = 16 cm	50 cm − 47 cm = 3 cm	36 cm − 18 cm = 18 cm	47 cm − 35 cm = 12 cm

Most of the subtraction exercises require regrouping. Make sure children remember to regroup correctly.

145 Properties of polygons

Circle the polygon that has the same number of sides.

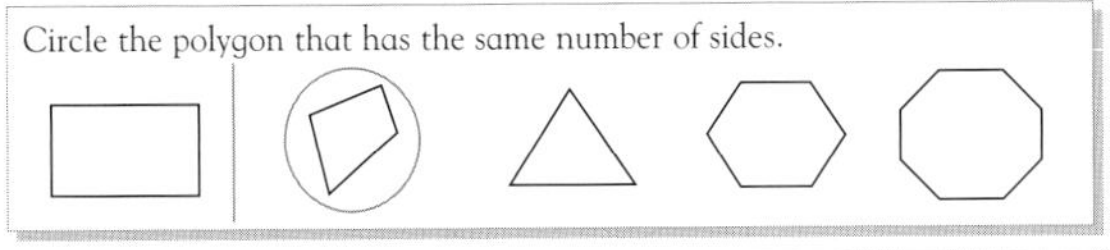

Circle the polygon that has the same number of sides.

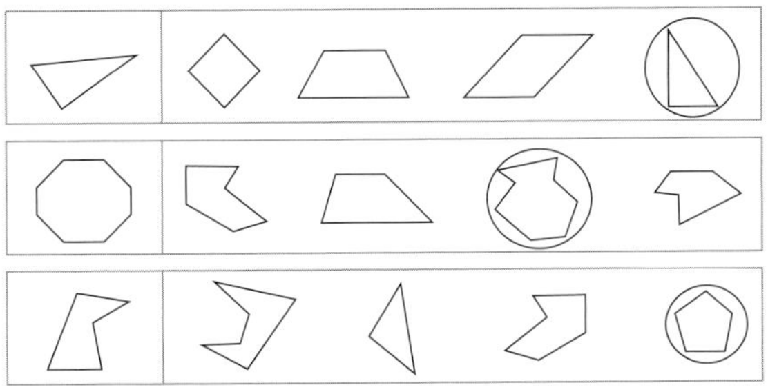

Circle the polygon that has a different number of sides.

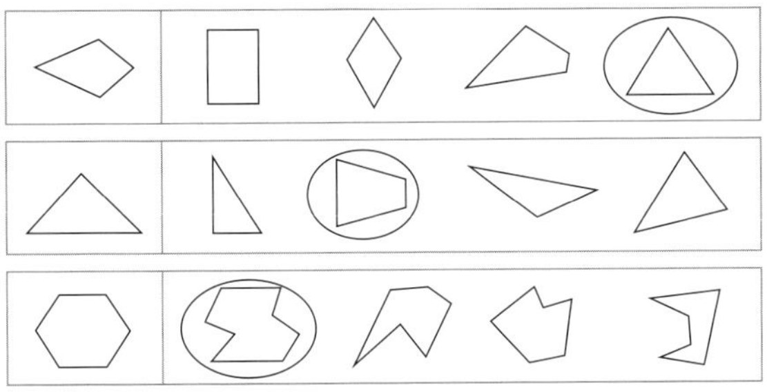

Make sure that children understand that they are not looking for identical shapes, but figures with the given number of sides.

146 Venn diagrams

Read the clues to find the secret number.

It is in both the rectangle and the circle.
It is greater than 3. What number is it? 5

Read the clues to find the secret number.

It is not in the square.
It is an even number.
It is less than 12. What number is it? 10

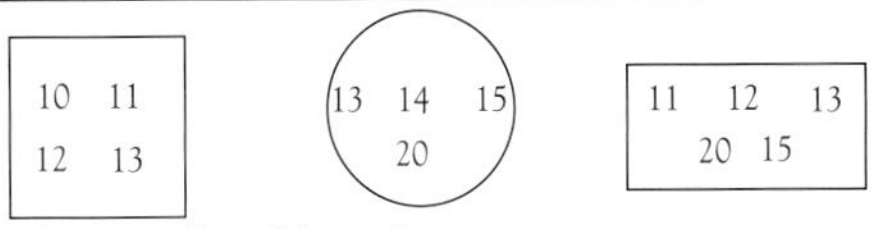

It is in the rectangle and the circle.
It is greater than 13 and less than 20.
It is an odd number. What number is it? 15

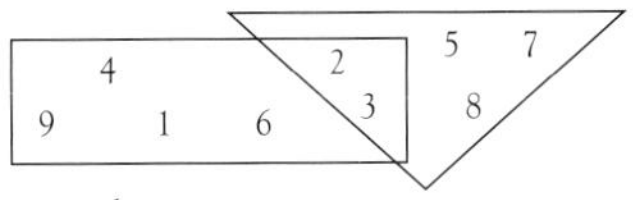

It is not an even number.
It is in the triangle.
It is in the rectangle. What number is it? 3

If children have difficulties, "walk" them through the example. The final question is a Venn diagram showing which numbers are in both figures. You may want to ask children which numbers are in both the triangle and the rectangle.

147 Most likely/least likely

Look at the marbles. Then answer the questions.

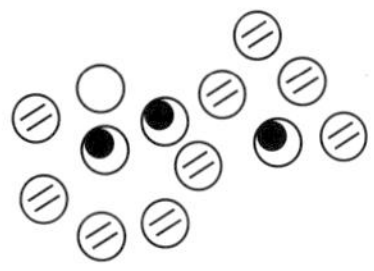

Which kind of marble would you be least likely to pick without looking?

Which kind of marble would you be most likely to pick without looking?

Look at the spinner. Then answer the questions.

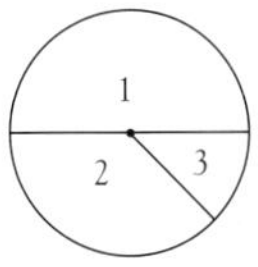

Is the spinner more likely to land on 1 or 2? 1

Is the spinner more likely to land on 2 or 3? 2

Which number is the spinner most likely to land on? 1

Which number is the spinner least likely to land on? 3

Look at the tally chart. Then answer the questions.

Imagine that each time you shake the bag, one coin falls out.

Tally of coins in the bag

COINS	TALLIES
Pennies	||||
Dimes	||
Nickels	𝍸 |||
Quarters	𝍸

Is a penny or a dime more likely to fall out? penny

Is a quarter or a nickel more likely to fall out? nickel

Which coin is most likely to fall out? nickel

Which coin is least likely to fall out? dime

Children should realize that the more of a particular item there is in a set, the more likely it is to be picked.

148 3-dimensional shapes

Write the name of each shape.

Sphere Cube

Write the name of each shape. Use the names in the Word Box.

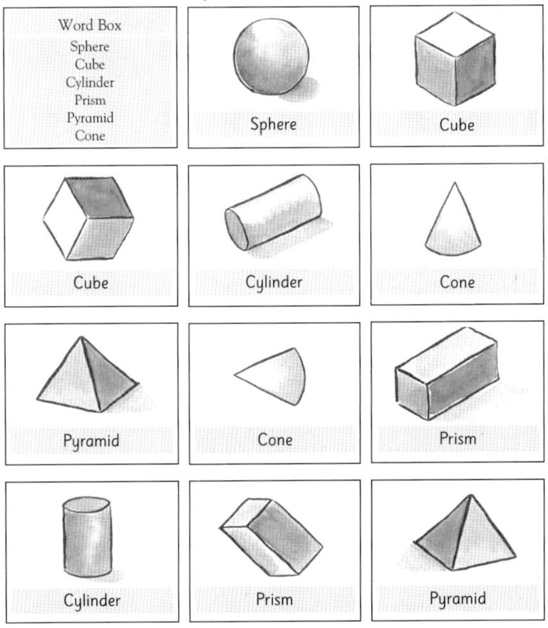

Children may confuse figures that have an unusual orientation. You may want to use real objects to help demonstrate this.

149 Counting

Write the missing number above each ↑.

23 – 24 – 25 – 26 – ○ – ○ – ○ – 30 – ○ – ○ – 33 – 34 – ○ – ○

Write the missing number above each ↑.

12 – ○ – 14 – ○ – ○ – 17 – ○ – ○ – ○ – 21 – ○ – 23 – 24 – ○

5 | 6 | □ | □ | 9 | 10 | □ | □ | □ | 14 | 15 | 16 | □ | 18

17 – 18 – 19 – ○ – ○ – ○ – 23 – 24 – ○ – ○ – 27 – ○ – ○ – 30

31 | □ | 33 | 34 | 35 | □ | □ | 38 | □ | 40 | 41 | □ | □ | 44

17 – ○ – ○ – 20 – ○ – 22 – 23 – 24 – ○ – ○ – ○ – 28 – 29 – 30

21 | 22 | □ | □ | □ | 26 | 27 | □ | 29 | □ | □ | □ | 33 | □

Each of the sequences involves counting by 1s. Children should fill in only the shapes marked with an arrow.

150 Finding patterns

Find the counting pattern. Write the missing numbers.

12 | 14 | 16 | 18 | 20 | 22 | 24 | 26 | 28 | 30

Find the counting pattern. Write the missing numbers.

5, 10, 15, 20, 25, 30, 35, 40, 45, 50

3, 6, 9, 12, 15, 18, 21, 24, 27, 30

11, 15, 19, 23, 27, 31, 35, 39, 43, 47

21, 23, 25, 27, 29, 31, 33, 35, 37, 39

19, 20, 21, 22, 23, 24, 25, 26, 27, 28

6, 12, 18, 24, 30, 36, 42, 48, 54, 60

19, 17, 15, 13, 11, 9, 7, 5, 3, 1

100, 90, 80, 70, 60, 50, 40, 30, 20, 10

10, 20, 30, 40, 50, 60, 70, 80, 90, 100

58, 55, 52, 49, 46, 43, 40, 37, 34, 31

50, 45, 40, 35, 30, 25, 20, 15, 10, 5

42, 38, 34, 30, 26, 22, 18, 14, 10, 6

It may be necessary to point out that some of the patterns show an increase and some a decrease. Children can see what operation turns a number into the next number in the pattern, and then perform the operation to continue the pattern.

151 Reading tally charts

Look at the tally chart. Then answer the questions.

Winners at Tag

Kelly	Mark	Sandy	Rita	Brad
卌||	|||	卌|	卌	卌||||

Who won the most games? Brad

Who won more games, Sandy or Kelly? Kelly

How many more games did Rita win than Mark? 2 more

Look at the tally chart. Then answer the questions.

Colours of T-Shirts sold

Blue	卌卌|
White	卌|||
Green	卌||||
Black	卌卌||

Which colour shirt was sold most? Black

How many green shirts were sold? Black

Which colour sold more, blue or green? Blue

How many black shirts were sold? 12

How many more green shirts were sold than white shirts? 1 more

How many more black shirts were sold than green shirts? 3 more

How many T-shirts were sold in all? 40

Look at the tally chart. Then answer the questions.

Snack choices

Chips	Cherries	Cheese	Cookie	Apple
卌||||	卌	卌卌|	卌||	卌||

How many people chose chips? 9

Which snack did 7 people choose? Apple

Did more people choose chips or cookies? Chips

Which snack did the fewest people choose? Cherries

How many more people chose cheese than chips? 2 more

How many people chose apples and cherries? 12

Children usually accept the concept of tally marks very quickly. They can count on by fives for completed tallies.

152 Same shape and size

Which figure has same shape and size?

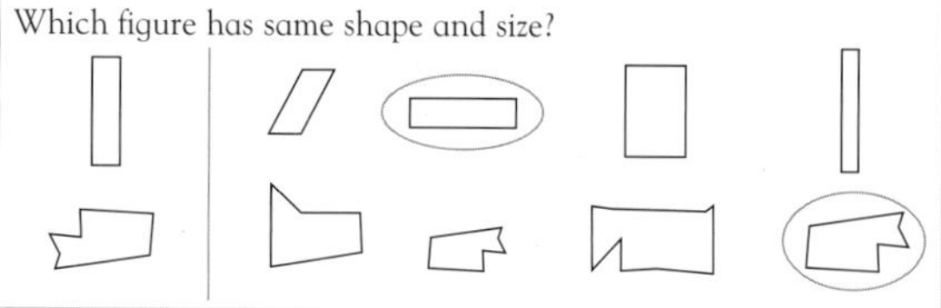

Circle the figure that has same shape and size.

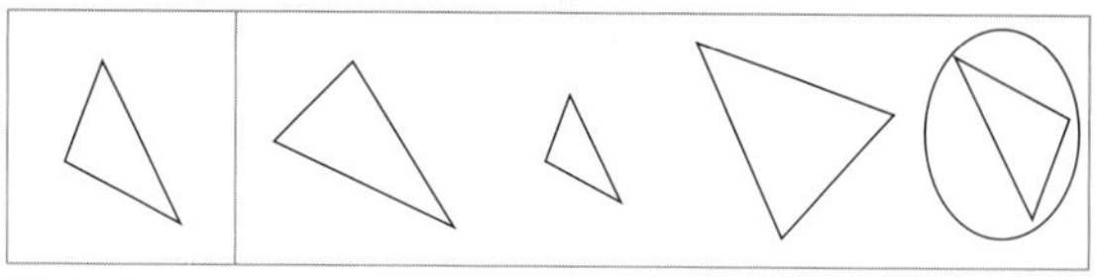

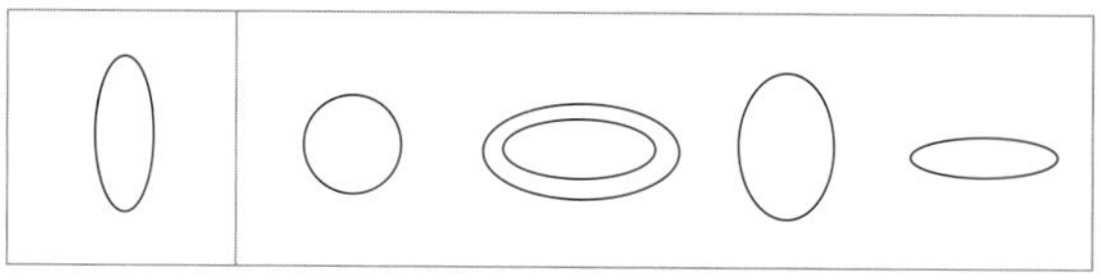

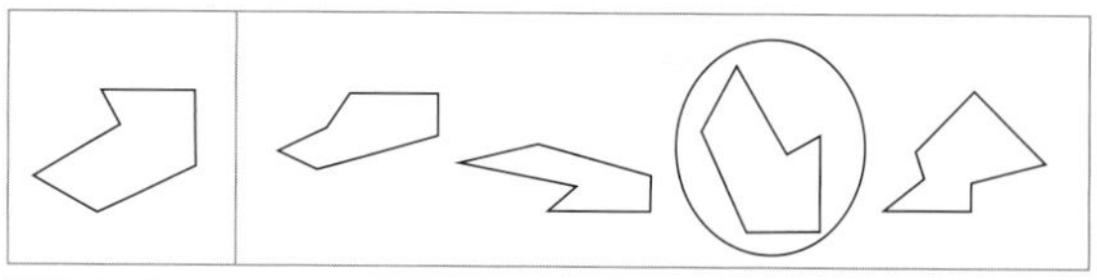

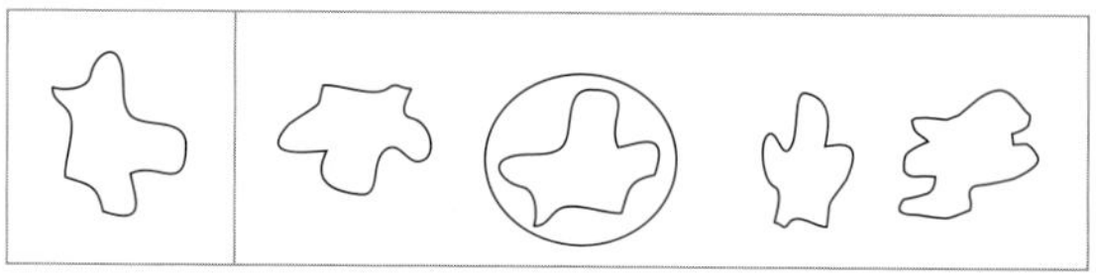

Make sure children look for both size and shape. They may have difficulty if the figures are drawn with different orientations.

153

Parts of a set

Write the fraction that shows the red part of the set.
How many of the fish are red?

How many [fish]? 3
How many fish in all? 4

Write the fraction. $\frac{3}{4}$ part of the set / whole set

Circle the fraction that shows the shaded part of the set.

(circled) $\frac{1}{3}$	$\frac{2}{3}$	$\frac{3}{2}$
$\frac{2}{3}$	(circled) $\frac{3}{5}$	$\frac{2}{5}$
$\frac{1}{4}$	(circled) $\frac{3}{4}$	$\frac{2}{4}$
$\frac{4}{5}$	(circled) $\frac{1}{5}$	$\frac{1}{4}$

Write the fraction that shows the shaded part of the set.

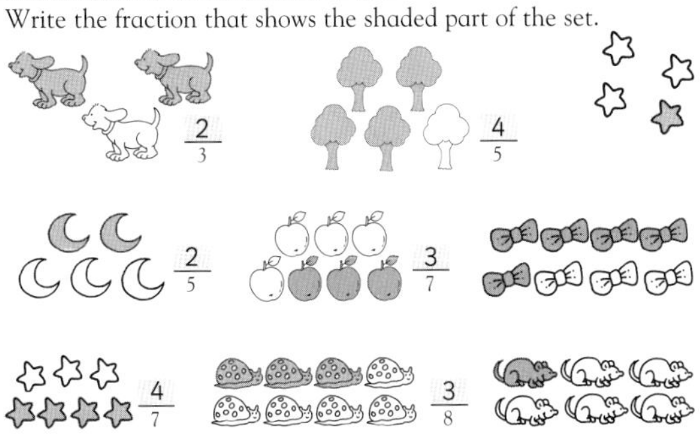

$\frac{2}{3}$ $\frac{4}{5}$ $\frac{1}{4}$

$\frac{2}{5}$ $\frac{3}{7}$ $\frac{5}{8}$

$\frac{4}{7}$ $\frac{3}{8}$ $\frac{1}{6}$

If children have difficulties, point out that the denominator—or bottom number of the fraction—is the total number of parts. The numerator—or top part of the fraction—is the number of shaded parts.

154

Symmetry

Hold a mirror along the dotted line. Does it show a line of symmetry?

yes no yes

Does the dotted line show a line of symmetry? Write yes or no.

yes	no	yes
yes	no	no
yes	yes	yes
yes	yes	yes

Some of these shapes have lines of symmetry in unusual positions. Let children use mirrors on the shapes if they are unsure of their answers.

155

Measurement problems

Write the measurement shown by the arrow. 3 cm

Write the measurement shown by the arrow.

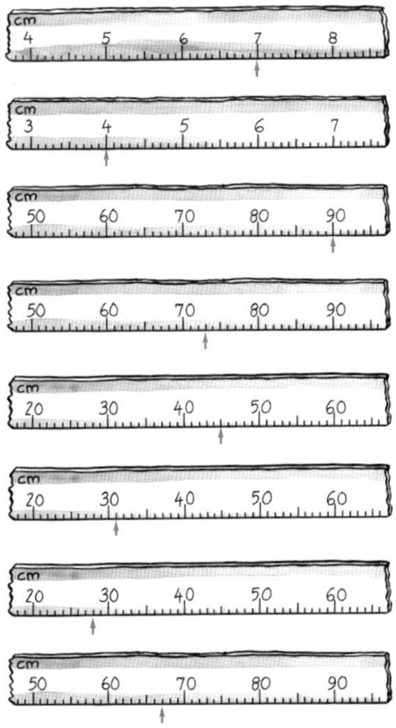

7 cm

4 cm

90 cm

73 cm

45 cm

31 cm

28 cm

67 cm

Children should be able to read off scales of this type relatively easily. Make sure that children include the units in their answers.

156

3-dimensional shapes

Write the name of each shape in the box.

prism sphere

Write the name of each shape in the box.

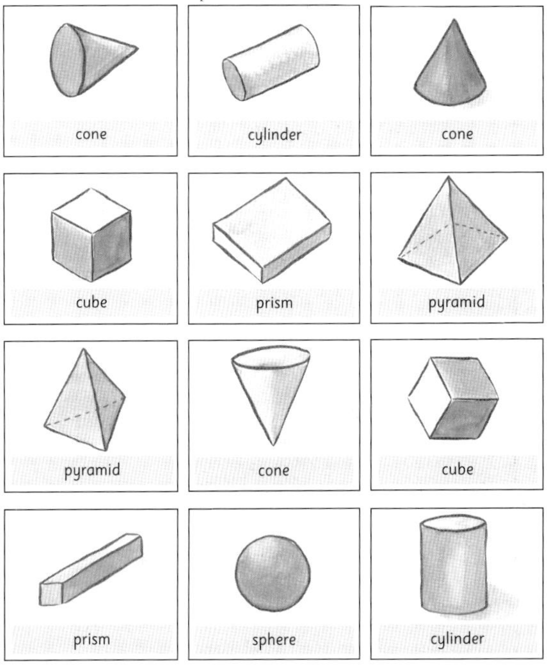

cone	cylinder	cone
cube	prism	pyramid
pyramid	cone	cube
prism	sphere	cylinder

Children may be uncertain of the terms *prism* and *pyramid*. Show them objects to demonstrate the difference.

EDITOR, CANADA	Julia Roles
PRODUCTION	Erica Rosen
EDITOR, INDIA	Aekta Jerath
DTP, INDIA	Balwant Singh, Pankaj Sharma
MANAGER, INDIA	Aparna Sharma

First Canadian Edition, 2005

Dorling Kindersley is represented in Canada by Tourmaline Editions Inc.,
662 King Street West, Suite 304, Toronto, Ontario M5V 1M7

Library and Archives Canada Cataloguing in Publication

Math made easy grade 1 : math workbook / Marilyn Wilson,
Canadian editor. -- Canadian ed.

"Ages 6-7".
ISBN 1-55363-049-1

1. Mathematics--Problems, exercises, etc.--Juvenile literature.
I. Wilson, Marilyn

QA107.2.M3882 2005 510'.76 C2004-906899-7

Colour reproduction by Colourscan
Printed and bound in China by L.Rex
05 06 07 6 5 4 3 2 1

The publisher would like to thank
Chris Houston for his illustrations of Canadian money.

Discover more at
www.dk.com